# Sway

## ADRIANA LOCKE

*Sway*
Copyright (c) Adriana Locke, 2016
ALL RIGHTS RESERVED

This book is a work of fiction. Any references to event, real people, or real places are used fictitiously. Other names, characters, places, and events are products of the author's imagination, and any resemblance to actual events or places or persons, living or dead, is entirely coincidental.

All rights reserved, including the right to reproduce this book or portions thereof in any form whatsoever.

Cover Art:
Kari March, Kari March Designs
*www.karimarchdesigns.com*

Cover Photos:
Adobe Stock

Editing:
Lisa Christman, Adept Edits

Interior Design & Formatting:
Christine Borgford, Perfectly Publishable
*www.perfectlypublishable.com*

# Also by
# ADRIANA LOCKE

THE EXCEPTION SERIES
The Exception (book 1)
The Connection, a novella (book 2)
The Perception (book 3)

STANDALONE NOVELS
Sacrifice
Wherever It Leads
Mine (coming Fall 2016)

COMING SOON!
Mine (a standalone)

Swing (book 2 in the Landry Family Series)
coming Winter 2016

To *Jennifer Costa*

You are so much more to me than any one word can describe. My friend, my beta, my sister, my sanity on most days. You are my Patriots enabler and my focus more times than not.

Thank you for who you are, for your love, support, and honesty.

And thank you for reading this twenty million times.

This one's for you.

xo

# Alison

"THIS IS A SINGLE GIRL'S paradise."

"No," I grimace, blotting the spilled cheese sauce from my shirt. "Paradise would be a tropical island with a hot cabana boy at my beck and call . . . and an endless supply of mojitos."

Lola laughs, the sound barely heard over the chaos of the kitchen. Chefs shouting instructions, event planners panicking, plates being dropped—the world of catering is a noisy endeavor.

I step to the side to allow Isaac, a fellow server and Lola's gorgeous friend with benefits, to scamper to the ballroom a few feet away. He's tall with a head full of dark curls and a laugh that makes you involuntarily smile. Lola is crazy for keeping him at arm's length, but that's how she operates. He has little money; she has limited interest.

"Cabana boys may have hot bodies and virility, Alison, but they lack two very important qualities: fame and fortune."

"So, what you're saying is that you'd take a limp dick over a hard one? Interesting," I say, rolling my eyes and tossing the sauce-soaked rag into the linen bin.

"No, that's not what I'm saying, smart ass. I'm saying I'd take a solid bank account over a solid cock. Think about it—with all that money, he could never fuck me at all and I wouldn't care."

"If that's the case," I retort, grabbing another tray of drinks, "there are tons of opportunities out there to not get fucked."

I laugh at the dreamy look on her face, partly because it's hilarious and partly because I know she's not kidding.

Lola and I are a lot alike. We both come from meager backgrounds and Luxor Foods is our second job. There's no doubt we both would rather not be here because serving rich bitches can be a very humbling experience. But they are also the best parties to work because they tip. Very well. Of course it's so they can feel above us most times, but we'll take it. It's money in our pockets, and if they get off on it in the process, good for them.

That being said, Lo took this job to afford her manicures, pedicures, and eyelash extensions. I do it to take care of my son, Huxley. Lola's first job is working at a salon and her career goals include marrying up in the world. I, on the other hand, work at Hillary's House restaurant during the day and go to school for journalism in hopes to one day write pieces that might inspire someone.

"Speaking of fucking," she says, her eyes aglow, "did you see Mayor Landry?"

"I love how you segued into that," I laugh.

"It's a linear comparison. Tell me that fucking isn't the first thing that comes to mind when you think of him, and I'll call you a liar."

Of course it's the truth. It's the first thing that comes to mind... and maybe the second and third too.

Thoughts of the recently crowned Most Eligible Bachelor make me a swoony mess. Barrett Landry's thick, sandy brown hair that always looks perfectly coiffed, his broad, friendly smile that makes you feel like you could tell him your darkest secrets without judgment, his tanned skin, tight body, wide shoulders—the list goes on. But it all leads, as Lo so candidly pointed out, to thoughts of him stripped down and wearing only his charismatic grin.

I shiver at the thought.

"See?" she grins, waggling her finger in my face. "Linear comparison."

"I'll give you that. He's so seriously fine."

"Have you had a chance to get close to him? To breathe him in?"

"Breathe him in?" My laughter catches the attention of our boss, Mr. Pickner. He twists his burly body our way, letting us know we'd better get to work.

"I haven't," I say, turning back to Lola. "Even though I've been around men like Landry before—well, not quite like him, but as close as a mortal can be—I don't think I could handle it, Lo. He scrambles my brain. I'd probably fall face first into him and dump the drinks in his lap. Then we'd *both* be wet."

She swipes a tray off the table and shoots a wink at Isaac as he walks back in. "It would so be worth it if you played your cards right. You could probably get away with running your hands through his hair and maybe even licking his stubbled jaw. A kiss would probably be over the top, but his Southern roots would keep him from causing a scene and asking for security."

"You've thought this through, haven't you?" I ask in mock horror.

"Of course I have and every other woman in here has too. Hell, half the men probably have," she giggles. "In my fantasy, he gazes at me with those emerald green eyes and leans in and—"

"Ladies! Back to work!"

We sigh as Mr. Pickner barrels by. He's an overweight, balding, temperamental asshole of a man, but he owns the premiere catering company in all of Georgia. So we deal. Barely.

Lola bumps me with her hip. "Seriously. Stop being so goody-two-shoes and go out there and snag you a man and a retirement plan."

I bite my tongue. We've had this conversation a number of times before and she just doesn't get it. I don't fault her though. Most people don't. They see the glitz and glamour, the designer labels and fine wine and get drawn in like a Siren's call. That life looks too good to resist, too good to be true.

The thing is—they're exactly right. It is.

She reads the look on my face and we start towards the door. "I know, I know. You lived like that once. It's a fantasy, smoke and mirrors . . ."

"Yup."

"Well, I say I'll play in the smoke as long as the mirrors make me pretty."

I snort, pushing open the door to the ballroom. "You go right ahead and dig that gold all the way down the aisle."

"I've got my shovel right here." She shimmies her backside in my direction. "See that one over there?"

Following her gaze across the room, I see a man I know is one of the Landry brothers. There are four of them and two sisters, twins, if I'm not mistaken. I don't really follow that kind of thing much, but they're basically Georgia royalty, and even avoiding current events as I do, you can't help but pick up on some of their lives. Every newscast, it seems, has something Landry-related even when it's not election season.

"I'm going to check him out," Lola says and takes off, leaving me standing with my tray of ridiculously overpriced champagne.

I roam the outer edges of the elegant ballroom, giving a practiced smile to each person that plucks a drink off the tray. Some smile widely, some try to chit-chat, some completely ignore me like they probably do the paid staff at home. It's fine by me.

A few years ago, I attended events like this. Married to my college sweetheart, a newly minted judge in Albuquerque, we went to balls and galas and swearing-in ceremonies often. It was a magical time in my life, before the magic wore off and everything exploded right in my face.

"Well, aren't you a pretty little thing?"

I spin to my right to see an older gentleman grinning at me like a snake ready to strike.

"Would you like a drink?" I offer, knowing good and well by the color in his cheeks that he's already had more than enough.

"No, no, that's fine. I was actually just admiring you."

Pasting on a smile and tossing my shoulders back, I try to keep my voice even. "Thank you, sir. Now, if you'll excuse me—"

"I was thinking," he says, cutting me off, "how about you and I take a little stroll? Do you get my drift?"

"With all due respect," I say through clenched teeth, glancing at the wedding ring sparkling on his finger, "how about you take a stroll with your wife?"

I swivel on my heels and head off as calmly as possible, blood roaring in my ears. I can hear his cackle behind me and I really want to turn around and slam my fist into his beefy face. It's behavior that's typical of people like this, thinking they can get away with whatever they want with the bourgeoisie. I just so happen to have an overdeveloped sensitivity to it, being that my husband did the same thing to me as soon as he got a little power.

Lola catches my attention as I pause to settle down. She points discreetly to the other end of the room and mouths, "Over there." The gleam in her eye tells me she's spotted the mayor, but I can't see him.

I shuffle through the crowd and finally spy the man of the hour walking out, his arm around the waist of a woman that's been acting crazy all night. Her head is leaning on his shoulder, her hand resting on his backside. Laughing, I catch Lola's eye and nod to the exit.

"Bitch," she mouths as she approaches the same man that approached me earlier. I want to warn her, but don't. For one, I know it won't do any good, and for two, I can't take my eyes off Landry.

People literally part for him to walk through. It's like he's Moses. They're more than willing to be led through the Red Sea, divided by his power and influence, and into the Promised Land.

I'm off in space about what precisely that land might entail, when my shoulder is bumped, rustling me out of my Landry-induced haze.

"Excuse me," I say. When I realize who I've just ignored, my cheeks heat in embarrassment. "I'm so sorry," I stutter, handing Camilla Landry, one of the Landry sisters, a glass of champagne.

She's even more beautiful in person, a textbook example of poise and sophistication. In the media a lot for charity work with her mother, her face is easily identifiable with her high cheekbones and sparkling smile.

"Don't worry about it," she breathes, waving me off. "I can't take my brothers anywhere without women getting all mesmerized. Especially that one," she laughs, nodding to the doorway Barrett just went through. "Although, between me and you, I don't get it."

Her grin is infectious, and I can't help but return it.

"I'm Camilla," she says, extending her long, well-manicured hand like I don't already know.

I balance the tray on one side and take her hand in mine. "I'm Alison. Alison Baker."

"You helped clean up a sauce spill earlier. You put the lady that had the accident at ease when you took the blame and kept the attention off her. I wanted you to know I saw and respected that."

"It really was no big deal."

"In this world, *everything* can be a big deal. Trust me. You probably just saved my brother a couple of votes."

"Just doing my part," I laugh.

She smiles again, her chic sky-blue dress matching her eyes and heels. "Well, on behalf of the mayor, thank you. He seems . . . occupied, at the moment."

I wink. "I have no idea what you're talking about. I didn't see a thing."

She nods, looking a touch relieved, and thanks me again before turning away and greeting the older lady from earlier, the one that spilled her dinner all over me. Camilla takes her hand and helps her into a chair.

Her elegance is breathtaking and she has a charm about her, an easiness even though she's clearly blue-blood, that I've never seen before. It's exactly what the kitchen is buzzing about with Barrett—a charisma you can't quite put your finger on.

# Barrett

"I'M WET FOR YOU, BARRETT."

"I'm sure you are."

I wrap my arm around Daphne's narrow waist, letting my fingers splay against the red satin fabric covering her body. She moans at the contact, her eyelashes fluttering closed, and her head resting against my shoulder.

"How could I not be? You are *so* sexy," Daphne purrs, grabbing the lapels of my jacket and trying to jerk me towards her. "Please, Mayor Landry. Fuck me."

Squeezing her hips to hold her steady, I'm afraid she's going to get sick before I can get her out of here.

"Take me home with you, sugar. Take me to the bathroom for all I care, just take me," Daphne thinks she whispers as I guide her to the foyer of the Savannah Room.

Her not-so-quiet request gains the attention of the men in suits lining the marble walls. They look at us, the Mayor of Savannah and the daughter of a United States Senator, over their tumblers of gin. A few crack a grin, but most just nod and turn back to their discussions about oil or the stock market.

Not one man with the requisite American flag pin on his suit jacket is appalled. This may be the South, where people like to think it's all gentility and manners, but it's also politics, and it has its own code of conduct that morality has no place in. Politics equals power, but it also equals fortune, a bit of fame, and a lot of pussy, and these men take full advantage of it all.

And so have I.

But these days, with the gubernatorial election on the horizon and my campaign numbers strong but not enough to make me a shoo-in, I have been more selective in my extracurricular activities. My eligible bachelor title earlier this year, along with some pesky pictures of me with a couple of models at a party in Atlanta, didn't help my campaign. My adversary, a bastard named Homer Hobbs, has taken the angle that I'm just some spoiled little rich kid that can't be trusted with the keys to the Governor's Mansion. That's one angle. There are others.

"Are you coming home with me?" Daphne slurs against my shoulder.

"You know I can't do that," I say, pausing while she catches her balance. "I have to stay here and entertain the masses."

She giggles. "Why don't you come entertain my ass instead?"

Fighting to hide my frustration, I hurry her along as best I can towards the exit.

"So many people came to see you," she gushes.

"Let's hope that translates to votes."

"You need my daddy's vote, Barrett?"

Her tone, a babyish whimper, makes me roll my eyes. I know exactly what she's on her way to pointing out.

Yeah, I've fucked her and I'm not saying I won't replay that. But I'm not fucking her tonight for her daddy's endorsement. It wouldn't be a sexual transaction tonight; it would be an implication of power, of necessity, and I'm not about to step into that.

The oversized door is pushed open by a man in a green-vested suit. He tips his hat. "Mr. Mayor, may I summon your ride?"

"No, thank you, I'll be staying for a while. Can you please see that Ms. Monroe gets home safely?"

I slide my arm from around her waist and watch her teeter on her heels. Her black hair is a mess, her dress wrinkled and clinging haphazardly to her body. She's starting to nod off, and I'm embarrassed for her. The daughter of Miles Monroe, she should know better than to publicly embarrass her family. It's the political Golden Rule, a rule that's simply not broken without severe consequences.

I slide a hundred dollar bill into the valet's palm. "Please get her out of here immediately."

"No problem, sir. I have a car waiting. Anything else?"

"That'll be all."

I turn on my heel to see my father across the hall. He winks, running one hand through his salt-and-pepper hair and excuses himself from the conversation that's taking place around him.

He falls in step beside me as I make my way into the banquet. I spy my mother, Vivian Landry, in conversation with a judge on the Georgia Supreme Court.

"Nice move, son," Dad drawls, patting me on the shoulder as we walk. "We're going to need Monroe's support. Your numbers are solid, but Monroe's endorsement would make sure you win. That precinct—"

"I know, Dad."

He shakes his head. "I know you know. I'm just saying I know he'll be appreciative of you getting her out of here. What in the hell was she thinking?"

I shrug, scanning the activity in the room. "I don't know what she was thinking, but I also don't know who let her drink that much," I say, turning my back to my father. It never ceases to amaze me how callous he can be about this entire process.

"Whoever it was just did you a favor, son."

"Well, I could use a few more favors. Hobbs is doing more damage with his accusations than I dreamed. Did you see the interview today?"

My father cringes. "Yes."

"He pulled up those pics from Atlanta. Again."

"It's just politics, Barrett. Propaganda."

"Fuck propaganda," I bite out.

Wrapping my hand over the back of my neck, I try to work out some of the tension. The last bit of an election is always tough—mentally and physically. Everyone warned me as I went up the ranks that it would just get harder, more vicious. I thought I was prepared. I thought wrong.

I wake up every day wondering what will be said about me in the media. I have to watch what I say, what I do, rethink every breath that comes out of my mouth because the wrong word to the wrong person can all be twisted. And you can trust essentially no one.

It's a constant state of defense and it's starting to wear on me a bit. Or a lot. Either way, there's nothing I can do about it.

This is my dream. I keep reminding myself of that.

"Don't look like that, Barrett."

"Like what, Dad? Like I'm tired of the bullshit? Like I just want to be able to speak freely, grab a cup of coffee, crack some jokes without worrying about who will spin it a hundred ways from Sunday?"

"You're in the big leagues now. This isn't a local election. There isn't a whole hell of a lot I can do for you like I can down here. You have to play the game."

"I'm trying to play the game, Dad, but I'm playing with people who have no rules. How could he support Hobbs anyway?" I ask, declining a glass of champagne.

"He'll support Hobbs if he's going to win." Dad takes a sip of his drink. "And Hobbs has already said he'll vote against the Land Bill."

I stop in my tracks and turn to face my father. The bill in question is one of the hottest areas of contention in this election. It would take a large swath of property near Savannah and convert it into a commercial zone. It would trigger construction, create jobs, create affordable housing, increase revenue. All in all, it's a win . . . except for the landholders who just so happen to be old money families, like mine and Monroe's.

And apparently I'm the only person that thinks the rich, like me, getting richer at the expense of the poor is a bad idea.

"I'm not ready to commit one way or the other on that," I say to my dad, not wanting to go into it again.

"I'm just telling you—if you'd just throw your weight against it, it would make this Monroe matter much simpler."

"So you think I should support it because our family stands to make more money if it doesn't pass? Funny, Dad, that's not what I thought I was being elected to do."

He chuckles, the gravel in his tone letting me know he's not pleased. He's also not about to cause a scene. "You won't be elected at all if you don't play your cards right. Remember that."

I give him a look that says all the things my genteel Southern upbringing forbids me to say out loud to my father.

His jaw tenses as he searches my face. "You gotta get your head straight, wrapped around the opportunity in front of you. You can't mess this up now, son. Not when we're this close."

I sigh and scan the room, feeling the incredible weight of all eyes on me. Under normal circumstances, being the center of attention is something I enjoy. It does an ego well to know every female wants you and every male wants to be you. I can't deny that. But this is not what that is. Not entirely. Half the people in here are deciding what they can get out of me, what favors I can offer them if I get elected and they back me.

Graham catches my eye from across the room. We exchange a look, one that we've exchanged a number of times over our lives.

It was Graham and I when we were younger, walking into our father's office after getting into a skirmish at school. It was the two of us when we came home late and our parents were waiting in the living room as we walked in, half lit. It was the two of us when we wrecked Dad's new Corvette when I was nineteen and Graham seventeen, and had to break the news to the old man that his 'Vette was wrapped around a tree on the outside of town. Out of all my siblings, it's Graham that I can count on and, right now, I'm counting on him to get me out of this conversation with our father.

"Hey," I say, exhaling sharply and nodding towards the corner, "I need to talk to Graham for a minute."

"Go ahead. And son, I'm proud of you." He beams with satisfaction. His face, wrinkled from years of politics, running Landry Holdings, and raising six kids, is split into a grin. "So damn proud."

I pat him on the shoulder and turn away.

Grinning at a couple of women, I try to remember if I should know them from somewhere. The one in the white dress looks vaguely familiar, but I can't place her. Ignoring the look in their eyes that tells me I could have them both, at the same time, if I prefer, I make my way to my brother.

Graham is standing with his hands in his pockets, looking serious and put together like the Vice President of Landry Holdings should.

"I think it's going well," Graham says as I approach, rocking back on his heels. "As long as you get Monroe on board, I'm pretty sure you're golden."

"I'll get Monroe on board, but I'm probably going to have to fuck Daphne again to make sure," I laugh.

"Oh, I bet it's so hard to stick your cock in that. Damn, brother, I almost feel bad for you."

I shrug, the grin on my face staying put, feeling my shoulders relax for the first time in hours. "I do what must be done for the greater good."

"Such a fool," he says, but I know he's kidding. "Ford sent me an email today. He said he's trying to come home around the election. It can't hurt to have a Landry in uniform standing next to you. Between him and Lincoln, you'll look like an All-American."

"Lincoln *was* an All-American," I point out about our brother that is currently the center fielder for the Tennessee Arrows.

"True."

"Speaking of our siblings, did you hear from Sienna?" She's the family wild card, eschewing all things political and Landry-centered for a life as an artist and fashion designer.

Sienna and Camilla are identical twins, but couldn't be any more different. Camilla is always around, meddling in our business, lending a hand to events or charities when needed. Sienna is usually jet-setting around the world and too busy to check in.

"No. Dad called her earlier and chewed her ass for not being here, I think. Lincoln got a pass because he's training and Ford's excused because he's in the Middle East. But you know Dad doesn't think painting and designing dresses are really work."

"He could've cut her some slack."

I'm cut short by Graham's smirk. His eyes slide right past me and light up.

"Would either of you like a glass of champagne?" a female voice nearly whispers behind me.

"I'm good," Graham mutters, looking at me out of the corner of his eye. "How about you, Barrett?"

I ignore him and let my eyes feast on the curves of the woman in front of me. Her black pants are belted at the waist, her white shirt hugging the bends of her body. She's not overly thin or overly heavy, just a damn-near perfect vision of what a woman should look like.

She has creamy skin and a spattering of freckles across the bridge of her nose. She tucks a strand of her straw-colored hair behind her ear and takes a deep breath. I think she's going to laugh, but she doesn't. Instead, a faint smile ghosts her full lips and she lifts her chin like she has a secret she won't tell.

Her gaze remains on Graham, almost like she's afraid to look my way. Finally, she turns to me, and when she does, a slight rise in her chest is noticeable as she sucks in a shaky breath.

I grin.

Her eyes are a deep blue. The color is stormy, swirling, moving like a shield between us.

"Would you, sir?" she asks, taking a half a step backwards.

"Would I what?" I press, enjoying the way her cheeks turn pink in the most real way. She's not reacting to me as part of a calculated plan or trying to endear herself to me for a gain in some way. It's an experience I haven't had for a long time and I want to live in it a moment longer.

"Would you like a drink?"

The words topple out of her lips, like she wants to say them and scoot away.

I take a step towards her, watching her beautiful eyes widen. This girl is naturally gorgeous, her features not hidden by a thick layer of make-up. "That depends on what you're offering."

I shouldn't be toying with her, but I can't help it. I want to keep her talking, to watch her reactions.

She wants to get away from me, I can feel it, and I can't help but wonder why. Most women clamor over each other, ready to knife anyone they need to in order to get to me, but this one is trying to run.

"I don't have much to offer," she says, a hint of nervousness in her voice. "Unless you like champagne."

"I like all sorts of things." I keep my gaze heavy against hers, not allowing her to look away. She fidgets with her tray and swallows hard, but never takes her eyes off mine like she's too defiant to look away. The longer our gazes match, the hotter my body becomes.

She licks her bottom lip slowly, her heated gaze boring into mine. "Is that so?"

Graham chuckles beside me and I watch her jump, like she forgot he was there. She clears her throat and glances around the room.

She turns back to us again, this time a practiced smile on her face. The easy grin and whispery laugh are both gone. This is the reaction I'm used to seeing on everyone, the look they think I want to see. I hate it on her.

"Gentlemen . . ." With a nod, she walks away as fast as she can. She doesn't look back, but I watch her until she's out of sight.

"You're the fucking mayor," Graham snickers, loosening his green silk tie.

"I bet she'd like to be fucking the mayor." I raise my eyebrows, and my brother laughs louder.

"Do you have any class whatsoever?"

"What? I like the look of her."

"Which ones do you not like the look of?"

"I'll let you know when I find one."

He quirks a brow. "Aren't you supposed to be playing the role of the good candidate, being serious about all the things that matter?"

"Now, Graham," I chide teasingly, "are you saying her vote is less important than anyone else's?"

He shakes his head and pulls out his ringing phone. "You should be worried about her vote, not the way your balls sound bouncing off her ass. Now, if you'll excuse me . . ."

I laugh as he exits through a side door and leaves me standing alone. Looking around the bustling room, I search for the blonde beauty.

My phone buzzes in my pocket, and I know without looking that it's Daphne, offering herself up again for the night. She may even dip as far as playing the lonely princess card. I don't even bother looking, just stick my hand in my pocket and push buttons on the side until I'm sure it's off. She'll keep calling, but I won't be answering. On a good day she's borderline clingy after a fuck. When she's drunk, it's only worse.

I scan the room again, but only see the usual faces. Paulina, a friend of my mother's that I've slept with a handful of times, gives me a blatant smile. I pretend like I don't see her. All I want to see is the waitress that wants nothing to do with me. And she's nowhere to be seen.

# Alison

THE CRYSTAL CLINKS TOGETHER AS I drop the tray on the nearest surface. Gripping the edge of the table, my hands are shaking and I try to calm the thundering of my heart, ignoring the champagne that drips onto the floor.

I squeeze my eyes shut. It was like he was stripping me naked in front of everyone in the room. Like he was dissecting everything I was thinking, every risqué thought running through my mind. The way his clear green eyes held me like a bailiff, giving me no option to look away. And all of it done in such an unapologetic fashion that I had to leave before I made a total fool of myself.

The Mayor of Savannah is head-over-heels more intense in person than even I thought he'd be—and I had high expectations. Watching him give a speech on television or interact in news clips, he exudes this crazy mix of power and sexiness. But Barrett Landry in person? It's almost enough to make you high.

I grab a towel and wipe up the champagne, trying to catch my breath. My head is spinning, my blood pumping so wildly I feel like I might pass out.

I've got to get a grip.

Righting the overturned flutes, my breathing finally evens out.

His hooded eyes weren't darkened for me. They were to gain a vote or a fifteen-minute romp in the limo waiting out front. I know how these things work. None of that was for me.

Not for me.

Not. For. Me.

A hip bumps mine and I look up into the animated face of Lola. "I saw you!"

"Saw me what?"

"Getting all flirty with the mayor!"

"I was so not getting all flirty with the mayor," I groan.

"I'm not blind, babe. But I *am* disappointed. I was waiting for the big moment! I was waiting for you to fall into him, for your hand to go to the side of his face . . ." She closes her eyes and sighs. "You missed an opportunity."

"I missed an opportunity to embarrass myself. Poor me." I roll my eyes and pick up another tray, this time a platter filled with canapés.

"For someone so fun, you're really not very fun when it counts," she huffs.

"What's Mr. Pickner say? *We aren't here to have fun,*" I intone. "I have work to do, Lo." I ignore her protests and head out of the kitchen. As soon as I step foot back into the Savannah Room, my elbow is snatched. I whip to the side to see Mr. Pickner guiding me off to the side.

The other servers flurry past us, giving me the side-eye. I'm not sure what I've done to be hauled off like this.

"Can I help you with something?" I ask, keeping my voice level.

"Have you forgotten the rules around here, Alison?"

"No, sir."

He tsks his tongue and releases my elbow. "I see and hear everything."

"Mr. Pickner, I have no idea what you're referring to, but I do have a tray that needs to be passed around the room. So if you'll excuse me . . ." I turn to leave, but his voice lets me know he's not done.

"It would serve you well to remember the contract you signed. You are to serve the guests and not engage them in conversation. You, Ms. Baker, are not a guest. You're not getting paid to entertain them. You're here to pass around appetizers, not yourself."

I whip around to face him head-on, my jaw slack. "Excuse me?"

"These people have nothing to say to you. If I catch you doing anything more than offering an appetizer, you'll be fired on the spot. Do you understand me?"

I open my mouth to respond, but my mouth feels lined with cotton. I want to tell him to take this plate of overly-priced smoked appetizers and shove them straight up his ass, but I'm not given the chance.

Before I can do anything, the energy in the space shifts. Mr. Pickner notices too, because he immediately takes a step away from me. Everything in the room seems to be drowned out, the air once filled with laughter and scooting chairs is now saturated with the scent of expensive spice.

My eyes flitter to my right to see Barrett Landry. His deep blue tie has been loosened a bit, his cufflinks gone, his sleeves rolled to his elbows. He looks elegant in his custom-fit suit. I've never seen a man look this put together and pull it off like he woke up this way.

He smiles and I immediately relax, my body instinctively responding to him. He holds my gaze for a long second, both stealing my breath and giving me oxygen at the same time, before a coolness falls over his face as he turns to my boss.

Mr. Pickner puts on his game face, the one he doesn't use with his employees, and outstretches a hand. His eyes are a bit wide, like he's as star-struck as the rest of us.

"Mr. Mayor! I do hope you're enjoying yourself. It's been an honor to cater this event for your campaign."

Barrett shakes his hand firmly, and I can see the muscles flex in his forearm. It's pure arm porn as I watch the veins pop and his tanned skin tighten.

"Tonight has been exemplary, thank you," Barrett says, letting his hand drop to his side. "I couldn't help but overhear a conversation between you and the lady by your side."

The vein in my boss's temple pulses and I know I'm screwed. My stomach twists, a pit of acid churning, as I wait to see where this conversation goes. I consider excusing myself, but I think that'll make things worse.

Instead, I throw back my shoulders and brace myself, preparing to hear my boss and this gorgeous man discuss some impropriety I've unknowingly committed and wait to be fired. My mind ticks off possible replacement jobs, a way to make the kind of money that is currently going into a fund to help pay for the rest of my schooling.

*God help me.*

"I'm sorry about that," Mr. Pickner says. "My employees are under strict orders not to disturb you or your guests. Please accept my apologies and assurance that I will deal with this and it won't happen again."

"I'd hope not," Barrett says, his voice stern. "I'd hope you wouldn't reprimand your employee for taking a few minutes to answer my questions. This is a social gathering, *Jim*," he says, looking pointedly at him, "and it is one *I'm* paying for. If I'd like to socialize with . . ."

He looks at me with raised eyebrows and waits on me to find my voice.

"Alison Baker," I say, trying to look away, but unable to pull my eyes away from his.

"If I'd like to socialize with Alison, it seems as though I'm paying for the honor."

Mr. Pickner's face pales. He stumbles to recover but fails spectacularly. "Oh, I, um, I'm sorry, Mr. Landry. I had no idea. I . . ."

"I'm sure you didn't, which is why I find your readiness to discipline her insulting. In business, it's best you have the facts before you leap into action." He watches Mr. Pickner's face fall further and further towards the plush carpeting until he's satisfied. "Let me also point out that it is never okay for you to put your hands on a woman."

"I just—" he begins, but Barrett cuts him off.

"Never okay." He takes the tray away from me and sits it on a table nearby. He picks up my arm gently, sending a ripple of shivers throughout my body. My voice is gone again, and I try to remember everything I once knew about keeping calm and maintaining courtesy.

"Are you okay, Alison?"

His voice wraps around me like a warm blanket, and I'm certain if I weren't okay, whatever would've been wrong would suddenly be healed. My hand tingles where his is touching it, all of my senses buzzing. He grins, not his usual wide, disarming smile, but a softer one I haven't had the pleasure of seeing before. It's the one I won't forget.

"I'm okay," I say, pulling my hand away. "Really."

Barrett pauses, his eyes narrowing again, searching me. "I'd like to take you for some fresh air, if that would be okay with you?"

I can hear the words my brain wants to say in my head. It's a long ramble of stuttered words laced with a string of lewd offers my body is demanding. I press my lips shut and opt not to risk it.

The mayor turns to my boss and they begin a conversation, but I don't hear them. I just watch Barrett, taking in the beauty in front of me—the dimple that's barely visible in his left cheek, the tiny scar above his right eye. He's clearly in charge, my boss now seeming no more than a little boy.

Finally, they turn to me and I gulp. I have no idea what's been discussed, and I feel like they expect me to know.

*Damn it.*

"Alison," Mr. Pickner says, "please forgive me for earlier. Feel free to enjoy the rest of your night." He dips his head and skitters back into the kitchen.

I look up into the handsome face of Mayor Landry. He's studying me, an intensity in his gaze that makes my stomach flutter.

*This is how I didn't pay attention. Gah! Pay attention, Ali!*

My breath comes out in stuttered wisps. I shouldn't be going anywhere with him. For about fifteen million reasons, I shouldn't leave this room with this man. "Thank you, Mayor Landry, but—"

"It's Barrett. Please, call me Barrett," he insists, stripping away my defenses.

"Okay, *Barrett*." I grasp the little bit of brain power I have left and stand tall. "A walk is really not necessary. I'm fine. He was just . . . helping me out of the way."

He smirks. "Ms. Baker, please, consider what I do for a living."

"What do you mean?"

"I'm a politician. I work with liars all day," he winks.

I can't help but laugh. "I'm sure you do. But, really, I'm good. Please, go enjoy your event and I'll get back to work."

He takes a step closer, the air between us on fire. "I would enjoy spending a few minutes with you."

I feel my cheeks heat under his gaze. His eyes brighten with amusement at my flush.

"Now, if you don't want to cause a scene, I'm going to suggest we duck out of here before we manage to gain a wider audience."

Glancing around the room, I notice a few people watching our interaction. A sick feeling erupts in my stomach as memories of being watched before creep in my mind.

*"Did you see the photographs of your husband with Ms. Murphy?"* The cameraman sticks a video recorder in my face. *"How does that make you feel?"*

I cringe.

Barrett offers me his arm and I start to take it, but pull it back in a flourish. "I spilled some alfredo on my sleeve earlier. You probably don't want to get that on you."

"It'll wash." His easy way lessens my anxiety. He's doing to me what he does to everyone—charming me, enchanting me. I like it way more than I should.

Images of him tossing his jacket off to the side, unbuttoning his shirt as he readies for the bath zoom through my mind. When my eyes meet his, I know he knows what I was thinking.

He closes the distance between us, lifting my arm and placing it through the crook in his.

The material is supple, his arm hard beneath. Being this close to him, I feel like I'm in a bubble, that it's just he and I, and everyone and everything else is suddenly on the outside.

His scent is intoxicating, his smile disarming. It's a blend of power and approachability, and the combination is mind-blowing.

My defenses crumble, hitting the ground with a hefty thump.

I glance nervously at a few men trying very hard not to notice us. Getting out of here suddenly seems like a good idea.

"Are you sure you want to do this?" I ask. "You don't have to, you know."

He studies me closely. "You're right. I don't have to. I want to."

## Alison

I FEEL GAZES HEAVY ON our backs, hear hushed whispers as Barrett leads me out of the ballroom. His eyes are fixed forward, his body tense, but he doesn't seem to second guess his decision, even when I give him another opportunity to bail. He simply clamps his free hand over mine on his arm and keeps moving.

Like a true gentleman, he holds the French doors open as I saunter through. The air is balmy for October, a barely noticeable wind breezing through the gardens of the estate. Crickets chirp now that the sun's gone down, and the midnight blue night sky is lit with a million twinkling stars. A path extends from the flagstone patio and twists through the property, lit dreamily by flickering torches.

The door closes behind me and I turn to see Barrett standing still, his hands in his pockets, a curious, yet soft, look on his face.

There are a handful of women on the far reach of the patio. I'm not sure if he doesn't see them or if he doesn't care that they're watching us. I force the ball of anxiety that sits in the middle of my stomach off to the side and instead focus on the dapper man that's *looking right at me*.

He smiles and I feel my knees go weak. I reach out and steady myself on the wooden railing, willing myself to keep it together. He's just a man.

I turn my back so he doesn't see me laugh.

*Just a man. Right.*

"Shall we?" His voice is thick, a honeyed Southern twang that melts me from the inside out. Before I can respond, he lifts my arm and laces it through his, as if we do this all the time. His touch is gentle, yet dominant, a combination that leaves me breathless.

I smile politely, giving myself kudos for not swooning outright. There's something completely intoxicating about being treated like a lady and manners are the best foreplay.

We take the steps slowly, descending into the night. Moving away from prying eyes, we begin down the path.

The night air feels like it cocoons us, separates us from everyone else. The stress of being under scrutiny drifts away, and I think he feels it too. His shoulders relax, his breathing eases. I find myself easily falling into step with him.

"It's nice out tonight," he says.

"It's beautiful. This venue is amazing."

"Have you been here before?" He looks down at me, his eyes sparkling in the light. His jaw line is clean-shaven, strong, and I wonder what it would look like with a dash of early morning stubble.

"I was here a few weeks ago for a wedding, actually."

"Anyone I know?"

"I don't know. I don't even remember their last name."

"I didn't have you pegged as a party crasher," he teases.

I laugh. "No, no party crasher here. I was working."

"Have you ever been here when you're not working?"

Shaking my head, I keep my eyes trained ahead. Surely he realizes that I don't hang out at the Savannah Room in my free time. My social circles don't encompass places and people like this—not anymore.

*"You and I have nothing to talk about anymore," Hayden said. "I'm a judge. You're a . . . I don't even know what you are, Alison. You've turned into nothing."*

*"Nothing?! You're kidding me, right? Because I surely wasn't nothing when I was working my ass off to pay your way through school! I've helped you get to where you are. I take care of our child. I . . . How dare you say that to*

*me?" I seethed.*

*He laughed like he didn't have a care in the world. "I can say anything I want to you. What are you going to do about it? Just . . . go home, Ali. Go be with your kind of people."*

"Hey," he says, shaking his arm and jostling me back to reality. "Are you okay? Did I say something?"

I smile at the concern in his eyes as I shake off the lingering sting of my ex-husband's contempt. "No. It's fine. Just . . . you know how it goes. Things pop up in your brain at the least convenient times."

"That happens to me all the time. Nearly every time I have to give a speech, I stand at the podium and open my mouth and think something completely absurd and have to recover in a couple of seconds."

He winks and I'm left wondering if that's true, or if he's saying it to make me feel better. Either way, I can't help but realize he's taken the pressure off me and made the entire situation feel less heavy.

"That's the reason you're a successful politician," I grin.

"So there's only one reason?"

Giggling, I say, "I only know you well enough for there to be one. Speak as you find."

"Speak as you find," he nods, rolling the premise around his brain. "I like that. A lot."

"My mother always says it. It was so annoying growing up. Every time she'd hear us gossip or speculate about people, she'd repeat that," I remember. "But now, I tell Huxley that all the time."

"Who's Huxley?"

We take a turn in the path and it grows darker. The spaces on the sides of the walkway grow wider, deeper, and fields are barely visible expanding to either side. I bet it's beautiful in the day, filled with flowers and birds.

"Huxley is my son." I pause, giving him time to absorb that little nugget. He cocks his head, running his bottom lip between his teeth, but says nothing. So I continue. "He's ten. He's insanely smart and a lover of all things baseball."

His lip pops free and he takes a deep breath. "So, is his father around? Your . . . ex-husband?"

"Ex-husband. Yes," I confirm. "No, he isn't around. It's a very long, dramatic story."

We stop walking and he turns to face me. He eyes me curiously, like he's dying to ask for details, but doesn't know if he should. I save him the decision.

"I don't really want to talk about that, if you don't mind."

"Absolutely. I'm sorry for bringing it up."

I sigh as casually as I can, hoping it downplays the situation. "It's just a topic that makes me pissy."

"Well, we don't want you pissy." He chuckles and turns to the side and points to the sky. "Right there. Do you see that?"

I gaze into the expanse of the sky, but have no idea what, exactly, he's referring to. "Um, one of the four trillion stars?"

"No," he laughs. "That entire little constellation. Do you see it? It looks like a baseball and a bat."

"I'm sorry," I say, trying not to laugh. "I don't see it. And I'm kind of worried about your sanity if you do."

His chest rises and falls with his laugh. "Well, Miss Baker, I'm worried about your creativity if you don't."

"It's just *baseball*," I say, twisting my lips together. "It's really boring. It's just . . ."

"The American way?"

"Boring?" I counter.

He shakes his head with a somber look on his face. "I'm not sure I can like you."

"Because I don't like baseball?" I laugh. "If that's the case, our friendship is hopeless. I can't like something that includes hours and hours of watching grown men hit a little ball with a stick."

"It's the all-American pastime! My brother is the center fielder of the Tennessee Arrows, for cryin' out loud. You have to like baseball, Alison. You must!"

The smile on my face is dopey, but I can't wipe it off. I know he doesn't really mean the insinuation that maybe there's some reason for me to like it because of his family, but still. Just hearing it come out of his mouth plays right to my inner romantic.

I need to change the subject to something neutral. He could suck me in with his charm and that's not going to do me any good. "So, you know some things about me. Tell me something about you."

He snickers and looks at the ground. "Why don't you tell me what you've read and I'll tell you if it's fact or fiction. It's probably easier that way."

"Sounds like a fun game," I tease. "Oh, the bits of truth I could glean."

"You aren't writing an article or anything, are you?"

"I *am* in school for journalism . . ."

His brows shoot to the sky.

"Barrett, I'm kidding. I mean, I am in school for that, but I would never do that." He relaxes, but still looks a touch apprehensive.

"No, I believe you. You're way too real to be a reporter. You speak off the cuff with no lead-ins. Trust me, I can pick a reporter out of a line-up."

"Well, trust me when I say I hate them as much as you do."

He quirks a brow. "Then why would you want to work in that industry? It seems almost as bad as politics."

I laugh, but know exactly what he means. "It probably is." Looking up at his face, the way his gaze peers into mine, so genuinely interested—maybe even concerned—I feel my guard dropping. "I want to make a difference," I shrug. "I want to be the person that gets it right, that reports the truth and tells the things that are important. Is that stupid?"

"No, not at all," he muses. "It's a great thing to want to do. It's what I want to do too—take this dirty career and try to be the voice of reason. It's a hard job, but someone needs to do it, right?"

"Right," I smile, feeling my cheeks flush.

"You'll be a trailblazer," he sighs, shaking his head. "God, those people are animals. They'll report anything if they think it'll sell a copy of their publication. There are no ethics anymore. None."

"You're telling me. They're vicious and hateful."

He slows his pace, the moon glancing over his features, making his jaw line look sharper, his eyes more powerful than ever before. "You've really been hurt, haven't you?"

"Oh, Mr. Mayor, you have no idea," I laugh. "But, once again, we aren't talking about me anymore. We are talking about you and your fact and fiction."

He rolls his eyes, looking adorable. I could just watch him move all night. Some people love to watch other people in malls and parks. I could watch Barrett read the newspaper.

"Go ahead. Fire away," he says.

"I hate to tell you this and burst some sort of ego you might have, but I really know nothing about you to ask," I wince. "I'm sorry."

His jaw drops. "Are you serious right now?"

"Yeah," I eke out. "I mean, I know the basics. I know who you are, bits and pieces of your family and things like that. But I don't really have time to read papers or watch television right now."

He presses his lips together, maybe to keep from smiling, and subtly nods his head. "Well, damn. I've found a unicorn."

"That's something I've never been called."

He looks at me and I make a face, causing him to burst into laughter. His voice rolls over the fields. A flock of birds take flight from a grouping of trees nearby.

"Can I just tell you how much I love that you know nothing about me?"

"I didn't say I know nothing about you. I just said I know nothing about you to ask."

"Um, the difference?"

I wink, but don't answer. I'm not going to tell him how insanely gorgeous he is or how he ignites a fire in my belly with one glance. There's no way I'm telling him I know, *I know*, he'd be great in bed and that I'm positive he could take over my mind and heart if I let him.

I have to stay focused on what I need and what's best for Huxley, and that's not falling in lust with some dapper politician. More than I already am.

"So, what do you do for fun?" I ask instead, pivoting and heading back towards the building.

"Well," he says, turning his head back and forth, "I don't get time for a lot of fun these days."

"That's sad."

He snorts. "Tell me about it. Right now my life is centered around this campaign."

I hear a grit in his voice, a slight twinge of frustration. "I'm sure that's a lot of work this close to the day of reckoning."

"It is. It's all anyone wants to talk about. Family dinner turns into a campaign staff meeting somehow and it's just . . . it's hard to get away from." We turn the bend, the building glowing ahead of us. "I love it, don't get me wrong. This is what I was born to do. I just haven't found the balance between this and my personal life." He takes a deep breath. "Sometimes I wonder if there is a balance, if you can really have both."

I think back to my marriage. "I don't have experience with politics specifically, but I know the struggle of being in the public domain and trying to lead a normal life. It's tough. It's hard to keep the stuff not job-related private, sacred. It kind of . . . poisons everything."

The venom in my voice is thick, but I don't even attempt keeping it out. I couldn't if I wanted to.

"One of these days, I'd like to know what happened to you," he whispers. "But I won't ask you tonight."

We exchange a smile. It isn't the wide, charming one he uses on his political adversaries, nor is it the sexy smirk he used on me before. It's something else, the one from earlier—something more private—and it sends a wave of warmth through me.

"Would you like to have dinner with me one night this week?" he asks, a drop of hesitation in his voice.

My throat burns as I prevent myself from answering right away. Of course I want to, who wouldn't? But what good will it do? There's very little chance he'd do or say something to make me not want to see him again, and the fact of the matter is, he's a candidate in an election. He isn't in a place for a relationship, and what I need, what Huxley needs, is for me to be serious and calculated in everything I do.

"Alison?"

"I'd love to," I say, taking a deep breath, "but I'm going to have to decline."

He's taken aback, his steps faltering beside mine. "So . . . no?"

"Yes, no," I laugh. "Is that the first time you've heard that or something?"

"Well, yes. More or less."

I laugh louder as the lights ahead of us get brighter.

"This isn't funny," he says with a grin spread across his cheeks. "I really would like to see you again."

I beam and hope that the darkness hides it. "I would like to see you again in a perfect world. But we both know that's not what this is."

"No, it's not. Because you just told me no."

"Oh my God," I sigh, amused. "The timing is just bad, Barrett. You're in the midst of a campaign and I . . ."

"You what?"

"I'm a single mom trying to do what's best for her kid. And that's not going to dinner with you."

He stops in his tracks, his head cocked to the side. "Forgive me for asking, but what does you being a single mom have to do with you not going to dinner with me?"

"Look, I didn't mean it like that," I breathe. "It's just that my marriage was sort of high-profile and it ended spectacularly bad. I have this fear of the media, of reporters, specifically," I gulp. Then, before I can think about it, I add, "It's not just my life that goes to dinner with you. Huxley's life kind of goes too."

"So you would rather not go to dinner with me than be tossed into magazines. That's what you're saying?"

I nod.

He grins devilishly.

"That just makes me want to go to dinner with you more, Alison."

With every centimeter his smile spreads, it tugs my lips right along with it.

"It's extremely hard to find someone that wants to have dinner with me—the stripped down version. Women want the photographs, everyone to know they're with me. And you . . . don't."

I try to pull my gaze from his, but it's near impossible. He searches me—not my facial expressions or the angle of my posture, but me. Through my eyes and deep into my soul.

Shivering at the feeling of exposure, I finally look away. "You're right. I don't," I whisper.

He considers this, rocking back on his heels like I saw his brother do earlier. "What if I promised you we could do it at a place no one would see us? Just you and I. No agenda. No media. No expectations. Just a dinner between two friends."

"We're friends now?"

"I just saved you from your boss! You owe me one. And if that display of heroism doesn't get me . . . *friended* . . . what will?"

"You, Mr. Landry, are lucky you chose the word *friended*."

"What did you think I was going to choose?" he asks wickedly.

"You're impossible."

My heart beats like crazy in my chest. I need to put space between us before the remnants of the wall I built around my heart break and I end up agreeing to dinner with this man. Pivoting on my heel, I head back up the path.

"Are you always a pain in the ass?"

"Mr. Landry, I think you just lost yourself a vote," I say, feigning disbelief.

He stops in his tracks, pulling me to a stop alongside him. He turns me without me ever realizing it's happening until we're face to face. "You could do the right thing and give me another chance to win it back."

His voice is low, his eyes boring into mine. I feel my body temperature spike, my pulse throbbing. An ache builds in my core, the flames growing hotter by the second.

"I want a chance to win you over," he breathes, peering at me. The way his eyes search mine make it seem like time stands still. "Will you let me try?"

He forces a swallow and the look of hesitation, the internal fight he's having, isn't lost on me. It's there, right beneath the surface, and when I add my concerns to the mix, it's enough to make me balk. Just a bit.

"I'll think about it," I whisper, holding on to the little strand of courage I have left.

"Say yes."

Instead of responding, I ask, "Where'd you get that scar over your right eye?" I reach out and press gently on the raised skin. I expect him to pull back, but he doesn't.

My hand shakes as I touch his warmed skin. His forehead is silky and smooth. I'd like to run my hands over every inch of it, feel it ripple beneath my fingertips.

The corner of his lips twitch. "Lincoln hit me in the head with a baseball."

"Bad reflexes on your part?"

"Wicked curveball on his," he says, his face breaking out into a full smile.

"I thought he played center field?"

"He does. But he pitched some growing up."

We stand inches apart, my hand gently brushing down the side of his face. Although I feel like he'd stand here all night and talk to me, it's not possible.

"I really need to get back to work," I say, trying to unlock my eyes from his.

"Dinner? This week?"

I can barely resist the look in his eye, the one that implores me to say yes. The one that makes me believe he really does want to have dinner and spend a few hours with me.

I need to get away, put some space between us while I can.

"We ran into each other tonight," I shrug. "If we're supposed to see each other again, then I guess we will." I start to turn away before I completely buckle under his gaze.

"How am I supposed to get ahold of you? I don't have your number," he calls after me.

Heading up the steps to the Savannah Room, I glance at him over my shoulder. "You're the Mayor. Figure it out."

## Alison

IT'S LATE WHEN I MAKE it back to my little two-bedroom rental across town. The light in the kitchen is on as I pull into the driveway and cut the engine. I see the curtains pull back and my mother peering out at me.

I make my way up the walkway, nearly tripping over one of Huxley's baseballs. My brain is scattered, still back on the path of the gardens with Barrett.

I'd forgotten what this feels like. The excitement of sparking someone's interest, the feeling of being desired by a man. Maybe Hayden made me feel this way early on, but if so, it was quickly replaced with something more . . . mundane. Even the handful of dates I've gone on since never set this kind of energy into play. The way he looks at me, the fire from his touch lingers on my skin even now.

The door swings open as I reach the threshold.

"How was work?" my mother asks, closing the door behind me.

"Good. Long," I reply, tossing my purse on the couch and heading into the kitchen. "How did things go here? How's Hux?"

"He did all his homework and fell asleep to cartoons. There's a permission slip for you to sign on the kitchen table."

The purple piece of paper is lying next to the salt and pepper shakers when we reach the kitchen. "Did he eat dinner?"

"I made spaghetti, so of course. It's his favorite. There's some in the fridge if you're hungry." She takes a step back and eyes me carefully in the way only a mother can. "What's going on with you, Ali?"

Turning my back to her, I run some water from the tap and take a long draw of the cool liquid, hoping it calms my reddened cheeks and stops me from blushing further.

"Nothing," I say, leaning against the fridge.

She taps her lips with her fingertip, something she's done my whole life. "You look flushed. Are you feeling well?"

I can't help but laugh. I'd love to tell her that I'm feeling particularly amazing, that I haven't felt this good, this woman-like, in years. But I don't because she'd get all hyped up, wanting details, and I've learned my lesson in that department. Besides, this *thing*, whatever it may be, will end with dinner in the best case scenario. And, if so, that'll be that. Nothing more.

"I'm fine, Mom. Stop."

"Stop what? Being a mom?" she sighs. "You know I worry about you. You run yourself ragged. Between work at the restaurant, catering, school, taking care of Huxley . . ." She shakes her head and grabs her purse off the chair.

"I have a lot going on. I know. But it's all a means to an end."

"I know, sweetheart. But I fear you're going to burn out."

"Not happening," I say, giving her a reassuring smile for the millionth time about this. "I'm not dipping into my savings to pay for school. That money is a rainy day fund, something I can build on for Huxley. Catering has to pay for school and school has to pay for my life someday so I can quit waitressing."

"I'd rather you use the savings for school and then—"

"I know. I know you would, and I appreciate your concern. But I have a plan. I'm setting myself up like I should've when I was younger. I need to do these things on my own so no one can take them away from me."

Her face sours at the reference to my ex-husband, her lips pressed tightly together. If anyone hates Hayden more than me, it's my parents. It was hard on them to see me humiliated and broken-hearted, but they helped me pick up the pieces of my broken life.

Not that there were many pieces to reconstruct. We had clothes and personal affects when we left New Mexico and a little money. And most of that was eaten up in attorney's fees after defending myself in Hayden's debauchery, finding a new home and new job. I had no nest egg, no safe place, no career or degree to fall back on. Hayden took everything from me. No one will take it from me again.

"Let's not go there, Mom. What's done is done."

"What's done is done," she repeats, tossing her purse on her shoulder. "If you're good, I'm going to head out now. It's late."

"Go. Tell Daddy I said hi."

She kisses my cheek and leaves me standing in the middle of the kitchen.

The house is quiet. I dread this part of the day, the moment I get in from work or school and Huxley is asleep and my mother is waiting on me to get home like I'm a teenager. It's the time of day when I'm forced to look in the proverbial mirror and see myself and my situation. I'm not happy with what I see but it's getting better.

My stomach growls, reminding me that it's empty. Even so, I don't feel hungry. I'm completely warm and fuzzy from head-to-toe, like I've taken a few swigs of cinnamon whiskey. But I haven't. I'm buzzed on a sexy politician.

Grabbing a pen and signing Huxley's permission slip, I pad down the hallway to his little bedroom. It's across the hall from mine and decked out in a baseball theme.

He's in his bed. The light from the moon shines in the windows, making his blonde hair look like it has a halo. I bend forward and listen to the slow breathing, the precious sound that never ceases to amaze me. I used to stand in his bedroom over his crib at night and just watch him sleep. After we left Hayden, I would sneak into his room late at night and try to convince myself things would be okay. That what he'd gone through at the hands of his own father wasn't going to ruin him forever.

"Mommy?" Huxley's tear-filled eyes met mine, both hope and misery swimming together. "Where's Daddy?" His little voice cracked, the words leaving his mouth on a sob half-repressed, only a moment away from being a wail. "He's coming back, right?"

I pulled him to me, wrapping my arms protectively around his shoulders. I intentionally buried his face in my stomach so he couldn't see the river of tears cascading down my cheeks and prayed he couldn't feel my heart breaking.

"It'll be okay, Hux," I whispered.

He didn't believe me. I didn't believe me, not really. It's hard to believe things will be okay when you watch everything you've worked for, all the things you believed in for so long, go up in flames because the man you pinned all your hopes on ripped them away and doused them with gasoline.

Huxley pulled away, his face stained with wetness. "Why doesn't Daddy love me?"

Whatever happens in my life, I won't let that happen to him again.

Huxley's long lashes flutter and he peers up at me with a sleepy grin. "Hey, Mom. You're home."

"Hi, buddy," I say, brushing a few stray locks of hair off his forehead, pushing away the memories that have my chest aching. "How was your night?"

"Good," he yawns, struggling to keep his eyes open. "How was work?"

"It was fine. Go back to sleep. I'll see you in the morning, okay?" Kissing him gently, I tuck his blankets around him and blow him a kiss before leaving. As soon as the door is pulled shut, my phone begins to ring. I scurry to retrieve it before Hux hears.

Swiping it from my purse, I see Lola's name and my spirits lift, a smile gracing my face.

"Hello?"

"I want the scoop."

I laugh and make my way into the kitchen, the room farthest from Huxley, and settle into a chair at the wooden table. "The scoop? Whatever do you mean, Lola?"

"Cut the crap, Ali. I want to know what you did with the mayor tonight. I want to know every position, every flick of the tongue."

"You will be sad to know that no tongues were flicking."

"That's not just sad. That's depressing."

"Even I have to agree with you there," I sigh.

I fiddle with the salt shaker on the table, thinking back to the last few hours. It's a little disconcerting that he was able to make me feel so relaxed around him. I knew he had charm, but not like that. How he makes you forget you're with *him*, until you look up at his face or he touches your arm.

"The entire staff was buzzing about how Jim got put in his place by Landry," Lola recalls. "Isaac overheard most of it, but I want firsthand information. Every word, every look—give it to me."

There's no way I'm going to be able to avoid discussing this with her, although I want to. I want to keep it my little memory of Barrett, something that feels like my own. Something that makes me feel special in a completely stupid way.

Still, it's Lola and she'll pester me until I relent, so I have to throw her some kind of bone to shut her up.

"Isaac must've heard Jim telling me not to socialize with the guests after seeing me serving Barrett champagne. But Barrett told him that he had initiated the conversation and it was his party to do what he wanted."

"*Barrett*? First name basis?"

"He asked me to call him by his first name. Not a big deal."

"Let's just say I served the sexy bastard champagne tonight too and I didn't get the first name treatment. What else happened? And don't leave out the good stuff."

"There is no good stuff, Lo. Not like you're thinking," I laugh. "We just took a walk. We talked about random things and that was it."

"Were any of those random things requests for sexual favors?"

"Nope."

She sighs dramatically and I laugh.

"I'd ask why you didn't offer to deliver sexual favors, but I know the answer," she says.

"And what's that?"

"You're lame," she says matter-of-factly.

"I am not!"

"Yes, you are. L-A-M-E, lame. You continue to let some dick and his dick antics ruin your life. That, my dear friend, is lame."

"No, it's not," I fight back. "I can't do what you do and just go have fun. It's not that easy for me, even if I wanted it to be."

I can't see her do it, but I know Lola rolls her eyes. She just doesn't get it. To her, life is one big party until she hits it big. To me, life is lying in a bedroom down the hall all snuggled up in his twin bed with baseball sheets. Whatever decisions I make directly affect him, and Huxley is more important to me than anything.

"Why wouldn't you want it to be?" Lola asks. "You getting off tonight has nothing to do with Huxley. Hell, it might make you relax a little bit. Did you ever think about that?"

"Yes, I've thought about that," I gruff into the phone. "But think about it with your head for a second, will you? You're the one that goes on and on about Landry. You know how easy it could be to get wound up in him."

"Did you mean the innuendo you just tossed out there? Because if so, yes. Yes. I do."

"Damn it, Lo!" I laugh. "Listen to me. Barrett isn't like Isaac or whatever guy you were with tonight. He's . . ."

"Perfect?"

"Yes," I breathe. "So far he seems to be. But that's the thing," I say, fueled by the point I'm ready to make. "He's not. He's just like the other men in his position. He's powerful, used to getting his way. Women are toys to men like him. And—" I say, cutting her off, "—I'm not saying I'm opposed to being with him. But if that happens, it has to be under a certain set of guidelines. I have to keep some control over it because he'll win this election and jet off to Atlanta and I'll never hear from him again."

She snorts. "That's not true."

"It is true. I've seen it. Hell, I've lived it. What happened in my marriage? With the man that promised to cherish me forever?" I pause for effect. "Oh, yeah, that's right—he got some power and forgot about me. *His wife*. He swapped Huxley for a prostitute and our life for some back room deals that got him indicted and me investigated with an assault charge."

"That didn't stick," she points out. "No one believed you assaulted that reporter."

"No, but my face was in the papers, my name was ripped to shreds for nothing," I groan. "Don't you see what I'm saying? To men like Hayden and Barrett, I'm sure people are just instruments for entertainment while they scale the ladder."

She doesn't respond. Her breathing sounds through the phone, so I know she's still there.

"Lo?"

"I just hate that you went through that," she says softly. "I do. And I hate it for my buddy Huxley too. But Ali, it's time to spread your wings farther than being a mom and figuring out your career. It's time to do something for you."

"So you think doing Landry is the answer?" I smirk.

"Absolutely," she laughs.

"I can't afford to let my heart get all tied up in a man like that again."

"Well, my friend, your heart and your vagina are two different things. You want to close off your heart—go for it. But keep your legs open."

"You are insane."

"No, I'm perfectly rational. You can have sex just for the sake of orgasms, you know. You don't have to tie yourself all up. You aren't sixteen."

I laugh and stand, walking to the back door and looking across the backyard. It, like the house, is small but has enough space to toss around a ball and catch lightning bugs in the summertime.

"I have plenty of meaningless sex," I counter.

"No, you don't. You've slept with two guys, each a handful of times, in the handful of years I've known you. That's not 'plenty.' That's grossly underwhelming."

I sigh, knowing she's right. "Maybe I'm over *meaningless sex*. Maybe I'm . . ." I look at my reflection and contemplate saying the one thing I've been toying with in my head aloud. Once I spew it into the universe, it's out there for good. And maybe that makes it true. "Maybe I'm ready to have *meaningful sex*."

"Why would you go and do something like that?"

"I've been through all the emotions of a divorce. I've been sad. Angry. I've grieved and had meaningless sex. But maybe that's not enough now. Maybe I know down deep I'm looking for something more real than a quickie, so I'm playing it smart so I don't get gobsmacked by a man just like the one that burned me. So I don't end up right back where I started. Maybe I'm trying to find someone that I'll be able to trust and that will be respectable enough to bring into Huxley's life. Maybe I'm working on that." The line is silent for a long while. "Lola?"

"Oh, I'm here. Just trying to figure out how that means you can't fuck Barrett."

I laugh and do a check of the house, making sure everything's locked tight. "You have a one-track mind."

"This is true. And on that note, I have to go. I'm meeting a guy I met last week for a round two. Because separate hearts and vaginas and all."

"Does he even have a name?" I yawn.

"Who cares? His cock is massive."

"Nice," I say, shaking my head. "I'll talk to you soon."

"Bye, love."

I walk into the bathroom and set the phone on the counter. Looking into the mirror, my long blonde hair is wild, as it usually is after a long shift. It's coming out of the tie I'd tried to use to tame it, so I pull it out and let it cascade over my shoulders.

My eyes are dark blue, but there's a sparkle in them I haven't seen in a long time.

*"What if I promised you we could do it at a place no one would see us? Just you and I. No agenda. No media. No expectations."*

I place my hands on the counter and bow my head.

Just thinking about him makes me feel tingly. The thought of his smile makes *me* smile, the recollection of his words making me crave the chance to hear more.

I wish I was Lola and could have just offered myself to him, no strings attached. But I'm not Lola with her confidence for days. I'm a divorcee with more self-doubt than I'd like to admit. I can't play off my feelings or shake off rejection, and if I'm smart, I know I certainly can't afford to tie up any part of myself, heart or vagina, with a man like Barrett Landry.

## Barrett

THE GLOW FROM THE LAMP on my bureau illuminates the room. I remove my jacket, tie, and dress shirt and toss them haphazardly onto the back of a chair. It feels good to be home, to be "off," to breathe. I haven't relaxed all night, except for the few minutes I was with Alison.

I should be rehashing the night, going over conversations, trying to get a feel as to who I can count in my corner. But I don't. My mind drifts to her every time, and if I'm honest, I like it there.

Flopping back on the California king mattress, my body sinks into the down comforter. I let my lids close and Alison's face pops up immediately in my mind. Her shy smile, the way her long lashes flutter when she's embarrassed, how the corners of her lips tug when she tries to pretend like I don't affect her as much as I know I do—the images blend together to form an amazing slideshow.

My phone rings on the table and I swipe at it with my hand until I find it. I glance at the clock and wonder who is calling me so late.

"Hello?" I ask. I clear my throat, my voice sounding gravelly from being up for the past twenty hours. I can feel every hour in the back of my neck, each frustration in the tightness of my muscles.

"Hey, brother. How are ya?"

"Hey, Linc. What's up?"

I prop my head up on a pillow and get comfortable.

"Fucked up my shoulder, actually. I threw a long one from center and something snapped. I don't think it's a big deal, but I gotta see the team doctor in the morning."

"Damn. I hope it's nothing," I say. "At least the season is over, right?"

He blows out a breath. "Yeah. Silver linings and shit. So, enough about me, how's the campaign? Sorry I couldn't make it tonight."

"Don't worry about it. It went well. I'll know more tomorrow when Nolan gets me the official report."

Lincoln laughs, his voice crackling through the receiver. He's never been a fan of Nolan. He thinks he's sneaky and uptight. He's probably right on the uptight part, but Nolan has worked for our family for years. He's the one with the blueprint to eventually get me into the White House.

"Yeah, you know how I feel about that. You don't need Nolan, man. Just turn shit over to Graham and you'll be fine."

"Graham doesn't have experience with this like Nolan."

"But you can trust G. And trust is the most important thing."

"Since when does my little baseball player brother know anything about business?" I laugh.

"I have investments," he reminds me. "But you don't have to know business to know about trust. If you have one person that has your back, you're a lucky son of a bitch."

"That's true."

Linc grimaces. He groans through the phone and I know he's working his shoulder, trying to convince himself that it isn't as bad as he's been told.

"You probably need to rest that," I point out.

"I am," he barks.

"No, you aren't. You're working it around, trying to do the mind over matter bullshit that isn't going to do anything but tear it up worse."

"It's fine."

Rolling my eyes, I move the phone to my other hand. "Whatever you say."

"Welp, not to cut this short or anything, but I have a call coming in I need to take."

I laugh at the hurriedness in his voice. "Piece of ass hitting you up?"

He clicks his tongue and I know I'm right. "Good to know I'm so high on your priority list," I joke.

"I'll be in town tomorrow afternoon. See you then."

"Be safe."

Setting the phone on the nightstand, I glance at my clothes on the back of the chair. I need to pick them up, to grab a shower, to process the night. Hell, I really need something to eat.

Instead of sitting down with my briefcase or heading to the kitchen or shower, I sit on the edge of my bed and toy with the idea of calling Alison. My fingers itch to dial the number Graham located for me a couple of hours ago. Naturally, he doesn't know why I asked for it, and he was too busy to look into exactly who it was, otherwise he never would've done it.

Glancing at the clock again, my spirits sink. It's too late. She said she has a kid and I'd probably wake him up.

I fall against the mattress and think back to her big blue eyes. The way they sparkled when she laughed, how it felt when she wrapped her fingers around my elbow and let me guide her. She didn't lead me, didn't try to press her own agenda.

An undeniable smile breaks across my cheeks.

I've forgotten what it's like to have someone around that's not jaded by everything. Everyone I know, everyone I deal with, knows what to say and when and how to say it. They toe the line, don't rock the boat, follow suit—pick your well-behaved cliché. They know what's expected of them and who not to piss off.

Alison seems to have some experience in this kind of life, yet she doesn't seem like it affects how she behaves.

*Focus*, Nolan said.

Grinning, I realize I'm following orders. I'm focusing, all right. Just not on what he wants me to.

## Barrett

THE EARLY AFTERNOON SUN FILTERS through the curtains, the fall breeze dancing through the window. A gust picks up a stack of papers and ruffles them, threatening to send them cascading off the corner of my large wooden desk.

It's perfectly quiet here, the sound of birds chirping and an occasional noise from Rose, my secretary, downstairs are the only two things that disturb me.

I inhale a long breath of fresh air and try to absorb the peace. Between the planning committee, opening the bids for a new recreational area downtown, reviewing license requests from businesses, and taking calls from my election committee, my head is spinning faster than usual. The morning has been the new normal level of chaos. Just getting into the office downtown to do the work I was elected to do was a feat. Camera crews blocked the doors to the office, reporters shouting questions in response to Hobbs' latest attack. It was a mess. By eleven, I couldn't take it anymore and grabbed Rose and headed here, to the Farm.

An old farmhouse that sits just outside the city, directly in the middle of a fifty-acre piece of property, this is my favorite place in the world. The front is heavily treed and it's impossible to see the house from the road. It's been the headquarters of my family's political campaigns and family gatherings for decades. It's now used by my father and Graham for business deals for Landry Holdings, by my brother, Ford, when he's home from the Marines and needs a place to decompress, and by me.

I close my eyes and feel the air on my skin, listen to the curtains sweep against the hardwood floors. I would love to take a walk through the woods, but there's no time for that these days. Each day that passes, the less inspired I am, the less I can remember what free time used to feel like and the more I struggle to remember why, exactly, this was a profession I wanted in the first place. Not being able to trust anyone, questioning everyone's motives, leaves me feeling completely alone. It's bizarre—the more public my life becomes, the more isolated I feel.

Adding to my distraction today is a certain beguiling girl. I think of things to say to hear her laugh, I come up with things to say just to get a response. I want to see her smile, smell her, hear her voice again so badly I can taste it and I don't know why.

This doesn't happen to *me*.

I'm the king at keeping things superficial with women. I've always been good at that, but it's a skill I've honed to a razor's edge in the last few years because I can't trust anyone anymore.

I replay our conversation from last night, smiling as her laugh rings through my ears. She was on my mind when I finally fell asleep and the first thing I thought of when I woke up with a smile and a raging hard-on.

I grab the desk phone and press the intercom.

"Can I help you, Mr. Landry?"

"Yes, Rose. Can you order some lunch, please? Have it delivered?"

"Sure, sir. Your usual?"

"No," I draw out. "Actually, I'd like to try someplace new. Have you heard of Hillary's House?"

"Yes. Of course."

I smile. "Excellent. Will you order me something? Get yourself some lunch too."

"Absolutely."

My grin grows deeper. "And can you see if an Alison Baker is working? If so, I'd like her to deliver."

"No problem."

"Rose?"

"Yes."

"Please keep my request quiet. Just tell the owner that I'll pay extra for the inconvenience, but I'd appreciate it, being that it's election season and all, that she doesn't know where she's going."

"Makes sense. I'll have something here soon."

## Alison

"FREE AT LAST!" I SING, smiling at my co-workers and tossing a towel in the laundry chute at Hillary's House. "That lunch rush just about killed me. The next time you make meatloaf, Opal, I'm calling in sick! I swear it brings them in from all over the city."

"Yeah, but you're done now," Opal sighs, sticking another tray of food in the warming drawer. "I'm here for another two hours."

"It'll go quick if you don't think about it," I wink. "Have fun! I'm out of here."

"Anything fun planned?"

"Just a long, over-filled bubble bath," I sigh dreamily. "Hux is with my dad this afternoon fishing and I'm caught up on my homework for once. So I'm taking a few minutes and just pampering myself."

Opal smiles. "Oh, honey, you need to do that. You never take time just for you."

"It's what mothers do, right?" I grab my timecard out of the slot and go to punch out. I stop, mid-air, when my boss comes around the corner. Her long, blonde hair is pulled back into a braid, her pink bottom lip in between her teeth. The way her eyebrows are scrunched, I know I'm screwed.

"Hey, Hillary," I say, my voice saturated with cheeriness. "How are you? I'm just *leaving*."

"Oh, is it time for you to go?" She acts surprised and checks her watch for emphasis. "Darn. It is."

"It is. *Darn*," I say, but I don't punch out. Hillary's House is a great job. Not to mention she's about the sweetest person I know. So if she wants me to stay, she knows I will. *Damn her.*

"You wouldn't happen to want to do me one little bitty ol' favor, would you?"

"*No*," I tease, shaking my head.

"I need an order delivered out on Hammersmith Road. That's out by you, isn't it?"

"Um, like ten miles past me. Where's Dylan? Why doesn't he deliver it?"

Hillary looks around the kitchen and clears her throat. "Dylan is out on another delivery and this one needs taken now."

I slump against the wall, my dreams of a hot bath fading. "It can't wait ten minutes?"

"I wouldn't ask you to do this, Ali, if it wasn't necessary. I'll pay you overtime to take it. I'll pay you triple if you need me to."

"I'll take it for triple," Opal yells from across the kitchen. "Hell, I'll take it for double!"

"You are making pies this afternoon. Hush," Hillary admonishes her. She turns back to me, tilting her head. "*Please*, Ali. I'll save you a piece of the pecan pie Opal is making in a little bit."

"She gets overtime and pecan pie? I hate you both," Opal moans.

I sigh and put the card back in my slot. "Fine. I'll do it for double pay and pecan pie."

She slings an arm around my shoulder and rests the side of her head against mine. "I'll give you triple," she whispers. "Thank you."

"Yeah, yeah, yeah."

## Alison

I HAVE NO IDEA WHERE I'm at.

I drive past the entrance three times before I even realize it's an entrance at all. The gate is on the other side of the tree line, and a security guard, dressed in a navy blue suit, greets me with a scowl. He wants to see my credentials, so I show him my Hillary's shirt and the large box in the back with food. After a couple of calls, he waves me in, and I start my trek down the mile-long driveway to the impressive home sitting at the end.

It's a three-story plantation-style house with black shutters and ferns hanging from hooks on the wrap-around porch. There are rocking chairs spaced evenly across the right side and a large table with what appears to be an oversized checkerboard to the left of the front door. A yellow dog comes running slo-mo from the side, his tail wagging and tongue sticking out. Another security guy, this one in a black suit and black tie, is waiting for me.

"Can I help you?" he asks. His eyes are a wicked shade of grey, his hair cropped close to his head. His skin is a smooth, olive-y color that's to die for.

"I'm here to deliver food," I say, letting my eyes sweep around the property. It's gorgeous and simple and quiet—the house of my dreams, basically. I can imagine myself sitting on one of the rockers on the porch with a glass of lemonade watching the sun set.

"Your name?"

"Alison Baker."

He steps out of my way. "I'm Troy. Go on in, Miss Baker. You don't need to knock."

I smile back, getting one final look at those beautiful eyes, and head inside. I would be more annoyed at the inconvenience of this little adventure if my curiosity weren't at an all-time high. *Who lives here? With security? And has lunch delivered by Hillary's?* I'd be a little concerned being so far out, but Hillary knows where I am and the security guy gives me a little peace that an axe murderer isn't going to jump out of the woods.

I'm wondering if Dylan comes here regularly as I push open the front door and step inside. It's as charming as the outside. Wooden floors and dark trim set off bright white walls, royal blue décor and dark brown accent pieces adding pops of color. There's a white desk in the corner with neatly-piled files and folders and a sofa to my other side.

No one comes to greet me, no one seems to even know I'm here besides security. I can't tell if this is a house or some kind of office.

The sound of footsteps against the hardwood makes me whirl around to see a grey-haired lady looking as surprised to see me as I am to see her.

"Well, hello," she says, taking the eyeglasses off her face. "Who might you be?"

"I'm Alison from Hillary's." I gesture with the box of food in my arms and shrug.

She smiles and it reminds me of my grandmother. Her face is calm and kind, her blush a little too heavy. She nods and takes the smaller box from me. "Take that one up the stairs, to the right, and to the door at the end of the hall, please."

"I . . ." I start to speak, to ask why she can't take it considering she knows where she's going, but the smile on her face stops me. I suddenly feel disrespectful. "Sure thing."

I shuffle past her and make my way up the stairs. My steps echo as I clamor to the top and take a right.

If I weren't so in love with the house, I'd probably be more nervous.

I have no idea where I'm going or who is awaiting me. I just hope it isn't a dying old woman like in an old movie because that's exactly what this reminds me of.

The door facing me at the end is closed and I glance around, but there's no one to be seen. All of the other doors are closed. There's just a table sitting on a white rug and a vase full of multicolored marbles on top.

I take a deep breath and knock, hoping this doesn't take long. There's still hope for that bath if I can get out of here in a snap.

"Come in," a man's voice barks from the other side. It's low with a touch of authority dripping from it in such a familiar way.

My stomach somersaults and I pull my hand away from the door. I stare at it like it's going to give me the answer to the question running through my mind—*why do I know that voice?*

Before the door can tell me like in a Disney movie, it swings wide. And there Barrett stands, poised like he's ready to have his picture taken.

*Oh. Fuck.*

One hand in the pocket of his dark grey pants, one resting against the door frame, his eyes shimmer as they wait for my reaction.

*My reaction . . .*

I start to speak but can only sort of laugh, the words stolen by the sight of him. A crimson-and-white gingham shirt, buttons open at the top to expose a tiny sliver of tanned chest, is nearly my undoing. How he can look better than he did in a suit and tie is beyond me, but it's clearly possible. He's standing in front of me, smirk deepening by the second, gaze dancing across my flushed skin.

*Waiting for my reaction . . .*

"You ordered food?" My head bobs with the words, my voice much cheerier than I intend it to be. It seems like such a strange question because obviously he did or security wouldn't have let me in here. But the odds of Barrett ordering food from Hillary's by chance and me ending up here are what? Zero? Negative three?

And then it hits me.

*"You're the Mayor. Figure it out."*

My words from last night ring through my head and my cheeks

flush in remembrance. Figure it out he did, but did he have to do it when I smell like a deep fryer and he looks like a fashion model?

He grins, flashing his perfectly white teeth, and takes a step away from the door. His shoulders seem to fall, a wash of relaxation waving across his features. "I believe Rose ordered it, but yes, I'm expecting lunch."

The gruffness in his tone from before is suddenly gone.

I take a few steps into his office. Barrett removes some papers from a table beneath a window and then leans against it. He crosses his arms, and much to my dismay, doesn't say a word. It's like he wants me to break the ice, but that fucking grin on his face is melting me faster than I can think.

"How are you today?" he asks carefully, feeling me out.

I consider the inappropriateness of my *real* answer. Telling him that my body is tingling, that the flame that's just been ignited in my core is smoldering, that the way he touched me in my dreams last night was the best I've ever felt would probably not be the right conversation opener.

"Where would you like me to set this?" I ask instead, holding the box in front of me.

"Right here." He steps out of the way and I place the box on the table. I'm so close to him, I can smell the same spicy scent from last night, the one I haven't been able to get out of my memory. My brain is fuzzy; the look, smell, and energy that surround him are more than my little wits can take. I need air. I need space.

I need a vibrator. Again.

"Enjoy," I say and wait for him to talk, but he doesn't. I flash him a smile and turn to go. My head is spinning like a top and instead of standing here, feeling awkward, I figure I'll just leave. But before I can take two steps, a gentle yet firm hand is on my shoulder.

Everything misfires at the connection and I physically jump. My eyes dart to his and I hope he hasn't seen my reaction. Like the gentleman I know he probably really isn't, he pretends not to notice.

"Do you have somewhere you have to be?" The way he asks the question does to me what it does to everyone else when he talks—it compels me to answer. He speaks in a way that somehow lifts your words right out of you, even if you don't want to say them, like they know better than to deny him.

"Yes." At least my words still remember how to lie.

"I was hoping you'd be able to have lunch with me."

My body screams to stay. Hell, it wants to *be* lunch. But a part of me is yelling to run while I can because getting swirled into the orbit of Barrett Landry is probably more than I'd bargain for.

He moves effortlessly around the table, not waiting on an answer, and pulls out a chair. I sink into the soft leather, my breathing ragged, as I realize I've just committed to lunch with him. As a bubble of panic starts to develop, he pauses, looking at me over his shoulder. His eyes shine, a quiet grin settling over his lips. The look is intimate, his guard down, and I don't think many people probably see it. My heart flutters.

He busies himself unpacking the containers and sits half of them in front of me, the other half in front of him. It affords me the opportunity to get ahold of myself, to calm down and realize . . . this is okay. I'm okay. It's just a quick, impromptu meal, albeit one I'm utterly unprepared for.

Unfolding himself gracefully into the leather chair across from me, he opens his lunch. He lifts his eyes and the corner of his lips follow. "This looks great."

I smile, but don't respond. I'm still figuring out how I ended up seated at the table with him.

"Aren't you going to eat?" He nods to my still-closed container.

"I remember telling you I didn't want to have dinner." I bite my bottom lip to keep from smiling and his eyes go straight to my mouth.

He grins, a mixture of a little boy getting his way and a sexy as hell man well on the way to getting his. "Good thing this isn't dinner then. This is lunch."

I laugh and his posture relaxes further. I find myself falling into a rhythm with him, just like I did before. "Semantics, Landry."

"You can't fault me for playing by the rules. You said if we were meant to see each other, it would happen. I just, you know, made it happen."

I try to not be swayed by his cheeky grin or his hooded eyes or the way the muscles in his forearm flex beneath the watch on his wrist. Or the way I'm fairly certain he just reached discreetly beneath the table and adjusted his cock.

"That you did," I say under my breath and pop open the container in front of me. The food looks beautiful, Opal having done a fantastic job at staging the entree, but I can't eat. There's no way. My appetite is for one thing and that's sitting across from me.

"How has your day been?" he asks.

"Lunch was crazy today," I say. "How about yours?"

"Getting better," he says vaguely and then wraps those gorgeous lips around the fork.

I die. Imagining his lips on my skin, moving across it like they're doing to the metal tines makes me shiver. I hope he doesn't notice, but it's not like I can control it. I can feel him watching me, but I don't look up. I can't. It'll confirm that what he thinks I'm thinking is true and I'll die of embarrassment.

The silence is awkward, more awkward than a conversation in which I make a fool out of myself, so I take a gamble. "How'd the event go last night? Was it a success?"

"It was. Lots of connections were made although, between you and me, those things are usually pretty boring."

"That's good."

He rests his fork on the side of his plate and sits back, studying me. "Did you do anything after work last night?"

"I went home and slept like a log," I say, conveniently leaving out the phone call to Lola and then the date with my vibrator afterwards. "And then I got up and went to work today. Just another day in the life, you know?"

"I do. But you know what they say? All work and no play makes Jack a dull boy."

"Is that so?"

"That's what they say."

"So what do you like to play, *Jack*?"

When his eyes light up immediately and his lips twitch, I admonish myself for asking that question.

*Why, why, why do I do this to myself?*

"I play a lot of things very well," he insinuates.

"Do you?"

*Shut. Up. Alison.*

"Wanna play with me?"

I laugh, trying to ease the sexual chemistry that's now whirling around us like a cyclone. One little nod and I'm sure he's going to pounce, and I'm not sure I'll do anything more than fall on my back and open my legs. And while that'll be fun for however long his stamina runs—which is classified under *things I'd like to know*—after that, it'll be a disaster. This I'm sure of.

"I don't think I'm up for that challenge," I grin.

"I'll let you win," he says, his eyes growing wider, tempting me to break.

"I'm going to call bullshit on that."

He laughs, running a hand through his hair. I can almost see a weight lift from his shoulders. He seems even more casual than last night while we walked in the dark. Watching him control a room yesterday was such a turn-on, but watching him like this, relaxed, is maybe even sexier.

An easy breeze floats through the room and my gaze is carried out the window. I can see a line of trees, pines, I think, in the back of the property. It's so peaceful.

"Do you live here?" I ask.

"No. This is where I come to work when the office is too crazy. We call it the Farm."

"This is your getaway? Very nice," I approve.

"This isn't where I grew up, but I feel more at home here than anywhere in the world."

His features morph, turning lighter, more playful. He looks like a little kid showing off his new bike. It's adorable.

"I had no idea it was even here," I say. "It's amazing. So quiet."

"That's the point. I—"

Our gazes land on his desk to a phone buzzing. He looks at me for permission to answer and I nod. He stands and lifts the receiver.

"Yes, Rose?" He pauses and stares at the wall, purposefully not at me. "Send him through." He pauses again. "Yeah, Nolan?"

His posture changes immediately. His back stiffens, his shoulders tense. His volley back and forth with Nolan is all political jargon, the harshness in his tone has returned, thicker than before.

I wonder if this is what he goes through every day. It's even more stressful, I'm sure, than what Hayden went through, and I can't begin to fathom what that must do to his life. I know it's a part of the job, but I wonder how much of himself Barrett has to give up to have *this* life. And I wonder if he enjoys it.

"My cell is off because I'm trying to get some actual work done," he bites out. He moves confidently around the desk, one hand stuck in the pocket of his pants. He looks in total control, completely assured, a touch aggressive, and it's nothing short of visual foreplay. This call is prepping my body for sex, even though it wasn't meant to.

"If that's the absolute only way to get the votes, then fine," he finally sighs. I can tell he isn't thrilled about whatever he's just agreed to. "Listen, I want a list of other options you've explored before this goes through. I want it perfectly clear that if another way becomes available to achieve this, I want to go with it instead. *This is a last resort.* You got it?" He listens before planting the receiver firmly in place. He turns to face me, the prior look of amusement long gone. I'm not sure what that call was about, whether he's had a bomb dropped in his lap he must take care of.

"Are you okay?" I ask, my voice low. When he doesn't respond with more than a furrowed brow, I say, "That wasn't a rhetorical question."

"The campaign is a—"

"Barrett," I interject, "your campaign isn't what I was asking about. I was asking about you."

A slow smile slides across his face and he sits down and leans back in his chair. "In that case, I'm better at the moment than I have been since, well, last night."

I grin.

He pauses for a moment and then leans on his elbows again. "I'm sorry about that call. I don't know what else to say other than *welcome to my life.*"

"Is it always so . . . stressful? Aren't you here to get away from that today?"

"Yeah," he says, blowing out a breath. "It's a part of the job. It's 24/7."

"That must be exhausting."

"It's what I was born to do. Do the things I'm doing now."

"Are you sure?"

"What do you mean, *am I sure*? Of course I'm sure."

I almost play Devil's Advocate with him, but I don't. I let him be "sure" because really, it's none of my business.

"What are *you* sure about?" he asks me.

"I'm sure I wasted my time delivering the food."

I would never tell him that the smile I get in reply is worth it in itself.

"Are you saying you don't like my company, Ms. Baker?"

"I'm saying, Mr. Landry, that you could've called and invited me to lunch, not . . . tricked me out here." I lean forward, pasting a serious look on my face. He leans in too, and I fight the smile on my lips.

"I didn't trick you out here," he replies. "I just didn't give you the choice to tell me no. Again."

My laughter catches him by surprise. "You're tricky, but smooth."

His grin turns wicked. "My moves are even smoother."

My cheeks heat, my core burning with a flame that's starting to burn like wildfire. "Are they now?"

"Smooth as silk. If you're ever inclined to see them," he shrugs, "I'd probably be willing to show you."

I roll my eyes.

"That . . . thing you do with your eyes," he says, pointing at my face, "is almost impressive."

"It's a good thing I didn't come here to impress you then, isn't it?"

His jaw drops slightly before he recovers with a smirk. "It's a good thing I didn't ask you here to impress me."

I start to answer, but he leans closer and cuts me off. The smirk is gone and a softer smile is in its place. It makes my heart stutter.

"I didn't need you to impress me today because you impressed me last night."

"I didn't try to impress you then either," I whisper.

"I know. That's exactly how you did it."

My hand begins to shake and I lay it on my lap so he doesn't see. I scramble for a response, knowing this is going to go one way or the other right here, right now. But before I can come up with something, his phone rings again.

"I should go." I push back from the table and stand. He's in front of me before I can move. His eyes are holding mine, just like they did when I first met him. My heart is beating so fast I'm afraid it's going to thump right out of my chest. He overtakes all of my senses—his burning eyes, his jagged breath that matches mine, the feeling of his hand on my arm, and, before I know it, the taste of his mouth against mine.

I take in a quick breath as our lips touch. The contact zips through me, making me tingle from head to toe. I try to pull back, but a hand is at the back of my head pressing me firmly against him. My will to fight flees as his hands fall to the small of my back. I'm completely pulled into his web and I like it. Too much. He kisses in the same way he does everything—with power and passion and with no relenting. It's completely and utterly overwhelming.

He tastes of heat and energy, of confidence and practice. He tastes like a man should taste, and my lips tremble as my senses are overtaken.

His body is as solid as I imagined, his lips as supple and sweet as I dreamed. His lips open mine slowly, leisurely, and he breathes into my mouth. The heat and intimacy cause my knees to buckle and I lean against him, feeling his cock hard against my stomach.

I bring a hand to the side of his face and let it skim across the stubble. He pulls me tighter into him, his hands caressing my back, playing with the hem of my shirt. My breath quickens as his fingertips ghost over the delicate skin of my back and dip beneath the top of my jeans.

A growl emits from his throat, coursing through me and shaking me back to reality.

I pull away . . . and he lets me.

The room feels ten times smaller than it did before.

His breathing is as erratic as mine. We face each other, ignoring the phone that's ringing yet again. There's a band pulling us together and I know he feels it too.

"Be ready at eight. Wear something I can get off of you quickly."

"What?" I take a step back, the lust clearing out of my head at his tone. It's a command, an instruction, and the sound of it brings back a lot of memories I don't want to recall . . . and a burst of reality I'd somehow forgotten.

"Tonight," he repeats. "I'll have Troy pick you up around eight."

Holding my hand in front of me, I shake my head. "Look, I think you misunderstand . . ."

The cocky grin on his face would've been adorable a few minutes ago. Now, it's frustrating. "Stop playing hard to get. It's cute, sure, but I've seen it a hundred times and it's just going to take longer to get to the end point. And, let's be honest, we will get to the end point with your back—"

I half-laugh, half-snort at his insinuation that he can just bowl me over, interrupting him mid-sentence.

"If the end result is you looking at my back as I walk out of here, then you're right," I say simply before taking the few steps to the door.

His brows are pulled together, a look of astonishment on his face. "What are you doing? I know you feel this. I know you want my cock as bad as I want it buried in you."

"What I want and what I feel aren't the problem. The problem is that you forgot your manners," I smile as sweetly as I can. "Apparently you want someone that will bend to your will, jump, fuck when you say so. And if that's what you want," I shrug, "try the girl in the red dress from last night, but it isn't going to be me."

A look of bewilderment on his face, he shakes his head from side to side. "I'm sorry, Alison. Really. I . . ."

"Don't be sorry. I get it. Women drop to their knees for you." I flick the handle and pull the door open. "Good luck in your campaign, Barrett."

I'm around the corner of the door before he realizes it.

"Alison!" he calls as I hit the landing and dart out the door, but I don't look back. And thankfully or not, he doesn't come after me.

## Barrett

"FUCK IT," I MUTTER, SHOVING away from my desk. My chair rolls back on the hardwood floor of my office, coming to a rest a few inches from the wall.

It's been three days since I saw Alison Baker. I figured I'd feel differently in a few days. I'd forget the sweet taste of her lips, the way her breasts pushed against my chest, and the sound of her laugh caressing my ears. Never did I think I'd still be replaying our conversations, jacking off every night to the vision of her body sitting on my cock.

Fuck. Me.

Her body is curvy perfection, her face is beautiful, her voice a call right to a place inside my chest that makes me feel like I light up on the inside when she speaks to me. But none of those reasons are why I'm a mess over this girl. I've seen banging bodies a hundred times before. Faces are a dime a dozen and I've heard the sexiest things, sweetest things, filthiest things whispered in my ear.

It's not what Alison looks like, it's not what she sounds like that has me messed up. It's what she's *not*.

She's not calculated or conniving. She doesn't have every word, every move thought out in advance. As crazy as it sounds, she's a real person and one I can't shake.

And that's what has me fucked up, feeling guilt over something I said to a woman for quite possibly the first time in my life.

I feel like a complete cocksucker for making her feel like just another girl because clearly she's not. I love that she has the confidence to not just be another girl. That makes her even more intriguing . . . and me even more of an asshole.

A soft thud raps against the door before it pushes open. Camilla's heels, a delicate tick against the hardwood, announce her arrival.

She slips inside my office and shuts the door securely behind her.

"Hey, big brother," she smiles, taking a seat across from my desk.

"How are you, Swink?"

"Good! Mom had some paperwork for Rose, so I brought it by on my way to meet a friend for lunch."

"A friend?" I ask, cocking a brow.

"A friend. Her name is Joy, so don't panic."

Laughing, I sit back in the chair and watch my sister fiddle with her watch. "How are things going around here?" she asks. "Anything you need help with?"

"Nope. Everything's peachy."

She assesses me quickly. "I'm gonna have to call you out on that, Barrett."

"Call me out on what?"

"That little 'peachy' comment. You don't say things like that," she smirks, "and your face just gave you away. So . . . *tell me*. What's up?"

"You've earned your nickname, Swink. Such a meddler."

"It's what I do. Now spill it, Barrett," she prompts.

Sighing, I try to consider getting around it, but I know she'll pick at it until I come clean.

"All right," I say, folding my hands on my desk, "I'm going to give you an opportunity to give me some advice."

Her jaw drops. "Really? You're really going to open up to me? Wow. Wait," she says, shaking her head, "don't overthink this. It's a monumental day for sure, but you just talk and I'll revel in the excitement afterwards."

I roll my eyes. "Let's say a guy you like says something that, I don't know, offends you. Nothing terrible, just . . . said things he's used to saying, but he obviously should've known better. And now he wants to apologize."

"Oh, God, Barrett. What did you do?"

I toss her a look and she motions like she's zipping her lips.

"How do I say I'm sorry?" I ask as she lifts a brow.

"Well," she says, "the fact you didn't just chase this girl and make her bend to your will is throwing me a bit. You're usually a more 'I'll take what I want' kind of guy."

"Maybe I'm changing tactics."

"Maybe I need to know who she is."

"Maybe not."

"Fine," she groans. "Okay, you should apologize. But here's the thing—you can say you're sorry all you want, but words are pretty useless. Everyone says they're sorry but rarely means it."

"So what do I do? I mean it, Camilla. I'm sorry as fuck. I feel . . . I think I feel guilty."

"Wow," she breathes.

"Yeah," I nod. "Wow."

"Okay, so what you need is a grand gesture," she exclaims, her eyes sparkling. "You need to convince her you aren't the douchebag you presented yourself to be. Make her think you were just having a bad day. And if she believes you, you can't go back to douchebag mode, okay?"

I sag. "Of course not. I . . . she . . . I . . ."

Camilla giggles at my stumbling.

"I don't want to make her feel like I think I did. I hate feeling like this," I admit, throwing a pen across my desk.

"You have to win her over and you do that by showing her you're still thinking about her. You need to demonstrate that you listen when she talks, that you care about what she has to say. That is, of course, if you really did listen to her."

Camilla flashes me a look like she expects me to laugh it off. I don't.

"Of course I listened to her."

"Well then, if that's true, find something she loves, something she's mentioned in conversation. Something small that she wouldn't expect you to remember, and then act on it."

I scratch my head. "So, I should send her flowers?"

"No," she scoffs. "Flowers are what you send your mother or, I guess, you can send to your wife for a holiday as long as you follow it up with something else." She starts to grin, but I put a stop to that, reading right through the lines.

"I can't discuss the follow-ups with you with that look in your eye. You're my baby sister."

"Good point." She fidgets in her seat before exhaling a breath. "Find something else. *Not flowers*. Something that will mean something to her. If you want to win her over, that's your plan."

It's not a bad plan. It's even a good plan, really. If only I could think of something to send her that's not flowers.

"You do realize I've never sent a woman something before, right?" I ask. "Rose sends people flowers—which we aren't doing," I add as she starts to object. "This is all new to me."

And overwhelming.

I glance at the stack of papers on my desk and wonder if I have enough energy left in me to expend on Alison.

"I love that it's new to you," my sister says. "That means she's special. Just tell me this isn't Daphne we're talking about."

Laughing, I stand and walk around my desk. "No, Swink. It's not Daphne."

"Thank God," she giggles. Standing up, she reaches for me and I pull her into a big hug. "I'm glad you've found someone that makes you want to do better."

"Do better?" I pull away and smirk. "You don't want to know—"

"Remember how you don't want to hear about certain things in my life?" she interrupts. "Well, that works both ways, Mayor Landry."

"Noted."

She heads to the door but pauses before she leaves. "If you need anything, call me. I love this romantic stuff."

"It isn't romance," I point out. "It's just . . . me trying to not be a jerk."

Camilla grins the same grin our mother gives us when she sees right through our fibs. "If you care enough that you looked like a jerk that you want to go out of your way to fix it, that's romantic, Barrett. Sorry to break the news to you."

I watch her leave, her words hitting me head-on.

If I go out of my way to apologize, that would lead her to believe I'm interested.

I am interested.

*But do I want to be that interested? Can I afford to be that interested?*

The sound of the door closing at the Farm as she walked out echoes through my memories.

# 10

## Alison

THE CHEESE OOZES DOWN THE side of the bowl, inching slowly down the china, before it globs on the plate below.

It looks divine.

I carry the leftover macaroni and cheese to the living room and sit at the coffee table, stretching my legs out in front of me. The television is playing a soap opera that my grandma used to watch growing up. I always find it hysterical that I can not watch it for months at a time and tune in and feel like I didn't miss a beat.

Glancing at the clock, I still have a few hours before Huxley gets home from school. After paying bills this morning and doing oddball household chores, I decided to indulge in my favorite food before taking a long bubble bath . . . the one I haven't had a chance to take since my missed opportunity three days ago.

My chest tightens at the thought.

So do my thighs.

Barrett is everything I knew he would be. Intense, mesmerizing, and at the end of the day, a bit arrogant. Who is he to think I would just roll over for him? Or under him?

I fan my face at the thought of being beneath his hard, chiseled body.

*Damn it!*

Even now, days later and with the knowledge that he has the same conceited vein I hated in Hayden, I can't stop thinking about him. Arrogant or not, I'd be lying if I said he didn't make me feel alive, that he didn't make me feel like switches were turned on in my life.

Up until he opened his mouth right before I left, I could've been convinced there was a chance that he was different. But he's not. And while I guess that kind of behavior is somewhat normal for men of his caliber—how could it not be when they always get what they want?—it's a deal breaker for me, plain and simple.

I dig my fork into the goopy pile of cheese and try not to let my spirits sink. I'm doing things the right way, building a future for Huxley. Protecting him from men that will only do damage to our lives . . . like his pathetic excuse of a father.

My chest pangs a little as I remember the life I thought we had. The comfortable, stable life that showered him with love and confidence. But his father went up the ladder and left us ducking the consequences of his activities as he scaled higher. Now, here we are in this little house hundreds of miles away, starting over.

Starting smarter.

I want to build a future for my son. I want to fall in love. I just want to do both things in a cohesive manner . . . which means staying away from men that have the potential of landing me and Hux right back where we started.

Groaning at the sound of the doorbell ringing, I scramble to my feet and glance down at my t-shirt, hoping it's clean.

"Who is it?" I call through the heavy wooden frame.

"A delivery for Alison Baker."

Curious, I pull open the door to see a local courier on my stoop with an envelope in his hand. "Are you Ms. Baker?"

"I am."

He smiles. "I have this for you. Sign here, please."

I give him a loopy signature and take the envelope. There's no return address, no indication who it's from or what's inside.

Once the door is shut tight and I'm back on the couch, I rip open the top. Pulling out a letter on Georgia Hornets, the professional baseball team in Atlanta, letterhead, I gasp.

Dear Ms. Baker,

It is with great pleasure that we inform you that we've set aside season tickets to all of our home games next season. Two passes will be available for you and a guest in Will Call before each and every game. If you're unable to attend, you're more than welcome to send someone in your place. Please give us a courtesy notice prior so we can have them appropriately saved.

We look forward to seeing you in the stands!

Go Hornets!

Peter Capinella, CEO

Oh my God!

I squeal a little, imagining Huxley's face. He's never been to a professional game before and—*season tickets*? Getting to see every home game? He'll be over the moon. Even I'm giddy about it and I hate baseball. We've been to a handful of minor league games, but never a professional one. I can't wait to see his face when he finds out.

And then reality hits and I have no idea *why* we now have season tickets to the Hornets' games. I dig through the envelope for another letter, an indication of what we won or how this happened, but it's empty.

Before I can think it through, the doorbell chimes again. Jumping up, I speed to the front door and pull it open. A bouquet of roses and a smiling delivery girl are waiting for me.

"Ms. Baker?" she chirps, thrusting the elaborate design at me.

"Yes."

"These are for you. Have a super day!"

I take the flowers with a shaky hand and go back inside. My head is swimming, my heart clattering in my chest, as I sit on the sofa and place the vase next to my food.

Spotting a card buried in the foliage, I pull it out and open it.

*Alison,*

*Camilla said I shouldn't send flowers as a form of apology, so I sent you something else instead. I hope it's something you can do with Huxley. I know he's a big baseball fan and I still have hope that you can find your love of the game.*

*I would appreciate the opportunity to apologize for my behavior. I'll leave my number at the bottom if you're willing to hear me grovel. Trust me, not many people have heard me do that before. And it would mean a lot to me to be able to do it for you.*

*It was very nice seeing you the other day.*

*Barrett*

Sure enough, his number is printed very carefully at the bottom of the card.

I look from the glass popping with oranges and pinks to the envelope from the Hornets. My jaw hangs open at the over-the-top gift. I can't fathom how much season tickets to the games would cost, let alone the fact that he remembered I have a son that likes baseball and I'm not a fan.

I laugh out loud. I can't help it. The entire thing is ridiculous in the most spectacular way. I find myself wondering if this is real or a well-practiced charm.

*But if it is charm, if you're him, why bother if you don't mean it?*

My phone mocks me from beside the flowers, my fingers itching to dial the digits.

I need to be reasonable.

He went out of his way to send these things, and I'm seriously touched that he remembered Huxley. That deserves a phone call.

Calling him doesn't mean anything specifically, just having the manners to say thank you and giving him the opportunity to apologize for being an asshole.

I can do that. Besides, hearing him humble himself will be fun.

Dialing his number, a grin slips across my lips. The line rings twice before he answers.

"Landry," he says, his voice as smooth and delicious as I remember.

"Hi, Barrett. It's Alison."

I can feel him smile through the line. "What a nice surprise."

"Is it really?" I laugh. "I'm pretty sure you expected this call."

"There's nothing I expect of you. Believe that," he mumbles.

A pause extends between us and I can imagine him cringing, knowing what has to happen, trying to think of a way around it.

Not happening.

"So . . ." I say, giving him an opening.

"So . . ."

I blow out a breath in exasperation even though I'm smiling. "You know, I expected more groveling."

"Yeah, about that." He chuckles under his breath. "Alison, I would like to apologize for acting out of line the other day. I . . . I was wrong."

I know he's wincing as he says this and it makes me smile wider. "How'd it taste to say those words?"

"Like vinegar."

Laughing, I settle back on the sofa with the letter from the Hornets in my lap. "Well, thank you for saying it."

"Thank you for calling me and allowing me to say it."

"Did I have a choice? You softened me with beautiful flowers and Major League baseball, both of which were unnecessary, for the record. I had to call and thank you."

He takes a deep breath. I close my eyes and imagine his face, the way the lines crinkle around his eyes before he speaks.

"You are very welcome," he says softly. "I know 'sorry' is an overused term, but I am. I just . . . I suppose I normally don't have to jump through a lot of hoops to get a woman to agree to spend time with me. And I just figured . . ."

"You figured I would cave to your charm and be an easy lay?"

"No," he rushes, but stops in his tracks. "Well, maybe. Obviously I was wrong."

"Obviously."

I hear papers shuffling in the background and the sound of an incoming email dinging. Wondering where he is and what he's doing, I catch myself.

I'm calling to thank him. That's it.

"Alison," he begins, his voice a little shaky, "can we start over? Well, not start over, exactly. I think I did pretty well at the event. I'd just appreciate having another opportunity to . . ."

"Not be an ass?" I suggest.

"To win back your vote," he volleys back cheekily. "I've regretted letting you leave the Farm without apologizing to you a million times these last few days. For not remembering who I was dealing with and treating you accordingly. Like a respectable woman that is honoring *me* by giving me her attention."

I smile. I swoon. But I don't lose my head. "You know what that sounds like?"

"A good idea?"

"A perfectly executed line."

He sighs into the phone, the sound of his breath rapping against the speaker making me shiver.

"My son will be home soon," I say, stretching the truth, "and I have a few things I need to do. So, if you don't mind, I need to be going."

"Sure." His tone is dejected and it tugs at my heartstrings a little bit. I have to resist the urge to do exactly what he wants and bend to his will, to agree to whatever proposition he puts forth. "I hope you and Huxley enjoy the tickets."

"Thank you again," I reply, my voice softer, lacking the spunk it had a few seconds ago. "It was entirely too kind of you."

"It was my pleasure." He waits a beat, to see if I actually end the call or give him something else to go on. "If you ever change your mind about dinner, the invitation stands."

"Thank you. Have a good evening, Barrett."

"You too Alison."

I end the call and settle against the cushions. In another time and place, maybe I would take a risk with the dashing politician. He makes me laugh and our banter is so, so easy. I can't ever recall feeling quite like this. But fear is a powerful emotion, maybe the most powerful of all, and I can't get around the risk of losing everything I've built. Again.

## Barrett

"WELL, TO WHAT DO I owe the pleasure of finding you in my office?" I ask, shutting the door behind me. It's been a long day, probably because my focus has been shit. Hearing Alison's voice, and her rebuff of my advances again earlier this afternoon, didn't help. But what it did do was reinvigorate me. I haven't found the way to win her over yet, but I will. I have to. She's the only person that makes me smile. I'm not sure what that means or how long it will last, but all I know is that she gives me a spark I haven't found anywhere else, and it's something I can't shake. Something I don't want to shake.

Graham is sitting at my desk, going through a massive stack of papers. "Dad. You can thank him."

"Not that it doesn't thrill me to find you making yourself at home," I say, tossing my briefcase on a chair, "but why?"

"I've been appointed your chaperone tonight."

"Chaperone?"

"Whatever the official title is," he grumbles, tossing a pen on the paper he was looking at. "We need to get out of here in about thirty. Is Troy still outside?"

I nod, pouring myself a glass of water from the pitcher Rose keeps in the little refrigerator in my office.

"Did you see your poll numbers?"

"Yeah," I say, smacking my lips together. "They don't look too bad."

"They're surprisingly good, actually," Graham says, standing. "I think we have a fighting chance at this seat. Just keep doing what you're doing. No big waves, no big surprises, and a nod from Monroe, and I think you're good to go."

I swipe a pen and a stack of papers out of my inbox and give them a quick once-over. Signing my name to the bottom of all but one, I stuff them in my outbox for Rose.

"What did you do today?" Graham eyes me suspiciously.

"Let's see," I say, clinking the ice in the glass. "I got in here before anyone else—except the media, naturally. Did a bunch of paperwork and went over reports for the new budget. Attended the ribbon cutting ceremony at the park. Worked on the contracts for the new sewage treatment plant and had some lunch, then did a few phone interviews with newspapers from Atlanta."

"Funny. I don't quite believe you."

"And why is that?"

"Because while you're not exactly smiling, you're not completely pissed off, either. And that, my big brother, is odd."

"What are you implying?" I grin.

"See?" he says, pointing his finger at me. "You're smiling and there are no cameras here to mug for. That's a genuine smile. Did you just put a hit out on Hobbs? If so, let a brother know so I can start crafting your alibi."

"And that's why you're my favorite," I laugh. "You always have a plan."

"Only because I've always needed one with you and Linc as brothers," he points out.

"You can rest assured I've committed no felonies today."

"So she was of legal age? That's what you mean?"

Laughing, I sit in the chair across from him. "Yes, she's of legal age. She's . . . intriguing."

"Define 'intriguing.'"

"You're the one with the master's degree," I tell him. "I'm pretty sure you know what it means."

He rubs his hands across his forehead, looking just like our father. "'Intriguing' is a word that, when coming out your mouth about a female, concerns me, Barrett. I'm not going to lie."

"Fine. I find her exciting. I find her different. I find her . . ."

"Conquestable?"

"That's not a word."

He groans and stands, walking to my refrigerator and pouring himself a drink. "Have you not been listening to anything Nolan's been telling you? About locking down your image? About not getting involved with anyone when we have just weeks left to go?"

"Yes," I say, letting the last sound drag out. "That's why I met her at the Farm. There's no one there to see anything."

"Smart. If you must do something stupid, at least don't do it in public."

"It's not stupid, Graham. I had lunch with her a few days ago. That's it."

He looks at me blankly, like I don't get it.

"She's not like Daphne or . . . or . . . what was the redhead's name I dated awhile back?"

"Candy. Hence, my point."

"Yeah, Candy. Man, she had a nice ass."

"Barrett, *please*," he sighs. "Listen to me. I'm sure she's not like the rest of them. They never are, until they are."

I shake my head emphatically. "Not this one. She's a single mom that's been through a nasty divorce. She doesn't want any publicity, has no agenda. She just, I don't know, makes me feel like I can breathe. Like I can be me."

"So," he chuckles, "you can be you and she still likes you? I stand corrected. You've found an angel. Keep her around."

"Such a comedian," I grumble, walking around my desk and taking my seat. "I'm being serious. I think I could really like her."

That's not entirely true. The taste of her mouth is seared into mine, the scent of her vanilla-laden perfume scorched into my memory, and I know she's already singed her name into my blood. I've never had this . . . need . . . to get to know a girl before. It's this prickly feeling that lets me know I am, without being, fucked.

"Please be careful. Be smart," Graham says, pulling me out of my reverie. "While I'm happy to see you happy over someone without cup size factoring into the top five reasons, this probably isn't the time to mess with this."

"It doesn't matter," I say, reordering a stack of papers Graham scattered. "I get this feeling from her that she doesn't want anything serious with me."

"I doubt that," he snorts.

"I'm serious. I'm going to try to see her again, but she's . . . respectable," I laugh, realizing it's the first time I've ever been able to use that word about a girl in a conversation with my brother.

Graham blows out a breath, obviously not hearing what he'd hoped for. By the time he looks at me again, his mouth forms a thin line. "I'll get the plan together to bail you out of whatever mess this becomes."

"Thanks. Now let's get out of here before we're late."

## Alison

THE STADIUM SMELLS LIKE HOT dogs and spilled beer, two of my least favorite things. Seems fitting, since they go with baseball.

Lola walks in front of me, sashaying her hips as we pass a hottie making our way down the stairs of Barridge Stadium, the local minor league baseball team's home. When Lo called shortly after I talked to Barrett and offered the tickets, I couldn't refuse. Free tickets to Huxley's favorite thing were a no brainer, especially when we've only been able to come to the stadium a handful of times.

I decided not to tell Huxley about the season tickets yet. I figure I'll save that gift for another day and spread the cheer. No sense in using all the goodness up in one day.

"This is so cool," Huxley gasps. "Someday I'm going to play in a stadium even bigger than this when I go to the Majors."

"If you do, I want season tickets," Lola says, handing him his drink. "And clubhouse passes. Can you make that happen?"

"Sure," he says, not paying any attention. His little face is taking in the seats, lighting, and fellow baseball fans.

Lola starts down the steps towards our seats and I nudge Hux along. We grab our seats right above the dugout and get situated.

"This is so awesome, Lola!" Hux says, his eyes wide. "Thanks for bringing me."

"You're welcome, little guy," she says, reaching over and messing with his hair. "You need a haircut."

"No, I don't," he groans. "Don't start. Mom keeps trying to get it cut, but I want it to be long like Joe Stalsbach." We lose him again to the wonders of the world of baseball.

"How did you get these tickets?" I ask, popping a piece of candy in my mouth.

"You mean, who did I have to come upon to get these seats?"

"Lo!" I exclaim, bumping her in the shoulder. "Little pitchers have big ears."

She tosses a handful of popcorn at me. "Isaac. He got called in to work tonight. It's just a charity game with the Sirens, so he couldn't sell them for anything. So, he offered them to me. And I offered them to you."

I smile at my best friend. She could be doing anything tonight, but she chose to go out of her way to make Huxley happy and that means more to me than anything in the world.

"Thanks for doing this. He'll talk about it for a month."

"Anything for the little guy. I mean, he's my back-up plan. If I don't figure out a way to take care of me, he's giving me all-access to the dugout. I'm looking at tonight as an insurance policy."

"Oh my God," I laugh, watching everyone take their seats around us.

"So, speaking of which . . ."

"Speaking of what? God?"

"Barrett."

"Shh," I say, rolling my eyes. "For real, Lo. Realize we're in a packed stadium. People eavesdrop."

"And no one would know what I'm talking about if you didn't react so obviously."

I pop another piece of candy and glare at her. She just gives me her blank stare, the one she uses when she waits for me to stop being shocked at her behavior and continue the conversation.

"I'm not talking about . . . that . . . here," I warn.

"You didn't bother to spring that little gem of information, the one where you had lunch with—"

"Lola!"

"With a friend," she modifies, "until I picked you up. What did you expect? You do know me, right?"

I feel a little elbow digging into my side and turn to see my sweet boy looking at me. His brown eyes, like his father's, peer up at me with a level of excitement that makes me excited too.

He points to the field where the players have taken their positions unbeknownst to me. They're tossing balls back and forth, some of them jogging to the stands to sign jerseys and hats for fans.

"Can I go get an autograph?" Hux asks. He bounces in his seat, one hand stuck in his baseball glove. "Please, Mom."

"I don't see anyone over here," I say, scanning the fence. "If someone comes over, we'll go see if we can get their attention, okay?"

"Yes!" he yells, fist pumping, making Lola and I laugh.

The speakers overhead rumble and the announcer's voice blazes through the stadium. "Welcome, baseball fans young and old, to tonight's charity game to benefit Casey's Children's Hospital!"

The crowd goes wild as some of their favorite players wave from the field and dugouts. They take their places as the announcer continues. "We'd like to give an especially warm welcome to Savannah's own center fielder for the major league Tennessee Arrows, Lincoln Landry!"

The crowd jumps to their feet as I sink back into my chair. Hux is waving his mitt in the air as I watch Lincoln appear from the dugout beneath us and wave to the crowd.

I lean forward, trying to get a good eyeful of him. He's taller, thinner, but more muscled than Barrett. That's all I can really tell from the back.

Lola watches my reaction. "Do you think Barrett's here?"

I let my shoulders rise and fall.

"Your hometown loves you, Lincoln! Thank you so much for coming home to support our hospital tonight!" the announcer booms.

Lincoln turns to face the booth, situated above our seats, and I realize how beautiful he is. A younger version of Barrett, Lincoln has a softer jaw line and more unruly hair. When he smiles and flashes the crowd a thumbs-up, Lola nearly dies.

"I take it back. That's the one I want," she breathes, her jaw hanging open. "My God. Those men have genetics that need reproduced and I volunteer for the job."

I ignore her, a peculiar feeling bubbling in my stomach. My attention is drawn like a magnet to the dugout. I'm not sure why, but I wait with bated breath.

And then I see the reason.

"Ladies and gentleman, let's now give a round of applause for Mayor Landry, who'll be tossing out the first pitch!"

I gasp.

Lola smashes me from the side, her gasp taking away all air from the immediate vicinity.

Huxley sits down, unimpressed.

Barrett gets situated on the mound as the fangirls in the crowd go crazy and I have half a notion to cover Huxley's ears at some of the lewd suggestions being spewed towards the dugout.

He waves to the fans before tossing the pitch. It bounces once before it makes it to the plate. The crowd cheers wildly and I watch as his lean body jogs halfway to the plate and he embraces the catcher in a half-hug.

"That guy can't throw a baseball," Huxley says. "They should've at least gotten someone that could make it to the plate."

"That's the mayor," Lola tells him because I'm still without words, my eyes glued to him as he makes his way to the clubhouse.

"He's not a baseball player, that's for sure," Hux scoffs.

Barrett is met at the steps by his brother. Side-by-side, they're breathtaking. I can't begin to imagine how beautiful their family pictures must be.

Lincoln slaps him on the shoulder and says something in his ear, making Barrett laugh and I'm jealous I can't hear it. Not the words, but the sound of his voice. I heard it just today but I already miss it . . . especially knowing I'll probably never hear it again.

Almost like he knows I'm watching, he looks up. His gaze falls right on me like I'm the only one sitting in the stands.

A look of confusion flickers across his features before he breaks out into a wide smile.

# Barrett

"NICE JOB, MAYOR," A PLAYER says before fleeing the dugout to take the field.

"Don't lie to him!" Lincoln shouts after him, making the rest of the departing guys laugh. "That was the shittiest pitch I've ever seen. I've been embarrassed by you before, but tonight tops them all. Fuck."

"Good thing I'm not a player then," I mutter.

*What's she doing here?*

"The next time you need anything baseball related, call me or Graham," Lincoln says, turning to our brother. "Shit, G. We should've had you stand in. Trade in your yuppie polo shirt and lose the glasses and you could pass as Barrett. It'd be close enough. At least you wouldn't embarrass me."

Graham leans against the wall and he and Linc engage in some conversation that probably involves making fun of me.

*How can I see her?*

I know it's risky and stupid to want to see her now, right here in the middle of the entire city, basically. But I can't help it. Just knowing she's feet away from me and not being able to see her kills me.

As does the idea of her being here with someone else.

I leap up the few steps to the field and steal a peek up the stands. She sits with a raven haired girl that looks vaguely familiar and a little blond boy with a mitt.

*Bingo!*

"Hey, Linc!" I say, whipping around and descending into the dugout. "Remember the time when we were kids and you were getting your ass beat and I saved you?"

"Uh, no," he says, his voice echoing off the now-empty walls of the room. The players not playing are talking to fans, doing promotional stuff. We're the only ones around. "That didn't happen."

"Well, let's pretend it did. And today is the day you pay me back."

"What the hell?" he laughs, looking at me like I'm crazy. Maybe I am.

"What's going on with you?" Graham asks, standing straight. He quirks a brow, just like our father, getting his contingency plan ready for action. "And don't even tell me it's . . . *that*."

"It's that," I grin widely.

"That? It's what? What's that?" Linc asks.

Graham groans.

I pace a small circle, trying to get a strategy in place to make everything work and not worse.

"Hello, assholes," Lincoln says, throwing his arms in front of him. "What's happening? I feel like you guys are talking in some language I don't understand."

"Linc, I need a favor."

"Fuck me," Graham mutters, collapsing back into the wall again. "You do realize whatever stupidity you pull tonight is on my watch, right?"

"You aren't my babysitter, Graham. I'm a grown man."

"So please make grown man decisions," he fires back.

Linc's head volleys back and forth. "You guys are losing me, but I do like the sound of this."

"There's a little boy about four rows back," I tell Linc. "Blond hair, wearing a mitt. He's sitting by his mom. She's my age, blonde hair, white t-shirt."

"And?"

"Go get the kid."

He steps away from me and laughs. "Why? What do you care about a kid sitting in the stands? You don't even like kids."

"That's not true. I just don't like Sienna's last boyfriend's little kid. Fucker vomited on my suit."

"Kids do that," Graham points out.

"Not that one. He's nine or ten or something."

Lincoln looks at me like I've lost my mind, but being the troublemaker he is, he kind of likes it. I can tell. The side of his mouth curls into a smirk. He shrugs, knowing his reaction, favorable to me, will piss off Graham and his carefully constructed and now void plans for the evening.

"I'm game," Lincoln says. "I'll get him. But what do you want me to do with him?"

"Just bring him down here like he's won some sort of prize or something."

"And his mother?" His smirk deepens, matching mine. "She'll never let him come down here alone."

"No," I agree. "She won't. I'll bet she's a good mom and won't let her kid out of her sight."

Graham pushes off the wall and stands between me and our youngest brother. "Are you sure you've thought this through? You realize that the wrong photograph can be, and will be, floated a million ways in the paper tomorrow."

"How? Lincoln is going to be seen with a little boy, doing his baseball thing and making this random kid's day. I'll never be photographed with Alison, so there's no problem."

"I don't like this. Just for the record," Graham contends, scrubbing his hands down his face.

"Ah, G," Lincoln teases, clapping him on the back. "Live a little, man."

"Yeah, sure. Then who'll take care of you assholes?"

"Mom," Linc says and bounds up the stairs.

# Alison

"MOM! LOOK! CAN I GO down there?" Huxley shoots from his seat, his finger pointing towards the field. "Please! Mom!"

I follow his gaze, my breath stalling, to see Lincoln Landry at the fence directly below us. Children scramble from their seats, thrusting hats and pictures and Sharpies in his direction. He takes it in stride, just like Barrett does in a crowd, and plays it off like he does it every day. Maybe he does.

"Mom! Please!"

"Yes, go on. I'll watch you from here."

He climbs over Lola and races to the fence, a spring in his little step that's impossible to miss.

"Look at him," Lola sighs.

"I know. I love watching him have so much joy. I wish I knew more about baseball, but it'll be the same way with cars and things that blow up some day. I hate it that his father was such an incredible asshole."

Lo gives me a look. "I was talking about Lincoln."

"Of course you were."

Huxley makes his way to the front of the line, one of the last kids left standing. Lincoln takes his glove, running a hand through his hair. He looks straight up in the stands, at me, his eyes full of mischief.

The smirk that spreads across his face is more playful and less sexy than Barrett's, but still a panty-dropper. He tosses me a wink before motioning for me to come down too.

"Oh my God he wants you," Lola nearly shrieks. "Go. Get your ass down there, Ali!"

I can't respond because you can't do that without air. I don't move, either, because I'm partially frozen in my seat.

Lincoln motions again and Huxley turns around, his face nearly swallowed by his smile. "Mom! Come here!"

Rising slowly, which garners another chuckle from Lincoln, I make my way to the fence. There's still no sign of Barrett, but I know he's close. I can feel it. His energy teases me from the shadows.

"Hey, there!" Lincoln says, his voice dripping with a little extra gusto. "I have Hux here and no Sharpie."

"Oh, no!" I say, feeling like I just struck the biggest mom-fail of all time.

"Good thing I'm always prepared," Linc grins.

"He has one, Mom! In the dugout!"

Lincoln smirks.

I give him my best *'I'm sure you do'* look.

He laughs.

I roll my eyes, but can't help but laugh as well. "Why does that not surprise me?"

"Well, my reputation as a real-life Superman does precede me. Now see that gate right down there? Go through that and meet me in the dugout."

"Can we do that?" I ask, looking for security.

"Yeah, this is a charity game. They don't care. Just don't charge the pitcher's mound or anything."

"I'll try to restrain myself," I mutter.

Hux grabs my arm, jerking it up and down. "Let's go!"

Lincoln watches with amusement as Huxley drags me down the stands and to the gate, jabbering endlessly the entire time. I pretend to follow along with his all-out fanboy antics, but I try to play it cool. To pretend like Barrett isn't waiting for me.

My heart strikes against my ribs, pounding out of control. I hear

Hux's voice, but not the words, over the roar of blood in my ears.

Whether I want to be or not, I'm excited to see him again. Even if it's in a dugout full of baseball players and a star-struck little boy, I can't deny it.

As if he were expecting us, a giant of a man lets us right through and tells us to stay on the gravel and not get into the line of play.

"A real dugout, Mom!" Hux exclaims as we get closer. "So cool! My friends at school will never believe me!"

"It's awesome, huh?" I smile.

"So awesome." He gives me a wide grin, one showcasing his missing tooth. Pure happiness drips off of him and, for a moment, I don't feel like I'm failing him. He's not with a babysitter while I work or missing out on activities that little boys with fathers get to do. For once, I'm with him in a moment he'll never forget, a moment he can brag to his little friends about.

The steps leading below are dirty and the air smells of sweat and salt. I try not to breathe it in, but as I shudder, I catch the notes of his cologne.

As Hux gasps, "Wow," I look up and into the face of Barrett.

He's smiling with more than a drop of hesitation, like he's afraid I'm going to be mad. How can I be, though, when he just made Hux's year? Twice.

The effects of my return smile are immediate and obvious. His shoulders relax and he visibly blows out a deep breath.

"Hey, there!" Lincoln says, coming over to Hux. He grabs his shoulders and shakes them in some sort of a guy welcome gesture. "Well, what do you think?"

"This is cool," Hux says, taking everything in.

"It is, right? Do you play?"

"Yeah. I play second base," he says proudly. "My arm isn't as strong as it needs to be to play pitcher or center."

"I'll show you some exercises before you go that'll help, if you want."

"For real?" Hux asks, bouncing on the balls of his feet.

"Yeah, for real," Lincoln chuckles. He looks up at me and extends a hand. "I'm Lincoln Landry."

We shake, his hand a bit smaller but more calloused than Barrett's. "I'm Alison Baker."

"Guys, this is Alison and Hux Baker. This is my brother, Graham, and my oldest brother, the mayor, Barrett."

"I knew you weren't a baseball player," Huxley says.

"Hux!" I exclaim, my cheeks reddening as Graham and Lincoln burst into laughter. Barrett just grins and shakes his head.

"You didn't even make it to the plate," Hux points out.

"You are now officially my favorite kid ever," Lincoln says, catching his breath. "Come on. Let's go play catch in the bullpen."

"Can I?" Hux pleads. "Please, Mom?"

I hesitate, but before I can think it through, Lincoln puts me at ease.

"It's safe. No one can get in there. And there aren't any balls that will hit him or anything. I promise I'll take care of him. I mean, after that crack at Barrett, I owe him one."

"Please?" Hux begs.

I glance at Barrett. He's standing with his back to the wall, his arms over his chest. He watches the interaction, purposefully staying out of it, letting me make the decision with no pressure from him.

"Sure," I relent. "I can wait in my seat."

"You can wait here," Barrett interjects. "There's a room in the back so you don't get trampled when the guys come in. Linc can bring him back there, right?"

"Sure thing," Lincoln says. He grabs Hux's shoulder and off they go, Graham trailing behind them, muttering under his breath.

I'm left standing with the mayor.

He starts to speak, but thinks better of it. Instead, he touches me lightly on the small of my back, a gesture that would seem innocuous to a bystander, but feels anything but. The warmth of his palm, the zing of the contact, makes my jaw slack and my knees weak.

Guiding me through a doorway in the back of the dugout, we enter a hallway. He leads me into a small room with a desk and a water cooler. The door is pulled shut behind him and when I turn around, his chest is rising and falling just like mine.

"I was going to ask what you're doing here, but you know what? I really don't care," he marvels. "I'm just glad you are."

He closes the distance between us and stops right in front of me. If I reached out, I could touch his face, run my fingers down his freshly-shaven cheeks. I could kiss his lips, the one his tongue is skimming over as I watch nervously, anxiously . . . breathlessly.

"Thank you," I say, getting lost in his emerald eyes. "I know you set that whole thing up with Lincoln and Huxley, and I can't thank you enough. This after the tickets today? You just made his year."

"It was my pleasure. But can I tell you a secret?"

I nod, my body temperature rising dangerously. His lips lower slowly until they hover just above the sensitive skin below my ear. I fight back a shiver, my chest rising as I hold my breath and wait for him to speak.

"It wasn't just for Hux. It was for me, too," he confesses, his words dancing along my cheek. "Want to know why?"

I nod again, my breath catching in my throat.

"Because I want to kiss you," he whispers.

"You're asking permission?" I breathe.

"I'm trying to play by the rules," he says sincerely, pulling back and looking into my eyes. "If there were none, I'd pick you up and press you against the wall and lose myself in you."

His words are erotica, a direct line of fire from his mouth to my core. He pulls back just enough for me to see into his eyes again, to see the caution, the self-control he's using.

My attraction to him was never the problem. The glimmer in his eye right now, the one of patience, is enough for me to somehow give myself permission to enjoy myself for a moment. After all, it's all I've been able to think about for days.

"May I?" he breathes, his chest rising and falling as quickly as mine.

His hand touches my cheek and I gasp. A slight nod of my head is all it takes before his lips land on mine, tenderly, at first, and I melt into his hard body.

Just like he said, he's playing by some set of rules, ones that keep him from devouring me like I want. Even though a voice in the back of my head tries to remind me that with every stroke of his tongue this becomes dangerous, I can't do anything about it but kiss him back.

His arms wrap around me, pulling me against him. I feel his palms pressed flat against my back. I give in, any defense I may have had obliterated, and let my fingers wind through his locks.

I fit against him like a puzzle piece, like we've practiced this dance so many times that we fall in step without any hesitation. We move together fluidly, effortlessly.

It's sensory overload. The taste of his minty breath, the scent of his cologne. The roughness of his hands and the incredible smoothness of his lips. A moan starts to slip passed my lips when we're interrupted.

*Knock!*

My shoulders sag at the intrusion, Barrett breaking the kiss and letting his forehead rest on mine. Our ragged breaths echo through the room.

*Knock!* "Barrett, I need to see you."

He pulls back but doesn't unlock me from his web. Just far enough to see into my eyes.

"Hang on, Graham," he calls, his eyes never leaving mine.

"I'll grab Hux and get back to my seat," I whisper, feeling reality crush the moment.

He takes a deep breath. "Alison . . ."

The rasp in his voice, the need that's tangible, slices its way to my core. He's trying to be a gentleman, trying not to take charge like I know he wants to do. If he did, it would be so much easier because I want him to. I want to be lost in him, even if I know it's not necessarily the best thing.

His pause, his *playing by the rules*, gives me a chance to think.

He releases his hands from my waist and looks at me softly. "I want to see you again."

"Barrett, I—"

"It's your call," he says in a rush. "And I won't ask you again. I don't want to pressure you and that's not at all what I'm trying to do. I just . . . is it cheesy for me to say I just want to spend time with you?"

My heart swells at the sincerity in his voice.

He runs a hand through his hair. "I know you have reservations and I get that. Trust me when I say I do respect that. But I've been thinking about you since I met you, and you've given me a reprieve from my life without even trying."

When he looks up at me, his eyes are wide and absolutely crystal clear. There's nothing hidden behind the green depths, no political bullshit. Just a man asking a woman to share a meal together.

"So if you really don't want to . . ."

"Can I think about it?"

A flicker of disappointment shoots across his features. It's a brief look, one that he recovers from quickly. "Absolutely. I'll call you tomorrow and we can discuss?"

I nod, taking his smile for all it's worth, and let him guide me back to the door. Before he pulls it open, he gives me one more sweet, delicate kiss. It's that kiss that hits me harder than any of the others, the one I won't soon forget.

# Barrett

THE WORDS BEGIN TO SWIM on the page of the proposal sitting in front of me. I've been working nonstop since before sunrise and I can't possibly read another sentence.

I sit back, trying to decide on coffee or an energy drink, when a rough knock sounds and the door swings open.

"Hey, Barrett," Lincoln says, Graham on his heels.

"I thought you were leaving today." I say.

"Nah, I figure I'll stay awhile. My shoulder is pretty sore, and if I go back to Tennessee, I'll try to train with the guys and that'll fuck it up worse than it is," he winces, rolling his shoulder around.

Standing, I do a little stretching of my own. It feels good to move, to get some blood flowing.

I didn't sleep worth shit last night, my mind running from the election to Alison and back again. By three a.m., I realized that the problem with Alison lies in the fact that she's simply not mine. And the fact that I'm bothered by this little technicality fucks with me.

The realization had me hitting the bottle of Jack a little heavy in the wee hours of the morning. This isn't the time or the place for me to decide to start thinking about monogamy. That ruins men. Clips their nuts, drains their testosterone, destroys the very things that make politicians good politicians.

I am a politician.

I need my nuts . . . buried in her.

Groaning, I look up at my brothers. Linc has made himself at home in my fridge, an apple in one hand and a glass of water in the other. Graham is sitting across from my desk, watching me.

"Before we get to what I came here for, let's get this over with," Graham sighs. "How deep are you in?"

"Deep in what?"

"Alison Baker."

"I'll tell you how deep I'd be in that," Linc says, taking a bite of the apple.

I glare at him and he just shrugs.

"I'm not," I say carefully.

Graham doesn't buy it because he's not stupid. "Do I need to run a background check?"

"I know everything about her," I promise.

He looks at me like I've lost my mind. "How can you? You've known her for what? A week?"

"Okay," I relent, "I don't know what her favorite color is, but—"

"Do you know what her pussy feels like?" Linc interrupts.

"Shut up, Linc," Graham and I say in unison. He snaps another bite of his fruit.

I sigh, trying to figure out how to skirt the issue. I know what he's going to say and he's right. I need to be smart. But I also need to figure out a way to make this work.

"I know I need to watch my image."

He nods and stands. "Yeah, you do. We've worked our tails off to get you to this place. You're on the cusp of achieving something no one in our family has done since our grandfather, and if you can get there, you have a chance at the White House eventually. This is not the time to take risks, brother. Not in this department."

I turn my back to him. I don't want him to see the look of frustration on my face. This is not a conversation we've had before. Usually it's him telling me to stop fucking a chick, and I laugh and agree. But this isn't that. I haven't even fucked her.

I'm the one that's getting fucked.

"Look," Graham says, his voice overly calm, "I get that you kind of like this girl. She's hot, she seems sweet, she's got a great kid."

"*Smart* kid," Linc chips in, laughing.

"But can't it wait a few weeks until this thing is over?"

Graham's question is cut short by another knock and the opening of the door. Nolan rushes in, his glasses hanging off the end of his long nose. A stack of files in his hand, his suit looking rumpled, he drops into a chair beside my brother.

"Can't what wait a few weeks?" he asks, looking from one of us to the other.

I shoot Graham a look. "A vacation. Lincoln wants to go to Australia and swim with the sharks."

He chokes on his apple.

"Good," Nolan says, flipping open a folder. "I thought you were talking about some girl you were seen with at the game last night."

My cheeks heat. "What do you know about that?"

"People tell me things," Nolan says. "This isn't my first walk in the park . . . or ballpark, either. I'm sure Graham is in here now trying to talk some sense into you, warning you to keep your nose clean. And he's right, Barrett. There's way too much riding on this for you to be stupid."

"I'm not being stupid," I protest. I glance at Lincoln and he rolls his eyes, his disdain for Nolan palpable. "I'm just friendly with her. That's all."

"Keep it that way. She's divorced, had assault charges leveled at her in New Mexico by a member of the press." Nolan takes his glasses off and looks at me like he's won some victory.

I narrow my gaze. "I understand you're doing this because it's your job. But I need you to back the fuck off, okay?"

My head spins with this new information, but I can't let him see that. It'll show a ding in my armor and I don't want him trying to exploit it. Still, I'm shocked at his accusation and wonder if it's true and, if it is, what the story is behind it.

"I'm going to assume," he mocks, pulling his hand away from his face, "that you're going to listen to your brother." He looks at Graham and Lincoln. "Graham. Not that one," he says, nodding to Linc. "And stop this before it causes us a lot of problems to fix. Years of work have boiled down to this moment, Barrett. Don't blow it for, well, a blow."

I laugh, but Nolan blanches at the anger laced none too quietly in the sound. "Here's your problem," I say through gritted teeth. "You know nothing about Alison other than the secondhand, or maybe thirdhand, information you've acquired through your back channels. And you, of all people, should know just how many times they get the facts right."

"Are you defending her?" he asks, his brows lifted.

"Yeah, I'm fucking defending her. She's a good person and it pisses me off to hear you act like she's some kind of cheap date."

"Let's be honest," Nolan says, standing, "that's your typical method of operation."

"I—" I start, but Graham stops me before I get going.

"Let's all just settle down," my brother says, looking me in the eye. "Our focus needs to be on the election, not Barrett's flavor of the week."

My mouth opens quickly to send him a message, but the look he flashes me stops me in my tracks.

"Now, let's talk about Monroe," Nolan says, sliding his glasses back on his face. "I know you're having some rebellious feelings towards the Land Bill, but if you want elected, you're going to have to be logical."

"Logic says that it's the wrong thing for the people of Georgia," I point out. Again. "If that bill gets passed, a bunch of wealthy families, like my own, make more money. If it doesn't, businesses come in. People go to work. The economy flourishes."

"That's great in theory, Barrett, but it's never going to happen. Hobbs has already guaranteed Monroe he'll vote for the bill. We know Monroe favors you, at least somewhat, because you're in the same party and your families have been friends. But this bill is important to him."

"Because he stands to make twenty million dollars," I snarl.

"He's right," Graham gruffs. "You're going to have to make some decisions. You have to decide what you want *in life* and make a plan and follow it."

The innuendo isn't lost on me and I want to lash out. But I don't. Because at the end of the day, these men want what's best for me.

"I'll think about it," I say. That seems to pacify them all, except Linc who looks disgusted by it all. "I have some meetings, so if you all can excuse me..."

They get the point and head to the door. Linc is the last to leave. Before he exits, he turns to me. "You know what I have to say about all that, yeah?"

"What's that?"

"Fuck it. Do what makes you happy."

The door closes behind him and for the first time in my life, I take my youngest brother's advice.

## Alison

"DID YOU GET EVERYTHING?" I ask, giving his backpack one final glance before zipping it up. "You guys are going to have so much fun."

"We will. Even if we catch nothing, it'll be great because I got to miss school today," Huxley points out.

It's ten in the morning and I need to be studying. Instead, I'm being a mom, my favorite job in the world. I'll have to catch up on the other part later.

"Tell Grandpa to make sure you wear a life jacket, okay?" I ask, kissing him on the head as he tries to bolt for the door. "If you fall out of the boat, we'll have to miss using up those season tickets."

He looks horrified. "Don't even joke about that. I wish it was time for baseball season already!"

"I know," I grin, remembering how he jumped up and down when I told him about the tickets. "But it's not, so have fun with Grandpa."

"Okay, Mom! Love you!" he says.

By the time I get to the door, he's in my father's truck. Dad rolls down his window.

"I'll make sure he wears a life jacket," he winks.

"And no leaning over the boat. I don't care how big the fish is," I wince. My heart wobbles in my chest. "Okay?"

"I'll keep him safe. I raised you, didn't I?"

"Yeah, but he's my baby."

"And you were mine." He winks and rolls up the window. I wave as they back out of the driveway and are out of sight.

My phone rings in the kitchen and I grab it on the fourth ring. "Hello?"

"Hey, Alison," Barrett's voice melts through the phone. "How are you?"

My stomach flurries, a smile painted on my face without me realizing it. I take a seat at the table and try to seem chill.

I've been thinking about him a lot, preparing for this phone call. It was hard to sleep last night after the game. I spent the endless night hours searching my heart for my truth, what I wanted and what I think I can and should handle. Even though I tried to talk myself out of it a hundred thousand ways, I always came back to wanting more of the feeling I get when I'm with him. I've missed it, the sensation of feeling like a woman.

Sometime around six this morning, I made a deal with myself: I'll see him again when he calls. And if he acts like an ass again, I'll walk away and feel good about it.

And if I happen to actually see his ass in the meantime, I'll consider it a bonus.

"I'm good. Well," I say, caving to my anxiety, "not really. I just sent Huxley off with my father for a little fishing. I'm a nervous wreck."

"Ah, skipping school for some sun? My kind of kid," he jokes.

"He never gets to do that kind of thing, so why not?"

"You can learn just as much outside the school walls as you can inside."

"Yeah, now if I can just block out the drowning aspect, it'll be great."

He laughs, a smooth, sexy sound that distracts me. I'm glad for it.

"We used to go boating every weekend in the summer," Barrett says. "It's good to have some experience with water in a controlled environment. I'm sure your dad will watch him."

"He will. I just feel like it all falls on my shoulders, you know? And I feel like I've let him down so many times in his life already that I need to be especially vigilant."

"I doubt that's true."

"It is, but let's not talk about it. What are you doing today?"

His sigh drifts through the line. "Meetings. Committees. Interviews. Battling back this statement from Hobbs' campaign today."

"Want to talk about it?"

"No. Not really."

I can tell he's bothered. It's in the strain in the edges of his voice, the grit that scratches at his tone.

"I'd rather talk about you. How are you? How was your day?"

"Good. Busy. A touch lonely," I hint.

"Have you given any thought to seeing me again?" he asks, his voice soft.

"A little," I lie because it's dominated my thoughts.

"I hope that it's only a little because it took you two seconds to realize it was a good idea."

"I want to . . ." I stand and try to keep my head clear.

"What are you afraid of, Alison? Talk to me."

I decide to bare my soul. Leave it all out there, and then, maybe, my decision will be made for me.

"When I'm with you . . ." I begin, trying to figure out where to start.

"You find yourself smiling? And then you leave me and all you can think about is how to manage to see me again?"

My ears are sure they're hearing things. "Barrett . . ."

"I'm not asking you for anything more than a bit of your time. I just want to see what it is between us that drives me insane. That keeps me up at night, that brings you to mind when I should be working on the campaign." He takes in a rushed breath. "If you aren't in the same boat, so to speak, then I'll stop this pursuit. But, Alison, I think we are paddling towards the same target. We just need to see if we can get there if we paddle together."

It's do or die time and I have to pick a direction. If I seriously don't want to see him again, I need to let him go. He's right. But the thought panics me, sickens me. The idea of not having a chance at it being him on the other end of the phone when it rings feels so bad.

"What time is dinner?" I ask.

I can hear him grin through the phone. "I can meet you later tonight, or if you'd rather, I can make an hour or so in my schedule this afternoon for lunch?"

"I need to finish this paper I started earlier, but I work at four. Can you make it at one o'clock?"

"I can make it twelve or one or six if that means you'll come."

I smile like a loon. "At the Farm?"

"Yes."

"I'll be there at one. See you then."

I hang up the phone and head to my closet to find something to wear.

# 15

## Alison

THE WHEELS OF THE CAR crunch the gravel of the driveway. My heart rate picks up as I reach the end and flip the engine off.

Troy comes around the corner of the Farm and I give him a tight smile as I climb out.

"Are you okay, Ms. Baker?"

"I'm fine," I say, nervously.

I am fine, just excited and nervous and ready to puke.

"I met Mr. Landry through his brother Ford. Have you met Ford?"

I shake my head, wondering why it matters to me how he knows Barrett.

"Ford and I were in the military together. Ford still is in the Marines, actually. Anyway, I opted out after a tour of duty overseas." He leads me towards the front of the house, his pace decidedly slow. "We saw some action over there, and let's just say it messed with me for awhile when I got home. I was pretty down and out, burned about every bridge I had ever built. And you know what?"

He stops in his tracks and looks at me, his grey eyes warm.

"Barrett was the only person that didn't turn their back on me. I'd only met him twice before when I came around looking for Ford—I'd heard he was on furlough. I was a mess," he grins. "And Barrett pulled me aside and helped me get cleaned up. He gave me a chance in his security detail." His jaw stiffens, his eyes narrowing. "I know you don't know him, and he may not like me even talking to you, and come to think of it, I'm not sure why I am other than I see a look of apprehension on your face. But trust me when I say, he's the best man I've ever known."

It does make me feel better, but it's not something I didn't already know. Barrett is a good man; I knew that from the moment he found me with Mr. Pickner. My nerves aren't from that. They're from just how good he might really be.

A fluffy yellow dog comes barreling towards us, his tongue sticking out of his mouth, from the other side of the house.

"Trigger, stop," Troy commands. The dog sits without hesitation.

"Wow. He's well trained," I comment, following him to the steps.

"Of course he is. Ford wouldn't have it any other way."

Troy steps to the side as the front door sweeps open. "I'll see you later. Enjoy." And he's gone.

I barely notice Troy's departure because my eyes are glued to Barrett. He leans against the frame, one arm stretched overhead, a playful smile on his face. The edge of his white dress shirt lifts just enough to show a sliver of tanned and toned skin between it and the top of his jeans.

I should go towards him, say hello, but it takes a second to become acclimated to him—to the energy that rolls off of him in waves.

"Good afternoon," he drawls. His voice is a mixture of sweet and simple, honeyed and complicated. It makes me go weak when I need to be strong. Taking a deep breath and gathering myself, I try to keep my hormones in check.

"Hey," I finally reply, much to his amusement. His lips twist together in a cheeky grin as he pushes away from the door.

"Thank you for coming all the way out here."

"Let's be honest," I say, the words struggling to get out as he draws near, "you weren't going to make it easy to say no."

His chest rumbles with a chuckle. "No, no, I wasn't."

He kisses my cheek. I want to turn my face and capture his decadently soft lips with my own.

"It's beautiful out here," I comment, feeling my cheeks heat from his touch.

"It is, isn't it? This is my favorite place in the world."

The wind breezes across the porch, a warm sputter of air that has just a touch of the autumn weather on its heels. The ferns rock in their hangers while Trigger walks beneath them, settling on a rocking chair in the corner of the porch.

Glancing up at Barrett, his eyes lock onto mine.

"Are you ready to go in?" he asks.

I nod and follow him inside. The soft thud of the door behind me echoing through the room.

I follow Barrett inside and through a cozy kitchen. We end up on the porch again, this time at the back of the house.

"Wow," I breathe, spying a little lake at the far end of the lawn. "This is incredible. You'd never know this exists."

"It's perfect, right? It was my grandfather's place and now it's my father's, technically. I probably use it more than anyone though. I stay out here a lot."

"I would too. It's so quiet."

Barrett motions for me to sit at a table to our left. It's a little round table with a white linen cloth surrounded by four wooden chairs. Two places have been set, each with a Styrofoam take-out container.

"I hope you don't mind eating with plastic," he grimaces. "I didn't want to be too presumptuous and have Yolanda come out and fix something. So when you accepted my offer, I had to think quick."

We exchange a smile, and once again, it's effortless. Everything about him is so smooth, so easy. I keep waiting for the moment I think it's a façade, but there are no cracks in his veneer.

"So, I'm guessing you don't cook?" I ask, lifting the lid to my container as he does the same. Crab cakes and slaw line the inside, and the scents that rise make my mouth water.

"Cooking is one of the very few things I don't do and have no interest in ever doing," he laughs. "My mom and sisters did the cooking, and we had a housekeeper to pick up the slack. Now I have Yolanda."

"You have people. That's what you're saying."

He raises his fork with a piece of crab cake to his mouth. "More or less."

"I'm taking it you don't do dishes or laundry either," I laugh.

"You'd be correct."

"I'm kind of jealous of you and kind of sad for you."

Laughing, he takes another bite. "I'd be sad about a few things in my life, but not having to do chores wouldn't be one of them."

"They're a pain for sure. But as much as I hate the drudgery of daily life, I wonder how different my life would be if I didn't do them. In a way, all of the chores of life mean you have someone to cook for, someone to love that needs laundry. If there were no bowls in the sink or little dirty shirts to be washed, that would mean I didn't have Huxley. They're just little reminders of a full life, you know?" I pause before continuing. "But I'm not saying I'd turn down maid service."

"Maybe I'll wash a bowl tomorrow after breakfast and see if it changes my perspective," he teases. "It might be a life-altering experience. Who knows?"

"Report back. Make sure you get a soap that will keep your hands nice and soft."

"Noted."

We sit quietly, eating our food and trading smiles with each other. I don't feel awkward or compelled to speak at all, which surprises me. It feels absolutely normal to just sit and enjoy each other's company like this is a routine afternoon.

I'm in my head, thinking about how comfortable I feel, when I look up and into his eyes. He's leaned back in his chair just watching me.

I flush. "What?"

"Just watching you."

"Obviously," I laugh nervously. "Why?"

He lifts his shoulders in a half-hearted attempt at shrugging. A smile curls the side of his face. "You're crazy beautiful."

"I . . ." I sit my fork down and place my hands on my lap. Forcing a swallow, I will myself to look back up at him. "Thank you."

"You don't take compliments well."

"They're always just unexpected. That's all."

His head cocks to the side, like he's working a puzzle. "Men don't tell you that all the time? I find that hard to believe."

"Sometimes, yes, I suppose," I say, searching for words. "I never really go out of my way to date or anything. So it's not like I'm in situations where someone is going to blurt it out there."

"You don't date? At all?"

Shaking my head, I smile sadly. "No. Occasionally, I guess. But they're few and far between. Intentionally," I toss in at the last minute, not wanting to seem like I'm bad goods.

"Trust me when I say I fully understand why someone wouldn't want to date at certain periods in their lives. I'm kind of there now." He touches his finger to his lip, trying to hide a smirk. "I'm *supposed* to be there now," he corrects himself.

I giggle, closing my container and sitting it off to the side. My appetite is now long gone, and I have a propensity to fiddle when I'm nervous. I don't want to be jacking with the slaw like a little kid, and I will be if I don't get it out of my face.

"I'm sure you are," I agree.

"I'm in this election and I have to lock down my image, as stupid as that sounds."

"Remember when I told you I don't know a lot about you?" I wink. "I do know enough to know you're portrayed as a playboy. So you 'locking down your image' seems like a good idea."

He rolls his eyes and it's obviously a point of contention with him. "Who I'm dating doesn't affect how I do my job."

"I can see both sides of the argument."

"A discussion for another day," he says, obviously not wanting to delve into it. "My question is this: why are *you* not dating?"

His hands form a steeple that his chin rests on. The dimple in his left cheek sinks in just a bit and I want to touch his skin, feel the smoothness under my own.

"Alison?"

"Lots of reasons," I say simply, knowing that's not going to be enough to get around the topic.

A part of me wants him to know so that maybe it'll make whatever happens next easier. Whether that's him never calling me again or us meeting for lunch or dinner, it'll be easier if he knows my hesitations to all of this.

"I told you I have a son. His father is out of the picture completely and I really need to make sure I'm focused on him. He deserves that from me and I'm the only parent he has."

"Can I ask where his father is?"

I force a swallow. "He's in prison."

Barrett's eyes fly open and he sits back in his seat again.

"He was a judge in Albuquerque," I continue, figuring I may as well get it out there and over with. "Got caught up in some big scandals and was eventually disbarred, convicted of tampering with evidence, bribery, solicitation of bribery, solicitation of prostitution, and possession of drugs. Among other things. That's the quick list."

"Nice guy," Barrett says, whistling through his teeth.

"Right? When all of that came to light, it was terrifying. The biggest scandal in New Mexico in a long time. I was even investigated for a short while because I was his wife, even though we were in the process of separating when it all came crashing down."

The memory turns my stomach and I look away, not wanting to see the disappointment or judgment in his eyes. I've seen it so many times in other people's—it would devastate me to see it in his.

"Alison," he breathes, not speaking until I turn my head and look at him again. "I'm sorry. That had to be rough."

My jaw drops, my brain unable to process his complete apparent rejection of my possible complicity. Of course I had nothing to do with that, but he doesn't know me.

"You aren't going to ask me about it?" I ask in disbelief. "Ask me if I was guilty? Ask me what the investigation found?"

His head shakes gently side to side. "I already know what it found."

"How do you know?"

My hand trembles beneath the table, nervous energy kicking in. I have nothing to hide. But if he's researched me and read everything they said, saw the pictures taken of Hayden leaving a hotel room with prostitutes, saw the inquiry into me, I'll never be able to look at him again. It's humiliation to an unbearable degree.

"I know because I know you," he says, chewing on his bottom lip.

"Barrett, that doesn't make any sense." The breeze kicks up, the edge of the cloth rippling between my fingers. Despite the coolness of the air, my cheeks are on fire. This is not the discussion I wanted to have, although I suppose it was inevitable.

"It makes perfect sense. I know who you are. I don't have to ask you what some prosecutor decided. I know they didn't find anything."

"So you didn't have me investigated? Vetted, I think they call that."

He shakes his head and picks up his water. "No."

I sit incredulous, watching him take a long drink. He watches me over the top, waiting for me to react.

"I promise you I had nothing to do with any of those things," I ramble, wanting to make it crystal clear that I was and am innocent. "I had no idea. If I had, I would've left him long before. I—"

"Hush," he says, a softness to his voice that dampens the interruption. "I just told you I know what happened. I can tell. This shit is my life. Don't forget that."

He means for that to reassure me, to make me relax and realize he understands how things go in the public realm. But his words do the very opposite.

This shit is my life.

Everything I want to avoid, everything I left behind, is sitting in front of me amplified.

"Why are you looking at me like that?" he asks.

"Like what?" I swallow.

"I don't know. Like you've just seen a ghost."

"Just memories, I guess."

"Those memories—that's why you don't date? You're afraid of being hurt again?"

"No, not specifically. Heartbreak is a part of life. I can handle that." I glance across the lawn, more away from him than at anything in particular. "I'm just being very picky this time around. Unless someone is one hundred percent worth it and in it the same as I am, I'm not taking my energy away from what I need to do for me and Hux. It just seems pointless."

He nods and sort of takes it all in before pushing away from the table. Startled, I watch him come around and offer me his hand.

Pulling me to my feet, we take the few steps down the porch and onto the lawn. The grass is soft under my shoes, the smell of fall dancing through the air.

"It will be winter soon," he says, more to himself than anything. "If there's one thing I've learned over the last few years, it's that you can never predict what life's going to throw at you one day to the next, just like you can't predict the weather."

I'm not sure where he's going with this, so I don't reply.

He looks at me through the corner of his bright green eyes. "Nothing you do in life, even the things you think you have figured out—they aren't guaranteed."

"True."

"But at the same time, you have to take some risks to reap rewards."

"I'm not much of a risk taker."

He turns to face me, searching me for something. I can smell his cologne heating under the warm afternoon sun as he rolls back the cufflinks of his shirt. His forearms are tanned and toned, adorned with his silver watch. It's a mix of casual and sophisticated, boy-next-door meets powerful enigma.

"Do you see me as a risk, Alison?"

My breath catches in my throat. "Absolutely."

"Why?"

"Because you're . . . you," I whisper.

Before I know what's happening, he takes the step that separates us. His body is nearly touching mine, a paper-thin margin the only thing between us.

I look up into his eyes, see the stubble dotting his hard jaw line, the slight angle to his nose that gives him more sex appeal than it takes away.

Our eyes lock. After a slight hesitation, his face lowers inch-by-torturous-inch.

I take in a quick breath as our lips touch. The contact zips through me, making me tingle from head to toe. His hands fall to the small of my back, gently yet firmly encouraging me to draw closer to him.

Pulling back shakily, I see his breathing is as erratic as mine. We watch each other like we don't know whether to devour the other or walk our separate ways.

I want the first, but know I need to do the second. The look in his eyes tells me he feels the same way. I can't be much good for his campaign either. As I turn over the options in my mind, what I want and what I need, the alarm goes off on my phone.

Barrett watches with confusion as I pull the device out of my pocket and turn it off.

"I have to go," I say, my tone mixed with regret and relief. "I'm working tonight for Luxor. I have to be there a little early, hence the alarm."

He runs his hand through his hair, mussing up the silky locks. His jaw opens and shuts before he finally looks resolved. "Okay."

With a little slump in his shoulders, he leads me around the side of the house.

The pace is quick and my nerves bound right along with it. I'm not sure how to wrap this up. My head spins a thousand different options, but before I know it, he stops and pulls me in front of him.

"Do you want to see me again?"

It's a simple question, yet one I stumble to answer.

"Barrett . . ."

"That's not a no."

"That's not a yes, either," I grin.

He smiles, too, and it ingrains itself in my memory. "I'll call you soon. Maybe we can find a day we both have open."

"Maybe."

"I'd like that."

"I think I'd like that, too," I whisper.

His eyes light up and he starts to speak, but seems to think better of it. Instead, he kisses my cheek again and walks me to my car.

## Barrett

MY BODY IS SWEATY FROM the workout with my personal trainer. Instead of going to the gym, he came here. We worked out with free weights and did some simple cardio.

I strip off my soaked t-shirt when my phone rings. I see it's Daphne, but I answer it anyway. I still need her father's endorsement, so I can't just ignore her like I want to. That wouldn't go over well.

"Hey," I say, sitting on a barstool at the kitchen island.

"Hey, Barrett," she sings in her melodramatic way. "How are you?"

"Good. Just finished a workout."

"Nice. Do you have any plans this evening?"

I look around the empty kitchen and shrug. "No, not really. Just some work I need to finish up. I got a little behind today."

Memories of Alison on the porch of my family home makes me feel warm all over. It's normally an off-putting feeling to have a woman anywhere near my family and our things, but with her, it seems normal. Organic.

"Barrett?"

I flip back to reality. "I'm sorry. What did you say?"

"I was saying that I have a thing with Daddy tonight and was hoping you'd be able to go with me. You know how it goes, all those stuffy men talking about boring stuff. I need someone to go with so I don't slit my throat."

"Is it the Raparasey Dinner?"

"Yeah, I think so. It's the one you went to with me a few times at Seaton Block. I just . . . I need your hot ass to go with me again."

Chuckling, I stand and head to the fridge for a bottle of water. "I'm sorry, Daph, but I can't."

"Why?" she pouts. I can hear the disappointment in her tone, maybe even a little anger.

"I told you I have work to do," I point out.

"Yeah, but you always go with me. And think of all the connections you can make, sugar. It's good for you. And Daddy will be there, of course, and I know he hasn't officially endorsed you yet . . ."

"I can't."

"You can't or you won't?" she presses.

"It's really the same thing, isn't it?"

"No!" she exclaims. "It isn't. You always go with me. We've always bailed each other out, Barrett, and tonight—I need you."

The last couple of words are so heavy, so full of implication, that I feel my shoulders fall with the weight.

"You don't need me," I scoff.

"I do."

She reminds me of a little girl, pouting to get her way. I wonder if she's always been this annoying, and if so, why I'm just realizing how bad it is.

I remember the way these things usually end, and that's with her ass up in the air, her big, fake tits bouncing around like the balloons they are. That, too, usually doesn't bother me, but tonight, it makes me feel uninspired to see it again.

"Look, Daphne, I'm sorry. I really am. But I'm really busy and I'm going to continue to be for the foreseeable future."

The air changes between us. I can feel it through the phone and the miles that separate us.

"Is this because of the campaign or that girl I've heard you're seeing?"

She catches me off guard. I don't respond.

"If you're the smart man I know you to be," she says, her voice dripping with sweetness, "you will realize where your bread is buttered, Barrett. And that's right here, sugar."

"I'm not your 'sugar.'"

She exhales a long, dramatic breath. "You and I have always been a thing. No matter who you see, who I date, it's your bed I always end up in. You know that. We've been in the same schools, through the same elections, through the same bullshit our entire lives. Don't act like you don't want me now—especially now when you need me."

It's the way she says it, like she has one over me. It infuriates me and I see red.

"I don't need anyone, Daphne," I spit out. "We can be friends if that's what you want. But we aren't going to be more than that and that's not for any reason other than we never were."

"You're fucking up."

It's my turn to laugh. "Maybe. But it won't be the first time and it probably won't be the last."

## Alison

I TYPE MY FAVORITE WORDS, The End, and finish my paper. Hitting save before I lose the last five hours of work, I close my computer and my eyes as well.

It's after two in the morning and I haven't slept more than a handful of hours over the past few days. Between work at Hillary's during the day, a host of papers due in my classes, and a few catering jobs mixed in, I'm bone tired.

I check on Huxley before heading into my room and slipping beneath the covers without even brushing my teeth.

My paper was on ethics in journalism, and the entire thing made me think of Barrett and the unethical practices that are aimed at him. I hate that his voice is often twisted and sometimes diminished based on the slant of the journalist writing the piece. It's true for all politicians and celebrities, I guess, but Barrett I know. Or I think I do.

He's wanted to see me this week, and maybe I've wanted to see him too, but it hasn't worked out. And I'm kind of glad for that. Over the past week, we've been able to get to know each other without any pressure. We've had a couple of phone calls and a boatload of texts, and I scroll through them and smile.

Like he senses I'm awake and thinking of him, my phone buzzes in my hand.

*Barrett: I think I would sleep better if I could roll over and see you.*

*Me: I snore.*

*Barrett: I can figure out how to occupy your mouth.*

*Me: So much for all the credit I was just giving you for being a gentleman.*

*Barrett: The veneer comes off late at night. ;)*

*Me: Why are you up?*

*Barrett: I'd like to give you a line like I was thinking about you or you were running through my mind, but really—I'm working.*

I laugh as I envision him stretched out on his bed. In my head, he's naked, his divine body on full display. His hair is wet from the shower, his abs cut to perfection.

Barrett's next message pings as it's received.

*Barrett: How was your day? How's Huxley?*

My heart is full as I type out my response.

*Me: It was good. Hux is good. I'm sorry I couldn't talk much today. Between Hillary's House and my paper for class and Hux's homework, today was a mess.*

Barrett: *Never apologize for putting you and Hux first, Alison. That's the way it should be.*

I look at the words for a long few seconds before I can gather myself to respond. He's so sweet, so considerate of Huxley that tears sting my eyes as I try to find the right keys to answer him.

Me: *I don't even know how to respond to that.*

Me: *Well, if that's the case, I'll make sure you stay solidly in second place. ;)*

Barrett: *I miss you.*

Me: *I miss you too.*

Barrett: *I would really like to see you tomorrow night. Do you think that's possible?*

My cheeks split and I give in. Maybe it's because he's charming or that he's so sweet about Huxley or because it's so late and my defenses are down, but, for the first time without hesitation, I reply.

Me: *I'd like that.*

Barrett: *That was way too easy. I'll send Troy to get you around eight. Okay?*

Me: *Okay. :)*

Barrett: *I'm going to quit while I'm ahead. Goodnight, Alison.*

Me: *Night, Barrett.*

# Alison

THE SUN IS DIPPING AS we pull to the front of the Farm. The evening rays spread from behind a few clouds, creating beams of pinks and oranges in the most breathtaking sunset.

We roll to a stop and Troy turns off the ignition. He's around the Rover before I can get my seatbelt off and opens the door for me.

"Mr. Landry asked that you meet him behind the house. Follow me," he says, leading the way.

The path, illuminated by solar lights, slips between the trees, scents of evergreen filling the air. Troy steps out of the way and I stop in my tracks.

Tucked away behind the trees, invisible from the house, is an open air structure. There are four masonry pillars on a concrete slab. White fabric is tied against each pillar like in a classical painting, and if they were untied, they'd give another layer of privacy to the interior. The back wall is solid with a large see-through fireplace built in.

Taking a step closer, I spot a large wooden table that could seat ten people running down the center of the room. Oversized outdoor sofas and chairs with royal blue covers and bright white pillows with gold accents create small, cozy spaces.

Overhead, a cupola caps off the structure, the glass reflecting both the final rays of sunshine and the light from the oversized crystal chandelier that hangs over the table.

It's incredible.

"If you need anything, I'll be in the house," Troy says. I begin to turn to reply when I'm halted in my tracks. Coming around the corner is the most spectacular thing I've seen all night.

Barrett gives me a smile as he saunters towards me. He's wearing dark wash jeans and a black t-shirt with black, leathery-looking edging.

He looks like he just walked off the pages of a magazine and not from around the corner of a fireplace. Sexy and edgy, beautiful and classic. He's everything.

"You are gorgeous," he says, just loud enough for me to hear.

My pulse quickens as he approaches, his cologne filling the air. His grin widens as he reaches me and kisses me gently on the cheek. The simple contact has my body rioting, my thighs clenching together to dull the ache that's rapidly growing between them.

He saunters by me and undoes the ties that hold the fabric back. In a few seconds, the front of the structure is draped with the gauzy, flowing fabric, and it only adds to the romantic ambiance of the setting.

When he turns to face me, a wicked grin lays on his lips. "Thank you for coming," he whispers, taking my hand. He holds it in his for a long second, letting the warmth of the contact mingle, before leading me to my chair.

We reach the elegantly set table with pillar candles in large, glass vases and white sand. Fresh flowers spring from containers in the center, as well as more food than either of us can possibly consume in one night.

"This is beautiful," I breathe. There are two places formally set at one end with crystal wine glasses and china that clearly didn't come out of the local department store. I glance down at my clearance rack sundress and release a breath.

At one point in my life, I would've been right at home in this scenario. I had a closet full of expensive clothes that wouldn't fit in my car when I left Hayden. I had routine visits with a hairdresser, fresh manicures, and expensive make-up.

I try not to get embarrassed in the comparison of the before and after because this is where I am now and this is who I am. And I'm for the better because of it in all the ways that matter.

Pulling out a chair, he motions for me to sit. "I hope steak and Petrus Pomeral will do."

"I'll be honest," I say as I lower myself into the chair. "I love steak but I have no idea what the other thing is."

His laugh fills the air, floating on the gentle breeze that flutters the candlelight. "It's a French wine. My favorite. You do like wine, don't you?"

"Do I like wine?" I scoff. "What kind of question is that?"

"A question someone asks someone else when they want to know more about them."

I grin as he sits across from me. I love watching him move, his muscles flex as he bends and pushes.

He lifts the silver lid in front of him and I do the same. Sitting beneath the cover is a large steak, heat still rising from the plate. I have no idea how he managed to put all of this together, but I suppose it's easy when you're a Landry.

"Did your day get any better?" I ask, watching a shadow roll over his face.

"Not really. It won't get any better for awhile." He looks up at me. "As far as work goes, anyway."

A smile stretches across my face and I'm happy to see it returned.

"How was yours?" he asks.

"I got a little studying done before I left for work. I'll have to finish it when I get home. But otherwise, it was good."

"You could've brought your homework here," he suggests. "I could've helped you study."

I can't help but laugh. "Sure. It would put you to sleep."

"If I can stay awake in meetings about a dog park, I'm pretty sure I can stay awake watching you read. I'd probably even like it."

Flushing, I take a sip of my wine. It's rich and delicious.

"Did your son have a good day fishing today with your father? They went again, right?"

"Yeah," I laugh, remembering his call on the way here. "They had fun."

"Did his father ever do that kind of thing with him?"

I look away. "No, not really. Hayden was always busy."

"I shouldn't have asked that. I'm sorry."

"No, it's fine. I just don't think about that any more than I have to. I avoid it at all costs, really."

"I can understand that," he smiles softly. "Hux just seems like a great kid. Lincoln loved him."

Laughing, I place my glass back on the table. "Because he called you out about your pitch."

Barrett chuckles.

"Hux liked Lincoln too. He pretty much thinks he met a rock star."

"Yeah, well, that's because they're probably interested in the same things. Baseball and girls."

"My son doesn't like girls!" I exclaim.

"Give it time," Barrett chuckles. "They'll be calling your phone all hours of the night."

"I'm not ready for that," I say, feeling a bit of panic. "I don't even have a gun."

Barrett bursts into a fit of laughter. "I'll let you borrow Troy. He can be Hux's new security guy."

He seems to think nothing about what he's just said, but I do. I watch him slice his steak, but I can't shake the idea that if something did happen between us, Hux might actually need a security guy. The thought really bothers me.

"What's the matter?" Barrett asks, setting his fork down.

"I know we're eating and conversation is usually kept light, but what you just said made me think."

"What I just said?" He scrunches his face, trying to figure out what I'm referring to. "About Troy?"

I lean back in my chair, putting a little distance between us. "We keep talking and seeing each other. And I can't imagine that stopping anytime soon."

"God, I hope not."

My cheeks flushing, I try not to swoon and stay focused. "But then what, Barrett? What would that mean for Huxley?"

He considers my question. He takes a sip of wine before responding. "Well, you're his mother. It's your decision."

"I mean, I know this might not go anywhere," I say hurriedly. "I know it's awful timing for you, and I'm not even sure I want it to go anywhere anyway—"

"I do."

I force a swallow. His bluntness, his quick interruption, startles me. I search his face for a moment of, Oh fuck, I didn't mean to say that, but I don't see it. It's not there.

"You do?"

"Even though you're right—this is the wrong time to be starting a relationship with someone. Not even just that, I'm basically the guy you've been avoiding and I know that puts extra pressure on things. I want this to go somewhere. I want to see if it can. And maybe it can't," he adds with a small smile, "but I don't want to always wonder."

My eyes squeeze shut. He's saying the things any woman in the world would love to hear him say, yet I don't know if I can reciprocate them.

"I'm scared," I admit. "I don't want to be in the media or Huxley to lose his freedom. I don't want to be harassed for questions and . . ." I look at him with as much seriousness as I can. "I don't want to be embarrassed publicly."

"I would never embarrass you."

"I know. I believe that. But sometimes, you know . . . What if you get elected? Then you move to Atlanta and all of a sudden there's media everywhere asking questions, sticking cameras where they don't belong? I'm getting déjà vu thinking about it."

"Why?" he snorts. "Because you married an imbecile that thought he was king because he got a job as a judge?"

"Yes, actually. Because what if you go up the ladder and leave me behind?"

The thought causes a flash of panic to tear through me and I have to look away. It's not the idea of being alone, that I can do. It's the feeling of being unnecessary.

He tosses the linen napkin from his lap onto the table. His eyes are fiery. "Why would I do that?"

"I know how these things work."

"No, you know what you've seen. But you haven't seen me. You haven't given me a chance to show you how I feel, how I act. How I feel about you won't change whether I win the election or not. I don't know exactly what will happen if I get the job. It's something we'd have to figure out then together." He grins. "What happened to that whole 'Speak as you find' thing?"

He's making it way too easy to cave in. I look away from his beautiful eyes and sexy smile, from all the temptations that lure me in.

"What about Huxley?" I ask, figuring if there's a deal breaker, it'll be him.

"What about him? I'll just have him do my baseball public relations work."

Chuckling, I look at him. His features are softened in the candle light, his smile so authentic it makes me swoon.

He wants me. And Hux.

"How can I make sure he's protected?"

"Protected how? Like physically?"

"Yes. In every way. I don't want him loving you and then having you walk away."

He looks away from me this time, and I hold my breath.

"If we take things slow, keep them out of the media, I don't think he'll have many ramifications to this. And taking it slow gives us a chance to see if it's going to work out before we go all in. I don't want to hurt either of you, Alison."

He leans towards me and picks up the golden peacock feather necklace that lies between my breasts. The back of his hand rests against me for a second longer than necessary, and I know he can feel the thundering of my heart beneath it. The contact stops my breathing, and I just watch his hand turn over the emblem.

"This is beautiful." He places it where he found it, gently pressing it into my dress. His gaze locks on to mine, and he sinks back in his chair.

The air between us is thick, like a warm blanket on a cool evening. I feel him looking at me, and my cheeks flush as my eyes find his.

"What do you want out of life, Alison?"

I think about it for a long second. "I want to build a good life for Huxley and I, one that I can be proud of. One that can't be taken away."

"Dig deeper."

"What?"

"Imagine yourself in fifty years," he instructs. "What stories do you want to tell your grandkids?"

"Well," I begin, trying to muddle through my mind, "I want to tell them about all the times I laughed, the times I cried because I was so happy. I hope I can show them pictures with lots of smiles and recall silly little picnics and tons of special moments."

"So you want to be happy?"

"Yes. I want to be happy."

"What does happy look like to you?"

You. Feeling like I feel when you look at me. Having this little ball of giddiness when I see you smile, this level of comfort that I haven't felt with a man before.

But I don't say that. Instead, I consider my options. "It looks like fall afternoons on a porch swing, summer afternoons with a glass of lemonade by a pool. Happy looks like late night talks under a pile of blankets with a man that loves me like I love him."

Barrett's lips twitch, but he doesn't smile. He just soaks in the words, the imagery, and leans forward. "You have a way with words."

"Why do you say that?"

"You just took the ideas in my head and said them more eloquently than I ever could've."

My breath catches, my heart thundering in my chest.

"Will you try to find those things with me? Just see if we can."

"Slowly?" I ask, my voice shaking.

I want this, I know I want this. Damn it, I want this so much it's strangling me. It's a risk, a shot in the dark, hope hung on the laurels of a devilishly handsome politician. But when I look in his eyes, I see something I've never seen in someone's eyes before. And I want to see that for a long time.

"Fast, slow, sideways, if that's what it takes. But I'm kind of dying over here," he mutters, a tremble in his voice too.

As soon as I respond, my heart and vagina are all tied up. I know this. But I get the binding ready.

"Yes," I breathe, my blood pressure soaring. "Let's try it."

## Barrett

I PUSH AWAY FROM THE table and walk behind her. She faces forward, but tilts her head, exposing her neck. I brush her hair off to the side and lay my hands firmly on her shoulders. The thin strip of the straps of her dress are the only barrier between us. When our skin touches, a flurry of goose bumps race across her skin. She shivers beneath my touch and I can feel it in my cock. I harden immediately, my length swelling against my jeans.

I have to play this right. She's not another woman in my life that I won't care if I see tomorrow or not. She's the woman in my life.

"I want you," I breathe, watching her react.

She turns her head and looks at me with a glimmer in her eye, the one I love so much normally but right now—it's even brighter. She tucks a strand of hair behind her ear, giving me a little grin.

I let my fingertips stroke the skin along the ridge of her shoulder. "I want you. All of you, Alison. I want the whole thing."

She looks across the space and takes in the ambiance I carefully constructed for her. I wanted her to feel special, to feel like I took the time to impress her. It was an odd feeling, wanting to impress a woman. I don't recall ever doing it before.

"I want you too," she says finally, a seductive smile planting across her gorgeous lips. She glances down at my cock before meeting my eyes again. "All of you."

I roll my hands down the front of her shoulders and let them dip into the front of her dress. The smooth fabric on top and silky skin below are fucking heaven.

"Ah," she moans, resting her head against my right arm. Her breasts overflow my hands, the voluptuousness driving me absolutely wild.

I trail lazy kisses from behind her ear down her neck. She's so delicate that I push away the thoughts of what this moment could do to this strong, yet fragile, girl. What the aftermath could be if something goes wrong.

Her gasps obliterate any thoughts other than the feel of her under my fingers.

"What are you doing to me?" she whispers, her voice filled with as much need as is coursing through my body.

I press my lips against her neck, right beneath her ear. "Exactly what you thought I was going to do you. What you were picturing in your mind when you agreed to be mine."

Alison shudders beneath my touch as I roll one of her nipples between my fingers. She turns her head to face me and I capture her mouth with mine. She moans into my mouth, and the sound reverberates through me. I feel it through every inch of my body, increasing the frantic need to be inside of her.

Our tongues dance together, a frenzied movement that takes advantage of all the times we've denied ourselves. She's intoxicating, the taste of wine fresh on her tongue. I pull my hands to her face, cupping each cheek, my fingers pressing into her skin, as I deepen the kiss.

She stands, the chair crashing to the floor behind us. The things on the table shake, some fall over, as she bumps it with her hip to angle towards me. Her hands slide up my neck, down my back, touching as much of me as she can.

It's the most intense feeling I've ever had. Everything is intensified to a level I've never felt before.

I cup her ass in my hands, squeeze, and nearly come apart as she pops her hips and works her tongue against mine. I lift her swiftly, her eyes flying open. She never breaks the kiss as I sit her on the table a couple of steps away from her plate.

Alison's lips pull at mine as I suspend the kiss. Her breathing is ragged, matching my own, as I run my fingertips up her arms. She peeks at me through her long lashes and waits for me to make my next move.

I really just want to burst into her and feel her body wrap around mine. I want to enjoy it, make it a memory worth having.

She's so fucking beautiful.

My fingertips reach the straps of her dress, and I lift them with the pads of my fingers. I slide them down her arms until the top of her dress is pooled at her waist. She's facing me wearing nothing but a red lace bra. I can make out her nipples through the lace and it puts me over the edge.

"You waiting on something?" she asks, her voice shaky.

A low chuckle escapes my throat as I close the half step distance between us. She bites her lip as I come forward. Lifting her ample breasts out of her bra, I let them sit on top, the nipples in stiff peaks pointing right at me.

So fucking perfect.

I take one into my mouth, rolling her nipple with my tongue. She yelps in pleasure, grabbing my hair and pressing my face into her harder. I nip and suck, feeling her smooth skin fill my mouth. My other hand goes to the other, palming it, feeling the weight of its fullness.

"Barrett," she moans, spreading her legs apart. Her head is tipped back, her hair spreading out behind her. It's the purest, most erotic display.

"Lay back," I command, standing in front of her. She raises her eyebrows and I subtly shake my head. "Back, Alison."

Lowering herself flat on the table, her quick breaths echo through the night. Her breasts bounce with each movement and my cock throbs so hard it's painful.

I lift one of her legs, her dress rolling up her thighs. Her pussy glimmers with wetness, completely uncovered.

I press a kiss against the inside of her ankle, and she jerks at the contact. I wrap my hand harder around her foot, pressing another kiss, and she doesn't move.

"Good girl," I whisper. I lick a light trail from her ankle to the bend in her leg, stopping to take a deep breath of her scent. The vanilla is mixed with a heady musky scent. I force a swallow, but my throat is tight. My entire body, every fucking piece of me, needs a release.

Licking my way up her thigh, her leg trembles under my touch. I flatten my tongue as I reach the top, slowing my journey to the apex of her thighs. Moving my hands to her waist, I knock back her dress so that it's bunched up just below her chest. I could remove it altogether and consider that, but I don't want to wait.

I can't.

My tongue slides from the top of her leg to her pussy, wet and waiting for me. I don't hesitate, don't stutter, as my tongue sinks deep inside her.

She cries out, her arms reaching for the table on either side of her head. The fruit tray topples over. Grapes, berries, and oranges roll past me and onto the floor.

I suck her clit into my mouth, biting lightly on the swollen bud. She arches her hips, and I slide my tongue back down to her opening and bury my face between her legs.

Her body riots, releasing all over me, and I lap it up. She trembles beneath my hands, her pussy gripping my tongue.

A bundle of grapes sits by my hand near her waist and I grab them. I pull back for a split second, remove a few of the fruits from the stem, then roll one of the grapes around her clit. She shudders, trying to pull away. I place a hand on her navel, warning her not to move. She lifts her head and looks at me over the round tops of her breasts. She tries to smile, but before she can, I slide a grape inside her.

"Ah!" Her head collapses to the table again. I push another, then a third, grape inside of her. She's so wet, so ready that they go inside easily. "Barrett!"

Nudging her legs open further, I slide one finger inside. The grapes are cool against the warmth of her skin. I move them with my finger, feeling them jostle inside.

"My God!"

Working her clit with another finger, I slide it down until it dips inside her too. She moans loudly, arching her back again. My cock struggles against my jeans, ready to fucking explode.

I watch as my fingers work inside her, sliding them in and out, feeling one grape burst. The juice rolls out of her and down my wrist.

I press harder this time, working the second grape to the side until it, too, pops. Alison is mumbling, thrashing, trying to grab at my hands with hers. Knowing that it's me doing this to her, it's me that's got her worked into such a frenzy, it's me that has her begging for my cock in that seductive voice is nearly unbearable.

Popping the final grape, I remove my fingers to a loud gasp from her. I lower my head to her pussy and lick her with the flat of my tongue. The contact has her moaning, gasping, pressing my face into her with her hands. I suck the juice that trickles from her opening before allowing her to pull my face up to meet hers.

She half sits as she holds my gaze for a second before kissing me for all she's worth. Her tongue dips into my mouth, taking me by surprise. When she pulls back, she's barely breathing.

"I want you." Her voice is ragged, dripping with desire. "I want your cock now, Barrett."

Her hands are digging at my zipper as I'm undoing the button and simultaneously grabbing a condom from my pocket. Once my pants are on the floor around my feet, she spreads her legs and works her ass to the edge of the table. I step forward, rolling the condom down my length. Her hands slide around my waist, her fingernails digging into my ass.

"Now," she whispers and I slide easily inside her.

"Fuck!" I cry, the slippery wetness allowing me all the way inside. She clenches around me, her body fitting snugly around my length.

My eyes are closed, enjoying the feeling as I slide gently out and back in, feeling every inch of her warmth as I move. She kisses me again, tenderly this time, her full lips parting my own. Before pulling back, she bites my bottom lip, bringing me out of the fog.

Quickening my pace, I push my hands beneath her. I squeeze her cheeks and find a rhythm. The slapping of our skin, the wetness coating my cock and groin, her breasts bouncing against me are more than I even dreamed. Still, I need more, to put my stamp on every part of her body.

I hook her legs around my arms and lift her up so I can bury myself deeper in her pussy. Her body spasms around mine, her orgasm building again. She'll get off again before I find mine.

My cock slides up and across her clit. That's all it takes. She constricts around me again and I let myself go.

Pushing as far into her as I can, I watch her face as my body explodes in every way imaginable. My legs shake. My hands tremble as I hold on to her hips. My head feels like it's going to blow off my body as the culmination of the entire night, the entire last few nights, comes to a point.

I rest her back on the table and look into her eyes.

"You okay?" I ask.

"Yes," she exhales. She untangles her body from mine and sweeps her hair off to one side. She gives me a soft smile that only makes me want to sweep her lips up again with mine. So I do.

"I think I need to clean up," she whispers as she pulls away.

"There's a restroom behind the fireplace." I help her off the table, fighting the urge to pull her into me instead.

She glances up at me through her thick lashes, her cheeks still blazing from the thorough fucking moments earlier.

I can only watch her go. I'm not sure what the hell just happened. I am sure I'm probably fucked in a lot more ways than one.

## Alison

"TELL ME THE GRAPES CAME out!" Lola giggles through the phone.

"Of course they did," I laugh, "but I'm not telling you how or where."

"This is the best story I've ever heard. I just have chills. I have legit chills, Ali."

"Me too. You don't even understand."

"I'm going to need to call Isaac now and try to replay this, although it'll never measure up. Oh. My. Lord."

I laugh, falling back on my bed. I close my eyes and enjoy the feeling of being happy. Of feeling sexy. Of feeling like my body just got rocked.

"I just . . . You've rendered me speechless! Here I thought I was the dirty bird!"

"He's everything." I remember the look in his eyes, the lust nearly palpable, as he kissed up my leg. I shiver, drawing my legs together. I can still feel his touch, the way his fingertips drew lightly up my skin. The way his tongue dipped inside me. The way his cock felt as it plunged deeply into me.

"Ali? Earth to Ali," Lola says, luring me out of my memory. "Am I talking to myself?"

"I'm here."

She snorts. "I think you're still in the quasi-winery. I know I would be. Hell, I kind of am and I haven't even been properly graped."

"I don't know how I'll ever forget that, Lola. It was just erotic. Completely mind-blowing."

"And you got to experience that."

I prop up on my elbows. "Thank God for small favors. Or not small. There's nothing small about him."

"Shut. Up," she sighs. "So when are you seeing him again?"

I pause, trying to figure out how to broach the subject. Apparently it's too long of a silence because Lola picks right up on it.

"Why do I get a feeling you're not telling me something huge?"

"I already told you he was huge," I deflect to the best of my ability.

"You know what I mean. Not talking cock size for once."

"We agreed to take things slowly," I state as simply as possible.

"Whoa!" Something crashes in the background, the sound of bottles being knocked against tile. "Does that mean what I think it means?"

Sighing, I brace myself. "If you think that means I'm dating, for a lack of a better word, the mayor, then yes. It does."

"What happened to you over the last twelve hours? You call me on the way to work, all sobbing about Huxley going fishing. Then you call me and just got a grape sucked out of your hoohah and are dating the most eligible bachelor in the country?"

"Yeah, that pretty much sums it up," I laugh, unable to believe it myself. Every time I think about it, I automatically try to panic. Yet the worry doesn't come. It just feels like I'm where I should be.

"What happened to separation of hearts and vaginas? Not that I'm against this by any means. Hell, you've taken my retirement plan to a whole new level . . ."

"That's not what this is," I warn.

"No, I know it's not. You're not like that, like me," she points out. "And that's a good thing, I think. But what changed your mind?"

The moon shines through the window, illuminating my cherry-colored bedspread. She asked the million dollar question and I fight for a million dollar answer.

"Him."

"And that means?"

How do I explain that, besides the fame and the fortune and the political connection, he's everything I've ever dreamed of?

"I mean, he's amazing. And I realize I'm just scared by all the outer trappings, and only because of what I've gone through before. I just think it's worth it to see if it works. And if it doesn't . . . I guess I'll figure out a way to survive. I did before."

"That's my girl! I knew you had it in you. Maybe you had to literally have it in you to have it in you."

I laugh, her antics impossible. "Just remind me of this when I'm crying on your shoulder."

"What about the media? What about Hux?"

"Everything should be fine if we just play it cool. Stay hidden. And if he wins the election, I guess we'll see what happens," I say, chewing on my bottom lip. My stomach twists at the idea, but I force it away. I'm focusing on the good. "And if he doesn't, it'll be easier to navigate."

My phone buzzes with an incoming call. "Hey, my mom is calling. I need to grab it in case something's wrong with Huxley."

"Go. Just know I'm proud of you, Ali!"

"Thanks, Lo. Bye."

"Bye."

◆◆◆

THE LIGHTS ARE OFF IN the cabana, but the solar lights are still burning along the path leading to it. The grounds are quiet and everyone is gone but me.

My briefcase is open on the desk. Swiping a file, the edges worn from looking at it so many times over the last month, I plop back on the bed I use when I stay here and look at it again.

I try to zero in on the words, but my mind keeps going to Alison. I'm not sure what in the hell I've gotten myself into, only that this is the first time in a very long time I've felt like I just made the right decision. My decision. A decision unmarred by suggestions and requests from everyone around me.

Even though we're keeping it quiet, I know shit will hit the fan if it becomes public knowledge. Nolan will be furious. My father disappointed. Graham, the most trusted voice out of them all, will think it's wrong.

I don't care.

If I think about it long enough, I realize that my lack of concern does, in fact, concern me. Their points are right. This could be a big fuck-up for my campaign. There are a million ways this could go wrong. So why am I not more anxious about this new relationship?

I have no fucking idea.

All I know is that there's a little peace in my stomach, a little levity in my step that I don't want to let go.

In a world of stress and assholes, a life of planned moves and compromises, she's the purest deal. The only person that just wants me. She looks at me and sees straight through to who I am on the inside, without the name, the looks, the smile, or influence I can flash and get my way.

I can't let that go. Regardless of what they say.

My phone rings and I grab it. I see my mother's name on the screen. Immediately, I smile and answer. "Hey, Mom."

"Hi, Barrett. Am I interrupting anything?"

"Nope," I say, shutting the file and tossing it on the edge of the bed. "And even if you were, I'd stop to talk to you."

"Ah, you're a charmer," she laughs. "How is my oldest child? Are you hanging in there? I know how the last weeks of a campaign can be."

"Yeah, I'm all right."

"Why do I know you're fibbing?"

Chuckling, I imagine her face. Her eyes are narrowed, her lips pressed together.

"Because you're my mom, I guess."

"What's wrong?" she asks, her voice soft.

"Just . . . shit." I contemplate telling her about Alison first. I want to discuss it with someone that won't judge me right off the bat.

"Is it that Land Bill? Your father was talking about it tonight. I know we own some of the land in play and he wants you to go against it."

Sighing, I nod. "Yeah. That's the main thing right now. I'm being pushed by everyone to brush it off, but I just . . ."

"Barrett, listen to me. This is your career. Whatever you choose to do is your legacy. You have to do what you feel is right, what you can be proud of having your name attached to."

"You know Dad will disown me if I don't go against it, right? You realize you'll personally lose a few million dollars?"

"You do know I have enough money so your future children never have to work. And you also know I will die after your father and it'll be me that decides who's in the will."

I can't help but laugh. I know she's joking, in part, but she's kind of telling the truth too.

"On a serious note," she says, "I understand and respect the fact that you care about what your father says. You're a good man, a good mayor, a good son. But your father has had his life to make his mark on the world, and when I look at you children, I have to say he's made six beautiful, smart impressions. But this is your life, not his. He tries to push you and guide you, but you can make your own decisions."

I think to the one decision I've already made that I also know he'll be against.

"What if this is the wrong decision too?" I ask.

"Too?"

"Forget it," I say, realizing my slip of the tongue. "I misspoke."

She pauses like she does before she imparts her infinite wisdom. I hated these long stretches of silent time growing up. I always knew she was going to wallop me with something I couldn't argue, something that would root in my brain and make me feel a certain way. I wait on it with the same trepidation now.

"You don't remember this and I don't want you to ever speak of it. But when I was pregnant with Ford, I had very high blood pressure. The doctors wanted me to abort the pregnancy; they said if I carried him, I might die. Your father wanted me to terminate it. He said it wasn't worth the risk to my life and that I had to think about the rest of you kids."

"I had no idea," I say in astonishment.

"I was frozen, Barrett. How could I choose what I wanted, which was to keep the baby, and risk so much that affected so many others? It was a terrible position to be in."

I nod, understanding her position way better than she even imagines.

"But at the end of the day, I was the one that had to live with it. And I couldn't live thinking that maybe, somehow, it would work out. And I valued that little baby's life as much as I valued yours, or Graham's. So I chose to go through with the pregnancy.

"Your father wasn't pleased. He thought I was being cavalier about it, risking my health for something that may or may not even be feasible. But I made my choice because it was mine to make. And, as we all know, it worked out."

"But what if it hadn't?" I say, my brain spinning. "What if you had died or Ford hadn't made it?"

"It was possible. Nothing is guaranteed. But living and not knowing would've been worse than playing it safe. Sometimes, Barrett, you have to take some risks."

A grin slides across my face, her words as poignant as ever.

"Thanks, Mom."

"You are very welcome. I want to have lunch with you soon if you can swing it. I miss seeing your handsome face."

"I'll figure something out this week. I have to meet Monroe in the morning . . ."

She takes in a quick breath. "One more thing—Paulina said she was happy to arrange a dinner for you with some of her friends. I know one's a prosecutor and one is a tremendous benefactor at the hospital in Mason. Maybe that would help?"

I know Paulina's dinners all too well, and they always end up with her and me getting it on. I'm normally game for that, but things have changed. Majorly.

"I really don't have any openings in my calendar for something like that," I say, trying to dissuade her from pushing the issue.

"She said it'd be something small, something intimate."

I bet.

I try to hide my chuckle. "It's probably not a good idea, but please thank her for me."

"Will do. Get some sleep. We'll talk soon."

"Love you," I say, kicking off my shoes.

"Barrett?"

"Yeah?"

"Trust your instincts. They'll never let you down."

## Barrett

STEAM ROLLS OUT OF THE bathroom as I push the door open. It follows me into the bedroom. I pull the towel tighter around my waist, feeling better after the near-scalding water beat down on me for awhile.

My phone buzzes on my nightstand and I scurry across the room to get it. I haven't seen Alison in a few days, not since the night she agreed to try things with me, and her calls and texts are the only bright spot in a never-ending life of exasperation.

The thought of her displayed just for me, her shy smile, her sweet voice makes my dick hard. I need to see her.

Picking up the phone and swiping it without looking at the screen, a wide grin is planted on my face when I answer. "Landry."

"Hey, Barrett," Daphne croons. "How are you, sugar?"

My eyes roll back in my head, my hand finding my hair. Stifling a groan that begs to erupt, I sit on the edge of my bed.

"Not much."

An awkward pause settles over the line. Finally, she huffs, taking my lack of interest in her pussy personally. "Barrett? What's going on?"

"What do you mean?"

"You know exactly what I mean. I haven't heard from you, haven't seen you around at all. What's gotten into you?"

"Nothing has gotten into me," I mutter. "Look, Daph, I'm just busy these days."

"Let me relieve some stress, sugar."

I suck in a deep breath and wish I hadn't answered this call. "That's okay."

"You never turned down pussy, especially when it's mine, and I promise to wear that black lacy thong you love so much."

Sighing, I try to keep composed. "I'm tired."

"Too tired to fuck me, huh?" she tempts. "Remember how much you like it when I ride your cock? How you tell me how tight I am, how you love to watch my ass bounce on you when I ride you reverse cowgirl?"

"Daphne. Stop."

"Why? It's true. You love how wet I get for you."

I look at the ceiling like there's some divine intervention that's going to happen by studying the crown moulding.

"Look," I say, my voice raspy, "let's not go there, Daph."

I need to make her feel good about getting brushed off. I need her Dad's endorsement; I can't have her pissed. That's not going to help anyone.

"Whoever you're fucking right now isn't going to last, Barrett. You know that. You always come back to me."

"Why make this hard, Daph?"

"I always make it hard. You know that."

I struggle to not roll my eyes. "Whether that's true or not, it doesn't change the fact that I'm busy tonight. And I will be tomorrow and the next night too, if you're wondering," I add.

"So it's true," she chirps. "You know our friends are saying she's not one of us. That she might even be a waitress."

"Excuse me?" I bellow. "What the fuck does that even mean and why in the hell is it any of your business?"

She laughs in the phone. "That says it all."

"Don't you talk about her like that. Like she's beneath you somehow."

"Defensive, are we? Wow. She must be a helluva lay to get the playboy Barrett Landry wound around her finger."

"Shut your fucking mouth, Daphne."

Her laugher gets louder, causing my blood to nearly boil.

"That's no way to talk to a lady," she snaps.

"It's a good thing I'm not talking to a lady then, isn't it?"

"Touché."

I hear her dog yap in the background, her doorbell rings. She laughs again.

"I gotta go, Barrett. I have company."

"Hey, Daph?"

"Yeah?"

"Don't call me again."

I end the call and toss my phone on the bed. It sinks into my blankets and I wish I could sink in with it.

There's a raw spot in my gut that I can't shake. Daphne is a cocktail waiting to explode. She always has been, it's a part of her DNA. Normally it doesn't matter, but now that Alison is woven in this situation, it's unnerving.

I've always handled Daphne with some charm and cock; I can't do that now. Moreover, withholding both from her will only direct any reaction to Alison, the one person I don't want to feel the crazy.

Picking my phone back up, Alison answers in a few rings.

"Hello?" she asks sleepily.

"Hey, you."

"Barrett," she says. I hear sheets and blankets being moved around. "Are you okay? It's late."

I press my fingertips to my forehead. "Did I wake you? Or Huxley? I'm sorry. Shit."

"No, no, it's fine," she says quickly. "You just scared me, that's all."

Blowing out a breath, I imagine what she looks like in bed with no makeup and some sleepy eyes. "I miss you."

"Ah, Barrett. I miss you too."

"How was your day? Did you get your paper done?"

"No," she groans. "I have another few pages left. I had to work a few extra hours at Hillary's and then Huxley's homework was out of control. You should see the amount of stuff he has to do every night.

It's incredible."

A vision of me sitting at a table with Hux going over science problems and history questions flashes through my brain. I can see it so clearly.

"Is he doing well though? Does he need a tutor or anything?" I volunteer.

"No. He's as sharp as a tack. It's just so much work that it cuts into the time I have for mine. It's the life of a single mother," she says easily. "Nothing I can't handle."

"If you need any help with any of it—"

"We're fine, Barrett."

I hear the warning in her voice, to not step too close. I hate it. I hate having a barrier between us, being told to keep any sort of distance. I want to help her, take the loads off that I can remove without any problem.

"I know you're fine, Alison. I'm just saying that I'm willing to help."

"I know and it's appreciated. But it's important to me that I do this on my own."

"Do what on your own? Life?" I gruff.

"No," she sighs. "Not exactly."

"You do realize I'm not trying to take anything from you right?" I ask. "I want to . . . add to it. Make it better, easier if I can."

She doesn't respond for a long while and I give her time to wrangle whatever it is she's thinking. I wish I were there with her, wrapping her up in my arms. It would make so many things so much better.

"I don't mean to push . . ." I say, letting my words fall.

"You aren't pushing, Barrett. I love that you care."

"Of course I care," I snort.

"I just don't need a knight in shining armor. In my world," she says, pausing, "I am the knight. I'm the one that saves the day."

"I can respect that. Just let me be the stallion you ride in on."

She laughs, a free, flowy kind of laugh that makes me join in. "Barrett Landry, you're impossible."

Relaxing back on my pillows, I close my eyes and listen to the sound of her voice. It's what I needed, my antidote.

"I do need to get back to bed," she yawns. "I have the breakfast shift in the morning, so my mom will be here super early to get Hux up and to her house to get ready for school."

"Okay. But I wish I were there with you."

"I do too," she whispers.

"I can only imagine what it's like to wake up next to you."

Her giggle races through the phone. "We wouldn't be able to get out of bed."

"I wouldn't let you get out of bed," I growl.

"Which is why it's a good thing you aren't next to me right now," she says. "Okay, I'm going. Call me tomorrow, okay?"

"Okay. Talk to you then."

"Goodnight, Barrett."

"Goodnight."

# Barrett

MY HEADACHE HAS STARTED TO wane after an incredibly long morning, but I can feel it lingering right behind my left eye. I'm in a bad mood, especially after reading a new article ripping me to shreds in the press.

I paste on a smile and wave to a little group of women eyeballing me from the corner of the hotel that houses Picante, a restaurant where Nolan and I are meeting Monroe.

Nolan keeps his face forward and pretends not to notice the waves and gestures from my little fan club. It makes the women happier, we've learned, to think they had a "moment" with me. Ridiculous but true.

I usually give them a quick once-over, just check them out a little bit, see what's being offered. Normally, if I'm feeling particularly interested, I'd mosey over, make small talk, and grab a phone number for later.

Or two.

Hell, sometimes three.

Today I have zero interest.

"Now, when we get in here, I want you to remember that you're here to appease him," Nolan says under his breath.

"We'll see," I mutter.

The elevator door opens and we walk inside. Nolan presses the button to close the doors before anyone can get on with us. We ride in silence for the few seconds until the door chimes and opens into Picante. It's a small restaurant that's used by the wealthy. You pay a membership and they provide you with excellent food and privacy to boot.

The hostess recognizes me immediately and I can see her replaying our rendezvous together a year or so ago. I can't help but remember her bent over the hood of my car either.

Her lips fall apart and her eyes glaze over, and I try to give her the least encouraging smile I can.

"Mayor Landry," she breathes, batting her lashes. "How nice to see you again."

Nolan bristles at my side as I clear my throat. "I believe we have a table waiting on us."

She nods, blushing, and leads us through the room. "I was hoping it was you and not one of your brothers when I saw the reservations," she says sweetly as Nolan sticks an elbow in my side.

"Don't forget," he whispers. "You have the Garalent Gala coming up."

The thought makes my temple start to throb again. I don't want to think about that. At all.

"Here you go." She steps to the side but manages to brush up against me. If Alison weren't in the picture and this conversation wasn't going to ruin my mood, I'd probably make plans to see her again.

I glance up at her and she winks.

Today's not her day.

Nolan pastes on a smile as Monroe stands to greet us. We shake hands and take our seats across from him.

"Nice to see you," he smiles. It's a predatory gesture. He smells blood and insisted I come along today for the kill. He's ready to stick me in his pocket and then use me for four years after I'm elected. More than ever, I don't want to make any concessions to him.

"Good to see you," I lie, placing my napkin on my lap.

The waitress comes by and takes our order, nearly rubbing her ass against my arm. I lean away and pick something random off the menu, a dish that includes grapes.

"So, Barrett, let's talk shop, shall we?" Monroe fights the urge to smile.

"Yes. Nolan tells me you're close to making your decision on your endorsement," I say, glancing at Nolan. "How are you feeling right now, Monroe?"

He chuckles. "Well, I'm not sure how I'm feeling. As you know, I don't necessarily follow the party ticket."

"That's why we're here," Nolan says. "What will it take for you to endorse your own party's candidate? There is a lot at stake coming up."

"That's very true, which is why I've held off on endorsing anyone."

His game-playing is getting under my skin. I grit my teeth, trying to keep from blurting out what I want to say. "You've held off so long that it nearly doesn't matter." When I say this, Nolan nudges me with his knee beneath the table. I don't look at him. I'm forcing the issue, but what I've said is true.

Monroe raises his eyebrows and thinks before he speaks. "I have faith that whomever I support will matter to my precinct, Mr. Landry. And I think you also believe that. That's why you're here."

"Look," I say, having enough of his self-aggrandizing attitude. "Why don't we cut to the chase and you tell me what you're looking for? I have a full schedule today and I bet you do too."

He guffaws, his voice catching the attention of some businessmen at a round table in the corner.

"One thing I like about you, kid, is your confidence. That's a point in your favor."

I can't help but laugh at his intended disrespect. "I'll take all the points I can get."

He studies me for a minute. He certainly didn't expect me to come in firing. Hell, I didn't either.

"I tell ya what, Barrett," he sighs, leaning forward. "There are two things in this race that are important to me. One is the Land Bill. The other is how well the candidate I endorse will perform in office. My word matters to me. You know that," he pauses. He's the fox in the henhouse. I watch his smirk grow as he keeps talking. "And I'll tell you the truth—I'm worried about your reputation. You're a rake, to put it bluntly. A bachelor that appears as interested in women as he is the work that must be done."

"I beg your pardon," I say, narrowing my eyes. "My approval rating as Mayor of Savannah is the highest it's been for any person in that post in modern history."

"Look," Nolan interjects, "we aren't here to argue what Landry does in his own time. We are here to see what it will take for you to back him. So, what's it going to be? Just cut the shit and give it to us straight."

"I need a commitment that you will vote against the Land Bill," he says, looking me straight in the eye.

I don't waver. I feel sick to my stomach, knowing that it will kill the local economy while putting money in his pocket if it's nixed.

"That Bill isn't even guaranteed to be on the table in the next five years."

"But if it is," he says, cocking his head, "I want full assurance that you won't support it. Come on, Barrett," he sighs. "Your own family has land out there. You won't seriously consider losing that kind of money, will you? Be smart about this. I know you're probably thinking you'll go in there and do some good for the people and you can. You can. But there's no sense in shooting yourself in the foot over it."

I glance at Nolan and he's watching me carefully. I rack my brain for an answer that will appease him.

"Hobbs has given me his word that he won't support it if it comes to that."

I clench my jaw. "I assure you I will talk with you about it then before any decision is made."

He blows out a breath as the waitress places our plates in front of us and leaves.

"That's fair," he says without sounding confident.

"Absolutely it is," I say.

He shakes his head and pulls his plate in front of him. "Very well. I can also assume that you will be taking Daphne to Garalent, correct?"

"He is," Nolan looks at me sternly. "We've already discussed that, remember?"

I cringe, my head feeling like it's going to explode. We fucking discussed it, all right, but that discussion was very much before Alison.

Looking at Monroe's face, his eyes are lit. Me taking his daughter is a huge boon to him, and if I back out now, it's the nail in my coffin.

He slices through his chicken breast. "She'll be pleased to know that."

"Gentlemen, if you don't mind," I say, scooting my chair back, "I'm going to have to take off. I have an appointment in a few minutes that I was going to call off, but since we seem to be finished here, I think I'll try to make it."

Monroe laughs, knowing I'm making it up. "No problem. Good to do business with you, Barrett."

"You too," I bite out. I don't bother looking at Nolan. I just slip through the restaurant, avoiding the hostess, and out the door.

## Alison

I SUBMIT MY FINAL PAPER of the day to my professor and close my laptop. I've been working at this all day, trying to nail the theme of the piece and I'm confident that I did. One more year of school and working two jobs and I'll be firmly on my own two feet.

Huxley is riding his bike in the backyard, creating a little trail around the one tree that stands almost in the middle. I can't wait to buy a bigger house in a better neighborhood with a great big space so he can play and move to his heart's delight.

The doorbell rings and I give one last look to Hux before heading to the entry way. A delivery man is standing on the other side, holding a vase filled with deep purple flowers and a satiny white ribbon.

"Ms. Baker?"

"That's me."

"These are for you."

He hands me the heavy vase, and before I can thank him, he's back in his van. I pull them to my nose, breathing in the wonderful scent, and close the door behind me.

With an excited step, I make my way to the kitchen, place them on the counter, and pull out the card written on white stationary.

*I hope you're thinking about me, because I'm thinking about you. —Barrett*

Bringing the card to my chest, I hold it over my heart and allow myself to smile, to bask in the feeling of being wanted. That this busy man, in the midst of the most strenuous moment of his career, took a second out of his day to make me feel like this.

We haven't seen each other since the cabana, but we've talked every day multiple times. He instigates conversations as much or more than I do, and that's refreshing. Sometimes he'll send me a text with an article he thinks I'll find interesting and sometimes it's just to say hey. Regardless, it's nice and has left a permanent smile etched on my face.

We're taking this slow, slower than I thought we could, and . . . I think it's working.

Huxley scrambles through the back door and catches me before I can compose myself. "Where'd those come from?" he asks, his knees dirty from the lawn.

"Someone sent them to me."

"They're nice."

"Thank you."

"Was it a boy?"

My brain fires on all cylinders, trying to figure out what to say to Hux without scaring him.

"It was," I say truthfully. "A man sent me flowers."

"I hope it's a nice one. Like Lincoln Landry," he says, opening the fridge. "He promised me we'd play baseball soon."

I smile as he rummages through the bins. "You do know he's probably really busy. Don't be disappointed if he doesn't call, okay?"

"He will," he says matter-of-factly. "We're best friends practically."

Laughing, I try to decide whether to segue that little Landry opening to who sent the flowers or not. Hux decides for me.

"It wasn't Lincoln, was it? That sent those?"

"No," I say carefully. "But you know his brother? The mayor?"

He nods, opening a string cheese.

"He sent them to me."

"The one that can't play baseball?"

"Yes," I giggle. "The one that can't play baseball."

Huxley shrugs like the ten-year-old boy eating string cheese that he is. "Well, at least he has a cool brother, I guess."

I walk across the room and give him a giant hug. "He's pretty cool, too, I think."

"Is he your boyfriend now?"

"No, nothing like that. We're just friends. Seeing if we like each other."

He peers up at me through his long lashes. There are spatters of dirt mixed in with the freckles that span the bridge of his nose. "He'll like you, Mom. Why wouldn't he?"

"Who knows," I smile. "But how do you feel about that? If a man would come around sometimes. Would that bother you?"

He chews the last bite and drops his wrapper in the trash. "No, I guess not." He looks at the ground before pulling his eyes to mine, hesitation swimming in them. "I don't say this because I think it might hurt your feelings and I don't mean it like that, Mom. But I miss having a dad. I miss doing boy stuff with a real guy. Not that you aren't the best—"

I pull him into me before he can finish. I know what he's going to say and I want to spare him the pain of saying it . . . and of me having to hear it.

"Mom, you're squishing me," he says, his voice muffled. He pulls back and looks into my eyes. "I'm going to Grandma's tonight, right?"

I nod, fighting back tears. "If you want to."

"I do. She's getting Grandpa's old guitar out and we're going to see if we can play it."

"She should be here soon. You better go get ready."

He takes off, but stops suddenly and faces me at the threshold. "Mom?"

"Yeah, buddy?"

"You are the best. And I'm old enough to know that grownups like to be together sometimes. It's been just me and you for a long time, but I think it's okay if you have a friend. Even if it's a boyfriend that doesn't like baseball."

All I can do is smile. He watches me closely, nods, and zooms up the stairs.

## Barrett

I YANK MY TIE FROM around my neck and send it flying across the bedroom. It lands across a lampshade and dangles there, like it's going to fall off but doesn't.

After an afternoon of more meetings and a conference with my father who not-so-subtly told me I'm a fucking idiot if I don't lock in Monroe immediately, I finally made it home.

I've always liked my space, having time alone. Being from a large family, time without interruptions was always a luxury and it's something I've protected since I moved out for college. Living alone was non-negotiable. I never lived with girlfriends, never entertained the idea, no matter how many times they suggested it. Privacy equals sanity, quiet means peace. Until tonight. Now it just feels lonely.

My phone buzzes with a text. I pick it up to see Alison's name on the screen. I feel the stress melt away as I open the app, just like it does every time she sends me a message. They aren't pushy, aren't prodding. They just make me laugh or feel good, and I've never had an interaction with a woman like this.

*Alison: Of course I'm still thinking of you. How could I not be?*

*Me: I'll send flowers every day if it keeps me on your mind.*

*Alison: They are so beautiful, but it's not the flowers that have made me smile today.*

*Me: Pray tell.*

*Alison: The color, this deep, grape-y purple is nice . . .*

Memories of being with her, the way she feels beneath my touch, my name on her swollen lips the last time I saw her has my entire body lighting up from the inside.

I don't just feel lonely now. I'm needy, craving to see her, touch her, hear her.

Taste her.

For the first time all week, I'm home relatively early and I must see her. It's taken every fiber of my being to go slow with this when what I want to do is take it as I feel. But I don't, because with Alison, that won't work . . . and that's precisely why I like her.

*Me: Can I see you tonight?*

*Alison: Hux just left to go with my mother.*

*Me: I can have Troy there in thirty minutes.*

*Alison: I can drive. LOL*

*Me: He's on his way. Be ready.*

Shooting a quick text to Troy, I jump in and out of the shower and am pacing the kitchen when the doorbell rings. I laugh at myself as I jog to the entrance and pull the door open.

Alison's standing on the stoop, a twinge of nervousness in her smile. Her fingers fiddle with the strap of her purse. She's dressed in a navy blue dress that hits at her knees.

"Come in," I grin, holding the door open. She shuffles inside, and when I close the door and turn to face her, the entire feeling in my house changes. It's warm and lively, the emptiness filled by her energy.

Her eyes are soft as she peers up at me. I close the distance and wrap her up in my arms.

"Hey," she grins, tilting her chin.

"Hey," I whisper, laying a kiss on her lips.

For the first time all day, I don't give a fuck about Monroe or the Land Bill or what my father's take on the situation is. None of it matters because right now, this is the treaty to end all the wars of the day.

"Did you have a good day?" she asks.

I shrug indifferently and her face drops.

"Do you want to tell me about it?"

"Just another day in paradise," I smile.

"You do like being mayor, right?" She searches my face. "I mean, you ran for office."

I take her hand and pull her into the living room. "Yeah, of course. I'm the eldest Landry. I was trained for this my whole life."

"That doesn't mean you like it."

We sit on the sofa and she surprises me again. She's never been here before and she doesn't bother to do a quick sweep of the place, to see what I have or what it looks like. She just looks at me—and not at my face or my body or my wallet.

At. Me.

I consider her statement. "No, I guess it doesn't mean that. But I do." Thinking back to when I first got into politics, my first year as a councilman, I realize how much things, how much I, have changed. "I've always enjoyed the process. I think now, I just enjoy it for different reasons."

She tries to hide her smile, but it tugs at the corner of her lips. "Do I want to know what that means?"

Laughing, I pull her legs over my lap. "Maybe."

"Maybe not," she laughs too.

"At first it was a good way to have fun. Being a Landry alone brings a certain amount of . . . let's say attention," I wink. "But being in office gives you another dimension. Now, though, I feel like I can do something with that power. I've seen kids not have a safe place to play, families really skimping to get by. I can do certain things to help fix that now."

"Which is why you'll make a great governor."

Her voice is careful, her words enunciated very crisply. I furrow my brow, but don't have time to call her out on it before she speaks again.

"You'll do all kinds of great things for the state."

The Land Bill crosses my mind and my spirits begin to sink. It's one huge thing I can possibly make happen, yet I know it'll be a battle from every angle.

"Barrett? Are you okay?"

"Yeah," I say and then look at her. Her eyes are filled with concern, not for the bill or for her agenda, but for me. "I'm more than okay."

I pull her up and position her so she's sitting on my lap. Her grin in infectious, her little peacock feather catching the light as it heaves with her rapid breath.

"I'm glad you're here," I whisper, pressing a kiss to her throat. "Today was really shitty and getting your text made it turn around."

"Getting beautiful flowers delivered today made mine. Thank you for thinking of me."

She wraps her arms around my neck, her vanilla scent filling the air. If I could pause time, I'd do it right this minute and sit here looking at her face for the rest of my life.

"I don't think I've stopped thinking about you at all," I grin. "I have some pretty vivid imagery in my brain of you and—"

"Stop!" she says, her cheeks turning pink. "Don't embarrass me."

"Baby, you have nothing to be embarrassed about."

Her chin drops, her face still flushed, and her realness is almost unbelievable. I want to squirrel her away from the world, keep her protected and just for me in some little box. My little treasure.

"Huxley saw your flowers," she says, her voice wavering a little.

I chew on my bottom lip, wondering if I fucked up. I didn't think about her kid and I kick myself for that. "Was it a problem?"

"The only problem was that you don't know how to play baseball," she teases, looking back up at me.

"Ah, hell. Why did I have to fall for the girl with a kid that's a fan of Linc's?"

She giggles, running her hands down my chest. Her eyes turn from an easy sparkle to a heated twinkle. "You fell for me?"

"Isn't it obvious?"

"Well . . . I mean . . ."

"I know we said slow and I'm all about going slow," I say, trying to assuage any second thoughts she might be having. Because of all the women I know, all the women I've been interested in, this is the one that might really walk away. "But going slow is still going, Alison. And every minute that ticks by is another I'm thinking of you. I want to see you, want to get to know you."

"I want to get to know you too."

She starts to move and the change in pressure on my cock, coupled with feeling her pussy brush over it through my workout pants, sends a jolt of energy through my body. I force a swallow, not wanting to push my luck or make her feel like all I want her for is her body. This is one girl that I have to deal with carefully, because more than anything, she deserves it.

"Barrett . . ." she whispers.

"Yeah," I gulp, trying to control my growing length.

"I know we're taking it slow . . ."

"Yeah . . ."

"But I'd really like you to fuck me right now. I just haven't stopped thinking—"

I capture the next words from her mouth with mine, the end of the sentence falling on a sigh. My hands skim down her body, roughing over her breasts, until they land at her waist.

"I don't have a condom," I groan, the words washing over her lips.

"I'm on the pill," she breathes back, her kisses never ceasing. "Are you clean?"

I nod, tugging at her bottom lip with my teeth. She pulls it away.

"Me too," she whispers, her hands digging at my hips.

Lifting my hips, I shove them over and twist until they're somewhere low enough so I can be free. Her lips roam over mine, our tongues melting together, lapping up the other's desire in a heated, passionate frenzy.

Her legs grip my thighs on either side of me. When my hands touch her soft skin, it's heaven on Earth. I sink back into the sofa and let myself enjoy this moment, her little moans, her hair brushing against my arms, the wetness from between her legs dripping on my cock as she brushes it teasingly against me.

My palms smooth against her thighs, committing the sensation to memory. I scoot my hands under the edge of her dress to feel no barrier between us.

Growling at her pantiless state, the concept such a fucking turn-on, she kisses me even harder, making it impossible to concentrate on any given part of this entire experience.

I typically stay in complete control of situations, but this little vixen in the form of an innocent little mommy, has me whipped into a mess.

Letting two of my fingertips wisp against her pubic bone, her breath catches in her throat. I bite on her bottom lip, tugging her mouth back to mine, and she yelps—half in pleasure, half in pain—before sucking my lip between her teeth.

One hand holds her hip, the other splays against her midsection. My thumb finds her clit and as soon as contact is made, she nearly falls apart in my hands.

She grinds her wetness up and down my shaft, so ready for me that I can't take it. She can't either because as I begin to lift her, she reaches down, palming my cock in her hands. Before I can say a word, she sits down on me. Her tightness pulses around me, her breath coming out in ragged bursts.

I pull my face away from hers, my hands finding the side of her angelic face. As much as I want to thrust into her sweet little pussy, I find myself wanting to savor the moment of feeling, for the first time in maybe forever, able to breathe.

## Barrett

THE TELEVISION IS ON, THE volume low, and Alison is giggling at my side. I have no idea what's actually happening in the movie or what made me bring a plate of Brie, crackers, and fruit into bed, effectively breaking a huge rule of my own.

I'm lost in the sound of her voice echoing off the walls of my bedroom. I'm perplexed by the fact that I'm not sure this room will feel the same without her in it now.

Women have been in my bed before. They've stayed the night, stayed the weekend. But as soon as they look at home propped up on my pillows, I'm usually ready to ship them out. So why do I want to lock her down so she can never leave?

She pops a strawberry in her mouth, her lips forming an 'o' over the fruit. Her features are animated, soft, uncomplicated. She catches me staring and drops her hands to the bed.

"What?" she asks, swallowing the bite of fruit.

"Nothing," I grin.

"You're looking at me weird."

"Looking at you like you're beautiful is weird now?"

Her grin widens and she tucks a strand of hair behind her ear. "You're a charmer, Landry."

"You're a beauty, Miss Baker."

I lean over the tray between us and kiss her lazily. Her mouth is sweet like the fruit and I could go back in for thirds, since I had her once we got in here too, but I don't.

My landline rings, the handset beside my bed rattling, making Alison jump.

"I didn't know people still used those!" she exclaims

"No one calls mine but my mother and Nolan. I'd just get rid of it, but it's wired somehow into the security system of the house or something."

"Do you need to get it?"

"Nah, it's too late to be Mom. My cell is off, so it's probably Nolan pissed he can't get me and wants to ride my ass about some campaign statement or interview."

She glances at the clock over my shoulder and presses her lips, still swollen from our kisses, together. "I probably need to be going home."

"Why?"

She swallows and I see the trepidation washing over her out of nowhere. "Because it's getting late?"

It's more of a question than a reason and one I won't let go.

"We aren't teenagers, although you could pull off the twenty-something look better than me," I tease. "Troy can take you home whenever I ask him to. You don't have to leave now."

"I probably should."

I watch her wrangle with her decision and I can tell she doesn't really want to. She won't look at me, won't let me see into her eyes.

"Babe, what's wrong?"

Although the words were harmless, she flutters her eyes up to mine and there's a spark of pain hidden inside the blue irises.

She doesn't answer me.

"You better talk to me," I lead, rubbing my thumb over her knuckle.

"I guess for awhile I forgot who you are."

"What's that mean?" I ask, looking at her like she's crazy. "Who I am?"

She takes a deep breath and the smile on her face is almost one of resignation. "I forgot about all of that," she says with a wave towards my phone.

"Alison, it's a part of my job. It's not going to go away."

"No, I know," she sighs. "I just got swept away and . . ." She giggles, a soft, sweet, little rasp. "I relaxed. Do you know the last time I relaxed like this?"

I kiss her again, squarely on the lips. "You can come here and relax like this any time you want."

She takes my hand in hers and draws little designs on my palm. She's thinking, lost in some world I'm not privy to, and I want to ask questions. My curiosity is off the charts and I want to fix whatever's bothering her, but I don't ask what it is because I'm afraid maybe I can't fix it.

"What scares you, Barrett?" she asks finally, putting both of her small hands around mine. The warmth from her skin floods into me and I want to wrap myself around her in every way.

"Election day," I half-joke.

She smiles, but I can tell that's not what she meant. Still, this is not a topic I'd like to delve into heavily.

"The words, 'It's your baby.'"

"Barrett!" she laughs, throwing a grape at me. "I'm being serious."

"Me too," I groan, but realize she's not going to let me dodge this question. I blow out a breath and think. "I guess I'm scared of failure."

The grin on her face dissolves and she leans back against the headboard. "Continue," she prompts.

I shrug. "I . . . I don't want to fail anyone. Being in my position, both as a Landry and as the mayor of the city, has all sorts of responsibilities, and I lay awake at night sometimes worrying about the best thing to do for everyone."

"What about for you?"

My brows pull together and I lean back in the bed and face her. "What do you mean, what about me?"

"What about doing what's best for you? Do you ever think about that?"

"Sure," I say, stumped by her question.

"I don't know how that's true. When is the last time you did something purely because it was in your best interest?" she asks, her voice tilted with sass. "When is the last time you didn't consider what was best for your campaign or your father or the city?"

I lean forward so my breath tickles the side of her neck. "When I sucked grapes out of your pussy."

"Ah!" she gasps, trying to pull away, but I don't let her. I pull her into me and she melts, letting me kiss her.

When we finally separate, we're both grinning like crazy and I hope that's the end of this questioning.

But it's not.

"So I'm your little form of rebellion?" she asks. She means it as a joke, as a taunt, but there's no denying the fear hidden beneath the surface.

"Maybe," I say, watching her for a reaction. "Or maybe you're the first thing I've thought was worth going after."

She relaxes, but looks away.

"Alison? What's the matter?"

Her head shakes from side-to-side, but the blankets are pulled higher up her waist. "Nothing. Nothing's the matter. Why would you ask?"

"Talk to me," I whisper, my gaze pleading with hers to talk to me. "What are you scared of?"

She bites her lip and gathers her courage. I watch her do it, the blues of her eyes solidifying, her shoulders quietly squaring. "You."

"Me? You're scared of me?" I laugh. "Why in the world would you be scared of me?"

"Because it's too easy to be with you. Even at this slow pace we say we're going at . . ."

I lift her chin with my fingertips. "It's crazy, huh?"

She nods, her eyes wide. "It's so crazy. I've spent the last few years making sure all of my ducks are in a row so I never get trampled by anyone again."

"The only place I'll trample you is in this bed," I grin.

"The parallels from what I went through and this are so similar. What if I get caught up in this, in you, and you get elected? Don't get me wrong—you should be elected. You're smart and funny and charming and have the best heart. But you move to Atlanta and . . . what then?"

"Then we figure it out," I say with as much confidence as I can muster. "What if I lose? Will you want to fuck a loser?"

She shakes her head. "Even if you don't win, you won't be a loser."

"Even if I win, that doesn't make me a winner." I say the words before I think about it, before I realize I've said them aloud. Something clicks and I know she's going to ask me to expound on the idea, and I grimace and wait for it.

"What does that mean?"

I huff a breath and think about lying to her, but the openness we have in conversation is nice. Cathartic, even.

"It just means," I say, grabbing a strawberry, "that sometimes in this business you have to agree to things you don't necessarily believe in."

"Like what?"

"Like a bill about some land around the state."

"Don't agree to it," she says simply. "If it's not what you believe in, how could you?"

"Because you have to sometimes give on things to win on others."

She bends over and presses a sweet kiss to my shoulder. "I don't think you believe in yourself enough."

The words hit me hard because it's true. I start speaking again without thinking. "It's hard to believe in yourself when you aren't sure you've ever accomplished anything on your own."

"How can you say that?" she asks. "You won the mayoral election."

"Did I?"

I raise my eyebrows and watch her face twist in confusion. Her mouth opens to reply, but she shuts it just as quickly.

"Yes, I'm the mayor," I say, my throat burning. "But did I win it on my own ideas? Or did I win because of my name or my looks?" I look away because I've never said these things aloud to anyone, although I've thought them nearly every day for years. "Or did my father influence it somehow?"

The last one is the kicker. It's something my opponents have projected a number of times, that my father paid off certain people and thereby bought the election. He denies it, but of course he would. I don't really think he'd do that, but there's always a niggle of doubt. My dream was his dream before it was mine.

The silence between us thickens and I switch off the television. I realize I've done what I can't do. I opened my mouth. It's Politics 101: Never Open Your Trap. Everything is kept close to the vest, everything in the dark.

So why in the hell did I just say that?

Her hand rolls mine over and she laces her fingers through mine. She doesn't respond for a long while, just holds my palm like it's enough. Maybe it is.

"Barrett?" she asks, her sweet voice barely audible.

I turn to look at her. Her features are soft, her lips still telegraphing that they've just been kissed. I love the look on her, like she's just been thoroughly adored. It's what she should always look like.

"Even if that is true, and I don't believe it," she says, taking a breath, "it just means even more that you need to prove to yourself that your ideas are enough."

"But what if they're not?"

"If you say what you feel, that you don't agree with the Land Bill, and you don't get elected—is that the worst thing that could happen?"

The answer to that is complicated and both yes and no. It would end the work of so many for so many years. I have no backup plan; politics has always been my career, the trajectory up the ranks as quickly as I've been able. But looking at her in my bed, trying to make me feel better, the answer is also this: the worst thing is losing the person that makes me feel alive and enough for the first time in maybe forever.

"It's not," she says, shaking her head. "The worst thing would be for you to have your legacy tainted by a bunch of half-truths. By your grandkids asking how you felt about this or that in your career and having to lie. It'd be better to not win."

It sounds so simple, but isn't. It seems to be true, but it's convoluted. It seems easy, but it's so damn hard that I don't want to think about it anymore. Not while she's here.

"You know what would be better?" I ask, feeling my lips twitch.

"What's that?"

"If we stop talking and instead make use of this fruit . . ."

She grins and I roll her over before she can object.

## Alison

"AND HE WOULDN'T DO IT! That bastard. He said he wasn't sticking fruit inside my body and slurping it out. So, I told him I'm not seeing him anymore," Lola laments, making me laugh.

"Maybe he's not into food play," I giggle, turning the car down the street the next afternoon. "It's not for everyone. I don't even think it's for me, Lo, really, but . . ."

"But it's Barrett Fucking Landry!"

"Exactly."

"So Isaac is on ice. I'm just going to find someone else that will indulge my newfound food fetishes."

Laughing, I shake my head. "But Isaac is such a nice guy, Lo."

"And apparently nice isn't what does it for me."

"You're impossible."

"Are you working the charity thing that hit the schedule at Luxor last night?"

"Yeah," I sigh. "I just switched days at Hillary's House today so I can be off. The tips will be astronomical; I can't say no."

She sighs too. "Right? I'm so over working these shitty jobs. I just need to land a rich man and be retired already."

I roll my eyes, but grin. The chatter with Lola is my tried and true way of relaxing from work before getting home to Hux. The stress of the job is diluted by her antics and it's my own form of therapy.

"You do that," I laugh.

"I expect to. But in the meantime, you need to corner Isaac and let him know he needs to—"

"I'll do no such thing!" I laugh. "I'm not about to tell him how to have sex with you, Lo!"

"You're simply not the friend I thought you were," she huffs.

"Apparently not. But I'm pulling in the driveway and am beat, so I need to get off of here."

"Okay. Talk later."

I end the call and pull up beside my mother's car. Every day it's the same feeling of being grateful she's here to help with Hux and frustration that I'm in the position of needing my mother so much to help with my child.

Opening the door to the house, I smell the aroma of freshly baked snickerdoodles. I follow the cinnamon scent to the kitchen where my mom and son are sitting at the table with a plate of cookies and tall glasses of milk.

"Hey, Mom," Hux says.

"Hey, buddy." I kiss the top of his head. "You smell like outside."

"He's been outside tossing a ball around all day. He even had me out there playing catch," my mother says.

"You? You played catch?" I laugh. "I bet that was a sight."

"Some man called here earlier this afternoon, shortly after Hux got home—"

"It was Lincoln!" he beams. "We're going to go work out today!"

I cast a confused glance at my mother. She twiddles her thumbs and looks at me with raised brows.

"He said you'd take me to see him when you got home," Hux says, standing. "So can we go, Mom? Please?"

"Go wash your face," my mother instructs him.

"But Grandma . . ."

"Huxley. Now."

He stalks towards the bathroom and when he's out of earshot, the room gets smaller. Much, much smaller.

"So . . ." she draws out, waiting for me to give her information. I don't.

"Alison, why is a Major League baseball player calling the house to play baseball with my grandson?"

I shrug like I have no idea, but she doesn't buy it.

"There's also a beautiful bouquet of flowers in your bedroom," she states. "Hux told me to take a look, said the mayor of Savannah sent them to you."

"It's nothing," I say, turning away from her.

I wait for the impending question and answer session, but nothing happens. The bathroom door closes down the hall and my mom's chair scoots against the tile floor. But she doesn't speak.

I can't take the anticipation any longer. Turning to face her, I see her looking at me, a wide smile on her face.

"What?" I say, fighting a grin of my own.

"I want to ask you a million questions . . ."

"There's nothing for me to answer. Not really," I add on, the grin getting harder to conceal. Just thinking about Barrett makes my stomach flutter and it's ridiculously hard to not show it.

"So you met him somehow and you're seeing him?"

"No," I gasp, then catch myself. "Actually, yes. Kind of. But if we—"

"Oh my gosh, Alison! You're kidding me!"

"Mom, please," I say, sounding like Hux when he's embarrassed. "It's nothing. We just met awhile ago and have been spending some time together."

"I can't say I'm sad about this," she teases. "He's handsome and well-to-do . . ."

"We're friends. That's it, Mother."

She tsks me and crosses her arms over her chest. "Being friends with someone doesn't put that look on your face," she teases.

Taking a deep breath, I know I can't hide anything from her. It's pointless. "We're trying things out, feeling our way through . . . whatever this is."

"I'm so happy for you, Ali."

"Don't get all crazy," I say, rolling my eyes. "And please don't mention it to anyone. It's nothing official and I don't want people asking about it."

We exchange a look, one filled with memories we'd both like to forget.

"Understood." She walks around the table and pulls me into a quick embrace. "I won't meddle, but if you need anything, just ask." She starts to leave but pauses at the doorway. "I knew someone would sweep you off your feet . . ."

"Friends, Mom!" I laugh, exasperated.

"Friends. Right," she shrugs, and shortly after, the front door closes.

Then it opens again.

"Alison, there's a man that's just pulled up in a Range Rover?" She peeks her head around the front door. "I'm guessing that's something to do with your friend?"

My jaw hangs open. I have no idea why Troy would be here, besides that Lincoln called, but I've had no time to get ready.

"Yeah," I say, "go on. It'll be fine."

She smiles too brightly and leaves, but the door stays partially open. Before I can get to it, Lincoln pops his head around the corner.

"Hey there," he grins in his adorable way. He chuckles when he realizes how gobsmacked I am. "Expecting me?"

"Not really," I laugh.

"Well, I called earlier because I need a good workout. I thought Hux could head to the Farm with me and play some ball, if that's all right?"

My brain scrambles for something to grasp on to. "Yeah, I guess. I mean . . ."

"And," he draws out, "my brother has had a terrible day. I'm sure he'd like to see you, if you don't mind accompanying us."

"He doesn't know you're here?"

His head shakes. "Nope. It'll be a surprise."

"Lincoln, with all due respect, I'm not sure this would be something Barrett would appreciate. I know he has work to do, and I don't want to intrude. Nor do I know how he'll take it if I bring Hux there."

He leans against the doorjamb and I'm glad Lola isn't here. If she were, she'd be tackling him and having her way with him. He's ridiculously handsome in a boy-next-door kind of way, if you live by a boy that could possibly show up on the cover of a magazine.

"Alison, with all due respect, you aren't intruding." He looks at the ceiling before finding me again. "You'll be my guest. How's that?"

He snickers at my reaction.

"Yeah, that'll go over really well," I say.

"Exactly. You show up with me, and I'll guarantee you Barrett will fall all over himself to be with you. He's not going to leave us alone together," he winks.

"I'm taking that to mean you've had arguments over girls before?"

"Nope," he says, popping the last sound, "because my brother has never had one before you that would've been worth my time."

My cheeks heat at his words and his cocky little grin goes wider. A dimple sinks into his cheek just like it does Barrett's.

"Today, my brother needs you," he says, laughing as Huxley comes barreling down the hallway with a grin a mile wide. "So if you think as much of him as I think you probably do, which is half as much as you should think of me," he smirks, "get your stuff and let's go."

◆ ◆ ◆

## *Barrett*

"MOTHERFUCKER," I GRIMACE, FEELING MY blood pressure soar through my veins. "You've got to be kidding me."

"I'm not kidding about any of it," Nolan says through the phone. "Apparently she's saying you knocked her up a couple of years ago and paid for her to abort the baby."

"It's bullshit," I say, exasperated. I fall back into my chair and peer at the lawn of the Farm through my office window. "I only dated her for a couple of months. I barely even remember her."

He laughs, but it's not one of amusement. "I'm sure. The faces must bleed together at some point."

"Very funny, Nolan," I groan. "Just deny it. I don't fucking know. Make her come up with proof because there is none that ties it to me."

"You know she volunteered to not say anything if you cut her a check for fifty thousand."

"I'm not paying her fifty cents. This is extortion."

"This is politics on a grand scale, Barrett. She won't be the last, so prepare yourself."

I can hear the judgment in his voice, the sound that says without saying that he'd be a lot happier managing Graham or Ford than me.

My head begins to pound harder than it's pounded all day. I've been working since before the sun came up with no break for lunch or even coffee. The bag of food Rose brought in at some point midday is sitting on the table by the window untouched.

He ends the call without a goodbye and I sit watching the driveway. Standing, I see Troy's Rover coming down the bend and I glance at the clock. "Shit," I mutter, looking at the stack of papers I have left to work on, even though the day is done.

The car rolls to a stop and a number of doors open and slam. I hear voices, more than Troy's, one in particular that's a little sweeter than the others.

What the hell?

I see Alison standing next to my driver as Lincoln and Huxley head to the lawn beside the house. She's wearing a pair of jeans and a loose-fitting t-shirt, her hair pulled into a messy knot, and has no make-up on. And I don't think I've ever found her to be more beautiful than I do right now.

She looks at me, a hesitant smile ghosting her lips. I flash her a finger to tell her to hold on and take the steps down the staircase two at a time. When I reach the porch, she's sitting on the swing, watching Hux and Linc.

"Hey, you," I grin, sliding into the seat beside her.

"Hi," she breathes, her hand falling into mine. We lace our fingers together and I give hers a gentle squeeze.

"I want to kiss you," I say, "but I don't know if I'm supposed to do that in front of Huxley or not."

The breeze picks up her laugh and carries it across the yard. Lincoln looks up and catches my eye and just nods. I nod back, knowing he arranged for this after seeing me nearly having a breakdown this morning.

"Well, I'd like to kiss you," she replies, "but I'm not sure if I'm even supposed to be here."

"Why wouldn't you be?"

Shrugging, she watches her son toss a ball back and forth with my brother. "Are we interrupting anything? Linc just showed up and basically dragged us over here . . ."

"So you didn't want to come?"

Her face twists to mine, her eyes soft. "Of course I did. But I don't want to be a thorn in your side. And Huxley is here, and I don't know—"

"I'm glad you're here, and I'm glad he's here too."

"You are?"

"He's part of the deal, right? I mean, I can't take you and not take him, even if he doesn't think I'm the coolest Landry brother," I wink.

"No, he certainly comes along with the package."

"And I happen to like your package," I whisper, making her laugh as a ball is overthrown and rolls to the porch.

Lincoln and Huxley race to retrieve it, landing in front of us. They're laughing, out of breath, and Linc leans on the railing. He has a shit-eating grin on his face, his Arrows hat pulled low over his eyes.

"So," he says, not looking anywhere but at me.

"So," I say back, trying to keep my face as blank as possible. This just amuses him more and I can't help but let my lips part into a grin. "Nice job."

"You're very welcome," he says, knowing exactly what I'm thanking him for. "I told Ali if you didn't want to see her, I'd be more than happy to hang out with her."

I start to respond with a big "Fuck you," but remember Huxley is standing right there. "You're pushing it, Linc."

He bursts into laughter and looks down at his new friend. "Can your mom play baseball?"

"No," Huxley groans. "I don't get a lot of practice in because she and my grandma kinda stink. Sorry, Mom."

Alison laughs beside me. "It's okay. It's true."

"So, your dad or uncle or brother aren't around?" Lincoln asks, making me cringe internally. I don't want the kid to have to start talking about things I know aren't easy for him or his mother.

"I don't have a dad," Huxley says, his words enunciated very carefully. "Or a brother or an uncle. I have a grandpa, but he works a lot. So it's just me and my mom and my grandma."

Hearing the words come out of his mouth twists at my heart. I can't imagine my life without my father or my brothers or sisters. They're a built-in network of support, even though half the time I want to kill them. But I'd rather have them annoying me than not have them at all.

My heart breaks for this kid, and as Linc forces a swallow and looks at me out of the corner of his eye, I know his does too.

"The next time you come out here, we'll bring a glove for your mom and Barrett, and we'll teach them to play. That way, when I have to go back to Tennessee, you'll have someone to practice with."

"When do you have to leave?" Huxley asks.

"In a few days. But I come back a lot to visit. Otherwise, my mom cries. You know how that goes," Lincoln says, rolling his eyes for effect.

"Yeah," Hux huffs, making us all laugh.

Lincoln takes off his cap, a purple hat with a golden A on it, and plops it on Huxley's messy head. "I gotta get a drink. I'll be right back."

He disappears in the house and as I start to speak, Alison's phone rings. She looks at the screen.

"It's Luxor calling," she says. "I need to get this and confirm my schedule for the next couple of weeks."

I nod but realize how much I hate it that she's catering jobs with assholes like me. She should be getting to stay home and take care of her kid and focus on school and whatever makes her happy.

Shaking those thoughts from my head, I look at Hux. We're alone, the two of us, and I have no idea what to say to a child. I don't watch cartoons. He doesn't read papers. What could we possibly have in common?

As my brain scrambles for something to say, Huxley does me a favor: he takes charge.

"You like my mom, huh?"

Shocked, I try to compose myself. "I do," I say, going for the truth. "She's pretty special."

He nods and ponders his next question. "How much do you like her?"

I can't help but laugh. "Well, I like her a lot. She's nice and smart and really pretty," I wink, hoping he at least kind of likes girls at his age. I liked them as soon as I could see, so I'm hoping we have some bond there.

He rolls his eyes.

I wince.

"I think my mom likes you too."

"Do you now?"

He nods, chewing on his bottom lip. "She's a lot happier lately. She sings songs in the shower and while she cooks and doesn't get so mad about the baseball cards all over my bed when I forget to put them up."

"I'm glad she's happy."

"Me too." He kicks at a rock. "You will be nice to her, right?" He looks at me with the most sincere little eyes I've ever seen.

I lift off the swing and kneel at the edge of the porch so we're eye-to-eye. "I promise you I'll be nice to her. And if you ever think otherwise, you can call me or come talk to me, and we'll discuss it."

"Really?"

"Really. She's your mom, Huxley. I respect you wanting to protect her. That's a very big job."

He grins, just like Alison when she's on the verge of being embarrassed. If I weren't trying to solidify my position in their world, I'd laugh.

"My dad wasn't very nice to her." The pain in his voice is raw, so visceral that it slices me to the quick. "She cried a lot, and I don't want her to cry, Mr. Landry."

I reach out, hesitantly at first, and adjust Lincoln's cap on his head. "I don't want her to cry either. And I don't want to make you worry, okay? I want to be her friend and make her keep singing while she cooks."

The lines around his eyes start to fade and I almost see a smile.

"And Huxley? I want to be your friend too. I know I'm not as cool as Lincoln, but if you give me a chance, I know some fun stuff. And I can get passes to the water park all summer."

"Really?" he asks, in total awe.

"Yup," I say, never more appreciative of the little perks of my job. "And, like I said, if you ever have problems with anything, you call me. Man to man."

"Man to man," he repeats. "I will, Mr. Landry."

"One more thing. Call me Barrett. Only people that want to fu—," I catch myself. "Only people that want something from me call me 'Mr. Landry.' Okay?"

"Okay," he grins a wide, toothy grin.

## Barrett

I TOSS THE FOLDER ACROSS the desk. It slides over the glass top and smacks the side of my pen holder.

"Damn it, Nolan. He had no problem with the budget until now. You know as well as I do that Monroe's called him and put pressure on him to, you know, put pressure on me."

"You're absolutely right." Nolan pushes his glasses to the end of his nose and looks at me from across my desk.

Groaning, I push my chair back and give myself some space.

He flips through some papers and pulls out another sheet. "This was sent today certified mail."

He tosses it on my desk and I sweep it up, a feeling of dread sinking into my stomach. "What's this?"

"It's a letter from the attorney of a Gabriella Winston, also known as the mother of your unwanted baby. She's raised her price to a hundred thousand," he sighs.

"Not happening." I wad the letter up and toss it into the garbage before looking at Nolan again. I shoot daggers, not necessarily at him, but at the idea that someone would use a topic so sensitive and make it up out of thin fucking air to hurt someone else. "Does she not have a fucking conscience?"

"These are things you ask yourself before you get involved,

Barrett."

"She's out of her damn mind if she thinks I'm enabling her on this. Fuck this and fuck her."

"She's going to go public."

"Good for her. Let her. And watch us torch her back in the press. She wants to play, we'll play."

"We can't do that, Barrett. Unlike her, you have a public image to consider."

"Which is exactly why she's doing this! She's going to tank my image to profit, using an abortion as the kicker. That's fucking sick."

He starts to argue when a knock raps at the door. Graham pokes his head around the corner. "Am I interrupting?" he asks.

"No," I grimace, sitting up in my chair. "Come on in."

He nods to Nolan and shuts the door behind him. Striding across my office, he takes a seat. "I come bearing bad news."

"Great," I sigh, wishing this day was over already. "Give it to me."

"There's a picture in the paper today." Graham lays a copy of the Savannah Dispatch on my desk. "That was taken outside the Farm yesterday."

Grabbing it and looking closely, I see Troy in the Rover. In the passenger seat is Lincoln and in the back, behind Linc, is Alison. Her face is kind of blurry, but it's her.

Thank God Huxley isn't visible.

I want to die. I want to crawl into a hole and just sleep until this entire fucking election is over, until everyone stops acting stupid—caring about what I do, what I say, what I support, pegging kids on me that aren't even mine.

Nolan glares from his spot next to my brother.

"Don't start," I grumble, putting my head in my hands. My mind is spinning about whether Alison has seen it or not and what she'll have to say about it. This is absolutely what she doesn't want and what I thought I could prevent.

*How fucking stupid.*

"Barrett," Nolan says, licking his lips, "this isn't going to go over well."

"She's not even officially coming to see me. She's technically with Lincoln."

"Even if she is with your brother, and we both know that's not true, the media will spin it to discredit you, especially with her history. You know that."

"Fuck."

"I'm going to need to get back to my desk and figure out how to deal with this," he huffs, sticking his paperwork back in his briefcase. "This is exactly what we didn't need and absolutely what I asked you not to do."

"I didn't do anything, Nolan. Nothing wrong."

He pauses, his hand midair, and looks at me like I'm a child. "You just cost me a day's work by not being able to control yourself for a little while longer."

"There's nothing remotely scandalous about this!"

The air in the room thickens, all of us waiting on someone else to make the next move. I want to get out of here, to find Alison, to make sure she's okay.

"I knew this was coming." Graham adjusts his tie and clears his throat. "I have a plan, one neither of you may like, but it's all I can come up with considering the extenuating circumstances. Let's use this to our advantage. I know there's no way Barrett is not going to keep seeing her."

"How do you know that?" Nolan asks. "He's seen her for a while now and that's indicative of the end."

"Trust me." Graham looks at me again. "Furthermore, there's no way the media won't find out about her past—innocent or not," he adds as I quirk a brow. "All we can do is to go with it, play it off. Defense in the form of offense."

"What are you saying?" I ask, leaning forward, my hands together on my desk.

He takes a deep breath and watches Nolan. "I propose we go all in. Make a statement that Barrett is in a relationship with a single mom, that he's this benevolent man that is taking care of her and her son. Let's swing the story our way, use it to our advantage."

Nolan seems to consider the absurdity of this.

"She doesn't want in the media," I say, nixing the idea. "There's no way she's going to agree to this."

"Are you going to keep seeing her?" Graham asks.

I think about it for a half of a second. "Yes."

"Then think of it like this—as much as you want to live in Lala Land and pretend like you can do what you want on the down low, you can't. It's ridiculous to even consider it, Barrett. So by doing it in the open, as much as she tells you she doesn't want to do that, you can protect her. Otherwise . . . you can't."

It makes so much sense coming from Graham. But I know, in the bottom of my gut, this won't be that simple to Alison.

"If it were just me, I'd be all in," I say, feeling my resolve wane. "But this decision isn't just mine."

"Since when?" Graham jokes. "You always just make decisions about shit and force everyone else to play your game. That's what this is, in fact. We've told you not to see her and yet, here we are, playing along with what you want."

I don't answer him, my mind already on the conversation I'm going to have with her.

"I think Graham has a point," Nolan says finally, standing up. "If you're hell-bent on seeing this thing through, let's run with it. Just until the election. It's not like you're seriously going to marry this girl or anything."

Something about the way he says that burns me. I stand too, my chair smacking the wall behind my desk. Graham notices my demeanor and inserts himself before I can blow.

"Exactly," he says, assuaging Nolan. "So let's convince Alison this is the right thing and just roll with it until Barrett is finished." He raises his eyebrows at me, his way of trying to keep me calm.

My chest heaves with frustration as I watch them walk to the door. Nolan turns to face me before he exits.

"You're going to need to convince her of this pretty quick so we can get our statement out and beat Hobbs to the punch. You know his guys are working on it now."

Once he's gone, Graham turns to me. "This is the best I can come up with. I knew this day was coming and I don't know how else to let you have what you want and keep you from blowing everything in the meantime."

My shoulders sag forward and I drop my eyes. Guilt trickles through me because he's right—this election doesn't just have my dreams attached to its success, but a host of other people's too.

When I look back up, he's gone. I buzz Rose to let her know to hold my calls and cancel my appointments for the rest of the day. I text Troy to pick me up out front. Once I'm in the Rover, I call Alison.

On the third ring, she picks up. I grin as soon as I hear her say hello.

"Hey, it's me," I say as Troy swerves through traffic towards her house.

"I was just thinking about you."

I take a large gulp of air. This could blow back in my face so bad, I know it. I feel it in the pit of my stomach. But it does seem like the most logical solution, and truth be told, I want to be with her. Making up my mind once and for all, I go all in. "Are you home?"

"Yeah, I'm just finishing up a bunch of homework. Why?"

"Would it be okay if I swung by for a minute? I want to talk to you."

"Uh, yeah," she says. "Is everything okay?"

"It's fine. Just want to run a few things by you."

"I'm here," she says, trying to sound confident.

I laugh because I'm trying to be sure this will work out too. "I'll be there in a second."

The Rover scurries through thankfully light late afternoon traffic and, before I know it, we're pulling up to a little white house with black shutters. I dart out the door and race up the steps, knocking a handful of rapid beats before Alison pulls it open.

She stands in front of me in a pair of jeans with holes in the knees and a light green shirt. She looks like she should be fixing dinner in the kitchen, helping Hux with his homework, and waiting on me to come home for dinner.

I shake the thoughts away because the conversation that's getting ready to happen could end that visual forever.

"Hey," she says, a lilt to her voice that lets me know she's as anxious as I am.

"Hey," I say, entering the house. It smells like her, like vanilla and cotton, and is decorated in a warm, homey way that makes me feel welcome immediately. "Is Huxley here?"

She shakes her head.

Knowing we're alone and this might not end well, I can't pass up the opportunity to kiss her. I begin to pull her to me, but she melts into my chest. Our lips find each other, like they could in the dark, and I memorize every movement, every tug, every feeling of peace she gives me by being her.

She leads me into the living room and we sit on a worn sofa. I think about saying something nice about her home and how pretty she looks, but I can tell she hasn't seen the article and I don't want to put it off any longer than necessary.

"So," I say, taking a deep breath. "Apparently someone snapped a picture last night of you and Linc entering the Farm."

Her face blanches and her eyes go wide. "How? Where?"

I shrug. "It's in the Dispatch. It's of Linc and Troy mostly, but you can see you. Your face isn't super clear, but it's you."

I give her time to process this before pushing the issue. She looks away, to a picture of her and Hux when he was much smaller, her eyes filling with tears. But they don't fall.

"I'm sorry," I say, the words making me want to die. "I know this is what you didn't want."

She nods her head and doesn't look at me. It's like a knife in my heart.

"It's not the pictures in the paper exactly," she says finally, her words barely above a whisper.

"Then what is it?"

"It's protecting Huxley's privacy more than anything," she says distantly. "But it's . . . more than that." When she looks at me, the sparkle in her eyes is gone. There are tight lines around her mouth letting me know she's in pain. "When I think of the media, it terrifies me. I have panic attacks, Barrett. It took a couple of years after I left New Mexico to be able to even leave the house without shaking and being ready to puke."

"I'll never let anything happen to you, Alison."

She doesn't tell me she knows I'm right. She doesn't say anything at all.

"I thought somehow I could prevent this," I say, taking her hand in mine. "Maybe it was wishful thinking."

"I don't know how I believed it wouldn't come to this."

"But hey," I say, looking at her until she looks at me. "It's to this now. And we have to choose whether what we have is worth fighting for or not."

She smiles and gathers the courage to speak again. "What do we have, Barrett?"

I kiss her lightly. "I'm just figuring it out. I don't know what it is because I've never felt it before. But I can tell you this for sure—it's not something I want to let go because we're afraid."

"Are you afraid of this?"

"My staff tells me I should be. They tell me getting involved with a woman can flip back around and kick me in the ass. They say it can ruin my reputation and lend more credence to Hobbs' claims that I'm a flighty decision maker."

Her face falls. "I don't want to hurt your career."

"You make me better. Don't you see that? You make me feel like I can conquer the world, Alison. You make me smile, give me little glimpses of something I'd never considered before."

She picks up on what I'm getting at and seems shocked at the idea. I want to tell her that yeah, I'm thinking of what a future could hold between us long-term, but I don't go there. I need to fight one battle at a time.

"You give me and my career way more than you'd ever take from it. But it's not just about me. It's about you. And Hux."

"I feel like I need to protect my boy," she says. "I know what being in the public eye can do. I don't know what hearing things said about his mother, about you if he grows close to you like I think he will—what will that do to him?" She frowns. "If I don't protect him, who will?"

"I'm fighting for you right now, to give me the chance to prove to you I'll protect you both. That I'm worth bringing into your lives."

Her face lights up. "Really? That's how you feel?"

"Definitely. I want to see where this goes, Alison, and I can't do that if I can't say you're mine. Look," I say, moving closer to her, "I can't protect you if I won't acknowledge we're together. If we're sneaking around, it's only going to make the media more curious as to who you are. But if I can come out and tell them I'm seeing you and ask them to respect your privacy, most of them will. Even though they're complete fucking dickheads to me, there's a general rule about keeping kids out of it. So you don't need to worry about Hux."

I can see her coming around, the idea not sounding so crazy. So I keep talking, praying that I say something that throws her to my side.

"I want you to be my girl in every sense of the word. We can still go slow, but just do it openly. I don't see the harm in that."

She sighs, a burden on her chest that she's clearly wrestling. It would be so much easier if this wasn't an election season and I wasn't in this big fight with Monroe and Hobbs. I wish, for a split second, I wasn't Barrett Landry, Mayor of Savannah.

"If you want to think about it, that's fine," I say sadly. "I'll understand."

She closes her eyes, taking a deep breath. Her hand trembles as she places it over mine. I can feel her pulse pounding, her skin heated. After a few failed attempts at speaking, her eyes fly open and the words pour out of her mouth.

"This is probably the stupidest thing I've ever done in the history of my life, especially since I feel this eerie sense of déjà vu, but," she says, taking a deep, lingering breath, "let's do it. Let's get it over with because the fear of not having you is worse than the fear of the press."

"Really?" I say, afraid I misheard.

She shrugs, a little grin smearing on her face. "If I think about not seeing you tomorrow, it kills me. And if I think about telling Hux he won't see Uncle Lincoln anymore, I want to die."

"Uncle Lincoln?" I ask, raising my brow.

"Apparently your brother told him to call him that."

Laughing, I pull her into my shoulder. I don't tell her how much I love the insinuations that makes. I don't let on that I'm going to call Linc when I get home and give him hell and a couple of thank-you's. I don't happen to say that it seems completely right to have my brother already intertwined in her life. But I do kiss the top of her head.

"Linc hated hearing that Hux didn't have a man in his life. We grew up with all these role models—our grandfather, our father, our uncle, and each other. And, you know, Linc's the youngest boy in the family, so he had to spend more time than any of us with Camilla and Sienna. I think he just seriously felt bad for your son."

"Huxley hasn't been this happy in his entire life," she sighs. "But I still want to go slow."

"Absolutely. Whatever makes you feel good about this."

She gazes in my eyes and cups both of my cheeks in her hands. "I'm still scared, Barrett."

"I'm scared too."

"Of going public?"

"No, of not winning your vote back." My smile falls a little. "And of having you break my heart."

She laughs like I'm kidding, but I'm not. I've never let my guard down with someone before.

I just hope it's worth it.

## Alison

THE MORNING'S PAPER STARES AT me from the kitchen table. The high I'd been riding over the way things have been going with Barrett, including our agreement to go public yesterday, has now evaporated into thin air.

My lip trembles as I turn the page, and for the hundredth time, read the side-by-side headlines.

*Mayor Landry is Off the Market* and *Mayor Landry Embroiled in an Abortion Debacle* scream at me in black and white.

"What are you thinking?" Lola asks, her hand on my shoulder.

"I don't know." My voice sounds so weak, even to me, and Lola squeezes my arm. She came as soon as I called her earlier, right after my mother called me with questions about the articles. Of course, I had no idea anything was happening and when Lola brought the papers by, I was blindsided.

"Did you read this?" I sniffle, pushing back tears.

"Yeah. Over your shoulder. I'm sorry."

"How could his own campaign do this to me? How could his own staff bring up everything I went through, paint me as some weak damsel in distress with a kid that needs saving? That's not what this is at all!"

"I know."

"And then this," I say, feeling the disbelief start to wane and anger taking its place. "There's a scandal about some ex he has trying to say he forced her to have an abortion?" I pace the kitchen, trying to wrap my mind around everything. "Do you think . . ." I'm almost afraid to say it out loud. The mere thought burns my windpipe, scorches my heart. "Do you think he used me to make himself look better because he knew this story," I say, jabbing the paper, making it pop, "was going to break?"

"I don't know . . ."

She watches me warily as my phone starts to chime on the table. I see it's Barrett and I don't want to talk to him. Not yet. Not until I make sense of this on my own. Silencing the call, I sit at the table and read over the words again.

"They call me straight out. They bring up the assault, they talk about Hayden's record, what I was investigated for. And it quotes a Nolan Bicknell as the source, Barrett's fucking campaign manager." I look at my best friend, my jaw hanging open. "How did I not see this coming?"

Lola blows out a breath and sits beside me. "You don't know what happened. Maybe it's just a strange coincidence."

I snort, knowing there's no such thing in politics. Everything is calculated, moved like a chess piece. And here I am again, being used as a pawn.

Tears pool in my eyes as my phone rings again and I just shut it off. My homework is sitting beside it and I pick it all up and carry it into my bedroom, dumping it on the bed. I don't want to look at anything right now—just the newspapers that remind me how stupid I've been.

"He used me," I say, believing it more and more as time goes on. "He allowed them to do this. The press release was supposed to say we were together and to respect our privacy, not call everything out . . ."

We both jump as a knock pounds on the front door. I know it's him and I know even more I don't want to see him.

"Want me to get it?" Lola asks, pressing her lips together. "Want me to get his balls?"

A grin touches my lips. "Just get it and tell him I'm not here."

"Got it."

She stands and marches to the door. I hear it swing open and his honeyed voice echoing through the hallway and around the corner to the table.

"Is Alison here?" he asks.

"Nope. She's not here."

"Where is she?"

"Not here," Lola barks. "Do you not get that? Should I put it out in a press release loaded with bullshit? You know, speak your language? Will that help?"

"Listen . . ."

"No, *you* listen. You need to go," she fires back.

"I know she's here," I hear him say. "I need to talk to her."

The sound of desperation in his voice breaks me and the tears begin to fall. I'm so hemmed up with feelings, the pain in the ass emotions I've tried to keep away.

Sitting quietly at the table, I hear them talk, their voices lowered, and can't make out what's being said until I hear Lo again.

"Leave, Landry."

"I want to talk to her. *Please*."

Everything goes quiet and I sniffle. It comes out louder than I expect and in my little one thousand-square-foot house, it doesn't take much for a sound to make it to the front door.

"Alison!" he yells. "Talk to me, baby. Please. Give me five minutes."

"What part of *leave* don't you understand? Does it equivocate in your mind with loyalty or honor? Because you clearly have neither of those."

"I had no idea," he says, obviously to me. "I didn't know Nolan was putting that out! I had *no idea!*"

I want to believe him, for things to go back to the way they've been, but doing that seems as careless as putting my heart out there to begin with.

"If you don't go, I'm going to call someone to get you out of here," Lola warns.

Scooting back from the table, I just want this to end with as little drama as possible. I don't want anyone called, I don't want a scene made. I just want to lick my wounds in peace.

I turn the corner of the kitchen and see him looking over Lola's shoulder. His eyes are wide, his blue tie hanging haphazardly off to one side. His hair is a wild mess like he's been running his fingers through it.

The sight of him twists my heart, but I have to stay strong.

This is the man that just fucked me over.

"What?" I asked, gathering as much anger as I can.

He storms by Lola, his Adam's apple bobbing in his throat. I take a step back before he reaches me and place my arms across my chest.

"Alison, let me explain."

"Talk," I instruct. "You have about three minutes to say your piece and then you're leaving."

His hands look like they want to reach for me, his lips twitch to kiss me. He fights himself not to whisk me in his arms, but he doesn't.

"I don't know where to start," he admits.

"How about the little article in the paper from your people that basically makes me out to be a pathetic, needy little gold digger."

"It doesn't do that!"

"No, it does. The entire article is slander!" The tears fill again and I blink back the red hot liquid. "I can't believe you allowed that!"

"I didn't," he insists. "I had no fucking idea Nolan was authorizing that. We were supposed to say I'm involved with a woman with a kid and to respect our privacy."

He gulps, his eyes begging me for forgiveness. It's heartbreaking . . . or would be if I weren't so angry.

"Don't think you can throw that out there and have me back down," I say, glaring at him. "You just completely embarrassed me, having my name, my history in people's mouths! People will be talking about me in depth now *because of you.*"

"Would you rather have snuck around and stolen minutes and hours with me here and there? Would you rather have looked over your shoulder for someone to take your picture?"

"No! I would rather have you just say what you said you were going to say!" I cry. "And then you say it at the moment this other article comes out? Tell me that's not convenient for you."

"Alison . . ." He takes a few steps towards me, reaching for me.

I nod my head with a fury burning inside. "You just used me. I'm not a chess piece, Barrett—"

"You're right," he cuts me off. "You're the damn board." He shakes his head, looking defeated. "Right now, every move I make has you in the back of my mind. What happens between us if I win? What if I lose? How does this affect you? When can I see you again? Should I send you flowers? How can I make Huxley like me more than Lincoln?"

"He's way hotter than you," Lola interjects, making us both jump.

"Lo," I sigh as Barrett glares at her. "Can you go? Please?"

"Are you sure? Because I've bounced people from events before."

"I'm sure," I say.

She shrugs and tosses her purse over her shoulder. "You just ruined the best thing that ever happened to you, you rich asshole." And she's gone.

The room seems to get smaller without Lola around. The air bubbles between us, like it always does, but maybe more heated because of the friction swirling around.

My mind is still reeling from the articles, from Barrett showing up here in the middle of the day when I know he has other things to do. I can't figure out how to see straight.

"I had no idea that story was going to break," he says earnestly. "I swear to God I about died when I saw it—next to the other article, no less."

"But you knew there was a chance of it? You knew this existed?"

He nods slowly.

"But that little blip of your reputation had nothing to do with you wanting to use me to solidify that very thing in the media, right?"

"No, it didn't. I swear to you."

"This conversation, of me wondering if you just used me, is part of why I hesitated to do this. And I told you that, made it very clear, this is what I was fearful of!"

"You have nothing to be embarrassed about!"

"You're not a stupid man, Landry," I snort. "Drop the act. Stupidity is the first thing I've found that doesn't look good on you."

He throws his hands in the air. "Alison, this is my mistake."

"You're damn right it is. But that doesn't make it any easier to swallow!"

"What do you want me to do?" he asks, tugging at his hair. "I don't know how to fix this, Alison."

"You can't. Don't you get it? The damage is done. *You* let this happen."

"*I* didn't. Nolan did, and trust me when I tell you he got his ass ripped twice by me already today. He was never authorized to put that information out there, and I'm considering firing him over it. I just can't do that this close to the election."

He rubs his hands down his face and groans.

"God forbid you stand up for what you want to Nolan," I say. He blanches at my words and I shrug. "It's true. You take his word, his ideas, like they matter more than your own. People vote for you, Barrett, not him."

"You sound like Lincoln."

"Well, Lincoln sounds smarter by the minute." I take a deep breath and try to calm down, to focus on the problem at hand. "You're here. I'm here. I'm giving you this chance to tell me about the abortion article."

"It's complete and utter bullshit." His voice is unwavering. "She's trying to extort me, and I won't pay her off because it's a fabrication."

"How do you know for sure?"

He shrugs. "I guess there's no way to know if she was pregnant, but if she was, she didn't tell me. If she had, I would've stepped up and taken care of the baby. I never would've pressured a woman to do something like that. Ever. It's a child . . ."

He stops moving, stops fiddling with his tie. His hands drop to his sides and he looks at me, his green eyes crystal clear. "I can't lie to you. I also can't make you believe me, but I'm telling you the truth." His gaze softens. "I'm glad I didn't have a child with her."

My breath stumbles, my eyes going wide because I can read into what he says. There's so much innuendo laced through that handful of words that I'm afraid to even touch it.

"Having kids is something I've never really given a lot of thought," he says, his voice soft. "I suppose I've always considered I would eventually, but never in the foreseeable future." He takes a quick breath. "Until now."

"Why now?" I ask, afraid to both ask it and not ask it, fearing the answer either way.

"Because you're the only person I can imagine having my child."

"Barrett... Don't say that. Don't use words like that to try to make me forget what happened. I'm not one of your constituents you can charm with a smile and baby kissing."

He takes a step towards me, his eyes on fire. "I'm not. I mean it."

"Why would you want to think those things about a helpless girl you have to protect?" I bite out.

"Alison, stop it."

"No, you stop it. I feel like I'm dealing with the mayor right now with your game face and pretty words and not my . . ."

The air stills as his eyes remain as steady as his tone. "Your what?"

I don't respond. I walked head-on into this and I don't know how to backtrack out.

"It doesn't matter how you fill in that blank because, like you said, they're just words. And no word could ever fill the spot you take up in my life. So call me your boyfriend or the mayor or an asshole for what happened today, but I'm still *yours*, however you want to define that.

"You don't have to like it or like me or take me back until this election is over, if you don't want. If that somehow proves I'm not using you, then fine. You can humiliate me by saying that was all bullshit. Think of what you can do to my campaign, and you know what? I won't care."

"You know I'd never do that to you," I say.

He takes a small step back and hangs his head.

"I can't lose you," he whispers, more vulnerability in his tone than I've ever heard. Gone is the confident man I know him to be, and in his place is a man that needs something that maybe I can give him. The sincerity in his voice pulls at me, tugs at my heart strings. I believe him because there's no way, even a master politician like himself, could fake the genuineness of those words.

"I had to be separated from Nolan this morning. I was this close to losing it on him, Alison. Trust me when I tell you that is not what he was authorized to put out there, and if we weren't this close to the election, I'd fire him. But the reality is, we are and I'm trying to be rational, to think about the big picture."

Looking away from him because the hurt in his eyes is too much to see, I allow the pain of seeing the words in black and white pierce me again. I don't want to feel it and it would be so much easier to pretend like it never happened. Falling into his arms, under his spell, would be head-and-shoulders more fun. But I can't. Because I know where that leads. Because I promised myself I would be stronger. Because I deserve more than this.

When I look in his face, I can't help but feel my heart break. I want to heal him, reassure him, but I can't. Not yet. Not until I'm sure I can withstand whatever the future could hold if this doesn't work out, because this pain? This is the tip of the iceberg if everything starts to melt.

"I know I come with a lot of 'extras.' I just . . . I'm sorry," he says again, the puffiness around his eyes making me wonder how much sleep he's getting.

"I believe you."

"You do?"

I nod, but take a step back. "I don't think you knew about this. Not really. But you know what? It hurts all the same, Barrett."

"I know. Let me fix it."

A small smile creeps across my face and he doesn't miss the sadness in the gesture. His eyes go wide, his face pale, and I think he's going to lunge at me and hold me against him. A part of me wouldn't object, but I don't get the choice because he doesn't move.

"There isn't some magic button that can fix this," I point out.

"I can't take it back now. I can't make this un-public," he groans. "What do I fucking do? What do you want me to do?"

The lines of his face shine in the sun streaming through the window. I see every crease, every line of stress, every pinch of frustration in his handsome face. My lips want to press against the wrinkles, my hands crave to smooth out his anxiety, but I hold back.

"I want you to give me some time to think about this."

"Why?" he says, his voice now touched with irritation. "You said you know I didn't do this on purpose."

"That's true. But that doesn't mean this didn't just change the game for me."

"This isn't a fucking game," he barks.

"No, it isn't." My voice stays calm as I watch him pace again. "But it is exactly, unequivocally what I didn't want. It would've been different if the article was right, and people knew who I was and gave me space. Now they'll look at me like I'm pathetic, and I refuse to be made the laughingstock of another city because of a man."

"No one is laughing at you," he gulps. "They're laughing at me."

A heavy breath leaves my lips. "The timing of this also makes me worried. Am I going to get asked about it or mocked because—"

"You better fucking not."

We face each other, the room pushing us closer, but we both fight it. Me out of self-preservation, him out of manners. The clock on the wall ticks softly and every second we stand there feels like an hour.

His chests rises and falls, his lips falling open as his breathing quickens. His nostrils flare just a bit as he bites down and the muscle in his jaw clenches.

"I need to pick Hux up from school," I say quietly. "He has a dentist appointment."

"We haven't finished talking."

"We have to be finished for now," I say, forcing myself to turn away from him. On some level, I'm grateful for the excuse to get away. I need to think.

"When can I see you again?"

I pick up my purse off the chair. The papers sit inches away and I make myself not look at them.

He takes a deep breath and blows it out. "If you want time to think about this, I get it. I'll give you that."

"I need to make sure this is something I can handle," I gulp. "All of a sudden, this just got very real."

His arms come around my waist from behind and I sink back into his chest. I breathe in his cologne and let it carry me away from reality for a few seconds.

"It was always real to me," he whispers and kisses the top of my head.

# 27

I CURL MY FEET UNDER me and look up at the stars. The moon is bright and high in the sky, yet the air chilly.

I tug the blanket closer to my body and look at Lola sitting on the other side of the patio furniture. She picks up the bottle of cheap wine and offers me more. I motion for her to fill it up.

"You've had three glasses," she points out, having grabbed some sort of logic on the way over after my frantic call when Huxley went to sleep. "You're a lightweight. We'd better cut you off."

"Don't even start making sense now, Lo. This is not the time."

She laughs and tosses the now-empty bottle into the trashcan by the door. It hits the bottom with a thud.

"So . . ." She waits on me to stop talking about the research paper I finished tonight and about my early shift at Hillary's. I've discussed why my oil needs changed in my car and how I'm suddenly craving hummus. Anything and everything has been toyed with tonight, except the reason I called her, a reason we both know.

"So . . ." I heave a breath, not sure how to bring it up or what part to bring up or if I even want to bring it up to start with. What I wanted was to not be alone with my thoughts.

"What happened after I left?" she asks carefully. "Did things go okay?"

I nod and down the rest of the wine in my glass.

"Why do I think you're lying? No, strike that—why do I know you're lying?"

"I don't know, maybe because I'm drinking wine like a fish?"

"Good point."

I sigh and rest my head on her shoulder, the low alcohol content in the inexpensive wine finally adding up to enough percentage to dull my senses. My thoughts aren't so jammed. They're clearer if not a little muddled, which makes no sense and all the sense in the world.

"He said he was sorry. He swore to me he didn't know the statement was going to say that, and the other article about the baby was a shocker." I shake my head. "No, not a shocker. He knew it was happening, just not today."

"Oh, shit."

"Yeah."

"Do you believe him?"

"Mhmm," I mumble, letting my eyelids drift closed. It's a delightful feeling to trust the peace of the dark.

"You do?"

"Yup," I say, fluttering open my lids. "I do. I don't think he knew it was going to be so unflattering to me and there's no part of me that really, truly believes he staged this to happen at the same time."

"So you don't think the timing was suspicious?"

I shrug. "Maybe it was a coincidence or maybe his people knew exactly what was happening with the ex-girlfriend or whoever in the hell she is or was. But did Barrett? I don't think so."

Her face scrunches in thought as we gaze across the yard. We sit like that a long time, both of us lost in thought, trying to make sense of this ridiculous situation with a man neither of us imagined we'd ever be discussing like this. Maybe it would be easier if we weren't.

"So boil it down for me," she requests. "If you believe him, what's the problem?"

I take a deep breath and look at Lo. She gives me a small smile, encouraging the words out of my mouth. They're on the tip of my tongue, but I hesitate. She's going to just tell me I'm stupid and, truthfully, maybe I am. Maybe it's ridiculous to feel the way I do, but I can't help it.

Once you've been burned by someone, the scars never leave. They become more sensitive to the same type of fire that got you once, tingling when you get too close to the heat. And as much as I'm starting to really, *really* adore Barrett Landry, the sensation is still there that maybe this is another fire.

It's possible I'm being overprotective of myself. There's a chance I'm overthinking things. But if I had overthought them a little more with Hayden, maybe my scars wouldn't run so deep.

My lips twist together, feeling swollen from the wine. My eyes wet, glaze over, and I fight hard not to cry.

"Ali?"

"Tell me I'm being stupid. Tell me I'm being completely idiotic for being scared."

"Oh, my friend," she says, amusement thick in her voice, "I'll never tell you that being scared is wrong. Being scared saves lives. Hell, it saves venereal diseases and unplanned pregnancies," she laughs. "But that doesn't mean it's always warranted either."

Looking up at the night sky, I try to find the stars that look like a baseball. I don't find it—the sky still looks like an erratic mess of twinkling lights. But it also causes my heart to beat wildly as I remember my first walk with Barrett.

"He makes me feel like I'm important to him. Barrett looks at me and sees me, Lo. He sees my heart. And he's so great with Hux. He makes me feel like I matter to him, he asks my opinions. He . . ."

"Sucks grapes out of your hoohah?"

I burst into a fit of laughter. "That too."

"So what you're saying here is that he convinced you he's this great guy, one that was good enough to lay aside your reservations and give it a whirl. And yet, at the first sign of struggle, you're rethinking everything?"

Gulping, I feel my cheeks heat. "I'm not necessarily rethinking everything. I'm trying to be smart, Lola. I'm trying to make sure I'm not walking into a replica of what I walked away from."

"No offense," she says, tipping back the rest of her wine. "But Barrett Landry is spades over Hayden Baker. Okay? Regardless of what Barrett's done to upset you, let's not put him on the level with your asshole ex. It's not like he has paraded up the steps of a swanky hotel with a hooker at his heels." She groans. "And with a hooker in ridiculously ugly heels."

I glare at her.

"What? They were. They actually looked Bedazzled, Ali. Who does that? And who fucks that?"

I roll my eyes, grateful for the bit of levity but knowing it's not enough to completely distract me.

She wraps her arm around my shoulder and snuggles into me like only a best friend can. I wonder absentmindedly what would've changed if I'd had her in New Mexico when I was going through everything. I was alone then. Would it have been easier if I'd had her there? Because this is a lot easier with her here.

"I think, in my infinite wisdom, you need to give the disastrously hot mayor the benefit of the doubt," she says matter-of-factly.

"What if it destroys me in the end?"

"Hey," she says, tugging the blanket around her waist. "You were the one that insisted on tangling up the heart and vagina. I believe my initial suggestion was to keep them separate."

"They're pretty wound together."

"I think they're more wound together than you even realize."

The stars twinkle a little brighter as I acknowledge that she's right. Every part of me is tangled up in this irresistibly handsome politician and I'm afraid there's no way out.

I'm really afraid I might not want a way out.

♦♦♦

## Barrett

THE HOUSE IS DARK, JUST the light over the cook top is on. I sit at the kitchen table and take another swig of bourbon.

The room is full of expensive pieces of furniture from a double oven to a restaurant-style refrigerator. The table I'm sitting at was handcrafted, as were the barstools lining the granite-topped bar. It's a warm room, the one everyone calls the heart of the home. Most assuredly the most expensive room in this house. Yet, when I think about sitting here or sitting at the little beat-up table at Alison's, there's no question where I'd rather be.

And it isn't fucking here.

My body aches. My shoulders are stiff, my head feels like I've gone a few rounds with my trainer. My throat is scratchy from yelling so much today, my knuckle a little ripped from hitting a punching bag at the gym with no gloves. The pain felt purifying, distracting from my true ailment—a blonde-haired, blue-eyed girl that I just might have ruined my chances with.

Not being able to smooth this over with her destroys me. Seeing the pain on her face, the little spec of insecurity in who I am and what I believe about her, hasn't left me all day. In fact, it's only pressurized, built, and now is bubbling over.

My phone buzzes and I only look at it in case it's her. But it's not. Of course it's not. It's Linc.

As much as I don't want to hear his stupidity, I really don't want to be alone. So I answer it.

"Hey," I say, flinching as the bourbon festers in my stomach.

"What's up?"

"Not much." I sit the glass on the table. "What about you?"

"Not much. Just seeing what's happening over there."

I look around the room and consider just how much of nothing is happening. No conversations, no plans for tomorrow, no lunch dates on the schedule that I actually want to attend. Not one damn thing.

"Graham called earlier and filled me in on the debacle with the papers and all that," he says, like he's just tossing that out there as a conversation piece. It's the reason he fucking called and as much as that annoys me, it's also a relief.

"Yeah, it's been a fucked up day."

"How'd you handle it?"

"What do you mean, 'How did I handle it?'" I snort. "I had a complete fucking come-apart in the middle of my office." I cringe as the memory washes over me, the fury I felt the moment I saw those headlines driving a nail into my skull.

"I can imagine," Lincoln says, no humor in his voice. "I have to say, I was a little disappointed no punches were thrown."

I scoff at my little brother, the one that nearly charged the mound last year when a pitcher hit him three times in one game.

"I know you don't like Nolan. Hell, I'm not sure how much I even like the son of a bitch right now. But I can't throw punches. I have a real job."

"Baseball is a real job, asshole. I make more than you do a year. Choke on that."

I laugh, even though I don't want to, because Lincoln is right. He makes more than I do doing a job that's a hell of a lot more fun and less stressful.

"How'd Alison take it?" he asks.

"How do you think she took it?"

"That good, huh?"

Rubbing my temples, I consider refilling my glass with liquor. It would absolutely dull the pain, but it would also mute my ability to think, to process, to plan, and that's nearly all I have on my side right now. I need to figure a way out of this.

"She's effectively not talking to me right now," I say, the words tasting as bitter as I expect them to. "A part of me feels like I need to act, to do something to make this better. It's what I do. There's a problem, I fix it. But you know, maybe this life I lead isn't what's best for her. I mean, fuck, Linc. My own people put out that article."

He chuckles under his breath. "The life you lead isn't the problem, brother. It's your quote-unquote 'own people' that are the issue. I'm not even going to start into a big lecture here on how much I hate Nolan and all the reasons I think he's poison to you."

"You're just mad he told dad you're the one that wrecked my BMW back in the day," I grin.

"Yeah because that shows his lack of loyalty! It was none of his fucking business. You and I had it worked out. It would've been fixed and that would've been the end of it. The cocksucker overhears us talking and snitches like the asshole he is."

Sighing, I stand and walk over to the island where I left the bottle of bourbon. I pour a little into my glass and swirl it around while I consider Lincoln's words.

"I'm *days* from this election. If I weren't, I would've fired him today."

"You should've fired him today."

I groan. "We've been working on this campaign for years, Linc. There are so many people's jobs riding on the line." Sighing, I slump against the counter. "I was reading him the riot act today, and Dad shoved me out of the room and told me to calm down."

Taking another swig of the liquor, I feel the burn as it trickles down my throat. "If I fire him now, my chances of losing this election triple. Maybe quadruple. So much time and money have been spent that I can't just blow it now because I'm pissed off. Those people have families to feed, bills to pay. That's not fair to anyone."

"It's fair to you. You gotta stand up for yourself, man."

"I did," I sigh. "I've done everything I can."

"Welp," Lincoln says, "if that's the case, have you done everything you can to tell Ali that?"

"Ali? You're on a nickname basis with my girl now?"

"Hey, she likes me. Probably better than you right now!"

"Go to hell." A pang of jealousy that their relationship is so easy taps my heart.

The line grows quiet, both of us trying to get some kind of game plan together. The problem is that neither of us plan as well as Graham, and this isn't something I can plan with my logical brother. I'm closest to Graham, but when you need someone to plan shenanigans, you have to go to Linc.

"You know, I've never understood why you like politics," Lincoln says.

"I'm not sure why I do right now either."

"Is it what you want to do? Do you want this life, worrying about what everyone says about you, picking you apart, going after your girl?"

Sitting back at the table again, I think about how many times I've asked myself that very question over the last few days.

"It's the only thing I ever considered doing," I point out.

"Because Dad pushed you."

"Not just that," I say. "I've always felt like this is what I'm supposed to do. And I've enjoyed it for the most part. You can do a lot of good things with the power it gives you. It's constantly moving, changing. You can't stand still or you get lost in the shuffle. And, before the last couple of months, I've had all the women and parties and opportunities I could ever want."

"That's all fine and dandy, but everything you've said has been past tense."

"Yeah," I sigh. "I know."

"So . . . why not drop out? Change courses. You don't have to do this. You don't have to try to save the world or give up your life and subject yourself to this craziness."

"I've considered it." My fingertips strum the table, lost in thought. "You know, I wonder what my life would've been like if Dad hadn't bought me the mayoral election."

"Barrett, don't even fucking go there. You won that thing on your own."

"Did I, Linc?" I ask. "I remember going to the debates, answering the questions at the interviews, and not really having a fucking clue what they were talking about. I said what I was supposed to say, smiled, and boom—I'm the mayor. Did you ever think about that?"

He groans into the phone. "You're just being stupid now."

I laugh, feeling like a weight is off my shoulders. "No, maybe I'm just being honest."

"If that's the case, maybe you shouldn't be in politics to start with."

"Maybe not. But I am and I can't back out now."

"You also can't risk losing her either, Barrett. I've never seen you happier than you have been lately. You're so normal when you're with her, almost like one of the guys I play ball with."

"Gee, thanks."

He laughs. "I'm serious. You're usually a stick in the mud, off burying your cock in some chick or huddled in a corner with Graham. You're actually kind of fun now."

Taking a swig of my drink, I feel it burn as it goes down. "I don't feel very fun right now."

"You're at the plate with a full count. You have to step to the plate ready to swing, Barrett."

"Baseball analogies? Really?"

"Listen to me. Be ready to swing. Don't let the third strike pass the plate. Because when that happens, you go to the dugout. Alone. And that's a cold and lonely place."

## Barrett

MY TIE IS OFF CENTER. I face the mirror and see the green and white striped fabric twisted like a twelve-year-old put it on.

It makes wonder if Huxley knows how to tie a tie. An image pops in my mind of us standing in front of a mirror and me showing him how to do it. I can't help but grin at the idea and the realization that the concept makes me happy.

Heaving a breath, I force myself to concentrate on getting myself presentable for another day at the office. It's early, a little past six, and I haven't slept. I'd hoped the bourbon would assist in that effort, but it didn't.

My phone was in my hand as much as it wasn't all night. I wanted to call her, to plead my case, to tell her how I'd do anything to fix the pain she felt yesterday. Then I got pissed off that this happened, from my staff, no less, and the fury coursed through me until I was exhausted.

Even though it killed me, I didn't call her. She said she needed space and I need to give her that. It's not something I've ever done before, played by a woman's rules.

I grab my briefcase off my desk and see a text from Troy that he's outside waiting on me. Before I get through the doorway, my phone rings in my hand. When I see it's her, I drop my briefcase to the floor.

"Hey," I say, my heart thumping in my chest.

"Hey," she whispers. Her voice is heavy, sleepy like mine, and I wonder if she's slept at all.

"How are you?"

"Okay."

I wait for her to talk, to navigate this conversation because I don't want to steer it the wrong way from the get-go. The silence kills me and I want to ramble a million different things, go into a word vomit, a speech of epic proportions on how I just want to fix this fuck-up. But I hold myself back. For the first time, maybe in my entire life, I keep quiet.

"I hope I'm not calling you too early," she says finally. The roughness in her voice is a clear sign that she's been crying, and that's like a punch to the gut.

"I haven't been to sleep yet," I admit.

"Me either."

"So I guess I could've called you at two a.m. when my finger was hovering over the call button?"

Her giggle through the phone is mixed with a sigh and it makes me smile and frown at the same time.

"I hate this," I say, wishing I could reach out and hold her.

"Me too."

The line goes quiet. Her breathing gets heavy and I know she's trying to decide how to approach whatever is on her mind.

"I took Hux for ice cream last night. I looked over my shoulder the entire time, Barrett."

"Did anything happen?" I ask, holding my breath.

"No, it didn't. We were fine."

"It will be fine," I assure her. "I won't let it be anything but fine."

"This could end so badly for me and Hux."

"But it could be amazing too. If you would just trust me and just—"

"You're right."

A lump appears in my throat and I have to squeeze the words out around it. "I am? I mean, I know I am. But you think so?"

"When you left last night and things were so . . . broken, something felt broken inside of me. I feel like all the colors of the rainbow are there when we're together. Does that make sense?"

"Absolutely."

"When I agreed to get involved with you, I did it knowing all the ways it could go wrong. I did it knowing you'd never intentionally hurt me, and at the end of the day, that's what Hayden did. He hurt me on purpose. He didn't give a single fuck about how his actions were going to affect me."

"I would never do—"

"Barrett," she interrupts. "Let me finish."

"Sorry."

She laughs. "I know you'd never do that. And I know there are things you aren't going to be able to control. But if I want to be with you, I have to realize that and not hold it against you."

"Damn it, Ali—"

"Ali?" she giggles. "You've never called me that before."

"If Linc is calling you Ali, so am I."

She laughs full-on now and it's music to my ears.

"So does this mean you forgive me?" I ask, hopeful.

"It means I don't have anything to forgive you for. Do I like what happened? No. But as long as I know what's real between us, I can't care what everyone else thinks. I can't let my fear hold me back. My insecurities are my problems to work through, not yours."

"I'll be right by your side holding your hand," I promise.

She doesn't respond, but she doesn't have to.

"Hey," I say, picking up my briefcase and heading to the car. "Does Hux know how to tie a tie?"

"No. What a weird question. Why are you asking?"

I laugh, shutting the door behind me and jogging toward the Rover. "No reason. Can I see you tonight?"

"You better."

## Alison

I PULL MY RAGGEDY RED robe around me and tie it snugly. It's my favorite, and most beat-up, piece of clothing but I needed it last night when I felt like my life might be breaking apart. Now, after talking to Barrett a little while ago, my heart feels like it's been glued back together, my hopes and dreams still intact. I'm not even sure what those dreams consist of, exactly, besides having Barrett in our lives.

I sing a little ditty from when I was a child softly until Huxley's eyes flutter open. He stretches and yawns, his sweet, sleepy smell making me smile harder.

He follows me to the kitchen where I have a plate of sausage links and a scrambled egg waiting on him.

"Wow, what happened to cereal?" he asks.

"What? You'd rather have a box of marshmallows?"

"No," he yawns, sitting down to dig in. "It's just . . . weird. You aren't a morning person, you know."

"I know, buddy." I hum a little tune and put the skillet in the sink when the doorbell rings. I look up at Hux who's looking at me. "I'll be right back. Grandma must've gotten her days mixed up."

Hux stuffs an entire sausage link in his mouth as a reply.

I pad down the hallway and pull the door open. When I see Barrett on the other side, my hand flies to my mouth.

He looks divine in his crisp grey suit and tie. His watch sparkles in the early morning sunlight, but it's outshone by his beautiful eyes which are looking at me.

The lips I love to kiss, love to hear form words in my ear, are pressed together in an undeniable smirk. He watches me for a minute before reaching for me and I fall into his arms.

Holding me with one hand, he steps inside and closes the door quietly behind him.

"I missed you," he whispers in my ear.

"What are you doing here?" I can't keep the amazement out of my voice, even though I don't want to give him the wrong impression.

Seeing him first thing, before the world has a chance to ruin our day, makes me happier than I could ever tell him.

"I needed to see you."

"Don't you have a million things to do?" I try to say as he kisses my lips, little taps in quick succession. I giggle as the last peck sinks deeper into my lips and I find my hands wrapping around his neck and pulling him into me.

"Mom, are you okay?" Hux shouts from the kitchen.

I pull back and laugh, resting my head on Barrett's chest. "Yeah, I'm good. I'll be right there."

Barrett nuzzles me against him, brushing my hair back with one of his large hands. "God, I needed this."

"You have no idea how much I needed it too."

"You look adorable in this robe," he grins.

I glance down at my clothing and grimace. "I can't believe I'm letting you see me in this!"

"Stop," he winks. "I want this."

"My holey robe?"

"Yes. And your morning rush with Huxley and your out-of-bed hair. I want it all, baby."

Grinning wildly, I start to comment without swooning, but I hear the sound of Hux's feet coming down the hallway. I feel Barrett tense, a nervous energy passing between us.

Turning to see Huxley coming towards us, I smile. "Hey, buddy. Barrett came to say good morning."

"Hey," my son says, giving Barrett a little wave.

"How are you?" Barrett asks him.

"Good. I was just, um, checking on my mom."

Barrett's face breaks into a smile as he steps towards Hux and stretches his hand. "You're a good man, Hux."

Hux beams, obviously liking being treated like a man, and shakes Barrett's hand. "Want some breakfast? Mom actually made food today."

"Did she?" He leans close to Hux and whispers, but loud enough for me to hear. "Did she sing while she made it?"

It's some kind of joke between them, I can tell, but I have no idea what it means. I raise my brows and they both laugh.

"I was asleep. But she doesn't make food in the morning, so I'm guessing yes."

"That's a good thing." Turning to me, Barrett's face sobers a bit. "I hate to run, but I have a meeting in about twenty minutes. Troy's going to have to drive like a bat out of hell to get me there the way it is."

"Go," I insist, shooing him towards the door. "But thank you for coming by today."

He watches me, wanting to kiss me but not sure if he should do it in front of Huxley. "Thank you for letting me."

"You can come here anytime," Huxley says. "But I'm going to go back in the kitchen now in case you're going to kiss her because I don't want to see that."

We laugh as he salutes Barrett and zooms back to the kitchen and out of sight.

"I like him," Barrett says, pulling me into him. He kisses me sweetly again, making me melt under his touch. "I still get to see you tonight right?"

"I was counting on it."

I kiss him one last time before he walks out the door.

My spirits soar and I walk to the kitchen like I'm walking on air. Huxley is putting his empty plate in the sink. He scratches his head, his morning hair wild. "He makes you happy, huh?"

"He does. But only if you like him."

He looks at me in a way that reminds me of Hayden. It's a careful look, calculating, and at another time in my life, my heart would have tugged in my chest. I would've thought back to a life we could've had and to all the things that went wrong. But today, I don't go there. I'm too worried about the life that we can have and all the things that just might go right if we're lucky.

"I like him," Hux announces simply.

Laughing, I amble towards my son and pull him into a hug. "I love you, Hux."

"I love you, Mom."

## Barrett

"DO ONE MORE," ACHILLES, MY trainer, demands, watching me like a hawk. I pay him a lot of money to put me through my paces, and he does, many times after hours in his gym. "Three, two, give it hell, Landry, one. Relax."

I blow out a breath and drop the dumbbell to the ground. Achilles watches in his camouflage pants and white tank top, his arms folded over his large chest. "You have a little steam behind you tonight, Landry."

"Pent up aggression," I say, wiping my face with a towel. "Better to leave it here than on a member of the media. Fuckers trailed me all afternoon. Hobbs has them all convinced I'm a gangster or something and it's nearly impossible to actually work."

"So, you aren't a gangster?" Achilles teases.

I glare and he snickers at my reaction. His Mohawk wobbles. "I kid, I kid. I actually had someone call me a few days ago and asked if I had any dirt on you."

"Are you serious?"

"Yeah, man. I set that bitch straight though. Told him he could go fuck himself."

"Did you say it like that?" I grin.

"Just like that."

"You wanna know how frustrated I am?" I ask, wiping my face with a towel. "I'm starting to think Lincoln makes sense."

"That's crazy talk," he laughs.

"Right?"

"You know what I always say," Achilles says, stuffing his hands in his pockets, "trust those that have proven their loyalty. Linc might be full of shit half the time, but he has your back. That's why I trust Robin. My wife is the only person in the world I trust explicitly. She's proven it."

He leans against the wall and tries hard not to smirk.

"What?" I ask.

"I see you're on your way to settling down now too. Have to say, I'm shocked."

"Yeah, well, I don't know about settling down for sure."

His chest shakes with his laugh. "You released a statement. I've known you for twenty years, Landry. You've never entertained doing something like that before."

"That fucking statement wasn't what it should've been," I grumble, feeling the anger work its way to the surface. "Nolan fucked me over on that. Alison was pissed as hell and I couldn't blame her. Do you even realize how bad it looked coming out with the other article like that? Fuck."

Achilles picks up a dumbbell and presses it overhead. "I wondered when I saw it, to be honest. Did you work it out with your girl?"

"Yeah," I grin. "I'm meeting her after I leave here. I have this big thing set up at the house with candles and a bubble bath. I just want to . . ." I look at him and he's wearing a teasing smile. "I sound like a pussy, don't I?"

He sets the weight down and laughs. "No, man. You sound like a guy that is getting his priorities together. Making your girl feel special should be the first thing you do in your day. I mean, if you lose her, what do you have left?"

He gets it.

I try to wrap my head around that when movement catches our attention outside the glass. Troy is coming towards the door. He pulls it open and steps to the side.

My face breaks into a wide, yet confused, smile.

Alison walks around him, her step stuttering as her eyes meet mine. Her cheeks blush to the color of her pink dress, a short little number that I want off of her body as quickly as possible. I drag my gaze down her round breasts, over the sinful curve of her hips, and down those legs I want wrapped around me so badly my cock is rock solid.

I need her. I need some kind of physical confirmation that we're okay. Call me stupid or call me a pussy but I need it like the air I breathe.

Glancing at Troy, he shrugs. "She called and asked if I knew where you were. I figured you wouldn't mind if I grabbed her for you," he says.

Achilles smacks his lips beside me. "Well, I'm guessing you don't need me anymore," he chuckles. "You remember the security code, right?"

I nod but don't look at him. I can't look anywhere but at her.

Before I know it, it's just the two of us. She's standing in front of me. It's everything I've wanted since I saw her this morning. I feel like a kid on his birthday, when the box that you know holds the one gift you've been begging for is suddenly placed on your lap.

"Hey," she says, her voice timid. I have no idea why the hell she's nervous. All I know is that my heart is racing like a man on crack and my fingers itch like a junkie looking for his next fix.

I have to touch her. I have to taste her.

I stalk towards her, watching her anticipate my arrival. Her eyes widen as I draw near, the peacock necklace moving in between the large breasts that I want my mouth on.

In a couple of long strides, I'm in front of her, our bodies nearly touching. She tips her head to look up at me and begins to speak, but I capture the words with my mouth. She gasps, melting into me with no hesitation. Our tongues lace together, her sweet perfume wrapping around me. My arms are tightly wound around her, pulling her into me like I can't get enough.

Because I can't.

She's all that exists in the world right now and I want to be so far into her, lose myself so deeply into her, that it takes an act of God to separate us.

My hands find the curves of her ass and I cup them, squeezing, appreciative of her continued pantiless style. She moans, my palms dragging roughly across her skin to her hips. My fingers dip into the curve of her body, her own finding the small of my back, her nails digging into me. Her fingertips trace a line across my lower back, leaving a rush of sparking skin beneath.

*This woman is going to kill me.*

"You don't mind I showed up here, do you?" she breathes.

I lean back and look into her eyes. "I couldn't be more happy that you did."

"Hux left and I just needed to see you. I needed this peace I feel when I'm with you."

My lips find hers and press against them tenderly. "I needed it too."

"You know what else I need?" she asks.

"Whatever you need, I'll deliver."

"I need you inside me, Barrett."

That's all it takes for her to go from sweetheart to siren.

Pulling her hands from around me, I nearly drag her across the room.

"Barrett!" she laughs, having trouble keeping up in her heels.

I bring her around a corner next to the sauna, the air pierced with only our breathing. A long table sits next to it for massages. I pull her in front of me, kiss her quickly on the lips, and turn her away to face the wall.

"Grab the edge of the table," I order, my voice giving away just how worked up I am. "And hold on."

A quick breath escapes her throat, but she complies. I take a second to take in how fucking sexy she looks while she waits on me to fuck her.

My cock hardens, throbs, as I take in her nude heels, her thick, tanned legs, and the way the bottom of her ass cheeks peek from beneath the hemline of her dress bent over like this. I palm my cock and stroke it as she glances at me over her shoulder.

"You look so fucking good, Ali."

Her cheeks flush, but a sexy grin slips across her lips. "Then what are you waiting for, Mr. Landry?" She leans further across the table, baring her ass for me. She taunts me, shaking it from side to side. "I asked you to get inside me. Do I need to ask again?"

I drop my shorts to the floor and stand directly behind her. Rubbing my cock up her slit, I coat myself with her wetness. I suck in a breath and fight the urge to bury myself in her immediately.

Her breath catches in her throat at the contact. Her back is to my front. My breath on the back of her neck results in a quiet sigh escaping her lips. I press my tongue against her skin and drag it slowly to just below her ear. Her skin heats up immediately, her heartbeat now pounding, matching mine. I nip the delicate skin under her ear before pulling away.

"Barrett . . ." she begs, widening her stance.

I grab the zipper between her shoulder blades and drag it down her body. As the cool air touches her skin, she gasps. I unsnap her bra, leaving her entire back exposed.

"Let it all fall," I demand. She stands, still facing the wall, and the garments slowly pool at her feet.

My cock is pulsing, demanding attention, and I feel like I'm about to go off just looking at her. Her skin is creamy and soft, unblemished perfection. I drag a finger from the nape of her neck down her spine, her body rolling beneath my touch. It's intimate and sensual, and I could watch her reaction to me always.

I cup her breasts from behind. Her nipples harden and I tug on them, twirling them between my fingers. Her head falls back on my shoulder, her eyes shut, mouth open.

"Bend over again," I whisper into her ear.

She stretches out, grabbing the edge of the table. I touch her opening with the tip of my finger. Her hips press back against it.

"Eager, are we?" I ask.

"Stop fucking with me and fuck me," she demands.

I tsk, reaching out and pressing one hand on the small of her back. "We'll get to that. But you're going to have to learn patience, Ms. Baker."

She groans, pulling her hair away from her face. "I've needed you for days. Don't make me wait. Please, make me know we're okay."

Hearing her say that, I nearly combust. I gather a pool of moisture on my finger from her slit. She's dripping wet for me, her tight body begging for my cock that's throbbing to be in her pussy.

I spread her wetness around lazily, watching her sweet ass move against my hand, before crouching down behind her. Increasing the pressure on her back, more symbolic than actually restraining, she flattens against the table. Her eyes find mine over her shoulder. Holding her gaze, I taste her sweetness, feeling her shiver as my tongue touches her opening. She rocks back against my face, desperate for contact.

She rocks back again and I press my thumb over her ass. As she rotates back, she feels the pressure. She half yelps, but the hitch in her breathing tells me she's not against it.

I suck on her clit, working my mouth against her velvety folds as my thumb puts the slightest pressure on her ass.

"Barrett . . ." My name is a moan, a pleading, a begging for more.

Her knees begin to shake, her legs quivering on her fuck-me heels.

Adding pressure to both spots, I work both my tongue and thumb in circles. Her whimpers grow louder, her hips swiveling faster, her wetness dripping. I lick from her vagina up her slit, my cock ready to explode. Removing my thumb as I pass, my tongue licks up the curve of her ass, and drags up her spine as I stand. Positioning myself behind her, I slap her juicy ass once, hearing her squeal, before I push fully into her with one hard movement.

"Ah!" She's barely heard over the sound of the table ramming against the wall. "Barrett!"

I thrust into her again and again, feeling her pussy massage me with every push. It's fucking heaven. It's what I've needed for days now, the balm to my ills.

Pushing again and again, I feel her body quicken around me. It's not going to take long for either of us to explode.

I stroke into her over and over, the doors to the cabinet on the wall falling open with the impact of the table to the wall. Bottles begin to spill out as I plunge into her.

"I'm coming!" she screams over the top of the destruction. Her pussy clamps around me, the muscles spasming in the sexiest way. Her head thrown back, her hair a sexy mess, her swollen lips fallen apart in a sultry breath. Knowing I just put her over the edge makes me topple over it too.

"Fuck!" I shout, stroking into her a few more times. As the crescendo of my orgasm hits, I slow the pace, milking the feeling for as long as possible.

My eyes open, my lids heavy. I watch her lips form a smile, her body relaxing as she lands from the ride. She looks like an angel, a perfect, beautiful, built-for-me creature that I'm falling for harder and harder.

Maybe I've already completely fallen. Maybe this tightness in my chest, the ferocity I feel about her is what everyone means when they say they've fallen in love.

"I needed that," she whispers. Her lips press together and she giggles a light, airy sound.

"Me too," I say, pulling out of her and helping her stand. I lay a kiss to the top of her head and feel her warmth cocoon me as her arms encapsulate my waist. She snuggles into me. "Are you okay?"

"Yeah. I'm good. Very good."

"You were better than good," I joke as she shoves away from me.

"Funny, Landry." She tosses me a grin.

We stand in silence, the floor around us littered with random objects rattled from our antics, our bodies sticky with sweat. Her hair is a mess, her skin flushed, and she's never looked more beautiful.

# 30

I GLANCE IN THE REARVIEW mirror. The blue sedan stays four or five car lengths back, just as it has since I left Hillary's. I swung by there after dropping Huxley off at my mom's to get my schedule and to ask to switch a couple of days around to accommodate a musical at Hux's school and a catering event. The sedan pulled out behind me and has followed me ever since.

Nearing the turnoff to my house, I consider calling Barrett. I haven't physically seen him in a few days, our schedules refusing to coincide. We've talked on the phone numerous times every day. The stress of his campaign and our ridiculous schedules have cramped our face time.

It's for the best though. Everything has been a whirlwind these past few months since we met at the charity event and the little break in our schedules has given me time to evaluate everything from a distance.

It's only made me miss him more.

Nothing is the same without him around. Hux has noticed it too.

When Barrett is around, things seem brighter. My life is enriched from more than just being a mother. I'm a woman wanted by a man that is everything I could ever want and then a little more. He respects me, he appreciates me, he cherishes me, and unless I'm completely wrong, he might be starting to fall in love with me.

And I'm starting to fall in love with him.

The thought is terrifying and exhilarating at once.

Glancing up again, the car is nowhere to be seen. I check twice, three times, but it's gone. Still, I grab my phone to call Barrett just as his number rings me. I smile as I answer it.

"Hey, you!"

"Hey, babe," he says, his voice husky. I can hear the exhaustion thick in his tone. It gets deeper every day. I'm worried about how he's taking the campaign and the pressures on him, but he always says he's fine. "Are you home?"

"Almost," I say, turning onto my street. "I had some errands to run."

"I'm ten minutes away and I'd like to stop by if that's all right."

"I'd love that," I grin. "I'll see you then."

I navigate the car into my driveway and race in with anticipation of seeing him. I glance in the entry mirror and try to get some semblance of style in my hair and plop on some lip gloss. Before I can do all the things I'd like to, he's knocking at the door.

Pulling it open, I'm met with his handsome face. He grins and steps inside, closing the door behind him. Our lips meet immediately, like there's no other way, and I sigh softly into his mouth.

"I've missed you," I whisper, feeling his lips work over mine.

"I've missed you."

He takes my hand and leads me in the living room. I follow, but the hair on the back of my neck stands on end.

"Is everything okay?" I ask.

We sit on the sofa and he looks at me and I know everything is not, in fact, okay. His eyes are filled with concern, his shoulders rigid, waiting on some assault I have no idea how to identify.

My stomach free-falls into an abyss.

"Did you see the news today?" he asks, his words careful.

"No. Why?"

His head bows slightly, his eyes going to the floor, before he looks at me again. "Fucking Hobbs."

"What did he say?"

Barrett's jaw clenches, his temple pulsing with frustration. I'm terrified by the look in his eye—one not directed at me, but it doesn't matter. He's ready to go unleashed.

"I'm going to cut to the chase," he gulps, looking away again. "He basically used you to get at me."

"What?" I say, shooting to my feet. My heart races, my mind going right along with it.

"He used your past—the assault, the investigation—to undermine me. To say that I was being careless and making bad decisions."

"Oh my God," I say, my hand going to my mouth. "I'm so sorry, Barrett. I . . ."

He sits on my sofa, his head in his hands. His fingers clench strands of hair and tug roughly. The suit stretching across his back is taut, a hint of the stress his body is holding beneath. He's been under so much pressure and now my past has added to the mix.

"I'm sorry," I start again but am quieted with one look from him.

"Don't," he warns. "Don't even apologize for that asshole."

"I'm not apologizing for him. I'm apologizing that I had anything to do with you being skewered."

A chuckle rumbles through the room. "Baby, I'm not worried about me. If anyone wants to believe that me being with you is a bad thing, then so be it."

"Barrett . . ." My mouth opens to speak, but I can't, and when his lips find mine, everything that needs to be said is. His kisses show me more than his words could ever express. I tell him right back, show him as passionately as he shows me, and by the time we break our connection, we're both panting.

His forehead rests against mine, his lips starting to twitch. Mine follow suit and slowly, our smiles encourage the other's until we both have wide grins on our faces.

Giggling, I wrap my arms around his trim waist and try to quiet the chaos in my mind. I don't know what this means or what's in store, but I know it's true. I love him. And I think he loves me.

"I'm okay with staying in the shadows," I say. "At least until the election is over."

He jerks away from me. "What the hell are you talking about?"

"Your campaign. I don't want to cause you any trouble, Barrett. I know where we stand. Don't think you have to go defend me or ha—"

"Stop," he commands. "We know where we stand. I don't give a fuck what anyone has to say about it."

"But..."

"For the first time in my life, I know, without a doubt, without a single shred of hesitation, that this, you and me, is the right thing. And if that makes me lose the election, then it does. As long as you're okay with me continuing it, they can say what they want."

"I want you to finish it. I want you to win it on your terms. To prove to yourself you can do it your way."

He kisses me again. "If it's too much for you to deal with me during this, I understand."

"I just don't want to cause you problems."

His laughter echoes off the room and he holds my hand up in the air and twirls me like we're dancing. "Cause me problems? Shit, you save me so many ways you don't even know." His head cocks to the side "Let's go out to dinner."

"What? Where?"

"I want to show you off."

"Barrett," I say, panicking. "You don't have to do that. It's fine. I—"

"I want to show them how proud I am to be with you. Let them take our picture. Let them see how beautiful you are."

"I don't know..."

He tilts my chin up with the tip of his finger. "Do you want to be with me?"

"Yes," I breathe.

"Then let's be together. You and me. Fuck them."

His smile is contagious and I give in. "Okay. You and me."

# 31

*Alison*

BARRETT LACES HIS FINGERS THROUGH mine, giving them a gentle squeeze. I look up into his handsome face and return his mega-watt smile.

"Are you okay?" he asks as we enter the restaurant.

I nod and try to concentrate on him and the absolute serenity in his gaze—not the hundreds of pairs of eyes gazing at us, not the hushed whispers swirling around the room.

"Me and you," he winks. "Just me and you, baby."

We are led to a table in the corner. Barrett pulls out my chair for me to sit before taking his across from me. Our drink orders are taken, menus placed in front of us.

The place is beautiful, filled to near capacity, and I can feel the weight of the stares on my back. Barrett is sitting in the corner so he can see the entire room; I'm thankful I can't.

"Your hand is shaking," he says, lifting it off the table and planting a sweet kiss to the center of my palm. "Will you relax? Please?"

"I'm trying," I whisper. "I just know they're all talking about us right now."

"I'm sure they are. Everyone always talks about the most beautiful girl in the room."

My cheeks heating, I pull my hand away. "I thought I was prepared for this. When I would go places with my ex-husband, things like this would happen."

"No offense, but I don't really want to think about you at dinner with him."

The grimace on his face makes me giggle.

"I'm not joking," he says.

"I know. But I like that it bothers you. Call me crazy."

"You're crazy to think it wouldn't," he smiles.

Drinks are placed in front of us and we order off the menu. The server is a man, but that doesn't stop him from flirting with Barrett.

Once we're alone again, Barrett looks at me with a seriousness in his eye. "Are you happy?" he asks me.

I run my finger along the edge of my glass. "Yes. Why would you ask me that?"

He pulls at the collar of his shirt. "Because it's the most important thing to me."

The earnestness of his tone hits me right in the middle of my heart. My cheeks split with a smile and I mean every inch of it. "I feel like, for the first time in my life, things might be going where I want them to go."

His hand drops to his lap and he takes a rough swallow. "Where's that?"

"To being happy."

"Do I make you happy, Alison?"

"Yes, you do."

"I know this whole thing is hard for you, me being a politician. And sometimes . . ." he looks at the ceiling before finding my eyes again. "Sometimes I feel like I maybe pushed you into this and that makes me—"

"You didn't push me into anything," I interject. "Yes, maybe you were a little aggressive in your methods. But every choice I've made, including being with you, is one *I* made. Okay?"

He nods and looks around the room. "You have no idea how proud I am to be sitting here with you." He looks at me again and takes my hand, holding it on top of the table. "You've made my life better. I just hope that your life is better because of it too."

I think about it for a long minute before responding. "My life is harder with you in it."

He tightens his grip on my hand, his eyes flickering with worry.

"It is, Barrett. I worry so much that things will go wrong. I stay up at night wondering if this has a chance to work out in the end. But," I say, just as his mouth opens to speak, "I always come to the same conclusion: it has to. Because I can't imagine not sitting here with you tonight or not getting your texts first thing in the morning. Regardless of how hard it is, it's worth it."

He starts to speak when the server approaches the table. "I'm sorry, sir. There's a man at the bar, a Miles Monroe, that has asked that you speak with him for a minute."

Barrett falls back in his chair and looks at me.

"Go if you need to," I say, noting how sexy he looks when he's on the verge of getting mad. "I'll be here when you get back."

"This is our date," he grumbles.

"And you're the mayor running for election. I can handle not being with you for a few minutes. I'll just check on Hux. It's fine."

He stands and stops in front of me. He bends down, a sinful look on his face, and kisses me, letting our lips linger for a moment longer than necessary. When he pulls back he whispers against my mouth, "That should serve a few purposes. One, it will remind you of the things to come after we get out of here. Two, it should tell you how fucking gorgeous you look tonight. And three, it will make it clear to every person in here that we are together, like it or not."

Before I can respond, he's gone. My heart is pounding in my chest, my cheeks flushed from his kiss. If I sit too long and feel the stares of the other patrons, I'll be a nervous wreck, so I pull my phone from my purse and send a quick text to my mom to check on Huxley. As soon as I hit send, a woman's voice, breathy a la Marilyn Monroe, speaks from my side.

"You must be Alison," she almost whispers.

I look up, her curvy body stuffed into a baby pink dress that must have cost more than my tuition this semester. I force a swallow and plaster on the practiced smile I've used many times over the past few years.

"I am," I say, my voice even. I recognize her as the girl Barrett escorted out of the Savannah House the night I met him. "Can I help you with something?"

"Uh, no," she laughs, like the idea is ridiculous. "I'm Daphne Monroe, but I'm sure you knew that." She licks her ruby red lips. "I just wanted to thank you for helping Barrett with his campaign. You've been such a blessing to him."

My mind scrambles and I catch my jaw from dropping right in time. I don't know what she's getting at and I'm not about to ask. Instead, I play along. "Not that he needs my help," I muse, "but I'm glad I can assist where I can."

Her eyes narrow and I know she's trying to keep the upper hand. Behind those heavily-lashed eyes is a breadth of fury. "I know what it's like to be in the middle of a campaign year," she says, her words tempered with a smile that's not at all genuine. "I can only imagine how . . . someone *like you* . . . is dealing with it. It will be over soon and you can go back to your life. Just hang in there."

My blood roasts my veins at her thinly-veiled insinuations. Her hand finds the bend of her hip, angling her hand so I can see the expensive jewels on her fingers.

I laugh.

"Someone . . . *like me* . . . is dealing with it very well," I smile sweetly. "But you're right—we are just waiting for it to be over so we can get some kind of normalcy in our lives. Although I suppose we'll have to find a new normal once we get moved," I add, hoping she gets the point that I will be going with him to Atlanta. "I just dread packing everything."

"Oh," she gushes, putting me on edge, "it's so nice of Barrett's people to get you a new house as payment. You must give great blow jobs because that's not usually in the deal. It's usually a quick check or a new car or something for you fillers," she smirks. "Fillers. That's what girls like you are called."

My lips spring open, my eyes wide, my fingers ready to rip her apart when I see Barrett walking up to us. His eyes are frantic, his steps hurried, as he makes his way to the table.

I give a quick look to Daphne, who has no idea he's behind her. I'm not about to play into her hand and start something in front of him. Everyone in this building knows her and her father and would surely take her side in any kind of argument. I'd lose.

And I'm not losing to this bitch.

"Hey, baby," I say when Barrett is just behind her.

"Is everything okay here?" he asks, eyeing Daphne carefully.

She whirls around, her hand flying to her chest, at the sound of his voice. "Hey, you," she says. "I was just meeting your date tonight."

He side-eyes her and takes his seat. "I take it you met then."

"We did," I laugh, making him more nervous. "It's nice meeting your friends, Barrett. It really puts some things in perspective."

"Does it now?"

Daphne cuts in, stepping to Barrett's side. "I'm going to get back to my table. I think our mothers are co-chairing an event this week. Maybe we'll see each other there, Barrett."

He shakes his head. "I think my week is booked solid. But it was good to see you, Daphne."

"You too." She glances at me, her eyes lethal. "Nice to meet you, Alison."

"That pleasure was all mine," I emphasize, watching her try to keep her composure as she skirts off across the room.

Barrett laughs and takes a sip of his wine. "I'd ask how that went, but I think I already know."

I consider telling him what she said, voicing to him what she just implied: that I was no more than a pawn in his career. Before the words can free themselves from my lips, I decide not to. It's bullshit, plain and simple and if I bring it up, I'm not sure what he'll do. I don't want to give that nasty woman any power.

Instead, I say, "How can you be friends with someone like that?"

"I'm not anymore," he insists, placing his glass back on the table. "We grew up together, went to the same schools all our lives. She was someone I could . . ."

I shake my head emphatically. "Nope. I don't want to hear this."

He laughs, his eyes shining with a sentiment I could get lost in if I let myself. "She was someone I could . . . forget," he whispers. "She was someone I couldn't care less about, someone that wasn't even a blip on my radar." He leans against the table, his features striking against the candlelight. "She was never anything to me. You, Alison Baker, are mine."

I bend forward, our lips finding each other's over the center of the table. For the first time, I don't care who is watching, I don't care who is whispering. I just want to revel in this man, his words, and the fact that I know he means it.

## Barrett

"YOU OKAY BACK THERE?" TROY asks, glancing at me through the rearview mirror.

"Yeah," I say, going back to my phone. "Why?"

"You just seem jittery, I guess. That's not normal for you. Even when you're stressed or pissed, you're always composed."

I toss my phone into my briefcase and lock it. Resting my head on the back of the Rover seat, I take a deep breath. "Just stressed the fuck out."

He clicks off the radio and turns down Alison's street. "So, if you don't mind me asking, how serious are we about this girl?"

"Serious."

"That's what I thought," he says, slowing to a stop along the curb. "For the record, I really like her. She reminds me of Camilla, but without the trust fund."

"She's nothing like Swink. She keeps to herself, wants no part of this world. Camilla eats it up."

"Yeah, but Camilla is the classiest woman I know. And Alison, she has that same vibe."

I open my door and smile at my friend. "Thanks, man."

He nods and as soon as I step out, he pulls away as I instructed him to do.

I make my way up the sidewalk to the front door, stepping over a baseball bat. It makes me smile because it's so normal, such a typical family-in-the-suburbs thing to see.

There's a chip in the front window of the house and I wonder as I knock if she'd be pissed if I had someone come over and fix it. And if I had them install a security system.

Before I can think too much about it, she pulls the door open. "Hey," she grins, letting me inside. "Are you hungry? We just ate, but there are leftovers in the kitchen."

"Yeah, actually. I am."

I kiss her in a more reserved way than I'd like. I sit my briefcase down by the door and follow her into the back, watching her ass sway in front of me as we go.

Huxley is sitting at the table, working on math problems. He looks up and smiles. "Hey, Barrett."

"Hi," I say, sitting across from him. "How's everything going?"

He shrugs. "Good, I guess. I hate math though. Are you good at it?"

"Nope," I laugh. "I had my brother Ford do all my math homework when I was a kid. I hated it too."

"I don't get it when numbers and letters go together. That's just . . . confusing."

"That it is," I laugh.

Alison puts a plate of meatloaf, mashed potatoes, and green beans in front of me. It looks delicious, like something I'd get in a diner, but more wholesome. She watches nervously as I take a bite.

The flavors blindside me, so much more than I expected. "This is great," I say honestly and take another bite. I didn't even realize how hungry I was until now.

A television plays in the living room and I feel myself relax. This is the atmosphere you see on television, the American life you see on sitcoms. A life I didn't even know was real until now. A life I didn't know I needed until recently.

We chitchat about Hux's school and the paper Alison just finished, but we stay away from the election. I'm grateful for that. Bringing that poison into this room would be wrong. It's so real and pure in this kitchen that I want to preserve it.

"Time to do dishes," Hux announces, taking my plate and going to the sink. I watch his little body move around—filling the sink, adding the bubbles, getting his towel laid out to catch the wet dishes.

Alison watches me with as much curiosity as I watch him. She raises her brows and I consider my next move, but know what I want to do.

Standing, I take off my watch and place it on the table. I roll my sleeves back to the elbows while I head towards Hux. He looks at me over his shoulder.

"You don't have to help me," he grins. "I do the dishes every night. It's my job."

"I'd like to help you, if you don't mind," I say, trying to figure out how to join into this perfected assembly he has going on. "I've never done this before."

He nearly drops a plate. "What?"

I shrug. "We had people that did it for us."

"Can we get people, Mom?"

Alison laughs, tucking her legs beneath her on the chair. "Sorry. No people for us," she tells him.

I want to interject that I want them to have people, my people. That one day, sooner rather than later if I can help it, I want our lives merged. I want to take care of them, have a little slice of this life for myself and give them the privileges of mine. But not yet. Not until this mess of a campaign is behind me. And then we'll go forward.

I look at Huxley, who's grinning at me.

*As a family.*

I grin back.

"A couple of moms were volunteering in my class today," Huxley announces. "They asked me about you."

I take a soapy plate from him and rinse it under the water. He motions for me to put it on the towel, so I do.

"They did, huh?" I say. "What did you say?"

"I just told them that I did know you and you were a nice guy. But I needed to study and gossiping isn't really a nice thing to do."

"Since when do you not gossip?" Alison asks. "I remember you coming home this afternoon telling me all about how Patrick stole the pen out of Nina's desk."

"That's not gossip, Mom," he says, rolling his eyes. "That's fact."

"Either way," I tell him, taking a glass, "I appreciate your loyalty and not saying anything."

He shrugs, but the corner of his lip twitches. "Speak as you find. And, well, you're like family now, kind of. And we protect each other. We don't let each other get bullied and that's what I felt like they were doing—getting information they could use against you."

I glance over at Ali, my heart stilled in my chest that this little boy would think of me as family. She bites her lip, looking like she's trying not to cry, so I try to change the topic for the sake of us all.

"So, tomorrow night I thought maybe you guys could come over to my house. I don't cook, but you know . . ."

"You have people," Hux laughs.

"I do. Or your mom can come over and cook something in my kitchen. Would you like that?"

"Yeah, but I have a program at school."

Alison stands and makes her way to the coffee pot. "Tomorrow night he has a fall music program." Her hand trembles a little as she pours herself a cup. "You could, you know, come if you want."

I take another plate and rinse it, considering my options. There's nothing more I'd rather do than see this kid that just came into my life sing or play the trombone or whatever it is he does. Because he deserves to have a man there watching him, encouraging him, showing him what it means to be a man. But it's not that easy.

"I have meetings and interviews tomorrow and my schedule is blocked until at least seven. What time is it?"

"Six."

My spirits sink. Even if I could've made it, I don't know if it would be the right thing to be seen publicly at his school. I have no idea where to draw the line at this type of thing at this point in our relationship.

"Maybe another night," Hux offers, watching my face.

A long silence stretches over the kitchen before Alison clears her throat. Huxley and I both look at her.

"You know those season tickets we got for the Hawks games?" she says to her son. Hux's head bounces up and down. "Those were a gift," Alison tells him, "from Barrett."

Huxley swings to face me, his eyes lit up like a Christmas tree. "Really? You gave those to us?"

I didn't realize she hadn't told him that little piece of the puzzle, and I'd have been fine if she hadn't. But I have to admit, seeing this look on his face is priceless.

"I did. I hope you enjoy them."

Before I know what's happening, I'm enclosed in a set of 10-year-old arms. His hands are wet from the dishwater, but the feeling of his face pressed into my stomach is worth it.

Chuckling, I look at Alison. Her eyes are damp with unshed tears, her hand over her mouth.

"Thank you," Hux says, pulling back. "It's the best thing anyone has ever given me."

"You are so welcome," I choke out, his gratitude making my throat squeeze shut. "Maybe I could take you to a game or two. We can leave Mom at home."

"Really?"

"If you'd like that."

"Yeah!" he says, pulling the plug from the sink and then drying off his hands. "That would be awesome."

He flashes me a huge smile before racing out the back door. Alison stands by my side and we watch him ride his bike around the back yard. I think how far he could ride at the Farm, how much fun he would have in all that space.

"He's a great kid," I comment as he ditches the bike for his mitt.

"Yeah, I'm partial to him."

"Do you want more?"

"More of what?" she asks, looking up at me.

"Kids."

She shrugs, her eyes just a touch wider than before. "I don't know. Maybe. I haven't really thought about it."

"Why haven't you? It's a normal thing, right?"

"Yeah, if you're in a relationship. I've been divorced for awhile now, and believe it or not, it's harder than you think to find someone when you have a kid."

"Good thing you found me then," I wink.

I don't push the kid issue because I don't even know how I feel about it for sure. It's not something I've thought a lot about specifically, but looking at her, I think I know the answer.

"I have a charity event in a couple of days. It's something my parents put on every year and I can't get out of it. The Garalent Gala," I say. "It's named after my mother's family. Proceeds benefit Alzheimer's."

"Sounds fun," she says, sipping her coffee.

My stomach churns a bit when I realize I always take Daphne to the Gala, and I've committed to doing that again this year.

Looking at her sweet face, I figure I'll get out of it.

"Want to come with me?" I ask.

"I can't," she replies easily. "I have to work."

"Alison, *please*."

She places her mug on the table and her hands go to her hips. "Please what?"

I blow out a breath, sensing the argument that's right there for the taking. I don't want to fight with her, but I do want things to start trending to what they are going to be.

"Can we talk really plainly for a minute?" I ask.

"Sure. Shoot."

"I think we both know where this is heading."

"This as in . . ."

I shake my head. "This as in me and you. And Huxley too." I lean against the sink, feeling my shirt get wet, but not caring. "Once this election is over, I really want us to take the next step."

She forces a swallow and takes a seat at the table. "As in what?"

"As in us being together." The words sound odd coming from my mouth, but I've never meant anything more. "I want to take care of you guys, try to be the man in both of your lives. You know, whatever that means."

"We don't need someone to take care of us, Barrett."

I blow out a long breath. "Fine then. I need someone to take care of me, and I'd like you to be the one to do that."

She watches me but doesn't speak. I'm not sure if that's a good thing or a bad thing, so I keep talking to try to sway her to my side.

"This thing is over in less than a week. For a lot of reasons, including the one that you won't need to work in catering anymore, another being I'd rather be comfortable knowing you're home and safe for these last few days, I really wish you'd consider quitting Luxor."

"No."

I'm shocked by the quickness, the simplicity of her answer. "No? Just . . . no?"

"No. I'm not quitting my job for anyone, not even you."

"Why? That's just dumb."

She laughs, but she doesn't find it funny. I can see that in her eyes. "I gave everything up once for a man. I put my dreams, my goals on hold to get him ahead, and once he did . . . poof. He was gone. And I had a child and a little divorce money that felt like severance pay. Never again, Barrett. Never again."

"So, what? If I'm elected, we're moving to Atlanta and you'll find a catering job there? That's ridiculous."

"First of all," she says, standing again, her ferocity back, "you don't know that you'll be elected for sure. Second, if you are, we'll have to figure it out then. Third, who said I'm moving with you? We haven't, you know, talked about that."

"I already know what I want. I want to take care of you, and I want you to be the girl that accompanies me to events and is home with dinner after work."

She raises her brow.

"Or I'll get us people," I laugh, pulling her into me. "It doesn't matter to me as long as I have you. And right now you working at Luxor makes me crazy and I'd rather you didn't."

"Why does Luxor bother you so much? You don't have a problem with my other job or school, right?"

I glance at the ceiling as her fingertips trail down my neck and try to decide how to explain it to her. "Because I know how people treat the catering staff. I've seen it. The people at those events act like they're above you somehow and when I think about that, about people talking down to you, I want to punch them in the face."

"Noted."

I sigh, resting my chin on her head. "But you're still going to work, aren't you?"

"Yup."

"Noted," I grumble.

## Barrett

IT'S BEEN A DAY FROM hell. Straight out of the fiery depths of Hades, this day has been nothing but one fucked up thing after another starting before I even got here.

Five thousand gallons per hour of sewage being spewed out of the ground in the middle of the city usually makes for a fun day. Add on top of that a new misconduct case being levied against the police department and a grant denied for a housing complex for the city, and the day goes to shit rather quickly and quite literally.

So, yeah, shitty all around.

My office door is shut, but the shuffle of staff members in the hallway outside sounds as loud as if they were in front of my desk. Everyone is on high alert, waiting for the latest poll numbers to drop. I'm trying to block it out, trying to work on the bill in front of me, but the interruption every six seconds by someone else is making it impossible. I can't even escape to the Farm. Too much work has had to be done today in the office, yet not a lot of it has actually been completed.

Another knock raps on the door and I toss my pen across the desk, watching it skid until it lands against a stack of files. "Yeah?" I ask, my voice more irritated than I care to let most people hear.

Nolan opens the door and lets it shut behind him with a slam. "Numbers are in."

By the look on his tightened face, they aren't good. I lean back in my chair and wait for the verdict.

"Hobbs gave a speech last night that was better than we predicted. He's gaining headway in the north more steadily than anticipated."

"How do we counteract that?" I sigh.

"You know how."

"Monroe."

"Yes, Monroe." He sits across from me, his face stiff. "Look, Barrett. I know you don't want to make concessions to him. I get it. But if you want to win this thing, you're going to have to bite the bullet and tell him what he wants to hear."

Squeezing my temples, trying to massage away the issue, I groan. This is something I had hoped I could put off long enough that it wouldn't be necessary. It's becoming apparent that's not happening.

"Is there any other way, Nolan? Anything?"

He shakes his head. "No, and you have Garalent coming up too. I'm not one hundred percent sure how Monroe's going to feel about you taking Alison."

"She's my girl. I'm not sure what that has to do with anything."

"Daphne has traditionally gone with you. For years now, it's been the two of you. It's kind of your show. People wait for those pictures, and Daphne gets a lot of press after it. You bowing out on her is going to diminish some of that."

"Not my problem."

He sits back in his chair, tapping his cheek with a pen. "So Alison is going with you?"

I don't want to answer that question. I'm afraid it'll open some door that I want permanently sealed. But the longer I look at Nolan, the more obvious it is he's going to wait for an answer.

"No, actually," I say. "She has to work." I raise a brow. "I'll be going *alone.*"

He catches his smile. "Well, in that case, I think we should consider—"

"We shouldn't."

"Barrett . . ."

"I am not taking Daphne Monroe to the Gala. Period."

Nolan rolls his eyes and stands. His jaw is twitching, frustrated with my sudden forcefulness. "Fine. No Daphne. But if you want to win this election, you're going to have to give in to her father."

Another knock, interruption number sixteen million, sounds at the door. Before I can respond, it pushes open and my father walks in. Dressed in a suit that mirrors mine, he flashes a look to Nolan, then to me.

"Son."

"Hey, Dad."

"I just saw the reports Nolan sent over. The polls are bad, Barrett."

"I'm still in the lead."

"Barely." He stands next to Nolan and they both look at me. "You have to be smart here. How many months do we have in this campaign? How many salaries are dependent on whether you get elected or not?"

"How about my legacy? How's it going to look if that bill passes and it fucks the entire economy, like I think it will?"

"It won't," my father says, his voice stern.

Groaning, I stand too, so we are eye to eye.

"Do you want to go out there and tell Rose she needs to look for a job?" Nolan asks. "We're all going to be looking for one come January if you don't act now. And we are down to days, Barrett. *Days.*"

He's right. This damn election is going to go to the person that sells their soul to the right bidder. I'm not going to have a chance to do the things I want to do as Governor, nor am I going to be able to make my family proud by winning the seat, if I don't do something. My ethics are keeping me from winning, and that's not fair to everyone that's worked so hard for this chance. Or me. And if Hobbs gets in office, fuck knows what he'll do.

"Give me the phone," I mutter.

## 34

### Alison

"EARTH TO ALISON."

I turn around to see my mother leaning on the doorframe to the living room. She's been watching me for who knows how long while I sit curled up on the sofa watching the sun set.

"Are you okay?" Mom sits beside me and gives me a questioning look.

I grin. "I'm good. Great, really. Just nervous."

"What about?"

I untwist my legs and sit up straight. Taking a deep breath, I ask the one person that I know that's been in a healthy marriage for most of her life with the same man. "How did you know that Daddy was The One? Like, I thought Hayden was, but now I know he wasn't. But how do you know your heart isn't being stupid?"

"You just know."

"Gee, thanks, Mom."

She pats me on the leg. "Are things getting serious with Mr. Landry?"

I nod and her smile widens further. Eventually, a grin tugs at my lips too.

"I really like him. Like, I love him. But I thought I was in love before, and it wasn't love, so what if it isn't this time either? I have Hux now; I can't just go falling in love."

"The fact that you got into a relationship with him in the first place speaks volumes."

"How's that?"

She shrugs. "Look, Ali. You never got involved with anyone seriously since Hayden. Why?"

"Because they weren't good enough for Huxley."

"Exactly. But you let your guard down with Barrett." She takes a deep breath. "You're a fantastic mother. I'm so proud to watch you with Hux and how you put him before anything and everyone. It just fills my heart with so much pride. I'll admit, when I heard you were seeing Barrett, I was a little anxious. He has quite a reputation."

"I know," I laugh.

"But if you trusted him enough to let him around my grandson, then that's enough for me." She considers her next words. "He talks about him. Says he likes him and that he talks to him like he matters."

"He's so good with Huxley," I say, my heart brimming in my chest.

She takes my hand and gives it a squeeze. "You have to trust yourself. Believe in yourself."

"That's what I tell Barrett."

"What?"

"To believe in himself. To know he can do things his way and win."

"Well, smarty-pants, take your own advice. Believe in yourself and believe in him enough to fight alongside him. Did you ever think that maybe no one has believed in him before?"

I roll my eyes. "Of course they have. He's supported by everyone. His entire family turns out to support him."

"Supporting someone and believing in them are two different things, Alison."

I gaze back at the sunset and think about what she said. The longer I mull it over, the more right she seems.

"I'm going to take off," she says.

"We need to leave soon for Huxley's program at school. You sure you don't want to come?"

She sighs. "I wish I could, honey. But your father will be home shortly and I really want to have a hot meal ready for him when he gets in."

"Okay." I watch her walk to the door. "Thanks, Mom. For everything."

"It's what I'm here for."

The door shuts behind her as I curl back up on the sofa. I wonder what life would be like with Barrett. How much of my daily life would change? How would I go about working and going to school if I was living with him?

Could I live with him? Without some sort of guarantee that things would work out? Do I want to be that girl that demands a guarantee?

My anxiety begins to spiral out of control when his name pops up on my phone. I swipe the screen.

"Hey, you," I say.

"Hey, baby. How's your day?"

His voice is gruff and I can hear frustration laced through every syllable. It pings at my heart.

"Good. But how was yours? You sound tired."

He huffs a laugh. "Tired. Pissed off. Frustrated."

"Why?"

"Well, I made a deal with the devil today."

"What do you mean?"

I pull the blanket around me, furrowing my brow. It's not so much the words that bother me, although they're ominous in themselves. It's the tone that he's using, the almost lack of warmth, the void of any sort of energy that has me biting my lip.

"I called Monroe. Made a deal on the Land Bill. It's done."

"Oh, Barrett . . ." My spirits sink to the floor, knowing just how much he didn't want to do this.

"I didn't have a choice," he sighs. "The poll numbers are too tight." He growls into the phone and I want to reach out and pull him into a giant hug.

"Why do you sound like you're trying to convince yourself? Not me?"

He chuckles. "Because that's exactly what I'm trying to do."

"Then why did you do it? Why did you go against what you wanted to do?"

"I had to."

"No, you didn't," I implore. "What you want, what you put your name on, that means something, Barrett. That means more than anything else. You aren't responsible for everyone's lives. People can find jobs. People will find a way to make it and you don't even know for sure if that would even happen."

"You're supposed to make me feel better about this," he laughs sadly.

"I'm not enabling your behavior. I'm not going to sit here and pretend like you did the right thing when I can hear in your voice that you don't think you did."

"I had to," he repeats.

I try to think of how to explain what I feel. It's so hard over the phone, nearly impossible to ascertain what he's thinking without seeing into his eyes.

"You have to start believing in yourself," I say, my voice soft. "Don't you realize how smart you are?"

He snorts, dismissing me. But I continue.

"You are. The people deserve to hear what you think, for you to do what's best for them, not what you think you have to say."

"I wish I could," he mumbles.

We sit for a long while, each of us quiet, each of us processing what he's done. My heart twists for him, hurting that he's in some self-inflicted prison. Finally, just as the back door opens and I hear Huxley rumbling through the fridge, Barrett speaks.

"You know the worst part of all of this?"

"What's that?"

"Hearing the disappointment in your voice."

"Oh, Barrett," I say. "I'm not disappointed in you."

"Yes, you are. I hear it. And if I were there, you'd be looking at me like everyone else looks at me. Like I'm just a fucking idiot for one reason or the other."

"Barrett, that's not true. I'm . . . I'm disappointed that you feel like you have to do things you don't want to do. When you're with me, you're strong, confident. You're happy and funny and kind. And then you go to work and you're still all those things, just with a buffer built around you to make you more . . . I don't know, palatable to the public?"

He takes a deep breath and blows it out steadily. "I need to go catch up on work. I got behind today. Can I call you later?"

"Of course you can," I whisper. "Anytime. I hope you do. I'm worried about you."

A long stretch of silence falls over us, but it's not a lonely type of feeling. It's swollen with a feeling that's so heavy, so comfortable, I can barely breathe.

"Ali?" he rasps.

"Yes, Barrett?"

"I love you," he whispers.

I gasp, the words not at all what I was expecting . . . but everything I'd hoped to hear come from his sweet lips.

He stutters at my reaction and I panic that he's going to recant his declaration before I can get my head together.

"Barrett," I say, interrupting his bobble of a response.

"Yeah?"

"I love you too."

The words sound like a song coming from my mouth, a set of words I was prepared to never utter to a man again. But the fact that I'm saying them and not just willingly, but with my entire heart and without a smidgen of regret, makes my heart sing too.

"You do?" he asks, a tremble in the words.

"I really do."

He laughs a weak, quiet rumble. "Damn it, Alison. I thought you were going to tell me to go fly a kite."

"Only if that kite is going to carry you over here," I breathe. "You just took me by surprise, that's all."

"But was it a good surprise?"

I grin until my cheeks ache. "The best surprise of my life."

# Barrett

THE DEFINITIVE SOUND OF HEELS against the hardwood tells me who just pulled up. The headlights had brushed past my office window, but I couldn't make out the model of the car before it pulled in. When the key was used and the alarm turned off, the possibilities narrowed tremendously. But the heels were a dead giveaway.

"Knock, knock." My mother's voice rings through my office. When I look up, she's standing in the doorway. Wearing a dark purple dress and pearls, she looks like she's sent straight from Central Casting. The perfect mother.

"Hey," I say, sinking back in my chair. "What brings you by this late?"

"Just checking on my eldest. I'm allowed to do that, aren't I?"

"Absolutely," I grin, happy to see her. "Come in."

She strides in the room with her usual grace, just like Camilla and Sienna do. They are beautiful and composed, yet can be lions when necessary. It's what I love most about them. It's what I love about Alison too.

Sliding into a leather chair facing my desk, she looks at me. Her eyes search me the way a mother's do, trying to decide how I am before she asks. "How are you?"

"Been better. Been worse."

"How's the campaign coming along?"

"Almost over."

"You say that like you're happy about it."

I shrug and kind of grimace. I don't even bother trying to hide shit from her. She always knows.

"I'm proud of you. You know that?" she asks and I know to brace myself. She always starts out with a compliment before really getting to what she means. "But this—what you're going through right now—is why I didn't want you in politics, honey."

"It's not terrible."

"And it's not great either. And what I want for you is a *great* life." She sighs and shakes her head, and I feel like a twelve-year-old boy again. "You've done an excellent job as Mayor, and I'd be thrilled for you to do the same things for the people of this state as you've done for the people in Savannah. You've gone up against some serious odds during your terms and you've beaten them all. But you've also managed to not lose yourself in the process and I'm worried that's going to happen." She eyes me curiously. "If it isn't already starting to happen."

She folds her arms and narrows her eyes. "I've watched my father work in this business and I've stood beside your father, through thick and thin, as he navigated this very same thing. None of them were as successful as you in a lot of ways. I like to think it's because you are part me," she teases.

"Probably true."

"You'll get as far as you want to. And I know your daddy pushes you, wants you to succeed in the ways he couldn't. But Barrett, my sweet boy, don't kill yourself for this unless you're sure it's what you want."

"I am sure."

"Are you? Are you really? I used to think so, but now . . . I look at your face tonight and I'm not so positive anymore."

I bury my head in my hands. "I made a deal with Monroe."

"And?"

"And I didn't want to make it. I did it because I thought I had to. But now, I have doubts, and I know it's not one I can follow through on."

"Barrett..."

"I know. But I'm responsible for all of these people that work for me, Mom. I feel obligated to do everything I can to make sure I win so they can feed their families."

"That's Nolan talking—"

"That's *me* talking," I cut her back off. "I have the opportunity in front of me that so many want, and I can do it! If I win this election, I can be in the running for a shot at the White House in a few years. If I don't do this, isn't that just stupid? To just quit on a dream so many have?"

"Not if it isn't *your* dream."

"It *is* my dream," I sigh. "I'm just stressed. I need a drink or something." I stand and walk to my dry bar and pour myself some Scotch.

I hear my mom stand and feel her walk towards me. She places a hand on my shoulder, and I look at her sideways.

"If this is your dream, I will help you achieve it. I will push you, pull you, put on events of every kind to get you to where you want to be. But if it isn't—" She shakes her head as I start to interrupt. "If this is your dad's dream or Nolan's dream or some crazy idea in your head that you have to do this, don't do it, honey. There's so much more to life than campaigns and legislature and politics."

"Is there? For a guy like me, is there?"

"Of course there is," she huffs. "There's happiness and vacations. There's falling in love with a lady, note I said *lady*, and having beautiful grandbabies that I can shop obsessively for." She winks, but I know she's not totally kidding. "You can have a tremendous life, Barrett, and not live in this world. And there's nothing wrong with that. I would be just as proud of you, and your father would deal. Trust me."

My mind starts to go down that path—of weddings and babies and strolls down tiki torch-lit paths, and I shake my head.

"What if I was already in love?" I ask, watching her for a reaction.

Her eyes light up and she places a hand on her hip. "That would make me very happy if it makes you happy."

I can't contain my grin, which makes hers grow wider.

"I'm not going to push. I'll just say that Camilla has met her and told me she's a delightful girl." She looks me over from head to toe before laughing. "This explains a lot."

"What does that mean?"

She shrugs, a grin still tugging at her lips. "You're rounding out, as a man. Thinking things through, considering ramifications for things on a broader scale than you would've before. It's nice to see. Now if we can only get Lincoln there . . ."

I laugh and let her pull me in for a quick hug. "You're making me feel like a little kid."

She squeezes my cheek for effect. "You are my little kid. And that's why I'm here at," she glances at her watch, "eight o'clock in the evening."

"Have you had dinner?" I ask.

"No. Your father is working late tonight with Graham, so I'm on my own. I'll probably just heat up some leftovers from last night."

I glance at the pile of papers on my desk and the four hundred requests in my email. I look back at my mother. "Let's order in. Me and you."

"Really?" she asks, her eyes lighting up.

"Really, Mom. I'd love to have dinner with you."

"I'd like that too."

◆◆◆

## Barrett

THE ANTIQUE GRANDFATHER CLOCK TICKS, reminding me of every second that passes. It feels like a million seconds have ticked by since I made the deal with Monroe yesterday, but, in reality, it's only been a little over twenty-four hours.

I've hated that walnut clock since I was a kid. My mother always said it was her prized possession, an heirloom from her own grandmother. She'd warn us not to toss balls or wrestle in the dining room because of that damn clock. There's a crack in the back of it that she doesn't know about thanks to Lincoln's handiwork.

"You listening to me, son?"

Dad nudges me in the arm and I snap back to the present. We've been going at this for hours. It feels like we're beating a dead horse. We go over every angle of the election frontwards and backwards, and every time, it winds up in the same spot: too close for comfort. On paper, I did the right thing by selling my soul to the devil himself. In reality, I feel less than stellar about it.

"Yeah, I'm listening, Dad."

"Good. So when Monroe endorses you, we'll watch the poll numbers. He should really clinch the north for you. They listen to that son of a bitch for whatever reason."

I nod, swishing the rest of my coffee in my mug. "It's going to be fine. I think it would've been fine anyway."

"I get doing what you need to do in order to win," Lincoln says, his eyes narrowed, "but I think this was a fuck-up."

"Linc, stay out of this," Dad warns.

"You push him and push him to do what you think is right. Has it ever occurred to you for one second that maybe he can make his own decisions?"

"He made the choice," Graham says, looking at Lincoln across the table.

Lincoln laughs. "Him 'making that decision' would be like a coach telling me to swing at the first three pitches without letting me get up there and get a good look at it first. It's asinine."

"We don't have time for baseball metaphors," Graham says, rolling his eyes. "This had to be done. It's not something we can explain to you in a matter of hours. This is not balls and strikes."

"You know what? Fuck you," Lincoln says, but he's not entirely kidding. "I may not know much about politics, but that was by choice. And not knowing shit about that doesn't mean I don't know what a good decision looks like."

I sigh, watching my brothers and father go at it right in front of me. Seeing them at odds over this campaign, the frustration in their eyes, makes me feel horrible.

Pushing away from the table, I stand and look down at my father. I know what I'll look like in another twenty years. I wonder how much I'll resemble him in other ways.

Giving him a tight smile, I nod and walk out. My mother grins at me from the kitchen as I walk by, but doesn't speak. She watches me, her brows pulled together.

Troy is standing outside the front door and pops open the back of the Rover. I slide in and he's in the driver's seat before I know it.

"Where to?" he asks, looking at me through the rearview mirror.

I shrug. Nowhere sounds good. I feel alone, completely fucking alone, and that's where I want to be.

"Just drive."

I don't tell him to take me to her place, but he does anyway. Maybe that means I'm a lost cause or maybe it means he knows me well enough to see what I need. Either way, when the Rover pulls up in front of the little white house, I can't help but feel relieved.

Troy catches my eyes in the rearview mirror.

"Thanks," I say, nodding.

He doesn't respond, just watches me climb out and make my way to the front door. I knock a few quick raps and she pulls it open right away. Her face lights up when she sees me and I step inside and waste no time getting my arms around her.

She buries her head in my chest and plants a kiss on my sternum. "I'm glad you're here," she whispers.

"Me too."

She closes the door behind us and we amble into the living room. I don't let go of her; I need her touch, her presence, to assuage some of the stress rioting through me.

"How are you?" she asks.

"Shitty." I sit down and pull her onto my lap. Nuzzling my face into her hair, I breathe her in and let it comfort me like it always does. "But I'm better at the moment."

"I've been thinking about you all day. You sounded so upset last night. If Hux hadn't been home, I would've come and found you."

"This not being with you all the time, not having you accessible to me, has got to end."

"One thing at a time, okay?" she whispers, kissing my cheek. "I'm here for you whenever you need me. You need to just focus on work for the next few days."

I hold her tight, this precious girl that dropped into my life with a tray of champagne. She has no idea what she means to me or that I need her every minute of every day.

"Can I just hold you right now?" I ask, feeling my nerves settle. "I don't want to think about anything other than what you feel like in my arms."

"Sounds good to me," she says and gets comfortable in my lap.

For the next half hour, I sit on her couch in the outskirts of Savannah and hold the one thing that I'm sure is the right thing.

# 36

## Alison

THE FRONT DOOR OPENS AND I hear my mother's voice. There's something off with the tone, something that has the hair on the back of my neck sticking up.

I put down the brush I'd been running through my hair. Hillary's House today was insane and I was able to get a quick shower in before Mom brought Huxley home from school.

Walking into the hallway, I see them both standing in the foyer. My mom looks as white as a ghost.

"What? What's wrong?" I ask, frozen in place.

"Some guy was taking my picture," Hux declares, like it was no big deal. "Grandma went crazy, Mom. She—"

"What?" I shriek.

Mom takes off her coat and then shrugs it right back on again, physically shivering, even though it's not that cold outside. "I got him off the bus like usual at my house. We started walking up the sidewalk—"

"And this man was in a van with a big camera," Huxley cuts her off. I'm too nervous to even reprimand him for manners.

"What was he doing?" I ask, looking at Mom.

She just nods. "I called the police. The guy took off, but I got his license plate number and they pulled him over a few streets away. He's being held downtown now."

My heart clenches. The room starts spinning. "Oh my God."

Hux's arms are around my waist before I can think. I hold on to him for dear life.

My precious boy, the child that doesn't deserve his privacy to be invaded because of my choices.

Guilt floods me, tears doing the same to my eyes. I feel like a piece of shit mother.

Every bad thing that could've happened today, every terrible thing that still could, sweeps through my mind all at once and I feel like I'm going to pass out. All I can do is hold on to Huxley.

"You wanna know something?" he asks, gazing up at me with his shining eyes.

"What's that?"

"It was kind of cool," he admits.

Shaking my head, I can't help but laugh. "No, it's not."

"It kind of is. They wanted my picture. I feel like a rock star or something."

"You're too young to be a rock star," I point out, trying to ease the fear that's still crippling my heart. "Now go put your bag up and let me figure this out."

He kisses his grandma's cheek and goes into his room, shutting the door softly behind him. I look at my mother.

"Things like this are going to happen," she says. "Barrett is too big of a catch not to think no one is going to pay attention."

"I can't go through this again, Mom. And not with Huxley."

"There are tradeoffs to everything, sweetie. It's up to you to decide what you can and can't handle."

Rubbing my forehead, I lean against the wall. "Think of all the things that could've happened. I don't want his face on a magazine or his name in papers. But . . . what if he tried to kidnap him, Mom?"

A tear trickles down my face at the thought.

"Every child has that risk, Alison. When your baby goes out the door, you run the risk of something tragic happening. It's a part of life."

"But does putting Huxley in the public eye make him more of a target?"

Her response is cut off by my phone ringing. I look down to see that it's Barrett.

"I'm going to go," Mom says. "I need to call the police station back. They'll probably call you too and make sure he's okay. I'll be back in an hour or so to watch Huxley when you go to work."

I nod and let her see herself out while I pick up the call. "Hey," I say.

"Hey, baby," he replies. The sound of his voice soothes me, makes my nerves ease just a bit. "How are you?"

I sigh and he picks up on my mood immediately.

"What's wrong, Alison?"

"Mom just dropped Hux off. Apparently someone was taking his picture today."

"What the fuck?" he booms. "Is he okay?"

"Yeah."

His fury is palpable and knowing he's as angry as I am makes me relieved in a weird way.

"Who was it? Did you call the police?"

"Mom did and the guy is at the station."

"I'm going down there," he bites out.

"No, you aren't. Let them handle it."

He groans through the line, but that's the only sound for a long while. We both seem to be mulling over the situation—him trying to fix it, me trying to absorb it.

"I'll make sure we make an example of him," he breathes, anger laced with every word. "I'll have his name and face ran through the mud every which way. Trust me."

The tears flow again, the fear resurging. I let out a little whimper, and I can hear him on the other end responding.

"Don't cry. I'm coming over there."

The one thing I want more than anything is to be wrapped in his arms. But I need time to think about this, and if he comes over here, he'll just convince me it's all going to be fine . . . and I need to know, by my own standards, that it will.

"I'm sure you have a million things to do," I say instead.

"None of them are as important as this."

My lip quivers. "I appreciate that. But I don't want to make any bigger deal out of this than it already is," I say truthfully. "And if you come over here like some kind of defender, ready to slay the dragon . . ."

"Oh, I'll slay the son of a bitch. That I promise you."

"See?" I laugh. "That's what I mean. Plus, I'm supposed to go to work at Luxor tonight. Don't you have some event or something?"

"Fuck," he hisses.

"See? Just take care of you, and I'll take care of us."

The pause makes me regret my choice of words.

"Barrett?"

He sighs into the line. "I hate that I'm not a part of 'us,' you know?"

"That's not what I meant."

"No, it is. You look at me like I'm separate from you and your son, and that . . . it pisses me off, Alison."

"That's not how I look at it," I retort. "But that is reality, Barrett. You have your thing you're working on, and I have school and a job and a side job and a son. Yes, you are . . . my boyfriend, for a lack of a more suitable word, but that doesn't mean . . ."

"What? That you don't want me around?"

My shoulders slump as I fall onto the sofa, my head going into my hand. "I do want you around. But . . . I just need to process this. My son's photo was taken by some asshole a little bit ago. I need to make sure Huxley is okay. I need to figure out what's going to happen." I take a deep breath.

"I'll send Troy over. He can be your—"

"I don't want Troy here. I can take care of this."

"Damn it, Alison. Let me help you!"

"You do help me. Look at you, ready to jump in and save the day. I love that about you, Barrett. But . . ."

I try to push back the thoughts rippling through my mind. Taking a deep breath, I know I'm going to have to confront the reality that's just smacked me in the face. Glancing at my watch, I realize I don't have a lot of time before I have to either go to Luxor or call off, and I need to talk to Huxley.

"Barrett? I really need to go. I need to talk to Huxley, call the police station, and then decide if I'm going to work tonight or not."

"Why do our lives feel so separate?" His voice is so lonely that it makes my heart hurt. "I want to take you with me tonight. I want to be able to see Huxley and make sure he's okay too."

"He will be. I'll make sure of it," I whisper. "I'll tell him you asked about him."

"I'll call you later?"

The way he asks it instead of states it hurts.

"Yes. Please call me later."

"Okay. Talk to you soon, baby."

"Bye, Barrett."

# 37

## Alison

"YOU'RE SURE YOU'RE OKAY? ARE you worried or scared or—"

"I'm fine, Mom," Hux replies, rolling his eyes awhile later. "I'm not a baby. And the guy just took my picture. You're kind of making a big deal out of this."

I mess with his hair as he ducks away, his nose buried in the book he's reading. "They arrested the guy. He's in a lot of trouble."

He doesn't act like he even cares.

"If you want me to stay home tonight, I will."

He peers at me over his book with a smile on his lips. "Will you please go so I can read in peace?"

"It's a good thing you're cute," I laugh, lifting up from his bed. "Grandma will take you to her house in a little bit, okay?"

He nods but doesn't look up. Laughing and saying a prayer of thanks that he doesn't seem to mind the drama of the day, I head into the kitchen. My mom looks at me from the kitchen table.

"You okay?" she asks.

I shrug. "I think so. Hux seems okay about it. I just . . . this is what I was afraid of, you know?"

"I do. That's because you're a good mom and you want to protect your boy. But you can't protect him from everything, Alison."

"I know that," I scoff. "But am I asking for trouble? Am I putting him in a position I'll regret?"

She crosses her arms over her pale green sweater and tilts her head. "Do you feel like you regret this?"

I start to tell her I don't know, that I haven't had time to think it through, that my head is still spinning like a top and I don't know what in the world is going on, but my phone rings.

It's Barrett.

"Hey," I say, holding it to my ear.

"I need to talk to you."

"Okay," I say, shooting my mom a look and leaving the room. "What's up?"

"First, how's Huxley?"

I smile. "He's fine. Acts like a little champion."

"Good," he says, blowing out a breath. "I have this fucking Gala tonight and I have a million things to do before then. But there's a story that will probably be breaking sometime tonight or tomorrow, and I wanted you to hear it from me."

I force a swallow past the lump the size of an avocado in my throat.

*This day just gets better.*

My hand grasps the back of a chair and I brace myself. "What kind of story?"

Something bangs in the background, possibly a glass on a table. My brain focuses on it instead of his words because it's easier to digest. "There's *another* girl saying she's pregnant by me."

"What?" I yelp, my chest caving in, the room spinning.

"It's not mine, Alison."

"Are you sure? Who is she? I. . . ."

"Her name is Lacy McKay, a girl I used to see off and on. I haven't been with her in months, so this baby isn't mine." His voice is so cool, so clinical, that I don't know how to process it.

I fall onto the sofa, squeezing my eyes shut. Taking a deep breath and blowing it out, all I can do is laugh a sad, resigned chuckle.

"This is an easy fix," he hisses. "I'll take a paternity test when the kid gets here and prove it isn't mine."

"But until then? What if it is?"

"Alison—it's not. She asked for a sizable check this afternoon. She just wants money."

"What are you going to do?"

"I'm not paying her for shit because it's garbage. What can she do? Go to the tabloids? And then what? Find out the baby's not mine when it's born and she'll look like the bitch she really is?"

I try to clear my head and keep my wits about me when I really want to run into my room and cry. My life a few hours ago was exactly where I wanted it to be. How quickly things can change.

He blows out a breath. "Look, she doesn't think I'll call her bluff. She thinks I'll pay her off and she can ride into the sunset *or* I will profess my undying love to her. I don't know. But neither option is happening."

"Oh, Barrett," I say, feeling sick. "I'm so sorry."

"Me fucking too." He clears his throat, his voice softening but not losing the sharpness. "I have to go get ready for this thing. Can I call you tonight? It'll be late. This thing goes on for fucking ever."

"Yeah. Sure. I'm working at Luxor 'til nine or so, then I'll be home."

He doesn't try to convince me not to go to work, he doesn't tell me to be careful or to think of him like he usually does. Instead, he takes a deep breath and says, "I'll call you later, babe."

"Okay. Try to have a good night, Barrett."

And the line goes dead.

THE LATE AFTERNOON SUN HAS lost its warmth as I pull into the parking lot of the location of tonight's catering job. Luxor's vans are parked by the curb and I spot Lola's car in the back of the lot by Isaac's. I pull in beside her, get out, and walk briskly to the back door.

This afternoon has thrown me for a loop. I hate this nagging feeling in the pit of my stomach that everything is falling apart, that things aren't capable of ending well. It just drums up so many bad feelings that I find myself wanting to vomit every few minutes.

"Mrs. Baker, did you see photos on Malarky's website? Did you see your husband snorting cocaine off a prostitute's tits?"

"Mommy, why did Daddy leave us? Doesn't he love me anymore?"

"You're a worthless piece of shit, Alison. You have nothing to offer a man like me."

My stomach rolls right along with the memories.

I walk around the side of the van and stop dead in my tracks. A woman is standing on the curb, a Cheshire cat-like smile carved on her glossy lips. She's beautiful—tanned skin and long, blonde hair. When she sees me, she turns to face me.

"You're Alison, aren't you?" she asks.

The disdain is undeniable in her tone, poison leaking off of each syllable. I throw my shoulders back and take a deep breath. "Yes, I am."

Keeping my head up, I quicken my pace, but she steps in front of me.

"I'm Lacy McKay," she voices, loud enough so that I can't pretend I didn't hear her. "I thought we should meet."

The air around us changes, sweeps from a normal fall evening to one of a horror movie. She can tell I know who she is because she smirks. That one little movement in the right corner of her lips changes everything.

"I don't see why." I'm stopped, unable to go forward without physically running into her, and I'm not giving her that. I narrow my eyes right along with hers.

She laughs a high-pitched squeak that makes me cringe. "Oh, honey, don't act like you don't know who I am." Her palm presses flat against her stomach, her eyes narrowing. "And that I'm having Barrett's baby. You did know that, right?"

Even though I knew this was coming and I know it's false, or that Barrett says it's false, still, it knocks the wind out of me. The thought of the possibility of Barrett's child in her stomach makes my entire body shiver, my entire self ready to come out of my skin.

I hate the smug look on her face. I loathe the entire concept behind this. I abhor being in this situation to begin with.

Still, I can't let her win. "Oh, *honey*," I say, giving her words back to her, "you can't get pregnant from fucking him in your dreams."

Her mouth drops open, and I soak up the small victory. She gets herself together much more quickly than I anticipate. "No, but you can get pregnant when he fucks you on his desk in the Mayor's office, can't you?" She takes another step closer, looking down at me from the good two inches she has on me. "It's just as well that you know now and can leave him before all of this comes out. He's never going to be with you anyway. I mean, shouldn't that be obvious to you by now? You're going into work," she says, making a face, *"in there.* If he were serious about you—"

"If he were serious about *you*," I bite out, "you wouldn't be in my face tonight."

She takes a step towards me, her breath hot on my face. "Guess where he is right now."

"Working, just like I need to be," I say, trying to take a step around her. "Now if you'll take your pathetic ass out of my way . . ."

She blocks my path. "He's with Daphne Monroe."

The pleasure she gets in informing me of this isn't lost on me. Her pupils shine with absolute delight.

I try to temper my reaction, not let my features show the surprise I feel, the blip of shock that's sitting right in the center of my core. "If that were true—"

"Oh, it's true," she snickers. "Pull it up online. It's her on his arm in front of the city tonight. Not. You."

I make myself laugh, even though I don't feel anything of the sort. But I want to make her feel stupid . . . and me feel stronger. "Well, it's not you either. So that makes you, what? At least number three on his list and you're supposedly *carrying his child*. What's that say about you?"

"You little . . ." She huffs a breath, her eyes blazing. "You think your shit doesn't stink, don't you?"

"Nice imagery," I snort. "Very classy. Now if you'll excuse me . . ."

As I'm walking around her, she grabs my shoulder. It throws me off balance and I stumble, just as her hand smacks me across the face.

"Ah!" I yelp, my cheek stinging from the contact. I turn quickly only to see her falling into the van behind her.

"You hit me!" she screams, her voice piercing the autumn air. "Someone help me!"

I can't move, frozen in place by the unbelievability of the situation. Shock stiffens my body, even though my brain tells me to run. I feel a hand on my arm, men's voices speaking, and my body being guided into the building.

The cool air hits my face, and I regain my bearings enough to see Lola running at me. Isaac is standing next to me, his arm on mine.

"Are ya okay?" he asks, his large brown eyes searching mine.

"I . . . I think," I stumble, my arms stretching for Lola. Collapsing into her, hearing her shout directions at Isaac and then to Mr. Pickner, the tears flow freely. All of the emotion of the day pours out of me with reckless abandon.

"What happened out there?" Mr. Pickner bellows.

"Some girl attacked her," Isaac says.

My face is buried in Lola's shirt, soaking it. She pats my hair and holds me tight.

"Shit," my boss hisses. "We don't need this kind of publicity."

"Are you seriously worried about *that* right now?" Lola barks. "She's a mess!"

"*She* is not my problem. My business is. I don't need a bunch of fucking camera trucks here wanting to get the scoop on the Mayor's fuck buddy."

"I can't believe you," Lola gasps. "What kind of man are you?"

"Not much of one," Isaac chips in from behind me. "You call her something like that again, and you'll be picking yourself up off the floor. You got it?"

"Is this over your boyfriend?" Mr. Pickner asks, scowling.

"My . . . what?" I ask, lifting my face and drying my eyes with the end of my shirt. I feel like I've been beaten with a whip and it has nothing to do with Ms. Third Place out there. The toll of the day, this life, has gotten to me. And I feel it everywhere.

"This spectacle you just caused—was it over Landry?"

His eyes are cool, his jaw set hard. He watches me with contempt, and I thank God I'm not alone with him because I don't trust him. Not at all.

"Yes," I sniffle.

His head shakes subtly, his eyes narrowing. "I'm going to suggest you give me your notice and get the hell out of here. If anyone asks, you were coming in tonight to quit."

"What?" I say, standing straight. "I need this job! I don't want to quit."

"You are a liability to me, Alison. Think of how this will look for me, won't you?" He chuckles. "Think about how *that*," he bites out, nodding through the door, "will look for Landry. Do you think that's going to help his public image?"

The realization of the words pummels me. My hand shakes as Lola takes it in hers.

"What Landry will care about, Pickner, is that you just fired her for no reason. I wouldn't want to be you when shit hits the fan."

He shrugs. "If you could please escort her out of here, I'd appreciate it."

"You can take your party tonight and shove it straight up your sweaty ass-crack," Lola fires back.

"You know what," Isaac says, looking down at our boss. "Lola and I will walk her out and neither of us will be back in. And you can bet when I'm interviewed about what happened out there tonight, I'll make sure I tell everyone what happened in here as well."

"Isaac . . ."

"Fuck you, Jim," Isaac says, wrapping his arm around my shoulders. "May God be with you when Landry finds out what you've said tonight." He looks down at me and smiles kindly. "Let's get out of here."

I look around his shoulder to see if anyone is on the sidewalk, but it's clear. I sigh a breath of relief.

Isaac smiles so sweetly, yet with a touch of ferocity, that I nearly kiss him. "Thanks, Isaac."

"Anytime. Now let's get you home in one piece."

## Alison

THE WATER IS COOL AS I splash it on my face. I pump some soap on my hands and wash off the make-up from what was supposed to be a night at work and clean everything away.

I just wish the memories were that easy to remove too.

Lola stands in the doorway of my bathroom and watches me. "Should we file a police report or something?"

"I don't know," I groan, patting my face dry. It feels swollen from the tears I cried as Lola drove me home. "I have no fucking idea what to do."

"Isaac saw everything. He said he ran across the parking lot to get to you as quickly as he could."

"Where is he now?" I ask, knowing he drove Lola's car behind us.

"I asked him to wait outside. I thought you'd need some privacy."

My shoulders ache, my head throbs, and all I want to do is go to bed and cry myself to sleep. There's so much to process, to think through, that I don't even know where to begin.

"What did she say to you?" Lola asks.

"That Barrett was with Daphne tonight," I say simply, trying to wrap my mind around it.

"That makes sense though," Lola says.

"And that she's pregnant with his baby," I mutter.

"What the ever-loving fuck?"

"He told me she was making a claim. He says it's not true."

"Oh, it better not be true!"

I nod, closing my eyes. As soon as I do, vivid memories of being surrounded by cameras in New Mexico, accusations being shouted, slam into me and I feel like I can't breathe.

Lola takes my arm and helps me to the sofa where I sit and try not to hyperventilate.

"You're having a panic attack, I think," she says, handing me a cool washcloth. "Here. Put this on your head or something."

"Did you guys seriously just quit for me?" I ask, fighting the rise in panic. Guilt starts to take over, adding to the panic and I struggle to sit up, but Lola puts a hand on my shoulder.

"We did. But that's nothing for you to worry about. Odds are he'll be calling us to come back to work by next week and we'll just demand a raise," she winks.

I'm not sure if that's true or not, but I choose to go with it. I need the reprieve from one of the burdens on me right now.

"I do think maybe you need to call the police," she says. "Just to be sure."

"But do I want to even bring them into it? I mean, that puts it on record." I lean my head back and place the washcloth on my face. "If I ignore it, maybe she will too."

Lola thinks about it, popping a piece of gum in her mouth. "I think you should try to get ahold of Barrett."

"He's at that event. With Daphne." The thought rolls my stomach, makes bile rise quickly. "I probably can't get him anyway."

"Try it. I really think you should. Someone in his campaign needs to know what happened in case he's asked about it. You know how fast word travels, Ali. Be smart. Use your head, not your heart."

I sit up, knowing she's right and feeling stupid not thinking about it sooner. I grab my phone and dial Barrett. It rings three times before it's answered. My heart leaps in my chest as I wait for him to speak.

"Hello?" a voice asks, but it's not Barrett. I pull the phone away from my face to make sure I've dialed the right number.

"I'm trying to find Barrett Landry. This is Alison Baker."

"He's occupied right now, Ms. Baker," a man says.

"There's no way I can speak with him?"

"No, there isn't. He's in the Garalent Gala with Ms. Monroe right now. I believe they're eating dinner as we speak."

"I . . ." I'm thrown for a loop, not expecting that. "Who am I talking to?"

"I'm sorry. This is Nolan, Mr. Landry's Chief-of-Staff. I apologize for my lack of manners this evening."

"Can you tell Barrett I called?" I squeak. I don't feel comfortable with this guy, not comfortable enough to tell him about my night or clue him into anything. Something's wrong, I feel it.

"I wanted to talk to you anyway, Ms. Baker, and thank you for doing your part in this campaign. You've done a splendid job, more than I ever expected."

"Excuse me?"

"Not many women would've been up for the challenge of playing the part of the Mayor's girlfriend like you have. It's benefitted his campaign immensely to look like a benefactor to you and your kid. You've helped us fortify his reputation, and I can't thank you enough. You can be assured we'll cut you a check for your services once the campaign is over."

Tears hit my eyes again, his words echoing Daphne's. I feel so used, that everything has been dual-purpose because I do believe Barrett likes me. But was this angle factored into it?

The tears fall harder after I look up at the television screen that Lola has just turned on. Barrett is on the screen, looking devilishly handsome in a navy suit and deep red and white tie. And beside him, looking as regal as the mayor himself, is Daphne Monroe.

She tilts her head to the side, her arm around his waist, and flashes him a wide smile. I can't see his face from that angle, but the display is enough to make me sick.

I don't respond to Nolan. I can't. I just end the call and run to the bathroom hoping to make it before I vomit on the floor.

# Barrett

MY FACE HURTS FROM THE pseudo-smile plastered across my cheeks. I don't let it slip despite the discomfort because if I allow a crack in the veneer, I know I won't be able to get it back. Although I've had to fake it a million times before, I've never had to put it on like this.

A man that's been waiting to talk to me for over an hour finally makes his way to my table. My food is untouched, my wine still full, as I gather my wits to entertain another possible voter.

Every part of me wants to leave, not a single thread of entertainment or desire to be here exists. I typically enjoy these little events. But not tonight.

Tonight I want to be at a little house across town, sitting on a tattered sofa in sweatpants, making sure Huxley is okay. I want my arm wrapped around Alison, my eyes on Hux as he sits on the little black beanbag chair in the corner he loves, and ensure that they are well and happy. Instead, I'm sitting at this ridiculous event waiting on the bald-headed man to approach my table.

"How are you, Mr. Landry?" he asks, extending his hand. We shake and I steady my features.

"Good, thank you. How are you?"

He begins chatting away about a project important to his district, just like everyone does. I try to zero in on what he's saying, gather a fuck or two, but when Daphne's arm lies against my shoulder and I hear her high-pitched laugh beside me, all my efforts dissolve.

My head feels like it's going to explode and I scan the room for Nolan. Every minute that passes, every second that ticks, is another moment I've gone through this charade.

Looking at Daphne by my side, not Alison, it swamps me how ridiculous this is. How ridiculous *I am. Is this what I've turned out to be?*

"If you can excuse me," I say to baldy, "I have something I need to take care of."

"No worries, Mayor. I just wanted to extend my congratulations on a job well done. Savannah will hate to lose you to the state, but it's with pride we watch you go."

I chuckle, pushing back my seat. "Nothing's definite yet."

"It will be, especially after that glowing endorsement from Monroe tonight," he grins. "You're a superstar waiting to happen on the national scale, Landry. Such a man to do things your way and not let the actual politics change you. It's an honor to support you."

My gaze follows him, my breathing strangled, as I watch him walk away. If he only knew how much of what he said isn't true.

Daphne's touch brings me back to the present. When I look at her, she's watching me with her sweetest smile.

"Need me to accompany you?" she asks, batting her eyelashes.

"Yes, actually," I say, taking her hand and helping her to her feet. "Let's get out of here. I've had enough of this for one night."

Her grin tells me she completely misunderstands my point, but I'm not setting her straight here, not in front of everyone.

We head through the venue, stopping briefly to shake a hand every few feet, until I spot Nolan against the wall. He quirks a brow.

"We're getting out of here," I say, motioning at Daphne.

Nolan stands. "Typically, I'd hate for you to bow out of an event early, but considering the circumstances . . ." He reaches in his pocket and pulls out my cell. "Here you go. Have an enjoyable night."

I immediately press the power button on my phone and go straight to my texts and shoot one to Troy to pick me up.

A scorching anger starts to boil in my gut, the feeling I've been trying to contain all night threatening to spill over.

"You are both complete assholes for setting this up," I fire to the two of them, my voice a little louder than I would like.

"No," Daphne fires back, "we remember who you are. We haven't forgotten all the things that are important to you because we aren't brainwashed by some piece of ass."

"Daphne, shut up," I hiss. Turning to my manager, I shoot him an icy glare. "I will call you tomorrow to discuss this."

He just grins. "Well, I happen to side with Ms. Monroe. You might not have liked our tactics, but this worked. Did you see the reception of the two of you? How well you were received tonight? You play off each other seamlessly, and tonight was just what we needed. It was priceless, Barrett."

Clenching my teeth, I say, "It might've fucking worked for whatever scheme you were trying to play. But God as my witness, Nolan, this conversation isn't over. I'm just not having it here."

Grabbing Daphne's hand, I guide her to the front door as hastily as possible. I don't want to take her with me, but I sure as shit can't leave her here. That would look bad and who knows what she'd do or say.

Fuck these people and fuck this day.

It's time I step to the plate and swing.

◆◆◆

## Barrett

THE ROVER PULLS INTO DAPHNE'S driveway in half the time it should've taken. I didn't need to say anything to Troy; the look in my eye must've said it all.

The sky is dark, but the glow from the lights inside the SUV allows me to see Daphne's eyes. She peers at me, a wicked grin on her face. "I wondered how long it would take you to bring me home. Want to take bets on how long it takes you to get this dress off me? Hell, Barrett. I might just bend over and let you get inside me from behind. I need you, sugar."

I run my hand through my hair. I knew this moment was coming and the argument coming up isn't one I can avoid. Not any longer. No matter what it does to my campaign or our friendship, the act is over. "Daphne, that's not going to happen."

She eyes me curiously and pulls back to get a better look. "Are you sure?" Her words are cocky, a challenge, letting me know that the choice I'm making will affect more than her ass . . . it'll affect my career.

She's playing with fire. She thinks she can strong arm me into doing what she wants—her. What she failed to realize is that I'm past the point of giving a shit about her or my career. I just need Ali.

"I'm absolutely sure," I say, keeping my voice level.

Her grin turns into a smirk. "Is this about *the girl?*"

"*The girl* has a name," I bite out. "But it doesn't matter."

"Oh, it *does* matter. It matters a lot, and I'm sure you understand that."

"Daphne . . ."

"I've given you the benefit of the doubt to get your act together, to stop trying to . . . look like one of them or whatever you're doing," she huffs, rolling her eyes. "But if I go inside, *alone*, I'm going to have a lot of time on my hands . . ."

My jaw drops to the floor. "Are you threatening me?"

I lean away from her, almost not believing what I'm hearing. This is Daphne. The Daphne I fuck because she knows how this shit works. And she's turning on me? I knew she was a loose cannon, but not like this.

"If you fuck up, my father *will* expose everything you've ever done. Remember—I know more about you than nearly anyone. And going down this path, the one of, you know, turning me down for a cheap piece of ass—"

"Shut your fucking mouth," I say, catching Troy's glance in the rearview mirror, but I don't give a shit about his warning. Daphne has crossed a line. "Don't ever talk about her like that. Don't talk about her at all. You know nothing about her."

She smirks, her head held high. "This is fucking up, Barrett. You might've gotten Daddy's endorsement tonight, but don't think that will necessarily hold. One little call . . ." She presses her lips together in a pout, like a child wanting a new toy. It's disgusting.

"You aren't serious right now, Daph."

She shrugs, her hand on the knob. "I know how these things work. Remember that, Barrett. I'm not some random chick you're fucking. Just keep in mind I'm not as stupid as you may think. I've been biding my time and making friends on the side. Just consider who I know and who's in my pocket . . . and what I'm capable of."

"What are you even talking about? Why would you do this?"

"I'd do this because I, too, have things I want to accomplish in my life. And I thought we were on the same page. But you're running around with trash now—"

"At the moment," I say, giving her a heavy once over, "I'd have to agree."

She laughs, her high-pitched trill making my skin crawl. "Fuck you, Barrett."

"Let's not forget," I burn, forcing myself to breathe, "that I know a few of your secrets too. I may even have a few pictures somewhere of you with a white little powder lining your nostrils . . ."

Her eyes dart around the car before landing on me, her knuckles turning white as she squeezes her fists. "You wouldn't dare."

"I wouldn't be able to help it if my phone landed in the wrong hands and those photos ended up public." I scratch at my chin in faux-thought. "I seem to remember a few, well, we could call them selfies, I suppose, that you sent me from a bathtub . . ."

"Don't you dare!"

"Then get the fuck out of my car and forget my name. Got it?"

She opens the door herself and slams it behind her.

Troy looks at me over his shoulder and, after one quick glance, he speeds us away from Daphne's house.

## Alison

*Lola: I can go with you.*

HER TEXT IS SIMPLE. AND I know she means it. She would be here in a second with her bags packed and ready to go if I wanted her to.

But this isn't a girl's weekend away. This is me trying to find some space to breathe without things coming at me from every direction. Between Huxley's photographer situation, Barrett being with Daphne, Lacy finding me at work and then losing my job on top of it, I'm just simply overwhelmed.

I'm not sure what will happen if the incident at Luxor goes to the press. Will they be here, camping out on my doorstep like before? It's not something I want to risk.

I just want to sort this all out somewhere safe and quiet and away from anyone that would have any input into my decisions. Whatever I decide has to come from me with no influence.

Quickly, I type back a message to Lo.

> *Me: I know you would. It just makes more sense right now to leave . . . him? I feel like this is all boiling down and I just need to get away.*

She responds right away.

*Lola: Just don't boil down with it.*

I leave a voice message for my mother, letting her know I'm fine and that we're taking a little getaway for the weekend. Trying to keep it light, I don't tell her about anything that happened. There's no need to worry her too. Lola went by and grabbed Huxley for me so she didn't have to see me crying.

My phone alerts me that the battery is dying as I slide it in my pocket and lock the door. I join Huxley in the car.

"Did you get everything?" I ask, starting it up and backing down the driveway.

"Yup. I guess. I mean, I don't know where we're going, so it's hard to know for sure."

"Well, where do you want to go?" I ask, taking off down the street.

He shrugs and looks at me from beneath his Arrows cap. "Why are we leaving, Mom? Did something happen?"

I pat his leg and give him my best smile. "No, baby. I just thought, you know, me and you could get away and have some fun for a couple of days."

"All right."

He hums along to the radio, watching the trees go by. I try to pay attention to the road and not let my mind get carried away. My head is throbbing from being sick and crying, my throat still raw. My nerves are completely frayed as we get farther out of town.

After a half hour, Hux looks at me, his eyes serious. "Mom?"

"Yeah, baby?"

"I know you've been crying."

My heart breaks at the worry in his eyes, the one thing I try desperately to never let him feel. I want him to grow up confident, knowing everything is okay. Not worrying about adult problems until he's an adult, and if I can keep him from it then, I know I will. Huxley is my life, comes before anything in my world, and the look on his face destroys me.

"Girls cry sometimes, Hux. You know that." I try to laugh and play it off, but he doesn't bite.

"I know. The girls in my class cry all the time about really stupid stuff. But you're not just a girl. You're my mom. You're tough. So if you cry . . . maybe I should worry."

"No, you shouldn't," I say. "Because no matter what happens, as long as I have you, everything will be okay."

He tilts his little head. "Did you have a fight with Barrett?"

"Not really. It's not anything you need to worry about, okay?"

"You don't have anyone else to worry about you. When I'm sick or sad, you take care of me. Who takes care of you?"

His words nearly bring fresh tears to my eyes. I fight them back, but it takes everything I have.

"I'm fine, Hux."

"Is this about the man with the camera? Because if it is, I'm fine, Mom."

Luckily, my phone ringing distracts the conversation. But when I pull it out of my pocket, I see Lincoln's name.

I only have a few percent left on my phone, so I answer it, figuring I can't get trapped into anything big. But I want to know if something has happened over the girl at Luxor, so I answer.

"Hello?"

"Where are you?" Linc asks.

"Driving. Is everything okay?"

"Where are you though? Specifically?"

"I don't know," I say, looking around. "Why? What's happening?"

He sighs. "For one, I'm standing on your porch and you aren't here."

"I already told you that."

"For two, Graham just got a call that you were involved in some altercation at work tonight. We wanted to make sure you were okay before we tell Barrett because he's going to go ape-shit when he finds out."

My spirits sink and I want to close my eyes and rest them, quiet the pounding in my skull, but I can't.

Huxley watches me from the other seat, not missing a thing. I have to choose my words carefully so I don't panic him.

"There was a little thing," I admit carefully. "I hope it's not causing you any issues."

"Is Huxley right there? Is that why you aren't answering me?"

"Yes."

"But you're okay? You aren't physically harmed or anything, right?"

"No."

"Did you fill out a police report?"

"No. I called Barrett to tell him, but . . ."

"But what?" he asks ominously.

"Nolan answered."

He exhales harshly and I know he too is choosing his words. "Did he fuck with you? I hate that son of a bitch."

I don't answer him. I can't say it out loud in front of Huxley, and I don't really want to hear the words ringing in the air myself again anyway.

"Ali?"

"He had things to say, yes, that I didn't expect."

"That fucker. That motherfucker. What did he say?"

"I. . . . really don't want to talk about it," I gulp.

"Where are you?" he asks, his voice taking on a level of authority I've never heard out of Lincoln. It's so reminiscent of Barrett that it makes my heart hurt. "I'm coming after you."

"No, you aren't. I'm taking Hux out of town for the weekend."

"Alison . . ." he sighs. "Barrett had no idea Daphne was going to be walking with him tonight at the Gala—"

My laughter, a sad, heavy chuckle, stops him.

"That's not even the biggest issue, Linc."

"What the fuck does that mean?"

"It means . . . it means that I'm overwhelmed and I need some space, okay?"

"No, no, it's not," he huffs. "Barrett left the event early because he wanted to find you, realizing what it probably looked like, especially on the heels of the baby thing earlier today. And when he finds out about the incident with you . . ."

I take a deep breath and hold tight to my guns. If I go back now,

I'm setting myself up for heartbreak. How do I know the thing with Lacy tonight doesn't just make Barrett feel bad? Maybe they want to spin that to make Barrett look better in the media too?

I can't back down. Not until I know for sure.

"Let him know I'm fine and that I'm not necessarily running from him," I say, gauging Huxley's response out of the corner of my eye. "I'm just overwhelmed right now, and I feel like I need to take Hux and just settle down."

"My brother loves you. I've never seen him like this about anyone. He's always been pretty hedonistic, to tell you the truth, and right now, all he's thinking about is you."

I fight back the tears again. "Well, if that's true, it will work out," I sniffle. "Just tell him I'll be back after the election and we can talk then. My phone is dying, Linc . . ."

"Ali, wait."

The line goes dead.

## Barrett

I PACE BACK AND FORTH across the living room of the Farm, my phone in my hand. I wish I had spent more time paying attention to her work schedule.

No, I wish I would've made her not fucking go to work tonight. I should've been *me*, the man I feel like when I'm with her. I should've taken charge, protected her, made her realize she's the most important thing to me in the world.

I should've been her man.

*Fuck!*

"Why is Alison not answering my calls?" I ask Graham.

"How do I know? She's not my girlfriend."

I stop in my tracks, ready to fire off some hasty comment when Lincoln clears his throat. Turning to look at him, he's sitting at the desk in the corner, facing the computer, his brows pulled together. He looks over his shoulder at us.

"Hey, who was here today?" he asks.

"I don't know. Why?"

"Humor me."

I blow out a breath, frustrated. "Dad. Nolan was here for a while with Rose, I think. Maybe Camilla?"

He nods his head, his bottom lip between his teeth, and flashes Graham a look before going back to checking sports scores or whatever he was doing.

"I need to talk to you for a second," Graham says, getting my attention.

"I'm here," I shrug, getting impatient. "Talk."

He lifts off the chair and squares his shoulders to mine. "Alison went to work tonight and there was an incident."

"Define incident," I growl, a chill tearing through every cell in my body.

"She was attacked."

"What?" I bellow. "Is she all right? Why am I just finding this out?"

"She's fine," Graham says. "There was a witness, a guy she works with and I've been talking with him off and on all night. He's filing a witness report now in case something happens. He saw it all." He thinks a second before speaking again. "He volunteered to answer any questions you might have."

"Alison is okay though, right?" I say, taking a step towards Graham. My heart is beating out of control. I knew something was wrong tonight. I felt it. Motherfucker, I knew it and I should've been with her or had her with me. *Fuck!*

"She's okay. Really. She . . . um . . ." Graham winces. "She was attacked by Lacy McKay."

"What!?" I boom.

"We don't know what was said," Graham says. "We just know what Isaac, the guy she works with, saw. And that was Lacy slapping her and then claiming Alison hit her back. But she didn't."

"Fuck," I hiss, grabbing my phone again to see if she's responded yet. "I need to see her. I need to be with her. Where's Troy? I need to get to her house."

"I'm sorry, Barrett. She's not there," Graham says simply.

"Where is she?"

"Hey, guys," Linc interrupts loudly. "You're gonna want to see this."

"Not now, Linc," Graham warns.

"Trust me."

"Lincoln, no one gives a fuck about golf scores, all right?"

He casts an angry look our way. "Okay, how about this? Does this get your attention?" He bends closer to the computer screen. "*I'll wire you another five thousand this morning. If Barrett pushes back about the pregnancy, we'll come up with fake ultrasounds. Don't be bothered by that. We've talked to Lacy and she's on board, ready to see this thing out until the very end.*"

"What the fuck is that?" I say, racing to the desk. I've broken out in a cold sweat, my stomach churning, as Graham and I look at the screen. Emails upon emails from a web-based account under Nolan's name. "Oh my God."

"It gets better," Linc says. He clicks another message.

"*Release the info about Baker. That should shake him up. Maybe it'll make him withdraw altogether.*"

Graham takes the mouse and clicks another message.

"*I'm having him tailed. As soon as we can get a decent shot of the girl, I'll have it sent anonymously to the media. Just play it cool, be supportive. I have a guy that's going to take some pics of the kid. Maybe that'll make him rethink this. Talk soon. Hobbs.*"

I step back, my hands shaking at my sides. My brothers watch me and I can see the fury in their eyes that I feel in mine.

"That son of a bitch," I growl.

"Why would he do this?" Graham mutters, shaking his head.

Lincoln stands and faces me. "Because he's a sneaky bastard. I told you not to trust him."

"I'm going to kill him." I grab my phone and send a quick text to Troy to come get me. I need to find Alison, find Nolan, do a million fucking things, and I don't know where to start.

My head snaps up as I listen to the front door open and my father's voice trickle down the hall. Graham, Linc, and I all look at each other, anger drifting between us all.

"That's true, Harris," I hear Nolan saying. "We just keep pressing forward. It'll all work out."

"What will work out?" Graham says as they turn the corner.

Dad looks around the room, obviously reading the mood correctly. It's not lost on Nolan either. He pales and takes a step back.

"Apparently Nolan talked to Alison tonight," Lincoln says, taking charge. He comes up next to me and stands shoulder to shoulder with Graham and I. Lincoln's voice is eerily calm and it sends a chill through me. "Want to tell us about that?"

I want to charge ahead, rip him a new asshole, but I can't. I'm frozen to the spot, unable to process everything that just happened.

My manager balks at Lincoln's question. "I just answered your phone and let her know you were unable to speak at the moment."

"Nah, Nolan, I don't think that was all that happened," Linc dismisses him.

"*He* talked to Alison?" I ask in disbelief. "What did he say?" I drag my gaze from Nolan to my brother, feeling my blood turn to ice. "Tell me, Linc."

A silence descends on the room.

"Nolan, what did you say to her?" my father asks his long-time friend.

He throws his hands up in the air. "I told her he was busy and that's what politician's lives are like."

Linc pops his knuckles beside me. "Nah, Nolan, I don't think that's all you had to say."

I take a step towards Nolan, but Linc grabs my arm.

"Linc was just online," Graham says, glancing at our father. "And he found something interesting."

"Like what?" Dad asks, setting his jaw. "What's going on in here, boys?"

"You want to tell me why you've been emailing Hobbs?" I look

Nolan in the eye and his face goes white. "I'd love to hear why you are talking about fake pregnancy tests and leaking pictures to the press. Come on, Nolan," I chuckle, the sound laced with fury, "I wanna hear it. Tell me. And if you had anything to do with Huxley being followed or her being fucked with by Lacy, I'm going to rip you into pieces so small they'll never put you back together. Do you understand what I'm saying?"

My dad spins on his heel and his jaw drops. "Nolan? What are they talking about?"

"I . . ." He grabs for the doorframe as Graham takes a step towards him. "I . . ." He stutters again, his eyes searching us for the weakest link. He lands on my father. "I was trying to make sure that Land Bill doesn't get passed. You know what that would do to you, Harris. He won't listen. He—"

"No," Graham corrects him, his tone as cool as a cucumber. "What I think you were doing was trying to implode Barrett's campaign. But why? I can't figure that out."

Nolan doesn't answer, just watches Graham move another step closer.

"Did you think we wouldn't find out? Did you think you'd get away with this?"

Graham's questions seem to break Nolan's stress, dissolve the last hanging shred of composure. He faces Graham head-on.

"How do you sit back and watch them build him up," Nolan asks, nodding at me. "You should be the candidate. You're the intelligent one, the one that will listen to logic . . ."

Graham smiles, but it's disingenuous. "So you decided to make sure he wouldn't win? Because you think he doesn't deserve it?"

Nolan relaxes a bit, tricked by Graham's easy tone. "No, *he* made sure he won't win. He won't listen. All of a sudden, he decides he wants to grow a damn conscience, and it's going to cost him the election! Then what?" He swings around to face my father whose eyes are bulging in disbelief. "I'll tell you what," Nolan growls, "I'll be out of a job! Just like a bunch of other people that rely on that kid," he spits, "to do what's best for the campaign. So, yeah, I took a few kickbacks to help end this mess of a campaign early. He wanted to lose so fucking bad, I figured I'd help him!"

He turns to face me, hatred in his eyes. "I considered the kickbacks I got from Hobbs my severance package."

I leap forward, fury bursting through my body when Lincoln jerks my shoulders back. I stumble into my brother's chest, my arms held behind my back.

"Let me at him!" I shout, my body shaking with anger. "I'm going to fucking kill you!"

"No, you aren't," Graham says, glancing at me over his shoulder. "You have an election to win if for no reason but to spite him. But I, on the other hand, *the logical one,* have no reason to not use logic here and—"

We all gasp as a smashing sound ricochets through the room. Nolan drops against the wall, his eyes bugging out. Our father shakes his hand from the impact to Nolan's face.

"I warned you a long time ago not to mess with my children," Dad rumbles, glaring down at his once-trusted advisor. "If there will be anyone going to jail tonight it'll be me."

"No," a voice booms from the doorway. We all whip our heads to the side to see Troy standing there. "If anyone is going to take a fall for that, it's me."

He bends down and helps Nolan to his feet. Blood trickles from his mouth and he wipes it with the back of his hand.

"If anyone asks, I'm the one that hit him." Troy gives us a look and turns back to Nolan. "I'm going to accompany you off the property and it would be best to go willingly and quietly."

Nolan shuffles immediately towards the door but stops, with his back to us, when I speak.

"This isn't over. If it would've been me, that would've been one thing. But you fucked with Alison and Huxley and you *will* pay for that. I promise you."

"You better hope we can't trace the guy taking pics of Huxley to you," Lincoln warns him. "Because I will personally find you before the police do and will use my exemplary bat skills on your fucking face."

Nolan flies down the steps and into his car. My father and Graham step outside, making calls to security, publicists, and others to let them know things have changed.

"Where is Ali?" I ask Linc.

He puts his hand on my shoulder. "I don't know."

"We have to find her."

## Alison

I PULL THE CURTAINS, A seventies floral print that probably wasn't even pretty then, closed. The television plays a cartoon Hux watches sometimes as he goes through every drawer in the hotel room.

"What are you looking for?" I ask, laughing.

"I don't know. That's why I'm looking."

"Fair enough."

It's getting late and I'm tired from the day's events. My entire body hurts, aches, throbs like I've been in an accident. My muscles are sore, my head pounding, and my heart cracked and possibly irreparable.

I've thought about turning around to go to Barrett all evening. At least calling him and seeing what he has to say. But a part of me, the prideful part, won't let me do it. What if he tells me Nolan is right? What if he admits Lacy's story is true? What if he just says the incident with her tonight, coupled with the Huxley situation, caused him a headache and he thinks we should stall things while he gets things figured out?

The answer is, I can't deal with it. Not tonight, not while my head feels cloudy like I've drank my weight's worth of vodka.

I look up to see Huxley opening a piece of candy from the vending machine.

"Do you want to go swimming downstairs?" I ask him.

He plops the candy in his mouth "Sure. After this show though, okay?"

Yawning, I grab my toiletries that Lola packed for me. "I'm going to get a shower while you watch."

He nods, engrossed in the plot. I kiss his head as I walk by and lock myself in the bathroom. Looking at my reflection, my swollen eyes and raggedy hair, I see the girl that looked back at me after my divorce.

My heart breaks as tears spill down my cheeks. I hope beyond all hope that somehow, by morning, some of this will sort itself out in the fog in my mind.

◆◆◆

THE SKY IS PITCH BLACK, not a star in it. I sit at the table where one night, what feels like years ago, I made love to Alison for the first time.

I remember the way she looked spread out on this very spot, the sounds she made, the feeling I had knowing that I was fucked in more ways than one.

I can't help but realize I may have sacrificed the one thing I wanted for a bunch of things I didn't. I should've done exactly what she told me to in regards to the election—trust my instincts and that my ideas are enough to win.

I should've done the same in my relationship with her.

My life falling apart hurts worse than anything I've ever dreamed I'd feel.

"Fuck," I say to the darkness around me.

Graham and Lincoln are trying to find her, Graham letting me know that he didn't have a plan for once because, as he put it, "Who would've thought she would've left you?" Not me. I suppose I thought she knew what she meant to me, but obviously she didn't. Or I gave her enough of a reason to question it.

That's a mistake I won't make twice.

I just hope I have another chance to prove it.

I pick up my phone and dial Graham. He answers immediately.

"I didn't find her yet," he says, forgoing a hello.

"You know," I say, "I'm tired."

"Tired of what?"

"Of everything. I'm sitting here thinking about all the things I want to do in my life, and yeah, I'm on the path to get some of them accomplished. But if I get in office where I can actually do those things and I'm set up so I can't, what's the point?"

"You're talking about the Land Bill?"

"Among other things. There's a chance I could lose Alison over this," I say, holding a breath.

He sighs. "She told Lincoln she just needed a little bit of time. Don't panic. We'll find her."

"I know we will. But that doesn't mean she'll consider me a good enough prize to risk everything she's giving up to be with me."

"You aren't a prize. That's your first mistake," he says.

"Fuck off, Graham."

He laughs harder and I eke out a smile.

"What are you getting at, Barrett?"

I take my shoes off the table, something my mother would have a fit about if she could see me, and stand. "I'm saying I'm tired of doing everything the way I should or the way I'm told to. If I'm going to do this—politics, campaigns, relationships—I want to do it on my own terms. I want to do it my way and then, you know, I sink or swim on my own laurels."

He doesn't answer, probably thinking I've been drinking.

"I'm not drunk."

"No, I know that." He pauses and exhales. "Okay. I agree. Let's do things your way. It's your career, your life to fuck up if that's what happens. So what do you want to do?"

"Schedule a press conference for me tomorrow. Early."

"Me? I don't have the contacts for that, Barrett."

"Call my publicist and Rose. They'll get the word out. I want to go on record first thing."

"Are you absolutely sure? You do realize this conference has the potential of doing more harm than good, right?"

I nod. "Yeah, I know. But if I lose this election based on who I am, then did I want it to start with?"

Graham sucks in a breath. "What about Alison? I mean, depending on what you say, there's a chance you could lose her over this too."

A grin touches my lips. "Someone told me to believe in myself. So I'm going to set the record straight on everything and . . . hope it all works out."

"If you're sure."

Before I can reply, my phone buzzes. I pull it away to see Alison's name. My heart stops. "Ali is calling." I don't bother saying goodbye, knowing he understands, and try to ignore the pounding in my chest as I click over. "Alison?"

The line is quiet. No response.

"Alison, talk to me, baby," I plead, my heart jumping to my throat.

"It's me. Huxley."

I spin in a circle, confused. "Hux? Are you okay?"

"Yeah."

"Is your mom there, buddy?"

"Yeah."

His voice is steady, strong, yet a little nervous. I have to calm the fuck down if I'm going to get anywhere with him.

"I've called you guys a few times tonight," I say. "I couldn't get through."

"Mom's phone was dead and it's been on the charger since we got here."

"Where are you?"

"I don't know."

I pull the phone away from my face and take a deep breath. I can't start barking orders, demanding shit. I have to walk a fine line. "Are you okay, Huxley? Is your mom okay?"

He doesn't answer me again. The line is quiet. I hear a television on in the background, but no other voices.

"Hux?"

"You made her cry."

My heart splinters, my shoulders slumping at his words. "I didn't mean to."

"You told me you wouldn't."

I pull the phone away and mutter a few profanities under my breath. How can a simple statement from a child make me feel like a kid myself?

"Sometimes," I start, my voice shakier than I'd like, "adults do things they don't mean to, just like kids do. But Huxley, I promised you, I would never make her cry on purpose and I didn't. Right now I'm at the Farm, where you played ball with Linc, remember? And I'm worried sick about you and your mom. If you tell me where you are, I'll come and get you. I'll make things okay."

"I can't tell you because I know she doesn't want you to know. And . . . I have to protect her."

I bite down on my bottom lip. "Yes, you do. And if you feel like you have to protect her from me, I'm not going to argue with you. Because if there's one thing in this life I want you to know, it's to trust your gut." I squeeze my eyes shut and wish to God I had taken my own advice sooner. "Don't let anyone tell you what to do or how to feel, okay?"

"Okay." He gets quiet, his little breath firing through the phone. "Barrett?" he asks, his voice unsure.

"Yeah, buddy?"

"Do you love her? For real?"

I drag in a hasty breath, my chest tightening at his words. "I do," I insist. "I love her very much. And I had planned next week to sit down with you, man to man, and ask you what you think about us being a family."

"Really?" His little voice sings through the phone and it nearly breaks me in half.

"Really. I love your mom, but she's *your* girl. I trust that you know what's best for her and if you don't think it's a good idea, I'll listen. Because I respect you. But I would love the opportunity to help you take care of her. And, you know, be there for you for the stuff girls suck at."

"So guy stuff other than baseball?"

I laugh. "Yeah. I'll use Linc for the baseball stuff because God knows I don't want to mess you up there."

I can tell he's grinning, but he doesn't say anything.

"Maybe when you get back to town, we can go to dinner, just the two of us, and you can tell me what you think about that, okay?"

"I think it's a good idea. I need some help with her," he says, a touch of exasperation in his little voice. "When she cries, I don't know what to do. I need an adult, and my grandma just cries too, and then I have two crying girls to deal with."

I wish he was here. But he's not. And that's a problem.

"I'll gladly be your help with her. And if you tell me where you are, I'll come now."

He waits a moment before responding. "I can't tell you tonight. She hasn't agreed to be a family yet, so, right now, I have to be loyal to her."

"Promise me one thing, okay?" I ask.

"Sure."

"If you need anything, if your mom needs anything, you will call me."

"Okay. But I need to go because she's getting out of the shower now."

"Hux?" I say quickly.

"Yeah?"

"Thanks for calling me. Call me anytime."

"Okay," he smiles. "But I do need to go."

"Bye, buddy."

"Bye."

I end the call and gaze into the night.

## Barrett

THE CROWD IS BUZZING BEHIND the closed door. A few people stand in the wings with me, ensuring the main television stations are present and that the journalists that will run the story on me are here. They may as well get the word straight from the jackass's mouth. Me. That's how I feel over this situation. It's time to make things right.

I'm in a black suit, customary red tie and flag pin, and have a bullet-point list of things to say in front of me that I scribbled out in the Rover on the way over here. From now on, I'm going with my gut, speaking from the heart, instead of relying on someone else's script.

I've found some peace since talking to Huxley last night, not as much as if I'd spoken with Ali, but more than I had.

"Are you sure you want to do this? Absolutely sure?" Graham eyes me carefully, sipping on a cup of coffee. He's wearing a suit like mine, blue tie, and a lot more worry lines. He knows what I'm doing, and while I think he disagrees, he's done what I knew he would do—he shut up and got behind me.

"Do I look sure?"

He blows out a breath and slips his phone from his pocket. His face shows a few more lines when he hands it to me. "It's Dad. I'll just step away while you take this."

"Pussy," I grumble, taking the phone and watching him walk away.

I scan the immediate area and duck inside a small room to my right. "Hey, Dad."

"Barrett, what in the hell are you doing? I'm on my way over there now after getting a call from Graham. What is this press conference about?"

"I'm taking matters into my own hands."

He sighs, the sound rattling through the phone. "Son, don't go out there and ruin what we've worked for. You are so close, and you can still do this. I don't know what's going on, if you're cracking under the pressure, but we got this. Just—"

"Hey, Dad?"

"What?"

"Just stop it, all right?"

"Barrett."

"No, seriously. Stop. You know I love you. You know I want to make you proud and do all the things you want me to do."

"Things *you* want to do."

"Things *I* want to do," I say, rolling my eyes. "But I also want to do those things my way."

"This can't wait for another couple of days? My Lord, Barrett! Have some sense about you. We've already lost Nolan and now you want to go out there and sink the rest of it? Why, son? Why? The election is *today!*"

I laugh at the fact that I don't feel like I'm letting him down. I don't feel like I'm dropping the line or failing at life. Because I know, without a doubt, that what I'm about to do is the right thing *for me*. "This is the most sensible thing I've ever done. Trust me."

He doesn't answer, and I know he's trying to wrap his head around the fact that I'm laying down the law. But it was time—we both know it.

Graham waves through the window in the door, and I heave a breath. "Dad, I gotta go."

"I want to talk to you about this later."

"That's fine, but I have a speech to give."

I click the phone off and open the door. Graham and I exchange a look, one I can't explain, but one that I know like the back of my hand.

Looking at him and seeing it, feeling it, let's me know that even if my father hates me over this, even if Nolan blasts me all over the place, my decision today was worth it. For the first time in a long time, I can be proud of what I'm doing, who I am, what I'm working for—and it has nothing to do with politics or careers or family vendettas.

"You have about ten minutes," Graham says, stepping inside. "They're making sure the microphones and shit work. Do you need anything?"

I shake my head, pulling my phone out of my pocket. "Let's turn this fucking thing off. Fuck it." I glance down and see Monroe's number flashing on the screen. "It's Monroe. Do I take it?"

Graham leans against the wall. "Hey, you're playing hardball today. Let's go big or go home."

I click the button and raise my brows at Graham. "What's going on, Monroe?"

"What the fuck do you think you're doing, Landry?"

"Oh, I don't know, taking my campaign back, maybe. That's what it feels like anyway."

"I got a call last night that you are losing your shit. That I should be worried about endorsing you."

I laugh, for the first time completely uncaring of what he thinks of me. "Maybe you should be. I am kind of reassessing my choices today."

"You know you won't win this election if I recant my support. I have enough time to change my mind on you publicly and I will. Don't test me."

"Tell you what, Monroe," I say, noticing a woman waving at us on the other side of the door. Graham slips out to deal with her. "Tune in to the news in a few minutes and you'll find out exactly what I've decided. Then you can feel free to blackmail me, torch me all you want in the press."

"*It's time,*" Graham mouths through the glass.

"Talk to ya later." I click the phone completely off and open the door. "It's show time."

# Barrett

THE ROOM IS MUCH FULLER than I expected. Chairs take up most of the center of the room, each one with a journalist awaiting my arrival. Camera crews line the floor in front of the makeshift podium, as well as the walls lining the sides and the back of the room. Lights are lit for better recording, and that, coupled with all the bodies crammed into such a small space, makes the air heated, the energy in the room boiling.

Graham goes ahead of me and announces that I'll be on in a few moments. I'm standing in a hallway to the side. The crowd buzz quiets as Graham finishes his remarks and exits the stage. Before I know it, he's in front of me.

"Last chance," he says.

"I got this." I start towards the room, but twist back around. "Hey, Graham?"

"Yeah?"

"Thank you."

"For what?"

I shrug. "For being there for me. This world I live in can feel pretty fucking lonely sometimes."

"You got this," he promises. "Go out there and set the bastards straight."

Popping open the door, I laugh. I'm strangely not nervous. My hands are completely calm as I glance down at the paper with my notes. I take the steps to the podium, feeling the anticipation in the air. I give myself a second to reassess my decision. *Do I want to do this?*

I know the ramifications might be ugly. A part of me even believes this will tank my career. If that happens, I have no plan B. I don't know what I'll do afterwards. And I find it very fucking strange that none of that changes my mind.

I stand behind the podium and adjust the microphone. Gazing across the crowd, there are a ton of familiar faces. Journalists I've been interviewed by over and over again. Reporters that have written pieces good and bad, some that have offered services that extend beyond the professional level. A couple of people I've fucked. Memories from my time as Mayor flash before my eyes, and I smile, knowing I've done the best job I could. Even if this is the end of my career, the stopping point of my political adventure, I'm fine with that.

Opening my mouth to speak, I notice the back door opening. My father and Lincoln walk in and lean against the back wall. I study my father's face, waiting for some indication as to what he's thinking, but it's blank. Our gazes break and I clear my throat, pasting on the mask for the cameras.

"Thank you all for coming on such short notice." I look up and smile, giving them a photo op. The cameras flash, taking advantage of me posed behind the podium. I look back down at my notes, take a deep breath, and go for it.

"It's been my honor to work for the people of Savannah. I'm humbled at the trust placed in me to make decisions on behalf of the people of this city. It's been a challenging, fulfilling, successful journey. Together, we have made our city one of the best cities in the country, and I'm proud to have had a hand in that.

"As you well know, there's an election today."

That earns a chuckle from the people in front of me and I pause to give them another photo op that they eat up.

"When I made the decision to run for Governor, I thought, 'What if we could take the lessons learned from Savannah and apply them over the entire state?' 'What if we take the Landry formula and turn Georgia into the gem it should and deserves to be?' So I tossed my name in the hat. Looking back, it's not a decision I regret, but one I wish I would've handled somewhat differently."

The clicks of the cameras along with murmuring fill the air, and I look up at Lincoln. The smile on his face gives me the courage I need to speak again, to bare my soul to these vultures and, quite possibly, end my career.

"Politics has a way of eating people up. So many good men have been sidelined and silenced because of pressures put on them by others in this world. It's a part of the game, a part of the industry, but I think that's common knowledge. The part that most don't realize, I know I didn't, is how it sneaks up on you. One day you know exactly what you want and the next," I shrug, "you aren't sure who you are anymore."

I look down, crumple my notes, and take a deep breath.

"It's hard to find people in life that will tell you the truth. That will look you in the eye when things get hard and tell you what you need to hear, not what everyone is saying and not what you want them to say. The truth—it's a rarity these days.

"Today, I want to make it absolutely clear who and what I am. Because if I am lucky enough to be chosen by the constituents of Georgia to be their Governor, I want you to know what I stand for and what I'll do on your behalf."

Cameras click away as I go through the Land Bill, letting them know I will support it and I will lose my endorsement from Monroe by saying as much. I let them know the platforms that mean the most to me—our economy and education—and what I intend to do to make them stronger if I'm in office.

"Some of this is new information, some of this is not," I say, taking a deep breath. "But at the end of the day, it was important to me that we get on the same page, so, if I'm elected, I know it's because you want me to do the things I think are best, not what I'm told to do."

Questions begin to be shouted towards me as they sense I'm finished and a mic is held in front of a woman I've been interviewed by a few times. "Mayor, a lot is being said in the last few days about your stability. We've been hearing that you're in a relationship, that you're having a baby with another woman, and then you were with Ms. Monroe last night. Since you're talking so off-the-cuff, would you mind addressing this for us?"

I lower the microphone to my mouth and look at Lincoln. He winks.

"Absolutely. I don't feel I should waste my time or yours with these baby rumors because they're just that—rumors. As for the third part of your question, Ms. Monroe is a friend from way back and she was with me last night because Ms. Baker wasn't available," I say, figuring it's the truth in a round-about way. "And since we're having to address my love life, I'd like to ask you to respect my privacy and Ms. Baker's, as I respect yours. I realize I work for the people and my activities that deal with public policy are fair game. But who I love, where she works, and what we have for dinner isn't anyone else's business."

"So you are still in a relationship?" someone shouts from the back.

"I am. Absolutely," I say, hoping to God it's the truth. "Alison Baker is, quite frankly, the love of my life. Let there be no question about that. And she has a little boy that I think the world of and I hope you can understand why he deserves to be left alone."

More questions are shouted, but my throat is squeezed tight. Saying her name throws me off my game, my stomach rumbling with worry. Graham picks up on my wobble and comes on stage and takes charge, letting them know I have work to do for the election.

I exit through the door off the side and look around. The hallway is empty. I'm not sure why, but I feel incredibly lonely.

Like I just struck out.

# 42

## Alison

A PLATTER OF PANCAKES AND bacon is placed in front of me, Hux's eyes lighting up when he sees his chocolate chip stack.

The server fills our drinks and scurries away to check on her other tables.

The diner is busy, the witching hour that straddles the breakfast and lunch rushes in full effect. We made it just in time for the first meal of the day, even though it's approaching lunch.

"This looks good," I say, drizzling syrup over my pancakes. I sound way more excited about this gooey pile of starch than I really am. My stomach churns with a mix of sadness and nerves, my head still not completely recovered from the day yesterday and staying up all night thinking. Regardless of the hundreds of times I rolled everything around, I'm still not sold on what to do.

I miss him. I miss him so damn much. My heart tells me to go back to him, to stop everything and go straight to the Farm. My brain tells me to take it slow, to think it all through, to remember reality. That I'll know when I know.

But I don't know.

Everyone is chattering about the election, their buttons pinned to their chests, stickers declaring they've exercised their constitutional right to vote displayed proudly. I wonder how Barrett's holding up, how he's doing, but I don't know whether I should call.

Hux takes a bite of his breakfast "How do you feel today, Mom?"

"Good!" I say as brightly as I can. "What do you want to do today?"

His fork hits the side of the plate and he looks at me. "Do you want the truth?"

"Of course I want the truth."

"I want to go home."

I watch the tentativeness in his eyes, the hesitation as he watches my reaction. Forcing a swallow, I take a hasty sip of my water.

"I know you think we need a break or whatever," Huxley says, "and I know that photographer thing made you nervous, but I really just want to go home."

"Well..."

"Why did we leave, Mom? For real." He waits for an answer but I'm not sure what to say. "I'm not a baby. I'm almost eleven. I can take it."

"Hux, it's complicated."

"Is it because of Barrett?"

Laughing, I take a bite of my pancake. "I'm not discussing Barrett with you."

"You're my mom," he says thoughtfully. "So you know that I pick you every time. But if Barrett made you mad or messed up, you should give him a second chance."

"What do you know about second chances, you little squirt?" I laugh.

"I know that I broke the vase you had in the living room with my baseball and you didn't ban me from bringing them in the house. You gave me another try. And I know when Grandma got mad at Grandpa for forgetting to renew the license plates on her car, she gave him another chance. And I gave you another chance when you forgot to sign me up for summer baseball last year, remember?"

"Those things are different than Barrett, Hux."

He shrugs. "Maybe. But he makes you smile a lot. And he makes me... he makes me feel like we aren't alone and I really like that. And I know that he's kind of popular or whatever and I know the picture guy was because of Barrett, but who cares, Mom? You tell me not to give in to bullies and here we are, letting the bullies win."

Tears hit me hard and fast, and I can't get a napkin fast enough. Hux watches the wetness slip down my face and his little eyes grow wide.

"I mean, if you want it to just be me and you, that's okay. We don't really need anyone else. But . . ."

"You like him?"

His smile breaks across his face, his eyes sparkling. "I do. He likes you, I can tell. And I think he likes me too."

"I think he does too." I pat my eyes, my heart filling in my chest.

*When you know, you know.*

"You want to go home today?" I ask.

He nods and grabs his Arrows cap off the back of the chair.

"Well, I guess I should go cast my vote today," I laugh, picking up my purse.

We exchange a look and then stand and head to the cash register.

# Barrett

THE FARM IS NOISY IN the way it only is when my brothers are home. Ford got in late last night but was still asleep earlier when Lincoln, Graham, and I left for the press conference.

There are bags and newspapers and empty water bottles everywhere. It's like the old days before we all grew up and went our separate ways. I usually love this feeling of having everyone I love in one place, except, this time, someone is missing.

Lincoln is in the living room watching the latest sports stories. Graham is up in my office getting an update on the polls today and the reaction from my speech.

I look at the stairs as Ford comes down. He's wearing a pair of grey sweats and no shirt. The fucker looks like Rambo with his chiseled abs and tanned skin.

"Hey," I say, pulling him into a one-armed hug.

He runs his hand across his buzz-cut. "There you are. Fucker didn't even wake me up this morning. I travel the world to show my support and you leave me in bed."

"I figured a few hours of rest wouldn't hurt you."

He walks past me to the coffee pot. "Graham and Lincoln filled me in, both about the press conference and your new girl. But between the two of us, you better watch leaving Lincoln alone with her!" He says that loud enough for Lincoln to hear, and Lincoln responds to him by flying the bird over his shoulder.

Ford pours us both a cup of coffee and drinks his black. I pour some creamer in mine and relax against the cabinet. "Have you heard from her?" he asks.

"No," I say, filling with dread. "I've been calling and texting her. It's ringing through now, which is a plus, but she's not answering."

"She'll come around," he grins.

I shrug and take another drink. "It's nice having you here."

"I'm up for discharge in a couple of months," he says over the brim of his mug. "I'm thinking about taking it."

"Are you really?"

He nods. "I am. I always thought I'd stay in until I retired, but I miss home. I miss having a normal life."

"You and I both."

He nods knowingly.

"Yeah, well, I probably just fucked up everything. I guess I should really start defining a new normal."

I feel the stress I'd managed to avoid for a while return. I stretch my neck, willing the kinks to go away.

"Have you heard from Dad?" Ford asks.

"He showed up with Linc. I haven't seen him since I got here though. Fuck knows what he's going to say."

"Look, Barrett, I know how Dad can be. But if whatever you said today is what you believe, then by God say it. I've seen people in places you can't imagine that never get the opportunity to speak their minds or stand for anything. You can."

"I know," I sigh. "And you're right. Politically and career-wise, I've done what I think is best. I just hope it doesn't cause a rift in our family."

"It won't." He slaps me on the back. "And now's the time you're gonna find out."

"What do you mean?"

"Dad's here." He walks away from me and into the foyer. I hear him greet our father. After a few minutes, Lincoln joins them and their laughter floats into the kitchen where I'm still standing. Finally, they all make their way to me. My father stops in the doorway, his face now somber.

"Barrett? Can I speak to you a minute alone?"

I shove off the cabinet and follow him through the foyer and out the front door. My father doesn't say anything as we walk, just surveys the grounds like we're taking a Sunday stroll. The nonchalance finally gets to me.

"Dad?"

He stops in his tracks and looks at me.

I sigh, looking at the ground. I shove my hands in my pockets and feel my shoulders fall.

"Barrett, son, I'm sorry I failed you."

"What?" My head whips to him. He's watching me, lines creasing his face.

"I never realized you didn't want to do this, not the way I pushed you to do it. I trusted Nolan and the team because they'd been with us forever." His eyes blur with unshed tears. "I left you to the wolves, son. I should've been more involved and helped you navigate this. This is my fault."

"Dad, no. It's not."

"It is. I won't lie—I was mad as hell at first. Then your mother sat me down, and we had a long talk and . . ." He shakes his head, his eyes sorrowful. "And I take full responsibility for this. You are my son and you're the best son a man could want."

His voice breaks and I can't take it. I pull him into a hug and fight not to cry. I've never seen my father like this and I don't know what to do.

"Dad. Stop. It's fine."

He sniffles and pulls away, wiping his eye with a handkerchief. "It's fine because you're a lot smarter than me. I've always known you were a better version of me, Barrett. But, even then, I didn't understand what kind of a man you've become. I couldn't be more proud of you today. Whether you win or lose, you won in my eyes for standing up to everyone . . . including your old man."

I can't say anything. I just stand there, feeling like a little boy that brought home a good report card. It's silly, yet it's the best feeling I've ever had.

"Barrett!" Graham shouts from the porch, Linc at his side with a shit-eating grin. They point down the driveway and I see a little red car, sounding like a bucket of screws, ambling towards us.

I take off running to the driveway and am at her door before she even gets it stopped. I pull it open and her into my arms. She melts into me, her arms around my waist.

A million things want to come out of my mouth, but none of them do. None of them can. I'm afraid to say the wrong thing, to get too serious too fast, or to apologize when I shouldn't. If I can just hold her, make her feel what I want to say, that might work best.

Hux gets out of the passenger seat and grins.

"Thank you," I mouth to him, reaching a hand out and motioning for him to come to me. Instead, he waves, and runs straight for Lincoln.

I can't help but laugh and realize this is the way things should be. Whether I win or not, this is my world being right.

Ali pulls back and I try to fight her on it, not wanting to spoil the moment, but eventually, I let her. Her eyes are filled with tears, a nervous smile on her face.

"I love you," I say, looking as deeply in her soul as I can. "I love you so much. I—"

"And I love you. I'm sorry for running."

"I understand."

"No," she says, shaking her head. "I should've had faith in you. I should've been stronger. I told you to believe in yourself and then I didn't. No, I did," she rambles, "I just—"

I kiss her lips, effectively silencing her with a simple gesture that's more to tell her it doesn't matter than anything else. "I should've listened to you. I should've believed in me and just done things the way I knew they should be done before today."

"Before today?"

"Well, yesterday," I grin. "I fired Nolan. I heard what he said to you and a bunch of other stuff I don't want to get into. Let's just say Nolan is at the police department this morning answering some questions."

"What?" she gasps.

I run my thumbs down her delicate jaw line. "I made a speech today where I said I *will* support the Land Bill and that you were the love of my life and that I kind of like your kid too."

"You did?" she whispers, her lip quivering.

"I did. Because I want everyone to know it from my mouth, not from some angled statement from Nolan or Rose or PR. From me."

She hugs me again and I squeeze her tight.

"I'm never letting you go," I tell her. "You know that right? If you can't handle me being overbearing and protecting you and Huxley, doing what I have to do to sleep at night, then you better just get over it."

"One thing at a time. You have an election today."

"The vote that means the most is yours," I say, leading her in the house.

"I'm pretty sure you've sealed the deal on mine, Mayor."

My brothers and father are in the kitchen when we enter. They see us and stop talking, waiting for the verdict.

Grinning, I go to her and pull her against my side. "Guys, meet Alison Baker. Ali, you know Graham and Lincoln." They exchange a small wave. "That's Ford, and my father, Harris."

"Nice to meet you," Ford says with a nod of his head.

My father extends his hand and smiles. "It's a pleasure to meet you, Alison."

"Likewise, Mr. Landry." She takes his hand and shakes it.

"Please. Call me Harris."

"Where's Huxley?" I ask, looking around.

Lincoln laughs. "Where do you think? Getting my baseball stuff out of my car. Come on, Ford," he says, "let's go play some catch."

"Sounds good."

My youngest brothers head outside and my father and Graham head into the den, leaving Ali and I together.

"What happens now?" she asks, biting her lip.

"My sisters will be coming in today and . . ."

"Not with that, Barrett. With *us*."

"Well," I grin, trying to compensate for my nervousness, "I had a talk with Huxley last night."

"What?" she exclaims.

I shrug. "He called me. We talked."

Gasping she says, "I had no idea!"

"Well, I told him he could call me anytime and he took me up on that. We talked about you and me and him and how we were going to deal with this whole thing."

Her cheeks turn pink and I stroke them with my thumbs.

"And we decided," I whisper, pressing a kiss to her lips, "that Hux needs help with you, so I volunteered for the job."

"He needs help with me?"

"Apparently you were crying in the shower . . ."

She looks to the floor, but I won't have it. I tip her head back so she's looking into my eyes.

"There will be no tears, Ali, unless they're from laughing so hard you cry. After tomorrow, we will sit down, you, me, and Huxley, and we'll decide where we go from there. Because wherever I go, you both are coming with me. Okay?"

The look on her face is better than any response she could give me.

## Alison

BARRETT LEADS ME UP THE stairs, going left at the top instead of right. We walk down the hall and into a room at the far end. I can hear the guys playing on the lawn and it makes me so ridiculously happy that Huxley is accepted in this family that I could burst.

We enter a plush bedroom, all done up in whites and pale yellows. The bed is oversized with the fluffiest looking blankets and pillows I've ever seen. It's almost like a cloud, a giant marshmallow of a room. The afternoon sun shining through the windows makes it seem like a dream, a vision of happiness.

The door closes behind me and his arms wrap around me at once.

"Thank you," he whispers, resting his chin on the top of my head.

"For what?"

I feel his body shrug behind me, a long breath escaping his lips. "For being you. For wanting me. For making me see the things I needed to see."

"I didn't make you see anything," I say. "You chose to do that."

"I never would've done it without you. Tonight is the first night I'll go to sleep without a million pounds of guilt sitting on my shoulders. I feel freer than I ever remember feeling."

I twist in his arms to face him. His jaw line looks more angular than I remember, his features edible. My hand cups the side of his face, my thumb stroking his cheek. "That makes me happy," I whisper.

"You know what would make me happy?"

"What's that?"

"Showing you how much you mean to me. Is that all right?"

My knees go weak as he licks his lips, his gaze boring into mine. "Yes. Please."

He scoops me up, my legs over the side of his arm, and carries me across the room. His gaze doesn't leave mine as he lowers me onto the bed, the blankets dipping with my weight. He covers my body with his, the heaviness mixed with his scent overwhelming my senses. He kisses me like he's never kissed me before—with precision, almost methodical. It's as if every movement he makes is a lesson to be learned, a point to be taken.

I lay back and feel his lips cross over my cheek, down my jaw, and down my neck. His lips lingering before moving on. My hands find his hair and twist in the sandy strands, feeling how real he is in my arms. For the first time, he's mine.

"You're so beautiful," he whispers in my ear as his fingers fumble with the button of my jeans. "So fucking beautiful and so fucking mine."

"I was just thinking that," I say, lifting my hips so he can slide the denim off my hips. He removes them, tosses them to the floor, and disposes of his pants as well. Before I know it, he's on the bed and I'm straddled over him.

His eyes twinkle. "I wouldn't want to be anywhere but right here right now."

My hips swivel, my pussy rubbing against his rock-hard cock. I feel his length under me, my body already wet for him. "Me either."

Barrett lifts me up, grabs his cock, and lowers me inch by inch over him. I feel my body expand, making room for his size. His eyes widen as he sucks in a breath through his teeth, his fingertips dipping into the curve of my hips.

"Damn it, Ali," he murmurs as he sinks completely into me.

I take a second to adjust, to feel the fullness. It's heady, a complete turn-on to feel him inside me while I look him in the eye and see *that*. That indefinable look in his eye that makes me feel like the most important, sexiest person in the universe.

"Ah," I breathe, grinding myself against him. His cock rubs against the walls of my vagina, the contact causing my clit to stroke against his body. His gaze is heavy on me, stroking my skin in its own way. I'm completely owned in this moment by Barrett Landry, and it feels unbelievable.

It's different this time—*more intimate, more sensual, more personal.*

"I feel it too," he says, reading my mind. He raises his hips, pressing farther into me. I can't stifle the moan that escapes my lips.

Pulling off of him in the most subtle way, I mix up my motion. I rock in a circle and then pump up and down, the differences in stimulation working me into a frenzy.

"That feels so good, babe," he says as he lifts my shirt off over my head. My breasts bounce inside the red lace covering them. "And that looks just as good. My God."

He meets me thrust for thrust, the intensity in his eyes picking up. My entire body is on fire from his touch, his cock, his gaze, and I feel like I'm going to combust.

I shift my weight onto my feet and slide my body down his shaft. A smirk covers his face.

"Keep it up and this will be over before it's really even begun."

"I can't help it," I whimper, feeling his cock stroke my clit as I lift up and then lower down again. "Fuck, this feels so good."

I bounce harder, his hands finding my breasts. He frees them from the lace, cupping them in his hands. His eyes squeeze shut, his mouth hanging open far enough so I can hear his quickened breaths.

His cock swells inside me. His muscles flex as his eyes shoot open. "I'm warning you. You better stop if you don't want me losing it."

"Lose it." I slam down, grinding my body against his. The friction hits every stimulus, his hands squeezing my breasts. He leans up just enough to take my mouth with his, pressing a kiss that's a tattoo on my lips.

"Ali . . ." Flopping back against the pillows, I watch him enjoy me and it's enough to put me over the edge.

I grind harder, trying to touch his body with mine at every possible point, and I light up from the inside out.

Warmth erupts from my groin, surging through my core and to my cheeks. Fireworks flash before my eyes, my head trying to comprehend all of the sensations and feeling like it's going to explode.

Barrett groans beneath me, the sexiest thing I've ever heard. It only intensifies everything I'm feeling.

The world-shattering high lasts longer than I expect and it seems like eternity before I float back to Earth. Once I do, my hair sticking to my skin with sweat, my breathing ragged, I find him watching me with a smile on his face.

I blush. "Don't look at me like that."

"Like what?"

"I don't know," I giggle, my cheeks flushing again.

"Like that was the first time that's ever felt that way to me?"

My heart swells because I believe it. I can tell he means it by the look in his eyes.

"That's what I'm looking forward to, babe. That's what I've been missing my entire life. But now I have it and I won't let it go."

I climb off of him and snuggle against his side. He pulls a blanket haphazardly over us before kissing my head.

"Thank you," I whisper.

"For what?"

"For being the first person to make me feel like I'm worthy."

"Oh, Ali, I believe it's the other way around."

"Hmmm . . ." My lashes flutter closed. The stress of the last few days disseminates as I lie in his arms.

"It's you that's changed me. In every damn way." He presses another kiss into my hair. "Make me a promise."

"What's that?"

"That we can start every day off with something like this. Without the speech, of course," he chuckles.

"I'd like that."

"Me too, baby. Me too."

## Barrett

EVERYONE IS IN THE DINING room when we go downstairs awhile later. Lincoln is eating a bowl of cereal, with Hux at his side, playing some kind of video game. Ford is messing around on a computer. Graham is at the head of the table, sorting through a stack of papers with a red pen. He looks up as we enter.

"Good news!" he says, smiling brightly. "The feedback from your little speech is altogether positive. People seem to have responded to your stupidity, one even going as far as to call you, and I quote, 'People's Choice.' They're saying you're the candidate of the people, the first real candidate in recent memory."

"So, like, he's the MVP of the race?" Lincoln asks, sitting his bowl on the table.

"Seriously, Lincoln?" Ford sighs, shaking his head. He looks up at me. "I'm reading about you right now. Listen to this, *Barrett Landry surprised us all when he gave a press conference this morning. Speculation ran rampant, some going so far as to say he'd be addressing rumors of a rift in his campaign and others expecting an engagement announcement. They were all right, yet wrong. The Mayor took to the podium and gave an off-the-cuff response to his candidacy, one that has resonated strongly with the people of Savannah. While his handlers looked apprehensive going into the conference, the voters looked confident heading into the polls today. The 'Vote Landry'* buttons we've been seeing spring up in the past few weeks are out in full force this morning."

My father beams, placing both hands on the table. "Well, I'll be."

"I'm shocked," Graham says, resting his hands on a stack of papers in front of him. "The early polling data is strong. Monroe made a statement right after your speech earlier, but I think it's too late to do much damage. Not to mention it was heavily tempered from what I expected. I think he's afraid of making you an enemy at this point."

"Fuck him," I snarl.

"I—" my father begins but is cut off by the door opening.

"Where y'all at?" With the muted Southern drawl, it's obvious it's Sienna. She took off for Los Angeles a few years ago and has adopted a semi-California accent now, much to my parents' dismay.

In a couple of seconds, she rounds the corner with a bright smile. She's identical to Camilla, except she's dyed her hair a richer blonde. She's dressed in camouflage pants, a tight black t-shirt, and Chucks. "I'm the last to show up. Naturally."

"Hey, I told you to come last night," Lincoln says.

"You should've come last night," my father says, standing straight and crossing his arms over his chest.

"I had things to do. Besides, it's not like I waited until the last second."

"Painting pictures isn't an acceptable excuse," Dad says.

She gives our father a look. "Hush, Daddy."

"Come here," Dad says, shaking his head. Sienna waltzes over, knowing he's putty in her hands, and kisses his cheek before turning to me.

"Good speech, B. I saw it online on my way over. I'm over the red ties, though. Let's freshen your style up a little," she teases.

"I'm good. Thanks," I laugh, taking a quick hug from my baby sister. "Sienna, this is Alison Baker." I take a step back and pull Alison towards me. "Ali, this is Sienna, the missing piece of the Landry puzzle."

Sienna flashes Alison a wide smile. "Nice to meet you."

"It's my pleasure," Alison says, returning Sienna's grin.

My sister looks at me and winks. "I'm going to grab a shower. The plane was delayed last night, so I had to grab one today." She raises her voice. "Thus explaining why I wasn't here then, Daddy."

He just shakes his head and Sienna kisses his cheek again. She flashes me a peace sign and bounds up the stairs.

"What happens now?" Lincoln asks, looking at his phone.

"Lincoln!" Sienna shouts from the second level. "You took my room!"

Everyone laughs as Lincoln cringes.

"Your shit is in the hall, fucker!" she yells. Items can be heard hitting the floor.

"Watch your language—" Dad booms up the stairs, but a door is slammed before he can finish.

"We won't know anything until late tonight," Graham says, unfazed by the outburst. "Don't forget, there's a news station coming by this afternoon to do a quick little piece on the family. If everyone could be dressed and happy and pretend to be the Cleavers, that would be great."

"Is there anything I can do?" Ford asks, pulling a red shirt over his head. "If not, I'm going to go for a run."

"Go on," I say, looking down at Alison. "It's going to be a long day."

# 45

I WALK TOWARDS THE HOUSE with my bags in hand. I'm sure one of the Landry's would've come out to help me, but I needed a few minutes to myself.

I've never felt so welcomed, so overwhelmingly accepted by a family like I do them. It's amazing to watch them play with Hux, tease him, joke around with him like they've known him all his life.

The house is lit up as I approach. It's beautiful in the evening darkness, like a picture painted by a talented artist. Troy is standing on the porch and opens the door for me with a smile.

"Thanks, Troy," I say.

"It's my pleasure. You've made my job a lot easier," he winks.

"How's that?"

He shrugs, furrowing his brows. "Barrett's usually a wild mess of coming and going. But since you came in the picture, he's focused. He's a better man now, Ms. Baker."

I can't respond. Words fail me. Grinning, I enter the house and it's sensory overload.

A number of televisions are on, all on different channels. The brothers are all in the dining room going over papers and discussing what the numbers and reports mean. A few people are now here that I haven't seen before. I'm guessing they work on the campaign because they flank Graham on either side and field calls left and right.

Barrett rushes to my side.

"It's going to be crazy for a few more hours. My mom and Camilla are probably in the kitchen. Do you want to go in there? It might be quieter."

"Uh, yeah," I say nervously. "I'll find something to do. Don't worry about me. Where's Hux? He was right here when I left and I don't want him getting in the way."

"Linc set him up in his room with a video game system. He's fine, trust me," he laughs.

"He'll be fine as long as he doesn't go through my phone," Linc says, looking worried. "Shit. I better just go get it." He jumps up and races upstairs, making us laugh.

I kiss Barrett on the cheek. "I'll just go find something to do."

Taking my hand before I walk away, Barrett says, "This might be boring for you, but I'd like you to stay. I'm so glad you're here."

I can't resist him. "Of course. I'll be here. For you."

He flashes me his sweet smile and presses a soft kiss to my cheek. "I'll be in here if you need anything." He grabs a seat next to Ford, and Graham slides him a sheet of paper.

"Alison," Harris says, looking at me over the top of his glasses. "That boy of yours is a good kid. I look forward to getting to know him."

I start to respond, but the smile on my face is all I can muster. Harris grins and goes back to his work.

I wander through the house towards the kitchen. My stomach is a ball of nerves at the prospect of meeting Mrs. Landry. She looks like she walked off the pages of Better Homes and Gardens in her pressed grey slacks and pink cardigan. Her hair is perfectly coiffed, pearls lining her neck. I'm flat-out intimidated by her already.

She's with Camilla in the kitchen when I enter. They're in the midst of a conversation I can't hear. Camilla looks up and sees me and breaks into a huge smile.

"Alison! There you are! I was wondering what happened to you!" She comes around the counter and pulls me into a hug. I know I'm stiff against her, but I'm a little taken aback.

"Hi, Camilla. It's nice to see you."

"I'm so glad you're here," she says, turning towards her mother. "Mom, this is Alison. Ali, this is my mother, Vivian."

She comes towards me, and I expect her to offer her hand. Instead, she too pulls me into a hug. She smells of expensive perfume and flowers as she lets me go.

"Alison, it's such a pleasure to meet you, darling." Her grin is reminiscent of her sons'.

"It's nice to meet you, Mrs. Landry."

"It's Vivian, please. Or Vivi. Some of my friends call me that." She turns away and picks up a pie server. "Would you like something to eat? If you've been here with these boys of mine all day, I'm sure no one has thought about feeding you."

I laugh. "I actually had Hillary's House deliver some things for lunch earlier. When Lincoln and Ford started fighting over a piece of cold pizza, I had to do something."

Camilla rolls her eyes. "They're animals. But I love them."

"I can see why. You all have a fantastic family."

"Thank you," Vivian says, beaming. "My boys are raucous and rowdy and loud as all get out, but they're good men. I'm pretty proud of them."

"I would imagine so."

"I met your son earlier. He's such a doll. So polite and well-mannered, and he seems to have taken up with Lincoln."

I laugh. "Yes, he loves baseball, so Linc is pretty much his idol."

"They're both good boys," she nods. "Maybe they can keep each other out of trouble."

She holds my gaze for a long second, before turning to her daughter. "Camilla, go in and see if the guys need more coffee, please."

Camilla grabs the pot and heads into the dining room. Once she's gone, Vivian turns to me.

My throat tightens immediately because I know this about to get real.

"Tell me about you, Alison."

"I . . . uh . . . well, I grew up here." I feel my face turn beet red. "I like to read when I'm not at work." *Oh my God, I'm so awkward.*

"Where do you work?"

"I go to school and work at Hillary's House downtown."

"Well, you have won the heart of my oldest son and get the stamp of approval from my exacting daughter, Camilla. And I don't know which is harder to accomplish," she winks. "I know it's too early to welcome you and your son to the family, but I'm glad to have you here for this momentous occasion."

She comes around the counter again and pulls me into another hug.

## Barrett

I GAZE AROUND THE LIVING room, a sense of pride washing over me like I've never felt. It's not just pride, but a sense of contentment, a sense of everything being right in my world.

Lincoln and Sienna are sitting on the floor, Huxley between them, watching the television. Ford is standing behind the sofa, his hands on the back of the furniture right behind our parents' heads. Graham is pacing one side of the room, fielding calls and texts as the night draws to a close. Camilla sits on a chair by Graham, watching everyone warily. And I sit on the love seat, Alison at my side, waiting for the results in what's being said to be one of the closest gubernatorial elections in state history.

Graham stops walking and his eyes snap to mine. "They say we have it, Barrett." His tone is hesitant, yet optimistic. He fights a grin, but his eyes give him away. "The last three counties to report are in the north, but I just got off the phone with our guy up there, and he says the early numbers are strong. Real strong, Barrett."

Camilla claps her hands. "I knew it!"

"Don't get excited yet, Swink," I warn. "Wait until it's official."

"Does anyone need a drink?" my mother asks, standing. These things still make her nervous, even though she's been through her fair share over the course of her life. It's not whether I win or lose that makes her anxious, it's how it'll affect me. It's what makes her the best mom I could imagine.

"You probably don't have any green juice, do you?" Lincoln asks.

"What the hell is green juice?" Ford snorts. "Have I been gone that long?"

"It's pureed spinach and shit, asshole," Lincoln says. "It's what makes me the best center fielder in baseball."

The news comes off a commercial break and we all hold our breath. Instead of an election update, they head into the weather.

"You'd think they could spare us the warm weather forecast," Graham mutters, not losing a step.

I laugh, pulling Ali closer to me. "They'll get to it."

"How can you be so calm?" Ali whispers. "Aren't you dying to know?"

"Usually I am. But you know what?" I pull her onto my lap and lock my hands around her waist. "I'm not. Because either way, I'm going to be fine."

"Shut up," Sienna says over the chatter. She points a manicured finger at the screen. "Look!"

The music plays that denotes an election decision has been made. A red, white, and blue banner rolls across the screen before the commentator comes on. "Ladies and gentleman, I'm being told that we are ready to call the gubernatorial race. The next governor of the state of Georgia will be . . . Barrett Landry."

The room erupts into a fit of cheers, everyone jumping to their feet. Everyone but me.

I pull Alison into me and hug her as tightly as I can as my family goes wild. She tries to talk, but I pull her so far into me that she can't.

"Just sit here with me," I whisper, breathing her in.

This is what I've risked everything for. Not the win in the election, though that's nice too. I've worked for this moment with her. For a life. For a future that's for me and not everyone around me. And I have it. I have her.

My eyes are closed when Huxley jumps on us, his arms wrapping around his mother and I. "You did it!" he exclaims as I pull him down between us.

"We did it," I correct him, watching his face beam.

"Congrats, son!" my father says, patting me on the shoulder. My brothers come and shake me, and Ali too, since I'm still holding on to her. She giggles, her face still in my shirt.

"Way to go, man!" Lincoln says, picking up Hux with his good arm.

I peer through the throngs of people until I see Graham. He's leaning against the wall, a look of relief on his face. We exchange that look, the one that says more than words could ever say.

"I have champagne in the kitchen!" my mother says. "Let's celebrate!"

Everyone follows her to the kitchen but me. Instead, I allow Ali to pull back. When she does, I press the deepest kiss I can onto her lips. She melts into me, her arms draping over my shoulders.

"Congratulations," she whispers. There's hesitation in her voice, and I'd wondered if that would come.

I look her directly in the eye and capture her attention. "I'll walk away from it."

"What?" she asks, puzzled.

"I'll walk away from the seat."

"You can't do that!"

"I can. And I will."

"Why would you do that? Barrett, have you lost your damn mind?"

Chewing on my bottom lip, I fight a grin. "I have. I met this girl and she stole just about every part of me, actually. My mind. My heart too."

Her cheeks turn a bright shade of pink and she looks at the ground. I tilt her chin up again so she's looking at me.

"This is your call, baby. Because this, you and me, means more to me than anything else. If you hate the idea of being my girl while I'm the most powerful man in the state," I smirk, "then I'll turn down the job. I just had to prove to myself that I could do it."

Her eyes narrow, her bottom lip between her teeth. The wheels turn as she mulls over the prospect, and I'm not sure which way she's going to go. A bubble of anxiety builds.

Her hands press against my cheeks, her thumb stroking the scar over my eye. "When Lincoln hit you with the ball, did you throw it back at him?"

"What?" I half laugh.

"When you got this scar, what did you do next?"

I shrug.

"Did you quit playing with him?"

I think back, confused as to why we're discussing this now. "No, actually, I don't think I did. I think I made him throw me another pitch so he hit the one hundred he was supposed to throw every day, and then I went inside and Mom took me to the ER."

She smiles and kisses me. "Take the job."

"What?"

"Take it. Be the governor."

"I'm so confused, Ali."

She takes my hand, lacing it with hers. "You aren't a quitter, Barrett. And you aren't scared. Those are two things I need to not be either."

"Do I scare you, baby?" I bring our hands to my mouth and kiss each knuckle.

"I think I'd be scared if you stopped looking at me like that."

I laugh and pick her up, tossing her legs over my right arm. Her hands fly around my neck, the air is pierced with her giggles.

"There's not a chance of that happening. So I think you're safe." I bend down and touch our lips together. "So you'll be my girl? Even though you once told me I'm the exact person you didn't want to be with?"

She grins. "I thought you once told me you could spot a liar from a mile away."

## Barrett

THE CELEBRATION WINDS DOWN INSIDE the house. It's been an insane day, capped off by a victory in so many ways. It's been one of the best days of my life.

So many people came by after the election was called in my favor. The house is full of people—friends, family, associates, even Ali's friend, Lola. I just need a few minutes to myself.

I slip out the back door and around the corner of the house. The night is calm, quiet, the air cool. It's just what I need to get my head wrapped around the new direction my life has taken. I'm at absolute peace for the first time, and I just want a moment away from everyone to soak it up.

I head to the tree line and the little bench that lurks right out of sight.

Pushing through the trees, I come face-to-face with Lincoln. He's sitting on the bench, his head in his hands. He looks up through his fingers and when he realizes it's me, he shakes his head.

"Busted," he sighs, sitting up straight.

"What's going on?" I take a seat next to him.

"Just getting a little peace and quiet." He glances at me over his shoulder. "I'm sure you do know. I'm sure you know better than me."

"Everything all right?"

He shrugs.

We stare off into the night, both of us avoiding the elephant in the room. Something's going on and I don't know what, nor do I want to push. But if he wants someone to open up to, I'll listen.

After a long while, he finally chuckles. "Life is funny, isn't it?"

"What makes you say that?"

"Just when you think you have it figured out, it pitches you a curveball."

"Are we talking baseball or life?"

"Baseball is one big analogy for life." He shrugs again. "Look at you. You thought you had everything figured out and then Alison walks in. Next thing you know, you're willing to walk away from everything if you have to. In one minute, everything changed."

"What's going on, Linc?" I turn to face him, eyeing him carefully. The usual playfulness in his features is gone and has been replaced with a look of dread. I've never seen my brother like this and it's disconcerting.

Blowing out a breath like the weight of the world is on his shoulders, he turns to me. "I just checked my messages from today. I have to head out tomorrow."

"Why?"

"I'm not sure. The owner of the Arrows said I need to meet with them first thing Monday."

"That's normal, right? A business meeting or something?"

"Yeah," he sighs. "Normally. But this has to do with my shoulder."

Lincoln reaches up and grabs it, wincing as he rolls it around. "I have a feeling they're going to either let me go or try to trade me. And if they trade me all jacked up like this, my contract will be shit, man."

"Ah, Linc."

"Yeah. If I can convince them I can get it rehabbed before spring training, I have a shot. But Barrett . . ." He looks into the night. "I don't know if I can. This fucking hurts. I've downplayed it, taken a shit ton of pain meds, but it's pretty mangled."

"Have you had scans and stuff?"

He nods. "The test results I got said it should heal. But the main one wasn't back when I left for here. I'm assuming the team got them and my copy is at my house."

"It'll work out," I say, patting his thigh. "You're the best centerfielder in baseball."

He shakes his head as if he's unsure and stands. "Watching you over the last couple of days has made me think. You just took everything in stride, just changed position and stepped to the plate." When he looks at me, his face is somber. "I don't know if I can do that."

"Don't get ahead of yourself—"

"I'm not. I feel it in my gut. This isn't just going to go away and I don't know how I'm going to handle that. I'm not like you, Ford, or Graham. All I can do is play baseball."

Watching his face fall unravels my happiness. I want to tell him it's going to be okay. I want to assure him that everything will be okay like I did when he had tendonitis in high school. But the man I'm looking at isn't my goofy little brother. He's a grown man with a career and his concerns are as serious as mine were about my own problems.

"Maybe it won't be okay," I say as easily as I can. "But want to know what I've learned lately?"

"Sure."

"Sometimes things look like they're all fucked up. There are times life throws you curveballs, as you say, and you have to swing or take the pitch. You're tempted just to swing so you won't strike out looking. But in your gut, you know it's going to be a ball. You just have to learn to trust your instincts."

A flicker of animation rolls across his features. "Nice analogy."

"Never mind that. Do you get what I'm saying, Linc?"

He starts to the house and I follow a step behind, giving him space. His head is bowed, his hands in his pockets, before he stops and faces me again.

"What if I get caught looking?"

I place my hand on his shoulder. "I'm not going to tell you this is going to be okay because I don't know if it will."

"Geez. Thanks."

"But I do know one thing for a fact. Regardless of whether you play baseball or if you have to figure out something else, you're going to do it with all of us behind you. And while that doesn't help in a lot of ways—you still have to figure things out yourself—you won't have to do it alone. You have a tribe of brothers and sisters behind you to help you along the way, just like you all came to bat for me this week."

His lips quirk. "So if I call you and need a job in the Governor's Mansion, you're fine with that? You'll let me be your Director of Sports or something?"

"There is no such thing," I groan, starting back to the house again.

"Maybe it's something we can start."

"Maybe we concentrate on getting you rehabbed so we aren't trying to fit you in the Governor's Mansion, all right?"

His grin is back in full force. "Barrett?"

"Yeah?"

"Thanks."

Glancing at him over my shoulder, we start up the steps. "That's what family's for."

## Alison

THE CLOCK CHANGES TO THREE o'clock in the morning. The party has dwindled down, all that's left of the celebration is a tremendous mess that someone's going to have to clean up later.

Huxley went to bed hours ago. Harris and Vivian left around one, escorted home by Troy.

Lincoln is lying on the sofa, his Tennessee Arrows hat pulled down over his eyes, snoring away. His right arm is draped across his body, his left hand on his right shoulder. I catch Barrett watching him.

"What's wrong?" I ask.

"Nothing, really."

"You're lying."

Barrett grins. "Lincoln's arm is fucked up worse than he's letting on. He has some major therapy to do coming up and if it doesn't get better, he might not get re-signed."

"Oh, Barrett." My heart pulls for Linc.

"It sucks. It's all he's ever wanted to do. He's had a ball in his hand since he could pick it up. He could rattle off stats as soon as he could talk."

"Can we help?"

"No. He has to do what the doctors say and hope he didn't completely ruin his shoulder."

"I'll say a prayer for him."

I look around the room, but we are the only ones left. Ford, the responsible one, went to bed upstairs with his dog. Graham headed home first, right around midnight, with a look of pure satisfaction on his face. Harris is the one that praised Barrett the most tonight, but I secretly think it's Graham that's the most proud.

Camilla left, escorted by a friend of their family just a few minutes ago. Barrett glared at the guy all night, so I'm not sure if he's going to be around much longer. Sienna is the only Landry, besides Barrett, still awake and she's sitting on the back porch with Lola, comparing tattoos the last time I eavesdropped. They have the same eclectic taste, the same free-spirited mentality. They've hung out together all night.

The excitement of the last few days has taken its toll and I feel completely exhausted. My bones hurt, much to my surprise. I'm utterly spent. The mixture of emotions, the worry, anxiety, pride, anger, fear have all sapped my energy, and I'm left standing in the living room of the Farm trying to figure out what's next.

Barrett comes up behind me, his arms wrapping around my waist. I tilt my head to the side automatically, and his lips find my ear.

"Ready to go to bed?" he asks, kissing me right behind my lobe. He's chewing on the inside of his cheek, a tell-tale sign that he's feeling me out. He's waiting on me to make the next move. But I don't know which move to make.

Barrett spins me around, wrapping his arms around my waist. "Ms. Baker, I'm getting impatient."

"Why?" I giggle.

"Are you ready to go to bed or not?"

"Are you sure it's okay for us to stay here? I mean, Hux is already asleep, but I could just take him home. I didn't realize—"

He silences me with a kiss, a lingering, sweet gesture that makes it impossible to not melt in his arms.

When he pulls back, he's smirking. "You're staying here. I'm not giving you an opportunity to overthink things or talk yourself out of this. This, you and me and Huxley together, is our new reality."

My exhale comes out in skittish waves, my anxiety palpable. "I can just go home and we can see each other soon."

"Yes. Yes, we will. Soon, as in, when I wake up and open my eyes and see you lying beside me in my bed. Then you can go downstairs and sing while you fix Hux and me breakfast."

It sounds wonderful, blissful, actually. But a part of me thinks it's too soon for that. He might need time to process this. I might need time to process this.

"Stop," he whispers, taking my face in his hands. "I don't."

"You don't what?"

"Need to think about this."

"I didn't say that," I point out.

"You didn't have to, babe."

Just like he did on the night I first met him, he breaks me down inch by inch. His charm softens my resolve, his smirk weakening me further. His touch and scent as he pulls me into him obliterate whatever objections I have left. It's ridiculously unfair and totally overwhelming . . . and only one of the reasons I fell in love with him.

Although he's different than any man I've known, and he's nothing like Hayden, I can't help but feel a little blip of uncertainty sweep over me. Knowing he deserves the opportunity, I give him a chance to sway me to his side.

"What if this is all wrong?" I ask.

"What if it's all right?"

"What if we mess this up a million different ways?"

"What if we nail it every way we go at it?" he smirks.

"What if you decide you hate me?"

He laughs, kissing me on the nose. "What if you decide you're going to love me forever? Because that, Ms. Baker, is what I'm going to make sure happens."

I rest my head against him, listening to his heartbeat. The room is quiet, the televisions off, and for the first time since this craziness started, it feels like it's just him and me.

Wrapped in his arms, I feel safe. Loved. Respected. Those are things I've not experienced before. More than that, he's worthy of all of those things in return.

"I have something to tell you too," I say, lifting my chin so I'm looking him in the eye.

"Yeah?"

"You won my vote back."

He laughs. "What finally convinced you?"

"Let's see . . ." I say, twisting my face in total concentration. "It might have been seeing you without a shirt on. Or it might have been watching you with Huxley. But, then again," I shrug, a smile touching my lips, "it might have been the grapes."

# Epilogue

## Barrett

IT'S EVERYTHING I THOUGHT IT would be.

Her arm lies across my chest, her hair spilling across the pillows. She's pressed as close as possible to my side, probably more my doing than hers, but I'm not complaining. Her chest rises and falls against me, and it's the most peaceful, beautiful moment of my life.

I place a kiss against her forehead and say a quiet prayer of thanks. I'm so grateful for all the things that have happened over the last few weeks, even the bad because even with them, I still got here. And I wouldn't risk redoing anything if that meant putting this moment in jeopardy. I wouldn't do that for all the money in the world.

Alison stirs beside me, her long lashes fluttering before her lids rise. It takes her a second to realize where she is and watching that realization spatter across her features is priceless.

A slow smile stretches across her lips that beg to be kissed. "Morning," she says sleepily.

"Morning, beautiful."

She stretches and starts to pull away and I just sink her in even closer, if that's possible. She understands my sentiment because she shakes her head, but relaxes, her head on my chest this time. "I could get used to this."

"You better get used to this," I reply, my tone sharper than I intended.

She gazes up at me, cocking a brow, and I shrug.

"What? You think you'll be out of bed before me in the morning?" I ask, a tease in my tone.

Before she can reply, the door flies open and Huxley leaps from the doorway, through the air, and lands on the foot of the bed. "Morning!" he almost shouts before jumping on top of his mother and I.

"Hux!" she says. "Easy, kiddo. It's early."

As he shimmies himself on top of the blankets between us, I catch her eye over the top of his head.

"And you're going to have to start knocking," she laughs.

"I can't help it," he says, giggling. "I have so much energy."

"What have you been into this morning? What time is it?" she asks.

"I don't know, but Uncle Linc made waffles with chocolate syrup this morning. Have you ever had that, Mom?"

Laughing, I roll onto my side so I can see them both. This would've seemed like the oddest picture a year ago but now, it's perfect.

"It's because he's really a little kid smashed into that big body," I say.

"I can see that," Hux replies, considering my words, making us laugh.

"You know, Huxley," I say, tapping him on the stomach. "We have a few things to discuss today."

"We do?"

"We do. We were going to have a conversation about what we were going to do with this mom of yours. Remember?" I glance at Alison and watch her blush.

"Oh, yeah," he says, looking at me. "What are we gonna do with her?"

"Hey, now!" Alison shoves at Huxley. "Be nice to your mother."

Hux doesn't glance her way, just watches me, his little eyes filled with anticipation.

"I'm going to have to move to Atlanta in a couple of months," I tell him, watching a wave of worry storm through his irises. "I have a lot of work to do there."

He looks at the ceiling, then the wall, then out the window. Anywhere but at me.

"I can't be in Atlanta if you guys are here," I whisper.

His head jerks towards me, a smile tickling the corner of his lips.

"I'll worry about you both, and I won't get anything done. It'll be hard for me to see you guys, and then she'll stop singing while she cooks, and then everything will go down the drain."

"So," he starts, his voice shaky, "what are we going to do? If you leave, she'll cry, and I've already told you I can't deal with that. Plus, you promised you wouldn't make her cry."

I know Alison is staring at me. I can feel her gaze heavy on my features, but I keep mine fixed on her son.

"I did promise you that. That's why I propose you both come to Atlanta with me."

"Really?"

Nodding, I reach across him and take Alison's extended hand. She squeezes it and holds on for dear life.

"Really, Hux. It would mean a new school for you, new friends. You'd be away from your grandparents a lot of the time and I know that would be tough for you. If you go with me, that would mean we would live together. Our lives would change. Do you understand all that?"

He doesn't look away this time. He doesn't smile either. He just searches my face for a lot longer than I expect.

My heart starts thumping because I thought I had this in the bag. I was sure I did. But the look on his face, the blank canvas, makes me think I overestimated myself.

"Barrett?" he asks finally.

"Yeah?"

"Are you going to marry my mom?"

I force a swallow and look at Alison. She wipes a tear at the corner of her eye and opens her mouth to speak, but nothing comes out.

My heart swells. The peace and love in this room is such a different feeling than I've ever felt, even with my own family. This gorgeous woman and her son support me and love me, even when I mess up and even when I might not deserve it.

I'll do anything in my power to ensure they're mine forever.

"Would that be okay with you, Hux?" I ask. "If I married your mom one day?"

"I'd really like that." His words are heavy, pressed around a lump in his throat. "I think that would be really great, actually."

Alison squeezes my hand and brings it to her mouth, planting a soft kiss against my knuckles.

"I'll have to talk to her about that and hope she agrees," I wink, "but if I have your blessing, that's a step in the right direction."

He leans over and wraps his arms around my neck, knocking the wind right out of me. Before I can respond, he leans away.

"I'm going to go find Lincoln. He has this app on his phone," he says happily, bouncing off the bed and scurrying toward the door, "that—"

"Stay off of Lincoln's phone!" Alison and I both shout in unison as Hux slams the door behind him.

Laughing, I pull Alison close to me again. "I'm not responsible for whatever he learns or sees from my brother."

"Lord, help us," she giggles. Tilting her head and looking at me, she smiles. "Did you mean what you said to Hux?"

"I meant every last word of it."

A sparkle glimmers in her eyes. "Really?"

"Speak as you find. Remember?" I grin. "As far as I'm concerned, we are together for the long haul. However you want to make that permanent is fine with me, as long as it is."

"It is," she whispers.

"Roll over here and show me you mean it."

She starts to straddle me, the heat of her pussy hot against my cock, when Huxley's voice shouts from the hallway.

"Maybe we should lock the door first."

The End

Swing, Lincoln Landry's story, coming Winter 2016!

# Acknowledgements

FIRST AND FOREMOST, I WOULD like to thank the Creator for all the blessings in my life. As a human, I'm always quick to 'ask for help'; I think it's also important to remember to say 'thank you' too.

As always, my family is the most supportive and encouraging bunch of people on the planet. Mr. Locke, the A-Team, my mother and in-laws: I love you all.

Jen, Susan, Michele, and Joy read this no fewer than a million times. Thank you is utterly insufficient. Ashley, Robin, and MaryLee also gave incredible feedback and attention to this story. Carleen and Kiki came in at the last minute and gave this story their valuable time. You are all so appreciated!

Mandi kept me going through this process. I'll be your faith, you be mine. It's how we roll, right, Pres?

Alison, I value your friendship more than you'll ever know. I love you.

I'm not sure I would've pulled this one off without the love and support from SL Scott. I love you and your phone calls and ab-mergencies.

My team, once again, rocked this project. Huge hugs to Kari with Kari March Designs, Christine with Perfectly Publishable, and Lisa C. with Adept Edits for lending your expertise to this project. Thank you to Kylie at Give Me Books for helping me get this out there, Jen at Kinky Girls Book Obsessions for everything you do, and Jillian with Jilly's Polished Proofs for making this sparkly. Hugs to Lisa W. for taking time away from everything you have going on, including your business A Bookish Life on Etsy, to make my frantic self teasers. I love you all.

Sending kisses, too, to Stephanie Gibson for being awesome, Candy Collins (Manning) for updating the Locke Library, and Jade Hyland (I didn't kill anyone!) for helping with All Locked Up. You guys rock!

My days are made better by knowing the following women: Angie McKeon, Jen Lynn, Dawn Costiera, Randa Lynn, Staci Hart, Kennedy Ryan, Gail McHugh, Gretchen de la O, Lili Valente, Serena McDonald, Lexy Storries, Kaitie Reister, and Kara Hildebrand. Thank you for being light in my life.

My Facebook group, Books by Adriana Locke, and Goodreads group, All Locked Up, are my escape. The readers in those groups give me so much love and energy that it would be impossible to do this without them! Thank you all for giving me so much energy and encouragement. (And if you're reading this and aren't in there—join us!)

My Instagram Girls keep my days full of smiles (and hotness!). There are so many of you now that I would worry I was leaving someone out. Thank you all for your posts and edits—you are the most talented group of women anywhere!

Blogging can be a tedious, thankless job. I want to extend a huge dose of gratitude for the blogs that have jumped on board and supported this release. You make this possible and I'm forever grateful.

And you—yes YOU! Thank you for choosing to pick up Sway. I know you have a million choices and I'm honored you chose my story. I hope you enjoyed it.

xo

Addy

# About the Author

USA TODAY BESTSELLING AUTHOR ADRIANA Locke lives and breathes books. After years of slightly obsessive relationships with the flawed bad boys created by other authors, Adriana has created her own.

She resides in the Midwest with her husband, sons, two dogs, two cats, and a bird. She spends a large amount of time playing with her kids, drinking coffee, and cooking. You can find her outside if the weather's nice and there's always a piece of candy in her pocket.

Besides cinnamon gummy bears, boxing, and random quotes, her next favorite thing is chatting with readers. She'd love to hear from you!

She has two groups where she's interactive daily! Join Books by Adriana Locke on Facebook ( *www.facebook.com/groups/booksbyadrianalocke* ) or All Locked Up on Goodreads (*https://www.goodreads.com/group/show/159694-all-locked-up* ) to talk books.

She can also be found hanging out at:

*www.adrianalocke.com*
Facebook—*www.facebook.com/authoradrianalocke*
Twitter—*www.twitter.com/authoralocke*
Instagram—*www.instagram.com/authoradrianalocke*
Pinterest—*www.pinterest.com/authoradrianalo*
Spotify—*www.spotify.com/adrianalocke*
SnapChat—adrianalocke
Google+—+AdrianaLocke

Continue on for an excerpt from Wherever It Leads, also by Adriana Locke.

# Wherever It Leads

## One

### Fenton

"TELL HIM I GOT HIS message yesterday and I don't need him to blow me. But thank him for the offer."

Grabbing the nearest shopping cart and sliding it in front of me, I toggle the phone against my shoulder. It nearly slides off my rigid muscles, a mix of workout fatigue and work stress setting up shop across my back.

Duke sighs through the phone, not even pretending to hide his frustration. "Fenton, that's not true," he says, exasperation thick in his voice. "He didn't ask to blow you."

"Obviously it's not fucking true. I just want to hear him have to deny it."

"You know what? Just forget I called. I'll come up with a response myself."

"That's probably the best idea you've had yet."

Duke sighs again, louder this time. I'm sure I've been an asshole to deal with since I hired him, but I gave him plenty of warning what he was getting into. This entire situation, the one he was hired to deal with, has been a complete clusterfuck from the start. There's nothing more vexing than being able to fix a problem and having your hands tied behind your back while being needled that the problem exists. I know it exists. I'm keenly aware and no one wants it fixed more than me.

"I'll just tell them the status hasn't changed."

"I could've taken care of this," I bite out.

"I know. I know."

"And they wouldn't let me."

"I. Know."

"I know *you* know. Try to impart some of that knowledge to *them*. I'm playing by their rules right now, but I'm starting to lose patience with their—"

"Fenton, you have to play by their rules. Otherwise—"

"I'm heading into the store," I interrupt. "The service is going to get shitty."

"Talk soon," Duke says, ready to end the conversation anyway, and the line clicks off. I shove my phone into the pocket of my black athletic pants. My jaw pulses, the buzz from this morning's workout now vanished.

Ignoring the eyes of an uptight man perusing the apples, I skirt my cart left to avoid interaction. I have no idea why I chose today of all days to do my own grocery shopping. I could've waited three damn days until my housekeeper gets back from vacation.

Steering clear of the apples and the negative energy rolling off the shopper, I head towards the bananas. I need to find the optimism I had five minutes ago before Duke called from the office and ruined my Saturday morning.

The bananas are organic and perfectly ripe, so I pluck a bunch off the podium. I start to push away, but the hairs on the back of my neck stand on end. A ruffle of unease scatters through my subconscious. I pause mid-step and glance around the store. People mill about, minding their own business, nothing out of the ordinary. I start to push away again when I spy the offender. A black piece of plastic peeks out from behind a bundle of bananas, the overhead light ricocheting off it and catching my eye.

I reach behind the produce and pull out a black cell phone. Turning it over in my hand, it looks no worse for wear. I press the round button on the bottom and the screen lights up.

Staring back at me are two gorgeous girls, probably a couple of years younger than me. Mid-twenties, I'd say. The dark-headed one is flashing a peace sign in a barely there white bikini. She's hot as fuck. But it's the blonde that draws my attention. She sits crossed-legged in shorts and a tank top on the beach, her hair falling around her narrow shoulders. Her body is covered, her stance demure, but there's something striking about her that I can't pinpoint. I almost can't look away. Her blue-green eyes taunt me, tease me with a look that's downright beguiling. The touches of vulnerability hidden behind her confidence intrigue me, make me want to hear her voice and know what she's thinking.

Laughing at my ridiculousness despite the heat rolling in my blood, I skim the store again. No one seems to be searching for the phone.

I glance back down and my gaze goes immediately to the blonde. The curve of her hip has my thumb gliding over the screen.

*I should turn the phone in to management. It's the logical, responsible thing to do.*

My feet don't move.

*Losing your phone in the bananas doesn't exactly shout responsibility.*

Taking a deep breath, I ponder my options. I can turn it in to Lost and Found and hope that they actually give it to her if she comes looking. Or . . . I could try to get in touch with her myself.

*Keep telling yourself you're playing the Good Samaritan.*

Leaning against the produce display, I do a quick analysis. The odds of her finding it at the Help Desk aren't great. Maybe fifty-fifty. Some bagger boy will probably see the lock screen and take it to the bathroom and jerk off. The odds of *that* are phenomenal. The odds of me breaking the passcode aren't great either, but if possible, would greatly increase her chances of getting it back.

*And the chance for me to see those eyes in person.*

I type in 0000.

"Try again" flashes on the screen.

1234.

"Try again."

Steering the cart with my elbows towards the customer service desk, I run through possible passwords before I commit to my final try. I have one more chance before it locks me out for good and I have no choice but to turn it over to Bagger Boy and his bathroom break.

I go for 1111, another overused password.

It makes a clicking sound and the lock screen opens. The phone toggles in my hands, my jaw dropping in disbelief. It worked. The home screen is filled with apps over shiny gold wallpaper, waiting to be explored.

*Should I or shouldn't I?*

My thumb glances over the photo album and I see the first photo.

*I definitely should.*

## AVAILABLE NOW!

CPSIA information can be obtained
at www.ICGtesting.com
Printed in the USA
LVHW080425290321
682800LV00035B/638